How to Catch a Rockstar

Arabella Quinn

Copyright © 2023 by Arabella Quinn

All rights reserved.

No part of this publication may be reproduced, distributed, or transmitted in any form or by any means, including photocopying, recording, or other electronic or mechanical methods, without the prior written permission of the publisher, except as permitted by U.S. copyright law.

If you purchased a copy of this eBook, thank you. Also, thank you for not sharing your copy of this book. This purchase allows you one legal copy for your own personal computer or device. You do not have the rights to resell, distribute, print, or transfer this book, in whole or in part, in any format, via methods either currently known or yet to be invented, or upload to a file sharing peer-to-peer program. It may not be re-sold or given away to other people. Such action is illegal and in violation of the U.S. Copyright Law. If you would like to share this book with another person, please purchase an additional copy for each recipient. If you're reading this book and did not purchase it, or it was not purchased for your use only, then please purchase your own copy. Thank you for respecting the hard work of this author.

The story, all names, characters, and incidents portrayed in this production are fictitious. No identification with actual persons (living or deceased), places, buildings, and products is intended or should be inferred.

Dedication

In loving memory of my dear mother,
The one who championed my writing journey,
These books stand as a testament to your never-ending belief in me.
As my biggest fan, your encouragement was unwavering throughout
the years I spent writing this book series. Though you're not here to
see the culmination of my efforts, I know you are watching over me,
cheering me on from a place where love transcends all boundaries.
Your absence is deeply felt, but I carry your love and support within
me, inspiring me and giving me the courage to chase my dreams.
You are forever in my heart.

Contents

Prologue	1
Chapter 1	13
Chapter 2	25
Chapter 3	36
Chapter 4	47
Chapter 5	60
Chapter 6	70
Chapter 7	78
Chapter 8	87
Chapter 9	101
Chapter 10	115
Chapter 11	126
Chapter 12	138
Chapter 13	148

Chapter 14	157
Chapter 15	168
Chapter 16	177
Chapter 17	190
Chapter 18	202
Chapter 19	210
Chapter 20	215
Chapter 21	227
Chapter 22	239
Chapter 23	252
Chapter 24	259
Chapter 25	272
Chapter 26	284
Chapter 27	292
Chapter 28	300
Chapter 29	309
Chapter 30	317
Chapter 31	328
Chapter 32	335
Chapter 33	349
Chapter 34	355
Chapter 35	364
Chapter 36	377
Chapter 37	389

Chapter 38	402
Chapter 39	413
Chapter 40	427
Next in series	438
Arabella Quinn Newsletter	440
Bad Boys of Rock Series	441
Also By Arabella Quinn	444
Other Novels by Arabella Quinn	446
About the Author	449
Excerpt	450

Prologue

Two Years Ago...

Ghost

Everyone was entirely focused on Ryder. He captivated the audience with his newly dyed, blond punk hairstyle and his electric performance of *Rebel Yell*. It was impressive. Maybe I felt a twinge of ... what? Not jealousy. Not resentment. I don't know what. My band was up on stage and I was watching from the audience. It just felt wrong. I was the face of Ghost Parker, but I'd stepped aside so that Ryder could shine in the spotlight — so that he could impress Talia.

I used the moment while everyone was caught up in the show to slip out the back of the room through some sliding glass doors onto the patio. The sun had set, so it was cooler outside, but not yet chilly.

The overhead patio lights were not on, but there was soft landscape lighting that highlighted the palm trees and greenery, and there were hidden fixtures that illuminated the paving stone pathways. I followed a path that passed by the pool and stopped in front of a railing looking out toward the blackness of the ocean in the distance.

In this hidden corner, I could hear the rhythmic sound of the relentless surf and only heard the faintest of notes from Ghost Parker jamming inside the house. It was a good place to escape the party.

I had only a few minutes of peace until I felt the weight of someone's eyes resting on me. My senses went on alert, but I didn't turn to see who it was. It was probably one of any number of girls who'd been watching me since I'd arrived at Tommy's house. The guest list was exclusive to friends; there were no random groupies here. It didn't matter though, guaranteed this person wanted only one thing — to get into my pants.

I rolled that thought around in my head. A good fuck might be a great distraction, but I'd have to ask the '15 minutes of questions' first. My therapist wanted me to stop having such utterly meaningless sex. She wanted me to get to know a girl, even if it was just for 15 minutes, before having sex. Baby steps, she called it. She was trying to teach me how to relate to people and how to build relationships.

The problem was that the more I got to know the girls, even after 15 minutes, the more I didn't want to sleep with them. Maybe that was the whole point my therapist was trying to make; I was making poor choices. But, sex was one of the few things in life that I enjoyed. The rush of being on stage in front of thousands was the only thing better than sex. And since they were the only two things in life that temporarily pushed me past the numbness, I wasn't about to give up either one.

With all the grappling in my head, it only took me an instant to make up my mind. I was going to let this chick blow me, whoever she was, and without the '15-minute getting to know her' bullshit. And I would enjoy it. Then I'd see if I wanted to stick around the party any longer or just disappear into the shadows of the night.

I turned, already flashing the smile that was guaranteed to make the ladies drop their panties but ended up raising an eyebrow in surprise. I could tell by the silhouette that this was no lady.

He took a step closer so that his face was out of the shadows. He held up a drink in each hand. "Jack and Coke or Whiskey Sour?"

I shrugged. "Either is fine."

He handed me the Jack and Coke and then took a healthy sip of his own drink.

I regarded him. "You're Talia's friend? We met on the party bus?"

"Grey," he confirmed.

I remembered watching him at the nightclub that night. The guy had really attracted the attention of the ladies. They had swarmed him so quickly, that our party had to leave the dance floor and head to the VIP section. He was almost too handsome and the skintight shirt he'd worn that night had shown off that he was in great shape, but guys like that were a dime a dozen in this town.

Maybe his popularity had intrigued me because that night I'd found myself watching him. I had a way of blending in with the crowd and avoiding notice when I wanted to, but several times I'd felt his scrutiny. It was as if he'd been aware of me all night. It'd made me slightly nervous, an emotion that almost never broke through the constant numbness. Still, I'd been curious about him. I'd even wondered what he was doing when I was busy getting a blowjob in the VIP restroom. When he left at the end of the night with a curvy redhead, it felt like the party fizzled. Everything seemed flat. No more weird nerves. I'd left the party, alone, right after.

I took a sip of the Jack and Coke and then leaned on the railing, gazing out toward the ocean. "I'm Johnny."

I surprised myself. I never introduced myself as Johnny. Maybe my therapist was finally getting through to me after all. She told me using my nickname, Ghost, was a way of hiding from intimacy. I wasn't looking for intimacy with this guy, so I immediately regretted saying it.

Grey rested his drink on the railing near my arm but remained facing me instead of looking out toward the ocean. "I've never seen you perform before tonight. You're ... just amazing. You mesmerize the audience. I was in awe."

His words weren't something that I hadn't heard a thousand times, but maybe because they came from a dude who was used to performing for an audience and weren't just tossed out by a woman that was trying to work her way into my bed, it felt like they meant something. Somehow, the words didn't feel so empty or calculating.

I took a hasty sip to stop myself from saying anything stupid. "Thanks, man. You didn't stay to watch Ryder?"

"No." He glanced down at his feet and suddenly he didn't look like the supremely self-confident guy that I'd observed all that night at Talia's goodbye party. His voice sounded gruff. "I saw you leaving. You looked lost. Like you could use a friend."

Something shifted inside me. I didn't know what I felt, but it wasn't something I was comfortable with. My heart beat faster. Maybe it was that he just got too close to my secrets. To my truths.

Surprisingly, my reaction was also physical. A flutter in my stomach. A tightness in my chest. A tightening of my cock inside my pants.

My jaw clenched as I snarled back at him. "Yeah? Well, you thought wrong."

Remi

I had nothing better going on, so after the end of the workday 'going on maternity leave' party for Celia, which consisted of cake in the break room, I accepted the invitation to go out with my coworkers to a local restaurant. Celia was a production assistant at Hollywood Exposé, the TV and online celebrity news conglomerate that I worked for as a feature story writer. She was one of those bubbly girls that everyone loved.

When I got to the restaurant twenty minutes later, Celia's table was full. I ended up at an ancillary table with other staff writers. Except for the two writers who wrote the script for Mindy Blakedale, the face of Hollywood Exposé, all the other writers and editors worked primarily alone. They were an observant and quiet bunch — not exactly the life of the party.

I'd asked a few of my colleagues what they were working on, but they all were a tight-lipped crew. No one wanted to give away their inside scoop, despite the fact we were all working for the same team.

I liked Celia and most of the people who worked behind the cameras at my job, but a majority of those friendly people were at the cool kid's table. I was stuck with the nerds. I probably could have barreled my way into that group, securing an empty chair from another table and shoehorning it in to be included with the fun group, but I was just too tired to make the effort. It had been a long and exhausting week.

I finished up my second drink and then started planning my exit strategy. I could just say goodbye and good luck to Celia and be on my way. There was no need for elaborate excuses even though it appeared that I would be the first to leave.

I said my goodbyes to the glum writer's table, then to Celia and several co-workers I was friendly with, and within a few minutes, I was slipping out the door into the fresh air.

It wasn't until I was in front of my apartment door digging through my purse and searching for my key that I found it.

It was a blue notecard with words scrawled in ugly black marker across it. The ink was badly smeared, but I could clearly make out what it said.

```
I know who you are
     REMINGTON
   watch your back
```

I couldn't help but hurriedly glance over my shoulder even though I was alone in the hallway. Fumbling with my keys, I nearly dropped them as I tried to unlock my door as quickly as I could. I didn't breathe until I got into my apartment and locked the door behind me.

My heart pounded as I stared at the card. *Remington.* Somebody knew. Who? And, what were they going to do about it? *Watch your back.* That sounded like a threat.

I let my purse drop to the floor. And then I slid down right next to it. I thought I'd left my past behind.

Greyson

I almost didn't go to the baby shower. *Because of him.*

But, in the end, I went. *Because of him.*

My friend, Talia, was hosting a baby shower for Sidney Anderson, the bassist for the rock band Ghost Parker. Out of the blue, less than a week ago, he found out he was a father. The mother had abandoned the baby on his doorstep claiming it was his. Now his friends were coming together to support him.

I was more of an acquaintance than a friend. I'd only met Sid a handful of times, but I was friends with Talia, and Talia was living in my beach house with her boyfriend, Ryder, who was a guitarist in Sid's band.

I liked Talia's friends. They partied a hell of a lot harder than me; they knew how to have a good time. Plus, with the whole rock star thing, they didn't make too much of my own fame. I was currently filming the 9th season of the primetime soap, *Devious*. I was the longest-running cast member, starring as bad boy titan, Colton Grimaldi, since episode 1 of the series. As my fame skyrocketed, it became nearly impossible to interact with people on a normal level, so having some friends outside of the acting world who knew me as Greyson and treated me like an ordinary person was refreshing.

So, here I was in my own house that I'd been avoiding since Talia moved in. I still wasn't too sure how Ryder felt about me. I usually stayed at my penthouse in Hollywood during filming anyway, so it was no big deal.

I carried my wrapped gifts, a baby monitor and a white-noise sound machine, up to the top floor where everyone was gathered waiting for Sid to arrive. Talia had done a great job decorating. There were balloons, ribbons, and streamers, all baby blue, everywhere. A huge banner draped across the wall exclaimed *It's a Boy!* And the tables were covered with *Oh, Baby!* printed tablecloths and piled with gifts. And, shit, there was blue confetti littering every surface of the house already.

I felt at home as soon as I stepped into the room. Right away, Talia hugged me, quickly followed by Kaylie. Ryder shook my hand and slapped me on the back. I was introduced to Ghost Parker's manager and his date and then greeted by a few others I'd met before.

The moment *he* walked into the room, I knew. *Johnny Parker*. He was the lead singer of Ghost Parker — known to almost everyone as Ghost. I kept my back to him, listening as his friends greeted him. My gut clenched when I heard his smooth baritone voice.

Fuck. I was so attracted to this guy.

It only took a second to disassociate myself from those feelings; I was a fucking good actor. I turned around, a neutral expression plastered on my face.

He was looking right at me. I didn't betray the riot of emotions that his gaze produced. Instead, my eyes swept right past him. I tried not to remember the last time I'd spoken to him — right after he performed live with his band at Talia's party. In just a few words, he'd left me shattered. Humiliated.

We never got close to each other during the baby shower, but I'd keenly felt his presence the entire time. He was amongst his best friends, in private, but he seemed so detached. It was so unlike when

I'd seen him perform with his band, where his overwhelming magnetism touched the entire crowd. I briefly wondered if today he was under the influence of drugs.

Even though he was acting so low-key, I swore that he had an extra awareness of me. He was better at checking his emotions than most actors I knew, but he couldn't hide the fact that he had some kind of reaction to me. Not when I was watching him so closely. His eyes followed me. He noticed me. Quite possibly, it was nervous energy or even contempt; I didn't know. Maybe he was picking up on my attraction and it was disdain directed back at me. He wasn't unaffected, that I knew.

Of course, I was immediately aware when he went out on the deck. Marie followed thirty seconds behind him. I watched them through the slider door; I had to move so I had the right angle to see them. They stood talking to each other.

Talia stopped to chat with me for a minute and when I looked back up, they'd disappeared. There was no way off the deck except through the main slider into this room or the slider at the end of the deck into the master bedroom.

He hadn't come back inside here, so I knew he must be in my bedroom with Marie. I grew antsy waiting for them to come out. I paced back and forth, keeping my eyes on the bedroom door. I waited a few more minutes. Finally, I just couldn't stand it any longer. The party was still going strong. People were drinking and having a good time. Right now they were bobbing for baby bottle nipples. No one was paying any attention to me.

I slipped into my bedroom. It was quiet in there. I quickly scanned the room; it was empty, but the bathroom door was open. I moved further into the room and finally, I could see them. Marie was on her knees on my bath mat. She was kneeling in front of Ghost, her head bobbing up and down on his dick.

Ghost looked like a bored god. He stood casually leaning against the wall, his hand braced against the vanity countertop. His head was flung back slightly, and his eyes were narrowed into slits. His expression was completely passive, but he was breathing slightly heavier than normal.

I was instantly hard as a rock. I stepped closer, just outside the bathroom door, to watch. I couldn't drag my eyes away.

When I came into view, his eyes snapped to me. "What the fuck are you doing?"

I lifted a brow. "You realize this is my bedroom, right?"

Marie popped off his dick and, yeah, I was staring at it. "Oh, my God! Greyson! Do you remember me? We met on the party bus. I'm a big fan of *Devious*. I'm Marie."

I couldn't pull my eyes away from Ghost's dick. "I remember."

Marie shifted on her knees. "This is not what it looks like. We're just friends..."

Ghost made an impatient exhalation. "Did I say you should stop sucking my cock?"

Marie giggled and then wrapped her lips around his cock again and went to work. With each bob of her head, I thought I might blow my load right in my jeans. Fuck, my cock was throbbing.

I didn't move. I couldn't. I just watched. I alternated between watching Ghost's cock disappearing into Marie's mouth and watching his face. The exquisite ache that built uncomfortably in my balls was torture.

Ghost's breath came a little heavier and his knuckles turned white as he gripped the counter harder. I was amazed at how in control he was. While I was sweating with the effort to keep my own cock from exploding, not once did he thrust into her mouth.

HOW TO CATCH A ROCKSTAR

He kept himself rigidly in check and his eyes never left mine.

It only took a couple more head bobs before he came. He threw back his head slightly and quietly groaned. I may have groaned with him. After milking him for a few seconds, Marie pulled off his cock looking pleased with herself.

She wiped her mouth while Ghost was tucking himself back into his pants. I was paralyzed with aching.

Marie turned on her knees and reached a hand for my pants.

Ghost blinked a few times. "What are you doing?"

Marie stopped, her hand resting on my jeans right over my painfully hard cock. She gazed up at me. "Tell me you want this? I want to do this so badly. This is so hot."

I just nodded. My dick was so hard; I desperately needed relief.

She quickly unbuckled my belt, unbuttoned and unzipped my pants, and had my cock out in seconds. It was thick and angry, the head glistening with pre-cum. Marie's mouth felt like heaven when she slid her tongue over my cock before taking me between her red swollen lips.

I was mesmerized by Ghost's face as he stared at my cock getting sucked off. It was no longer distant or vacant. His eyes were half-lidded with lust and tension coiled his lips. His cheeks were flushed and his nostrils flared. His intoxicating beauty hit me like a physical blow, ratcheting up the unbearable pressure in my balls, especially with his eyes zeroed in on my cock.

My hand wrapped around a hunk of Marie's hair, but it was Ghost's mouth I was imagining on me when Marie took me deep, the tip of my dick hitting the back of her throat.

A grunt escaped my lips and then a long hiss when she did it again.

The noise I made broke the spell surrounding us. Ghost tore his eyes from my cock and looked me right in the eyes. He suddenly looked pissed, a damaged immortal hell-bent on vengeance. I sucked in a breath, retreating from his wrath. I was about to come, but Ghost was already turning away from me. He stormed out of the room.

I closed my eyes and imagined his face. I imagined his mouth on me.

I spurted long and hard. Marie did a good job milking every last tremor from me, but she wasn't who I was thinking about.

Chapter 1

***

Present Day

Ghost

Whoop! Whoop! Whoop!

The high-pitched blaring sound was splitting my head open. I grunted with disgust and rolled onto my side, burying my head under the pillow in the process.

Whoop! Whoop! Whoop!

It was loud. Deafening. And it wasn't letting up.

Whoop! Whoop! Whoop!

Somebody. Make. It. Stop.

It wasn't an alarm clock. It was so damn loud — way too loud to ignore. My foggy mind insisted it must be something more important. Was it a police siren? Fuck. Did I do something wrong?

Whoop! Whoop! Whoop!

I forced myself to think as I burrowed deeper under the pillow, trying to block out the shrillest part of the noise. I'd had my share of brushes with the law, so getting arrested wasn't a completely insane scenario to contemplate.

Where had I been last night? What did I do? I feebly tried to piece together the puzzle against the backdrop of the incessant noise.

Whoop! Whoop! Whoop!

Suddenly, the pillow was yanked roughly from my head. The frantic alarm blasted in my ears ten times louder without the pillow to muffle it. Fuck.

Someone was tugging on my arm. It was a girl. I heard a few of the words she was yelling at me, but the alarm drowned out most of what she said.

"Ghost, you—"

Whoop! Whoop! Whoop!

"Please!"

Whoop! Whoop! Whoop!

"We gotta—"

Whoop! Whoop! Whoop!

After a few thumps on my back and less than a minute of arm tugging, the girl gave up. Without opening my eyes, I felt around the bed fruitlessly searching for the pillow so I could block out the fucking noise.

Whoop! Whoop! Whoop!

Just when I realized I was going to have to actually open my eyes to locate the missing pillow, what felt like an entire bucket of ice-cold water was dumped on my head. Holy fuck!

Whoop! Whoop! Whoop!

My eyes jolted open from the shock of the water assaulting my face.

HOW TO CATCH A ROCKSTAR 15

The adrenaline that simultaneously surged through my veins had my body springing from the bed, my fists sailing through the air, ready to defend myself to the death.

Whoop! Whoop! Whoop!

I took in the girl who stood before me as I tried to steady my breathing. She was gesticulating wildly as she yelled at me, frenzy overtaking her face. A flash of memory from the night before came back to me. This girl. A sexy black dress. Lots of long leg showing.

Now she was wearing a baggy sweatshirt over leggings. No makeup. Messy hair. She was damn cute. I wanted to drag her back into bed with me.

Whoop! Whoop! Whoop!

I felt my cock jump as I remembered flashes from our night between the sheets. And. Oh shit. I was naked. I never slept naked with a girl overnight. What if she snapped a picture of my cock while I was sleeping? It'd be all over social media in a heartbeat. Ryder had learned that lesson early on for our band.

Whoop! Whoop! Whoop!

She had something in her hand, which was still flapping around wildly as she yelled. A cup. It looked like one of those plastic cups to rinse your mouth out after you brushed your teeth. A small cup. She'd dumped a small cup of water on my face. I grunted at the realization. Jesus, it'd felt like I'd been waterboarded, but it was probably only a few ounces of water at most.

Whoop! Whoop! Whoop!

Between the damn alarm endlessly clattering and the pounding of the pulse in my ears from my adrenaline rush, I couldn't really make out what this girl was screaming at me. There was one word that was coming through crystal clear, though.

"Fire!"

My brain was finally catching up. The fire alarm was going off. It was time to bounce.

Whoop! Whoop! Whoop!

As the realization sunk in, the girl turned from me, her arms still waving in the air above her head as she bolted out the bedroom door. I almost laughed out loud because she looked like a deranged muppet with crazy wiggling arms flapping around as she disappeared.

Whoop! Whoop! Whoop!

I looked around the room for my clothes. Her room wasn't clean, so it wasn't like my clothing rested in a pile on her pristine floor. There were clothes everywhere. And other junk girls tended to accumulate was littered everywhere — on dressers, on the floor, and absolutely overflowing a chair. Jesus, the more I looked, the more of a pig I realized this girl was. There were old plates with leftover moldy food on them scattered about. Soda cans everywhere. A few beer bottles. Papers, books, and notebooks strewn around the room. Lots of shoes. Just shit everywhere.

Whoop! Whoop! Whoop!

Near the foot of the bed, I saw what looked like a pair of men's jeans. I picked them up and recognized them at once. One of my favorite pairs. Well worn. Ripped in all the right places, not by a razor, but by years of use. They fit my body perfectly. I'd wear these jeans until they disintegrated. I poked around the clothes lying near where I found my jeans, searching for my boxer briefs.

I didn't find them, but fished my wallet from the bottom of the pile. Thank goodness. Luckily, my jeans were broken in and comfortable because I'd have to go commando. I didn't have time to dick around here.

Whoop! Whoop! Whoop!

I slipped on my jeans while scanning the ground for my T-shirt, but quickly realized that was hopeless. I'd never find it in this mess. As I moved toward the door, I glanced out the narrow window in the bedroom. I was up on about the fifth floor. I had been focused on other things when we'd stumbled in last night, so I was surprised to see that this must be a big apartment building. A ton of people had gathered on the lawn and road in front of the building. Some were wearing jackets. Some had blankets draped over their shoulders. This was Los Angeles, but November could be damn cold at times. Most of the crowd was looking up toward the apartment building. Some were even pointing. Two things hit me. I needed more clothes, and I needed to get the fuck out of here. Right now.

Whoop! Whoop! Whoop!

My eyes landed on a sweatshirt. I grabbed it and held it up, inspecting its size. It was probably huge on the girl — I still couldn't remember her name — but it wasn't quite my size. It would do in an emergency. I pulled it on as I stepped through the bedroom door into the rest of her apartment.

Whoop! Whoop! Whoop!

The apartment was clear. No smoke. No fire. No sign of the girl or any roommates. I crossed the front room toward the entry door and felt for heat before I cautiously opened it. Peeked into the hall. All clear.

Whoop! Whoop! Whoop!

I followed the exit signs toward the stairwell, pleased my brain was making the right choices — checking for fire and not using the elevator. I jogged down five flights of stairs, all while the blaring alarm spurred me on to move even faster.

Finally, I pushed out into the brisk fresh air, where the sound of the alarm was more muted. It no longer felt like it was boring into my brain. Outside, it was cold, and I was grateful I'd grabbed the sweatshirt. Unfortunately, it was a salmon-pink color. I glanced down at it. It was way too tight. The sleeves were too short. It had the word 'Princess' written across the chest in a shiny gold script.

I probably could have found something better to wear if I'd searched for a few more minutes, but the place was on fucking fire. So...

I took a step and felt the shocking cold of the concrete on my bare feet. Shit, I'd forgotten my shoes in the rush to get out. As I'd torn down the stairwell, I hadn't even realized I was barefoot. I grimaced as I looked up from staring at my feet and noticed the crowd.

I was used to being the center of attention. Used to thousands of eyes focused on me and every move that I made. I loved it. Made a living from it. Drew my energy from it. Performing was my lifeblood.

Yet, I felt a rumble of uneasiness as I saw a few phones lift up. Aimed at me. Some people had recognized me. It was only a matter of time before the entire crowd knew who I was. My head was pounding with renewed vigor. And I was wearing this awful, ill-fitting sweatshirt to boot.

It was time to disappear like a ghost into the mist. I took a few steps into the crowd. Blending in was better. Fuck, I didn't have my phone. I asked the nearest star-struck girl if I could borrow her phone to make a call. She nodded mutely and handed it over. I quickly punched in Bishop's number, which I had conveniently memorized for just such emergencies.

Bishop was my personal security guard. Last night, I'd purposefully left my cell phone in the men's bathroom and exited the club out the back door. It wasn't the first time I'd ditched Bishop. I was expecting an earful from him when he picked me up, but he was a consummate professional. He wouldn't take it personally, but he'd double down on his efforts to keep me under tabs. It was getting harder and harder to outmaneuver him. He was great at his job and I trusted him, but more importantly, he'd become more of a friend than an employee. Regardless, I vowed to keep him on his toes.

Bishop chuckled when I let him know it was me calling. I had to get the address from the phone's owner and then I told him I'd be waiting for him a block east. A few seconds later, Bishop promised to pick me up within 15 minutes.

Fifteen minutes was a huge wait, especially with half the damn cell phones in the vicinity recording my every move. While I'd been securing a ride, the crowd began to coalesce around me. Even more phones were aimed at me. A girl — my girl from last night with the unknown name — pushed through the crowd to reach me. She wrapped me in an enormous hug.

"Ghost! You made it out. I'm so sorry about the whole water thing. I didn't know what to do! You wouldn't wake up."

Fuck. That didn't sound good. I had to shut her up. Wrapping my arms around her to return her hug, I whispered into her ear, "Hey, babe. I gotta get out of here. Too many cameras on me. I'll see you around."

I pulled back. A sad look passed over her face, but then it brightened. "I had fun last night. Take my number and call me. Anytime."

"I had fun too." I pretended to enter her number into the phone, which wasn't actually my phone, as she dictated it.

She nodded at me. "And my last name is Buchanan. Dina Buchanan."

"Buchanan. Got it." I fake-entered her last name.

Other girls were watching our interaction. They got bolder. Soon, they were snapping selfies with me. This was turning into a meet-and-greet right before my eyes — the most hated part of my job. The atmosphere outside turned even more festive when the rumor circulated that the fire was a false alarm. Someone had supposedly burned some popcorn, which triggered the alarm.

My head was still throbbing as I chatted with yet another fan. At some point, the cell phone girl snatched back her phone and began snapping a million pictures of me.

I noticed a tall girl at the periphery of the crowd patiently waiting her turn to get a selfie with me, but other girls kept cutting in. After ten minutes of being mauled by girls and even a few guys, I caught her eye again. She finally stepped up.

"Can I get a picture with you?" she asked meekly.

I noticed her flip-flops right away. Some dick had stepped on my bare foot as soon as the crowd tightened around me and it had been throbbing in time with my head ever since. I'd been vigilant since then, trying to keep my bruised and freezing feet from any more abuse. I'd had one eye latched onto where everyone's feet were for self-preservation purposes.

She had pretty big feet for a girl. Her flip-flops had silver, sparkly straps.

"You can get a picture with me if you do me a favor."

Her eyes bugged out. "What do you mean?"

"I'll trade you." My eyebrows lifted. "A picture with me for your flip-flops."

"You want my flip-flops? You have a fetish or something?" She looked confused.

"Something."

She giggled, but then kicked off her flip-flops and handed them over to me. She handed over her phone to her friend and then we posed together. Her friend snapped a ton of shots. She thanked me and was about to leave when I grabbed her arm and pulled her back.

She had to be just under 6 feet tall. I didn't feel that much taller than her when I usually dwarfed other girls. Still, I was able to dip her and land a surprise kiss on her lips.

Her shock turned to glee as I righted her again. She squealed as her friend cried out that she'd gotten it all on camera.

Just then, some new siren sounds mixed with the unrelenting fire alarm from the building. Fire trucks were now coming down the street to join the melee. I glanced over my shoulder at the building but still couldn't see any blazing fire. All of this was for burnt popcorn. Who ate fucking popcorn for breakfast, anyway?

The noisy and chaotic arrival of the several fire engines momentarily distracted the crowd. Timing it just right, I made my escape and melted off toward the pickup spot.

The black Lincoln Navigator with the tinted windows pulled up to me. I hopped into the back seat and before my back even hit the black leather of the seat, the behemoth car smoothly pulled away.

Bishop had a crooked grin on his face. "Tell me you had nothing to do with the fire engines? Oh shit, what the hell are you wearing?"

Distracted, I ran a hand through my hair. "Don't even ask."

Bishop passed my cell phone back to me. "Keep ditching your phone like that, and I'm gonna have to chip you."

Tracking our phones was a safety measure that our security team employed. None of us liked it, but it had proved invaluable a few times.

I laid my head back against the butter-soft leather. "You can yell at me after I get a cup of coffee in me."

"You're cutting it close." Bishop glanced at me in the rear-view mirror. "Your appointment with the head shrinker is in 20 minutes."

My therapy session. Fuck. I closed my eyes. I forgot about that. We were in the middle of a 3-week break from the tour, and I always tried to see Maggie in person when I could. I briefly thought about canceling, but I knew she would bust my balls if I did.

I moaned with irritation. "Do I have time to make it home for a quick change of clothes?"

"Nope."

I glanced out the window when the car came to a stop. Bishop double-parked in front of a donut shop. "Don't get out of the damn car."

I snorted. I wasn't planning on going anywhere. "Pick up a donut for me. Lemon with lemon glaze."

Bishop muttered something while shaking his head before he headed into the shop. I took the time to send a quick text to Trudy, our PR rep, to warn her to keep an eye on social media.

Her reply came back quickly.

> **Trudy:** Really? What did you do? It's not even 10 a.m. yet.
> **Me:** I didn't do anything.
> **Me:** It may involve cross-dressing though.
> **Me:** Lots of photos and videos.
> **Trudy:** Fine. I'll check #ghostsightings and see how much damage you did.

Bishop had come back with my coffee and donut and we were on our way to Maggie's office when I got Trudy's next text.

> **Trudy:** Awww. You look so cute. You could have brushed your hair, though.

I took a sip of my coffee and watched the three dots as I waited for more from her.

> **TRUDY:** My, weren't you busy! At least 12 girls from that apartment building claimed to have fucked you last night.
> **TRUDY:** #GhostParker and #ghostsightings, and #ghostsmokeout LOL
> **TRUDY:** You're trending, but everything looks fine. No biggie. Fans are eating it up. I'll monitor it.

I quickly typed a reply into my phone.

> **ME:** Thanks, Tru.

Running my fingers through my hair, I tried to tamp down my bedhead but gave up a few seconds later. I looked like a crazy person, but therapists were used to crazy, so no biggie, as Trudy put it.

I couldn't help but add another text.

> **ME:** And for the record, I only fucked 4 girls last night.

A few minutes later, we were pulling up to the nondescript building that housed Maggie's office. There were no signs announcing her practice; she had plenty of high-profile clients, so she was discreet.

After thoroughly scanning the area for paparazzi, Bishop deemed it safe for me to leave. He would be waiting at the rear exit when I was finished. Maggie's whole setup was designed to get clientele in and out without them ever being seen.

I grabbed the bag containing the donut, hopped out of the car, and waited at the door for Maggie to buzz me in.

Chapter 2

Remi

WHAT DID MY AUDIENCE want? Gossip. Scandal. Juicy tidbits. A peek inside celebrity lives. An occasional sprinkling of feel-good stories where celebrities made a difference in the real world. Warmth and humanity could only be doled out in small doses.

Social media had preconditioned my audience to respond to entertainment delivered in neat 30-second sound bites. How did I keep them engaged enough to read an entire article that might take 5 minutes? Humor. Wit. Sensationalism. And, it needed to be written at a fifth-grade reading level, at least according to my boss.

I was writing a feature story about another reality TV family that just wouldn't go away. It was my third time writing about them. I'd rather poke my eye out with a rusty nail dripping with tetanus, but I had no choice.

So far, my article was more vapid than the family it was covering. I took a deep breath. Instead of getting frustrated, I needed to view this as a challenge. If I could take this story and spin it into gold, I'd prove what a talented writer I was. I needed to stop tormenting myself by recalling my degree in investigative journalism and ignore just how far I'd drifted from my dreams.

The article was technically finished. I'd hit my word count, but it contained nothing of value. It needed something more. Just like my mom used to finely chop up vegetables to hide in the meatloaf, I always tried to sneak into my pieces some tidbits of wisdom, some truths, or moral lessons that a tiny segment of my audience might pick up. This piece had nothing.

I had to attempt to redeem it. The problem was that this family didn't excite me one bit. I didn't watch their reality show. I didn't follow them on social media. My greatest wish was that they'd fade into obscurity, so I'd never have to write about them again. For now, I was stuck covering them — it was trying to craft sophisticated entertainment out of The Three Stooges.

I stared at my laptop screen. It was seemingly impossible. My brain screamed with defeat. It was like turning meatloaf into chateaubriand.

Speaking of meatloaf again, I was getting hungry. Maybe a Twix bar would kick-start my creativity. I leaned over to reach into my purse, which was shoehorned in the bottom right drawer of my desk, when my phone rang.

Darn, it was my boss. "Hi, Caroline."

"In my office." She wasn't one to mince words.

"Okay. I'll be right..." My voice trailed off. She'd already hung up.

It was fairly unusual to be summoned to her office, but I wasn't worried. My job here was secure. I produced quality pieces and my output was consistent. Maybe, fingers crossed, she had a new assignment for me.

HOW TO CATCH A ROCKSTAR

I snatched a pad of paper and a pen from my desk and wound my way through the newsroom. The newsroom was a giant open space crammed with bumper-to-bumper desks, each containing at least two monitors. For as hectic as it all looked, it was a controlled chaos. Phones rang constantly, but most people wore headsets as they worked, so only a few one-sided conversations could be heard.

Caroline's office was only one floor up, so I took the stairs. She was on the phone when I arrived at her open door, so I knocked lightly on the door frame to get her attention. She looked up and waved me into the chair in front of her desk while she finished with her call.

My boss wasn't a stylish person. She looked like she spent a grand total of about five minutes on her appearance each morning. Her pin-straight, but thick blonde hair was cut in the shape of a helmet around her head. Her clothes were loose and boxy and always seemed randomly selected. She never wore a stitch of makeup or any jewelry.

Her appearance wasn't a priority; she channeled all her energy into her job. And she was absolutely amazing at it. She wasn't just my boss; I considered her a mentor as well. Plus, she'd taken a big chance on me. I owed her so much.

She hung up the phone and glanced up at me. "Would you close the door, please?"

I closed the office door and then returned to my chair, inhaling deeply to calm the skittering of nerves that had settled over me.

She looked me directly in the eye. "What I'm about to tell you doesn't leave this office."

I nodded my agreement.

She got straight to the point. "Mindy Blakedale is retiring. Losing her is a blow. She's been the beating heart of Hollywood Exposé for 12 years. Of course, we'll milk it for everything we can, but we have six months to transition to the new face of Hollywood Exposé."

I had met Mindy a few times but never worked directly with her. She was a minor celebrity in her own right and Hollywood Exposé treated her like a queen. She mingled with the peasants only when necessary. It helped that she was married to a famous movie producer who came from old Hollywood royalty. She was a true industry insider.

She folded her arms on top of her desk. "Jack Hoffman and I have been discussing her replacement."

Mr. Hoffman, as most of the staff called him, was the CEO and controlling shareholder of Hollywood Exposé.

Caroline tapped her thumb twice against the desktop. "As you know, Margot was being groomed as a successor to the position, but then she got snapped up by WCAU. The fool. She'd be sitting pretty right now if she wasn't so damn impatient."

My mind was racing. I didn't want to get ahead of myself, but why was Caroline telling me all this? Was it even possible that I was going to get the mother of all jobs at Hollywood Exposé? A silent squeal of amazement rippled through my brain, but I shut it down quickly. I needed to be on my game. Professional.

"Regardless,"—Caroline waved her hands to dismiss the subject of Margot—"I met with Jack last night and he wants Dawn Chambers to take Mindy's place. While she's an excellent choice, I did put in a word on your behalf."

The ecstatic thrill that had been buzzing in my body was quickly replaced by the sting of rejection. "That was really kind of you. Thanks."

Caroline smirked. "Dawn has seniority over you. She's got more time punched and more experience. She's a great field reporter with terrific instincts, and she's sat in for Mindy dozens of times over the years. Plus, she scores well behind the camera according to our focus groups."

Ah, it all made sense. If Dawn wasn't so damn short, she could be a runway model. She was gorgeous, petite, and stick thin. I had at least 15 pounds on her.

Caroline steepled her fingers. She vaguely looked like a supervillain. "You haven't had as much on-air work, but the field reports, red carpets, and on-air interviews you've done have gone well. And you think more quickly on your feet. Dawn has stumbled a few times in that respect."

My heart was thumping double time in my chest. I waited for Caroline to continue.

"You're very natural and composed behind the camera. We think you are very relatable to the audience. Warm and real."

I knew what her buzzwords meant. I wasn't a skinny twig, like Dawn, but maybe the audience would appreciate that. Ugh.

I'd watched my interview with Greyson Durant, who was now my boyfriend, at his penthouse when it aired. Grey scoffed when I groaned and said I looked fat. Let's just say, with the way I looked on screen, I hoped the camera really did add ten pounds. The wardrobe people made the unfortunate choice of putting me in a button-down sleeveless shell that made my upper arms look fat.

I needed to do some weight lifting to tone my arms, but who had the time? Maybe when days suddenly contained 25 hours, then I'd find some time to slip that into the schedule. God, I hated working out. I was more interested in shopping for cute workout clothes than working out in them.

"Jack has always valued my opinion, so he has agreed to consider you for the job."

She delivered the news in such an off-hand manner that I just sat open-mouthed and stunned.

One side of her mouth quirked upwards. "You've been working so hard, you deserve a shot at this."

"Is that wise?" I tried to hold back my doubts, but I couldn't. "Given my circumstances, I mean. I've been more behind the scenes here on purpose—"

She held up a hand to stop me. "Have there been any more threats?"

I shook my head. "Not since two years ago."

"See?" She raised her brows. "I did discuss that aspect of it with Jack. We've done some test runs, putting you on some high-profile pieces like the exclusive interview with Grayson Durant and we haven't received any blowback. Jack has his finger on the pulse of the industry; he'd know if this was going to be a problem. In fact, he thinks your—shall we call them 'detractors'—would be happier to see you in plain sight, reporting on entertainment news, rather than wondering what you were up to."

It made sense in a twisted sort of way. And there was no way Mr. Hoffman would take a chance on me if he thought I'd be a liability to the company. Maybe it was time to let my past go and put it all behind me.

Nearly ten years ago, I left Northwestern University a naïve young girl, ready to take on the world and make it a better place through investigative journalism. Only a few years into my job at a prestigious national newspaper, I attempted to break the biggest political scandal to hit in years.

Originally, I received an anonymous tip that pointed me to dig in a certain direction regarding a sitting U.S. Senator. It took me ten months to gather all the information I needed to take this despicable man down. Even after I was warned, not so gently, to back off over and over, I pursued leads until I had an airtight case against him.

The accusations were salacious. Charges of sexual assault, kinky sex, a secret child with an alleged Chinese spy, and liberal use of the so-called taxpayer-funded sexual assault hush fund being paid out to actual enemies of the state to keep it all quiet.

I had publicly available financial records, corroborating communication through FOIA requests, and unimpeachable witnesses. I had the receipts. It was there, almost right out in the open, but no one had the balls to go after this guy.

God, I look back in pity on my young, stupid self. Yes, even before the term 'fake news' was being bandied about, I knew that ideological partisanship ran rampant in the newsrooms. Hell, my journalism professors actually celebrated it, so seeing it out in the real world was not a shocking revelation to me.

In my naivety, I thought this particular politician had the correct letter next to his name so that I'd be championed as a hero for bringing him down. It was a hard lesson to learn, but some politicians were untouchable. At the top, there weren't two sides. They were all on the same team; it didn't matter if there was a D or R next to their name.

The prestigious newspaper I worked for would not touch the story with a ten-foot pole. Instead, I was demoted for my efforts. Same workload, lower rank, less pay.

In a fit of righteous ambition, I published all the material online exposing the Senator for all the world to see and judge.

The retribution that rained down on me was swift and severe. I was chewed up and spit out in a brutal fashion. Fired. Blacklisted everywhere, even from supposed independent papers and networks. No one would even talk to me. It was career suicide. I was told in no uncertain terms that no one bounced back from that.

What happened to the dirty Senator? Nothing. All the proof I'd collected was 'disappeared'. Destroyed. Wiped clean. My accusations hadn't even been a blip on his radar. He was still a member of the Senate to this day and was currently chairman of one of the most powerful Senate Committees. My work had absolutely no effect on the blatant corruption, but I'd destroyed my career.

It had been my red-pill moment — when my ideals were crushed and my eyes opened. I was forced to move back home with my mom, where I tried to start my own informational news site, reporting only on 'approved' stories under a pen name. I was constantly attacked by bots, shut down, canceled, and sent death threats.

So, I finally gave up. I worked menial jobs for almost a year until my mom remembered she had an old friend named Caroline who worked at Hollywood Exposé. Luckily, Caroline took a chance and hired me, knowing the whole sordid story. I packed up and moved to L.A. That was nearly five years ago.

It was no wonder I was a little hesitant to rock the boat now.

I swallowed nervously. "When is the decision going to be made? Can I do anything to convince Mr. Hoffman I'm the right choice?"

Caroline beamed at me. "Here's the exciting part: there's going to be a competition between you and Dawn. The winner will be taking over Mindy's position."

My nose crunched in confusion. "Competition?"

"You're each getting a long-term assignment with full creative control. You'll each have to develop a print piece and an online campaign dedicated to your subject to highlight a two-block slot during prime-time TV. It'll be a ton of exposure, so I hope you're ready."

"Wow." I was stunned. "That's huge. What are the timelines? What resources am I going to have?"

She pursed her lips in thought. "We haven't ironed out all the details yet. We're being very careful to make sure neither of you gets an unfair advantage. The budget, resources, and timelines will all be identical. Right now, we're thinking of four months to get the project completed. You'll only have the bare minimum of help, maybe a limited amount of hours with a camera operator, editor, and photographer each, because we want to see what you can do on your own."

Was I ready for this kind of pressure? This was a gigantic project. I'd done all of it in pieces for various projects, but never put it all together in one cohesive package. "What's the subject I'll be reporting on?"

Caroline grimaced. "Jack picked the subjects for each of you. He has a file of hundreds of story pitches that he's kept sitting on the back burner. He pulled out two that he felt were intriguing and topical."

"Why are you wincing like that?'

A puff of air escaped her lips. "Well, personally, I'm not a fan of either topic. And I think Dawn has a slight advantage with her material. But, I think it all depends on what story angle you choose. In my estimation, that will determine who wins."

"Okay." I nodded in agreement.

"I won't be giving out any advice, so don't ask. And, just so you're aware, Jack and I will be 100% neutral in choosing the winner. It will be based on the better story, the better presentation, the better reception by the audience, and the bigger buzz. Personal relationships will not come into play."

"Understood. So, what are the assignments?"

She rapped twice on her desk with her knuckles. "Jack assigned Dawn to 'black sheep royals'. You know how well royals always resonate with our audience."

My mind started creating hundreds of different creative story angles about royals. Shit, that was a good topic. "Hmm."

"You're doing a story about a haunted rock band." Her face was blank even after she dropped that dud on me.

I inhaled slowly. "What? Could you repeat that?"

She reached into her desk drawer, pulled out a file folder, and handed it to me. "It's all in there. The pitch that Jack's been holding onto. It's not much to work with, so you'll have to spin some magic. Have you heard of Ghost Parker?"

I thought for a moment. "Yeah. They sing that huge hit song 'Okay Babe'."

"Oh right," she replied. Then she started singing in a high-pitched voice, "Baby, baby, baby, oh, like, baby, baby, baby, oh..."

"No." I stopped her. "That's Justin Bieber. From a hundred years ago. When he was like 12 years old."

She shrugged. "Oh. I don't keep up with rock bands."

Clearly.

So, what did I know about Ghost Parker? I wracked my brain. They were pretty popular right now. They had that crazy hit song that had finally died down a bit. Thankfully. And they were the epitome of every rock band cliche: trashing hotel rooms, substance abuse, womanizing, and of course, egotistical, insensitive, and immature young male behavior. There was nothing special about them.

What a turd of an assignment.

"You're going to have to dig deep on this one. Dig up some skeletons in their closets and use them ruthlessly. The band isn't forthcoming about this haunting rumor, so you're going to have to be sly about it. Anything goes as long as you walk close to the line but stay on the legal side of it. We both know that Dawn is a complete pit bull, so you can't hold back, Remi. If you don't unearth something scandalous, you're toast in this competition."

We spent the next 20 minutes going over the particulars of my assignment. Even after I read through the preliminary research that had come with the original story pitch, I felt no better about it. Would this once-in-a-lifetime chance for major exposure in the entertainment journalism world turn into a giant flop in front of millions on national TV?

Ugh. I couldn't give up before I'd even begun. There had to be a way to turn this thing around. It was time to kick some ass.

Chapter 3

Greyson

I STOOD AS STILL as a statue, my hip leaning up against the gigantic kitchen island that was topped with an impressive marble slab. I stared at the small, red Cartier box resting in the palm of my hand. Taking a deep breath, I flipped open the top of the dainty box to reveal the diamond ring nestled in a black velvet cushion, sparkling brilliantly under the bright kitchen lights.

My heart beat rapidly against my chest, and my stomach fluttered. Was it nerves? I smiled faintly to myself. I couldn't remember the last time I was nervous.

Yes, I could. But I was letting all of that go. I grit my teeth with determination.

Okay, instead, let's go with — I couldn't remember the last time a woman had made me nervous.

I was an international TV star. Nerves weren't something I was overly familiar with. I didn't have to deal with that, since confidence was as necessary to my survival as food and water.

So what was this emotion swirling in my gut, making a cold sweat break out on my forehead? Could it be true love? Was this the grand culmination of two soulmates uniting? Was this charge pumping riotously through my veins, the giddy blush of love blooming inside me?

Or was this merely the natural trepidation a man felt when he contemplated baring the soft underbelly of his soul to the possibility of utter rejection, otherwise known as a marriage proposal?

I tried to examine my feelings, to pinpoint the exact nature of them. But I was so much more adept at burying them. Christ, I was such an expert at faking shit, even to myself, that I could no longer recognize a true feeling, even if it smacked me in the face. My entire life felt like one big act of make-believe. Professionally acting since the age of eight and lying to the public about my personal life had screwed me up good until my head was spinning. I hardly knew what was real anymore.

Fuck, I shouldn't feel so goddamned disillusioned with every-fucking-thing when I was about to ask someone to commit themselves to me for the rest of their life. Before I took such a big step, I had to be sure.

I'd had the engagement ring in my possession for more than a month now. I'd done nothing but think about it and I thought I'd come to a decision, but now I was second-guessing myself. Getting cold feet was normal, right? Or was that just with the wedding?

I loved Remi. I had no doubt about that. Sparks flew between us the first time I met her. I knew at that very moment that I wanted to have sex with her, but I didn't trust her enough yet.

Remi was — and still is — a reporter for Hollywood Exposé. She was tasked with interviewing me when my name got linked to a notorious A-list movie actress. I didn't give a damn when rumors started flying about me and the actress; it was par for the course in this business, but apparently, the infamous diva was having marital problems with her husband. She took her anger out on me, making things seem very personal between us, even though we'd barely ever spoken a few words to each other.

My agent was gleeful. The very public spat and airing of our tumultuous relationship, which was totally fictitious, only served to catapult my popularity into the stratosphere. The powers that be at *Devious* wanted to capitalize on that. I was told to do the interview with Hollywood Exposé and to 'dance around' any questions about the actress. Neither confirm nor deny an affair. I balked for about five minutes before I caved. The studio always got what it wanted in the end.

Remi didn't just interview me for the story that one time; she came back several times to meet with me and go over notes. Including me in the creative process, she consulted me about which direction I thought the story should go. Her vision was to craft a story that was more than a fluff piece, to give the fans a glimpse of the real Greyson Durant. She painted a glowing picture of a worthy man that, frankly; I didn't even see myself.

We talked a lot. We had coffee and shared laughs. I suspected that she was drawing out the process just so she could see me again. And it felt good because I loved being with her. I smiled when I thought about her and missed her when I was alone with my thoughts.

When we met for the last time to brush up on some last-minute details, I asked her out to dinner. She turned me down. She felt it was a gray area, ethically, to date the subject of her interview. But, after the story ran, and she'd cleared it with her boss, she agreed to go out on a date with me.

We had sex that night, and it was as sensational as I suspected it would be. She was sexy as fuck and slightly shy in bed, which was unexpected but refreshing.

We began dating discreetly. Instead of getting mad at the paparazzi that made dating near impossible, we made it a game to sneak around them. She wasn't looking for attention or fame and I never saw dollar signs dancing in her eyes like I'd seen in so many others before her.

Over the next few months, we got to know each other better. She was a very intelligent and compassionate person and damn good at her job. The article she'd written about me was a hit with the public and had shown me in the most flattering light. Her knack for ferreting out hidden truths and certain qualities and delicately highlighting them was impressive. I'd started reading her older work. There was no doubt what a talented writer and reporter she was. The quality of her work stood out.

She'd confided in me the entire story about her previous job as an investigative reporter, where her digging had unearthed a huge political scandal that ended up getting her blacklisted when she wouldn't back down. Eventually, the crushing machine of power politics, a full-court intimidation campaign, institutional corruption, and a few death threats ground her career to dust, but she never sold out her integrity. She was knocked down in the worst way but managed to get back up again to start over.

I loved her honesty and integrity. I loved her fun-loving spirit. She made me laugh. She made me feel like a superhero when she looked at me with stars in her eyes. Most of all, I loved how my heart hitched when I sunk into her.

Did I mention that she looked like a sex goddess? She was all lush curves and soft flesh. No matter how many times I told her she was absolutely perfect and not to lose a single pound of weight, I knew she didn't quite believe me. She'd seen the pictures of the girls I'd been photographed with. My supposed love life was plastered all over entertainment media for the entire world to see. With her job, she'd been front and center to witness it over the years, even before she knew me.

My last relationship, which in reality had only been a brief fling, was with my co-star, Stella. The media couldn't get enough of us. They kept our relationship going for months and months, long after it had burnt out.

Stella was the beautiful ingenue that the villainous bad boy that I played on *Devious* had ensnared. The fan base shipped us hard. It was tough not to get caught up in it all when our on-screen emotions blazed like fire.

She wasn't the first actress I dated. A lot of actresses were enviably gorgeous on the screen, but in real life, they were way too thin for my taste. I could actually count Stella's ribs, her hip bones jutted out unattractively, and I could hang a rack of clothing from her collarbone. I was legitimately scared that I might break her. She was also years younger than me and immature as fuck.

Remi wasn't obsessed with her appearance, like most of the women in my occupation. She lived a healthy lifestyle, though not quite as rigorous as mine, of moderation in eating and regular exercise without going overboard. It was refreshing not to hear someone purging the meal I'd just treated them to or obsessively reading every critique or nasty comment about their weight or appearance on social media.

As much as I'd told Remi how much her body turned me on, I think it was finally beginning to sink in now that I'd been able to show her over and over again. I couldn't get enough of her and that luscious body. My dick was stirring just thinking about it.

Tonight, after she accepted my proposal, I was going to take my time making love to her. My cock thickened in response to the thought.

Maybe I'd rip off her clothes and take her on the kitchen counter first. No, I wasn't going to propose in the kitchen. I'd been thinking in front of the fireplace. Then, we could celebrate with the expensive bottle of champagne that was currently chilling in the refrigerator before I dragged her down to the rug and fucked her to climax with my tongue. Then I'd carry her to my bed for the real celebration.

I was attracted to sexy women like any other guy. I'd had sex with too many of them to even remember all of their names, and I'd had long-term relationships with a few of them, too. But I'd never fallen in love with a woman before Remi.

So, why did I hesitate for even a single heartbeat with this proposal? Because fuck me, I'd fallen in love with men before. Several, in fact.

Was it real love or just lust? Oh, I definitely had severe crushes on men before. Feelings that felt an awful lot like love. The relationships I'd had with men were a lot trickier, mainly because of my profession. The audience that watched *Devious* didn't know that I was bisexual, and that's how the studio wanted it, according to my agent.

Honestly, I didn't think it'd be that big of a deal if anyone found out. No one gave a shit about sexual orientation anymore. It would be a big splashy headline at first because it'd been a secret for so long, but it would fade out of the spotlight fast. Women would still lust after Colton Grimaldi.

My agent, who was seriously old school, was always cautioning me to keep it private, and since I didn't really date that many men, I was hardly ever seen in public with another man, so it was easy. I told myself that the main reason I kept it under wraps was that my sexuality was not the world's business. It was my personal life. I wasn't ashamed of it, but I sure as shit didn't owe anyone an inside look-see at my sex life.

Remi knew I was bisexual, and she was okay with it. During the interview process, I'd told her that I was in love with someone unattainable and it was a great source of pain for me. I'd bared my soul to her, and she accepted me. All of me.

And I knew Remi. We'd confided in each other and shared our secrets, hopes, and dreams, and I could feel the depth of our bond. We trusted each other. I loved her.

It was just him that wouldn't get out of my head. The biggest fucking asshole to walk the planet. I didn't love him. It was pure lust.

It was just dumb fucking hormones.

How could it be love if he never fucking acknowledged me? He couldn't even be bothered to turn his head in my direction when I was certain he knew I was there. How could it be love if I really didn't even know him? I only knew what was on the surface. He would never let me in, and he knew next to nothing about me. He didn't want to.

I'd suffered for two years with these unrequited feelings. Whether it was true love or not, the heartbreak it came with was real. And I was sick of it. I wanted to move on from it. I wanted to not give a single fuck about him. Not feel a single thing when I heard him singing on the radio. Not feel one twitch when I caught a glimpse of him on TV. Not a pang when someone mentioned his name.

He was haunting me. He was the one I couldn't force out of my head even while I was staring at the engagement ring that I intended to give to the woman I loved.

It was his electric blue eyes that I dreamed about at night. It was his presence that I felt in a room even before I laid eyes on him. He exuded the jolting charge that rolled through every nerve ending in my body and had me gasping for breath when he was near. He was quite possibly the straightest guy I knew, and it had to be him that made my cock throb and my balls ache with need.

Fuck this.

HOW TO CATCH A ROCKSTAR 43

I was done wasting another thought on that asshole. I wasn't going to let him fuck up my life. Remi was my future.

Just then, I heard a quick knock on the front door. Remi had a key, so I only had a few seconds before she would be in my kitchen.

My heart skipped a beat as I opened up the drawer closest to me on the island and stuffed the Cartier box in with the potholders. I closed the small drawer and smoothed the panic off my face seconds before she entered my house.

"Oh my God, Grey," she shouted, "you won't believe what happened today!"

I raised my voice so she could hear me. "I'm in the kitchen."

She strolled into the kitchen with a sassy sway to her hips, rounded the island, and walked straight into my arms. She wrapped her arms around my neck and smiled up at me. Having her pressed against my body calmed the turbulent emotions that had been ripping through me like a tornado moments before.

Our lips met and the simple hello kiss suddenly turned more heated. Lust flared between us. My tongue pressed into her mouth and she gave a little moan that had my cock pressing against the zipper of my jeans. Fuck, yeah, she was what I wanted.

She pulled back with a little breathless gasp. I let her mouth retreat, but kept her tucked in my arms, pulling her firmly against my body.

"Hmm," she hummed. "We'll get right back to that in a moment. First, I have to tell you something incredible."

"Okay."

I studied her gorgeous face for a moment. It almost hurt to look at her; she was so stunning. Her dark brown eyes were surrounded by long, sooty lashes and could melt my insides with one look. My gaze was drawn to her plump, rosy lips, which were parted and slightly swollen by my hungry kiss. Her complexion had a golden hue, and her long, dark hair cascaded down her back like a silken waterfall. She looked like a goddess. A beaming, radiant goddess put on this earth to tempt mankind.

Her perfect white teeth flashed with a smile. "Mindy Blakedale is retiring." She bounced on her toes as her voice rose an octave. "Caroline said I'm in the running to replace her. It's between me and Dawn. I might be the new face of Hollywood Exposé!"

"What?" A bolt of excited laughter rumbled from my chest. I picked her up and spun her around. "That is incredible news!"

"I know!" she squealed. "We each have an assignment and whoever does the better job is getting the promotion. It's a competition of sorts."

"Okay?" I put her down. "That's a little weird. Who's judging the competition?"

"Caroline and Mr. Hoffman, the owner, are going to decide the winner. She wouldn't tell me what, if any, criteria they were going to use, but she did say they would take into consideration the amount of buzz we generated from the viewers with our stories.

"I feel like I might have a slight edge because Caroline is my mentor, but Dawn does have a few years of seniority on me. Either way, I absolutely have to kick ass on this crazy assignment."

I tapped the tip of her nose with my finger. "And what is this crazy assignment?"

She bit on her lower lip. "At first, I thought Dawn had the advantage. She's assigned something about royals living in America. I was nervous at first because royals are always really popular stories with the viewers."

My lips twitched. "But..."

"But I'm going to turn my story into something fabulous. I'm doing a piece on a haunted rock band. Supposedly, years ago, something tragic happened and numerous people spotted a ghost hanging around the band, haunting them. I haven't really looked into any of the details yet."

"A haunted band?" I gave her the side-eye. "That doesn't really sound too exciting, Rems."

"It will be, at least when I'm done with it!" She spun out of my arms and laughed. "Apparently, the band is a little touchy on the subject, so I'm going to go in under the cover of doing a day-in-the-life / human interest story on the band, but all the while I'll be secretly ghost hunting."

I groaned. "I'm not a fan of royalty in general, but it does sound more interesting than imaginary ghosts. You have your work cut out for you." I made sure to keep my voice teasing and light.

She brushed off my comment and continued, "I'll have to do extensive background research on the band members beforehand to dig up anything juicy I can find. I'm going to be embedded with their tour, so I should have plenty of time to uncover any ghostly dirt that I can. The story is going to have a featured print spot, a huge online presence, and a coveted TV block on Hollywood Exposé. I'll be creatively responsible for everything: the interviews, photos, and video. It'll be the biggest story I've ever done. It'll get me huge exposure and just might push me to the top. I could be the next face of Hollywood Exposé!"

An uneasy feeling was creeping in and twisting my stomach. "Embedded in the tour? For how long?"

"Weeks. Maybe months. However long it takes! I've got five months to wrap up the package for air." She began wringing her hands together. "I have so much research to do before the tour starts. I don't have much time. Can you believe it? I'll be living on a tour bus with some serious rock and rollers. How crazy is that?"

"It's pretty crazy." I hoped she didn't hear the waver in my voice.

"Who is this band?"

"Ghost Parker. Isn't it ironic that they have the word 'ghost' in their name? It just makes..."

I didn't hear the rest of what she was saying. I was too busy trying to contain my shock. Life really was a bag of dicks sometimes.

"Grey? Are you okay?" Her hand rested on my arm, trying to get my attention.

I snapped out of it quickly. I didn't even have to think about acting anymore. It came automatically. "Yeah, I was just surprised. Did I ever mention that I sort of know them? Ghost Parker? My friend, Talia, is married to one of the guitarists."

"Talia?" She smiled big. "The girl that used to live in your beach house? Small world, huh?"

I pulled her back into my arms and smiled back at her. "Well, this calls for a celebration. I've got a bottle of champagne chilling in the fridge. Let's sit in front of the fireplace and you can tell me all about your big plans for the story."

"Perfect!" Her eyes were sparkling. "How convenient! Why do you have champagne chilling in the fridge?"

"No special reason."

Chapter 4

Ghost

THE MOMENT I STEPPED into Maggie's office, her eyes widened at the sight of my ill-fitted pink sweatshirt that read 'Princess' across the chest, and the sparkly flip-flops adorning my feet. I couldn't help but grin at her reaction; it felt like a small victory in my ongoing battle to break through her professional exterior.

"Nice outfit, Ghost," she said, smirking as she gestured for me to take a seat on her plush couch. "Did you lose a bet?"

"Something like that," I replied, chuckling as I settled onto the couch. "Let's just say last night's company had an interesting taste in fashion."

Maggie raised an eyebrow, amused but not surprised by my antics. "Well, I hope you at least got her number before borrowing her wardrobe."

I laughed, shaking my head. "Nah, we both knew it was a one-time thing. Besides, these flip-flops are kinda growing on me."

She smiled, making a note on her clipboard.

I tossed the bag from the donut shop onto the table between us. "Lemon donut with lemon glaze."

She clapped her hands together, looking like a little kid on Christmas morning. "You shouldn't have!"

Stretching my legs out in front of me, I chuckled. "You need better taste in donuts. There are so many other choices, yet you're so set on the double lemon. There must be some deep-seated psychological reason for it."

She tapped her pen on her chin. "All right, let's move past your analysis of me for now. How have you been feeling lately? You know, with Christmas coming up and being on break from the tour..."

I sighed, my playful demeanor fading as I considered her question. It was true — having some time off from the constant chaos of touring life left me with too much time to think, to feel, to get lost in my own head.

"Truthfully?" I began, rubbing my hands together nervously. "It's been rough. I thought I'd enjoy the downtime, but without the structure of the tour, I find myself slipping back into old habits. The loneliness creeps in, you know?"

Maggie nodded empathetically, her gaze steady and reassuring. "That's completely normal, Ghost. The holidays can be a challenging time for many people, and it's easy to feel adrift when your usual routine is disrupted."

I appreciated her understanding, but it didn't change the fact that I felt like a lost soul, aimlessly wandering through life while everyone around me seemed to have things figured out. And yet, in this cheerful, airy office, I always felt a glimmer of hope — that there was a chance for me to confront my demons and work towards something better.

"Yeah," I murmured, feeling a strange mix of calmness and agitation.

Her pen was poised above her clipboard, as she prepared to dive deeper into the tangled web of my emotions. "So how were things on the road with the band?"

"Mostly the same as usual. It was a little different with Knox. He used to be my main partner in crime — I guess you could say, my wingman — but he's cut back on his partying, so it was a bit weird."

Knox had recently revealed some things to the band that he'd kept buried in his past but were messing with his head, and I'd referred him to Maggie. I knew he was slowly working through his shit and it hadn't been easy, but I was jealous of how quickly he seemed to be healing. I thought that it had to do with Summer; she was good for him. He was in love with Summer and it left me feeling odd man out at times. Without Knox to party with, I felt even more isolated.

I leaned back against the beige couch and sighed, feeling the weight of my loneliness amplified as my friends all took the next steps expected in adulthood. "You know, it's funny," I began, trying to keep the bitterness out of my voice. "Sid just got married, and Knox is head over heels for Summer. It seems like everyone around me is finding love, settling down ... except for Bash and me."

"Interesting," Maggie said, her eyes narrowing slightly as she considered my words. "And how does that make you feel?"

I hesitated, unsure if I should admit the deep-seated envy that had been gnawing at me for months. But Maggie had a way of making even the most painful confessions feel safe, so I took a deep breath and let the truth spill out. "Happy, of course, but also ... envious, I guess. It's like they've cracked the code to forming these deep connections with people, while I'm still floundering."

She nodded thoughtfully, her pen tapping against her clipboard.

"Well, Ghost, remember when we talked about working on your own connections? How have your 'interviews' been going? Have you been reaching out to women and talking to them for at least 15 minutes?"

I couldn't help but chuckle at the memory of Maggie's seemingly ridiculous assignment. It seemed so simple — just talk to people, really get to know them — and yet it had proven to be a challenging task and a source of aggravation for me.

"Sure, I've been talking to women more," I admitted, running a hand through my hair in frustration. "But it doesn't make me feel any more connected to them. If anything, it makes me realize just how different I am from everyone else."

Maggie studied me closely, her gaze never wavering as she searched for the hidden meaning behind my words. "Ghost, there's nothing wrong with being different. But it's important to remember that connection isn't something that happens overnight. It takes time and effort on both sides."

I knew she was right, but the thought of putting in all that work only to end up feeling nothing, was enough to make me want to quit trying. My eyes flicked to the clock on the wall, counting down the minutes until I could escape this unrelenting self-examination and retreat to the familiar comforts of solitude.

"Let's try a different approach," Maggie suggested gently. "Instead of focusing on romantic connections, think about the friendships you've formed within your band. How do you maintain those relationships?"

"Easy — we're all stuck together on a tour bus for months at a time," I joked, trying to lighten the mood. But Maggie wasn't deterred. She just smiled patiently and waited for me to continue.

"Seriously, though ... I guess we just have each other's backs. We've been through so much together, and it's hard not to form bonds when you're living in such close quarters. But it's different with other people, especially with women. There's always this barrier between us, this unspoken expectation that I can't seem to break through."

"Maybe the key is to approach these new relationships in the same way you approach your friendships," Maggie mused, her pen flying across the page as she jotted down notes. "Take the time to get to know someone without any expectations or pressure. You might be surprised by the connections you're able to form when you let go of the idea that love is something that can be forced."

I wasn't sure I was actually seeking love, just a little belonging. My fingers drummed against the armrest on the couch. "You know what, Maggie? I think I'm just not meant to love anyone." My words hung heavy in the air, a cloud of vulnerability settling around me.

Maggie's pen paused above her notepad, her eyes meeting mine with genuine concern. "What makes you say that, Ghost?"

"Every woman I've been with ... they don't give a damn about who I am. They only want me for the fame and money," I admitted, my voice hard. The truth stung like a slap to the face, but there was no use pretending any different.

"Have you ever considered why you attract these kinds of relationships?" Maggie asked, her voice gentle yet probing.

I shrugged, feeling defensive but also curious. "Maybe it's because I'm afraid to let anyone see the real me, the messed-up train wreck underneath this rock star facade."

"Ghost, we've talked about this before — your past does not define you. But understanding how it affects your present relationships can help you move forward. Let's explore where this fear of vulnerability might come from," she suggested, leaning forward slightly.

I hesitated, knowing exactly where she was going with this. It wasn't the first time she'd tried to get me to open up about the past. The memories of my father and the abuse I endured at his hands were locked away in a mental vault, one that I rarely dared to open. But maybe it was time to crack it open, just a little more.

"Fine," I muttered, swallowing the lump in my throat. "It probably has something to do with my asshole of a father."

Maggie's voice was soothing, yet insistent, "I'd like you to try to go back to that time in your life when things were difficult with your father." She clicked her pen, poised to jot down notes as I hesitated.

My chest tightened as I tried to breathe through the memories, and my eyes squeezed shut in a futile attempt to block them out. But like a relentless tide, they came crashing through me, dragging me under. "He was never sober," I choked out, my voice barely audible. "And when he drank ... he'd become this ... monster."

"Take your time, Ghost," Maggie said softly, her soothing tone a lifeline amidst the storm of emotions threatening to drown me.

"It's like he was always lurking in the shadows, waiting for an excuse to lash out," I continued, my voice trembling with the effort to maintain control. "Sometimes I'd lie awake at night, just listening for the sound of his footsteps down the hall. It felt like I was constantly on edge."

Maggie knew that he had abused me, but I'd never given her any details. Taking a deep breath, I closed my eyes and let the memories flood back, trying to maintain my composure. "He was an angry man — always drunk, always looking for a reason to lash out. I never knew when he'd snap, so I learned to keep my distance." My voice wavered, betraying how hard it was to relive the nightmare. "It seemed like every night, he would stumble through the door, reeking of alcohol, and just ... unleash his anger on whoever happened to be nearby."

"Did that include you?" Maggie asked gently, not wanting to push me too far, but needing the details to understand.

I looked down, picking at the frayed threads of the sweatshirt. "Most of the time," I admitted, feeling the old wounds reopening. "But a lot of the time it was Adam, my stepbrother, who took the brunt of his fury."

My jaw clenched as the weight of suppressed emotions threatened to crush me from within. But instead of recoiling, I allowed myself to feel — just for a brief moment — the pain that I had buried for so long.

"It's not easy to revisit those memories," Maggie said sincerely, "but understanding how your past impacts your present relationships can be incredibly valuable. Emotional intimacy was a luxury you couldn't afford back then, and it's shaped you. Realizing that is a big step to healing yourself."

"He's dead. Why couldn't I bury all this shit with him?" I asked, more to myself than to Maggie.

"It's not easy." She adjusted her glasses as she watched me. "You have the power to change your life, Ghost. You just need to believe in yourself and take that first step toward healing. How did you feel about your father's death?"

"His death..." I faltered, taking a moment to collect myself. "In some ways, it was a relief. I was finally free from his torment. But it was too late for Adam. And, even though he's gone, he's still there, inside me, haunting my thoughts and dreams. I can't seem to escape him."

"Ghost," Maggie said, placing her pen down on her notepad, "it's important for you to understand that your father's actions were not your fault. You didn't deserve the abuse you suffered, and it's okay to feel a mix of emotions about his passing. Grief is complicated, and healing takes time."

I nodded. I didn't tell Maggie that I didn't feel an ounce of grief for the man and I'd been glad when he died. Frankly, I didn't feel guilty about it either. He was a fucked up man that had carelessly ruined many lives and even when I was younger, I had understood that.

"Your father's alcoholism and abuse have clearly left deep scars," Maggie acknowledged, her eyes filled with empathy. "But remember that you're safe here — you can share your feelings without fear of judgment or retribution."

A bitter laugh escaped my lips. Safe? The concept felt so foreign, even now. Yet there was something undeniably comforting about Maggie's presence, her years of unwavering support providing a sense of stability I had never known. In a strange way, it almost made me feel invincible.

"You're doing so great, Ghost. I want to gently shift our focus to Adam. You mentioned him and you've never talked about him before. I'd like to hear a bit about him." Maggie paused, giving me a moment to process. "Let's talk about your relationship with him."

At the mention of my stepbrother, my breath hitched. The guilt and sadness that swirled beneath the surface threatened to burst forth. My eyes darted around the room, avoiding Maggie's gaze. Her office was filled with books and the faint smell of lavender, which did little to calm my frayed nerves. This was new territory, and I didn't really want to explore it right now.

I fought to keep my voice steady as I spoke. "We were close ... as close as two people could be in that hellhole we called home. He was my rock, my confidant — the one person who understood what it was like to live in constant fear of our father's wrath. He was always trying to protect me. "

"Sounds like you two had a strong bond," Maggie remarked, probing but cautious. "I understand that he took his own life some years ago."

I nodded, swallowing hard. My grip on my own arm tightened, nails digging into my flesh, seeking grounding in the pain. I hadn't ever spoken to anyone about his suicide. "When he ... committed suicide, it was like a part of me died with him. I've never really forgiven myself for not being there when he needed me the most."

She shifted in her seat. "Ghost, it's important to remember that your stepbrother's decision was his own. You bear no responsibility for it. It's natural to feel guilt and sadness, but those emotions don't define you or your worth as a person," Maggie reassured, her eyes locked onto mine, unwavering in their sincerity.

"Maybe," I conceded, my voice thick with emotion. "But the truth is, I still struggle to process his loss. It's like this gaping wound that refuses to heal, a constant reminder of the pain and suffering we both endured."

"Sharing this with me is a huge breakthrough, Ghost. I'm proud of you." She was studying me with a mix of compassion and curiosity. "Tell me, do you think Adam would blame you for his suicide if he were here today?"

At first, I was shocked by her question. But then I sat back and thought about it. Deep in my heart, I knew Adam didn't blame me. "No."

Her gaze was intense. "Would he want you to blame yourself?"

"No." The answer was simple in its truth.

She nodded. "Did you share any interests or hobbies with Adam?"

"Yeah," I said, managing a weak smile at the thought of our shared moments. "We both loved music, writing songs together. It's part of what led me to where I am today. He was so talented, Maggie. He deserved so much better than the life we had."

"Yes, you both did." She paused for a long moment."Can you tell me about how you learned about Adam's suicide?" Her eyes never left mine, offering a sense of safety despite the despair that threatened to swallow me whole.

"Found him," I choked out, my heart pounding against my chest. "I found him hanging in his room. There was no note, no explanation. Just... gone."

"Ghost," Maggie said, her voice thick with empathy, "it's not uncommon for survivors of suicide to experience feelings of guilt and sadness. But remember, none of it was your fault."

"Intellectually, I know that," I admitted, feeling like I'd been stabbed in the chest. "But my heart... It feels like I failed him somehow. Like if I'd just been there more, or listened better ... maybe he'd still be here."

"Survivor's guilt is a powerful emotion, Ghost. It's natural for you to feel this way, but healing from the loss is possible." As she spoke, I could see the sincerity in her eyes, a flicker of hope struggling to hold on amidst the darkness. Was it possible that I'd ever escape the pain or the ghosts of my past?

"Thank you for sharing these memories and feelings with me," Maggie nodded encouragingly. "It takes immense courage to confront the demons of our past, but doing so can pave the way for healing and personal growth. Healing is a gradual process, and it takes time to work through everything. I want you to know that you've come a long way since we first started working together. Do you remember when you first started seeing me?"

Her words made me pause for a moment, the memory of our first few encounters lightening the heavy mood that had descended. A brief smile flickered across my face as I remembered our first session. I hadn't exactly been a model patient back then. I'd been ordered by a judge to see Maggie for anger management after getting arrested for disorderly conduct. Scoffing at the idea of therapy, I dismissed Maggie and her entire profession as a waste of time.

"I remember. I was an absolute nightmare." A hint of self-deprecation colored my tone. "I didn't believe in any of this 'touchy-feely' stuff, and I definitely didn't believe that you could help me."

Maggie chuckled softly. "Yes, I remember. But you were also someone who was hurting, even if you refused to admit it at the time. And I saw potential in you, Ghost — potential for growth and change."

"Sometimes I wonder how you managed to put up with me," I mused, shaking my head in disbelief. "But you did. You didn't give up on me, even when I was hell-bent on pushing you away."

"Because I believed in you," she replied, her eyes warm and steady. "And I still do. You've come a long way, and you should be proud of yourself. Change doesn't happen overnight, but you're making progress."

"Progress..." I echoed, rolling the word around in my mouth like a foreign concept. "I guess I have changed, in some ways. But sometimes it feels like I'm still so numb to the world, like I'm just going through the motions."

"Change is a slow process," Maggie said gently, a reassuring smile gracing her lips. "And it's okay to feel that way sometimes. The important thing is that you're taking steps to confront your past and work towards a more open, emotionally honest self."

"Thanks, Maggie," I murmured, gratitude swelling in my chest. She had been the one constant in my chaotic life, the rock upon which I could anchor myself when the storms of my past threatened to overwhelm me. I knew I still had a long way to go; I still hadn't revealed my worst secret to her, but I felt that maybe I was on the cusp of a breakthrough. Thinking about telling her my greatest shame didn't send me into a blinding panic.

"Remember to be patient with yourself," she added. "You're

stronger than you give yourself credit for, Ghost. And I know that you'll find your way through this — one step at a time."

I tried to soak in all her confidence and belief in me. Optimism didn't come naturally to me.

"Time's almost up," Maggie glanced at the clock on the wall. "But before you go, I want to remind you of the importance of self-compassion."

"Self-compassion?" I raised an eyebrow, my mind still swirling with the emotions we had delved into during our session. "Sounds kinky."

"Not exactly." She leaned back in her chair. "It's about recognizing that you're human, and it's okay to feel pain and make mistakes. You can't change what happened, but you can work on accepting yourself — flaws and all."

"Sounds like a lot to ask from someone like me," I quipped, trying to lighten the mood, but Maggie remained serious.

"I've seen you make tremendous progress," she said kindly, her eyes meeting mine. "You may not see the changes in yourself, but they're there. And as you continue to explore your emotions and past experiences, I believe you'll be ready to open up even more of yourself to me and others."

"Thanks, Maggie." I tried to sound hopeful, though I couldn't shake the lingering doubts that clung to me like cobwebs in an abandoned house.

"Change is slow, but it's happening," she reassured me. "Don't give up on yourself, Ghost. You deserve happiness just as much as anyone else does."

"Alright, Doc," I said with a grin, standing up and stretching my stiff limbs. "I'll give this self-compassion thing a shot."

Maggie smiled, rising from her own seat. "Good. And remember, I'm always here if you need anything. Take care of yourself, Ghost."

"Will do." With a final nod, I left Maggie's office feeling raw and exposed, yet at the same time, inexplicably lighter.

As I walked away, I felt a mix of emotions bubbling inside me. Sadness lingered from the memories we had unearthed, but there was also hope — a fragile, flickering flame that refused to be snuffed out. I wouldn't keep coming back here if there was no hope. I was determined to confront my past and work towards a better future, no matter how long it took or how difficult it would be.

I paused for a moment in the hallway, taking a deep breath as if to inhale the promise of change that Maggie had instilled in me. Then, with newfound determination propelling me forward, I strode toward the exit, ready to face whatever life had in store for me.

"Self-compassion," I muttered to myself, letting the word sink into my consciousness.

It was a concept I had never considered before, but now I understood that it could be the key to unlocking a better version of myself. Maybe it was time to give it a try.

Chapter 5

Remi

THE NEWSROOM AT HOLLYWOOD Exposé buzzed with life, the familiar cacophony of ringing phones and clattering keyboards providing a lively soundtrack to my day. I leaned back in my chair, soaking in the frenetic energy that swirled around me like a whirlwind. This is where I felt alive, where I felt powerful. Each keystroke, each sentence weaved by my nimble fingers, held the potential to inform readers, shift perceptions, and maybe, just maybe, make a positive difference in the world.

"Remi, you've got a package!" Sheila, our group admin, called out as she approached my desk, her hands cradling a small box wrapped in brown paper.

"Thanks, Sheila," I replied, taking the package from her with a curious smile. I'd never received a wrapped package at work before; I had no idea what it could be. As I tore off the paper, anticipation bubbled inside me like champagne.

Inside, I found a beautiful leather journal, its cover a deep teal hue that seemed to shimmer under the fluorescent lights. Delicate gold vines were embossed on the front, their tendrils reaching towards the spine as if yearning for an embrace. The pages, creamy and smooth beneath my fingertips, breathed with the whisper of countless untold stories.

A small envelope fell onto my lap as I admired the journal, and I quickly opened it to find a note written in my mother's neat cursive.

```
Dearest Remi,


I saw this journal and thought it
would be perfect for you. I wanted
to remind you how proud I am of all
your accomplishments and wish you
the best of luck in the promotion
competition. Remember to always
reach for your dreams. You have
the power to change people's lives
with your words. Use it wisely.


Love,
Mom
```

My chest tightened at the warmth of her words, and I couldn't help but smile. Mom always knew how to lift my spirits, even from miles away. The journal was perfect for my new assignment.

"Alright, Remi," I whispered to myself, running a hand through my hair. "Let's do this. "

I placed the journal to the right of my keyboard, its presence a constant reminder of my mother's faith in me. With renewed determination, I turned my attention back to the task at hand, fingers poised above the keyboard, ready to chase after my dreams and make a difference — one story at a time.

I plunged into the depths of the internet, sifting through old articles and social media posts about Ghost Parker and its band members, searching for potential story angles. According to my assignment, I needed to manufacture a ghost that was haunting the band.

The rumor mill started churning years ago when the negative image of a promotional photograph of the band surfaced online, where some eagle-eyed fans claimed to see a ghostly figure looming behind the five musicians. The negative image was from the cover art from their first album, which had been turned into promotional T-shirts for their first big tour. After rumors of the ghost surfaced, sales of merchandise exploded. The band had denied any type of haunting or ghost attached to them, but I was determined to make this non-existent ghost into a global sensation that consumed the world with its captivating story.

"Come on, you elusive specter," I muttered under my breath, my fingers flying across the keyboard. *Let's find out who you are and why you're haunting these poor rock stars.*

As I delved deeper into each of the lives of the band members, I began uncovering tidbits of information that could be relevant to my assignment. Sidney, the bass player, grew up in foster care, a detail that tugged at my heartstrings but could potentially add an interesting twist to the story.

Ryder, on the other hand, had a cousin that died just before the supposed ghost photograph was taken — now there was a lead worth pursuing. If I could tie the cousin to the band somehow, I could make something work from it.

Bash, the drummer, recently became a father, but strangely, the baby's mother remained unmentioned in the media. A secret love affair, perhaps? I'd have to track down that information and see where it led. My mind raced with possibilities as I scribbled notes into my new journal.

As for Knox, he dealt with his own tragedy when his fiancée died in a car accident, making her another great choice for a potential spook out for revenge. Besides his fiancée's death, which was reported locally in Scotland, Knox seemed to keep himself out of the limelight.

And then there was Ghost himself, who had a penchant for minor skirmishes with the law, especially during the time period I was interested in. There wasn't much information about his private life that was publicly available. I would need to travel to his hometown to uncover some juicy information. If I could find a death tied to Ghost, my story would be that much stronger. He was the lead singer, and he was nicknamed Ghost, after all.

I didn't find any reported incidents at any of Ghost Parker's concerts that could be attributed to a ghost. There were no lights crashing down on stage, no major malfunctions, and no flat tires on the tour buses. I planned to interview the road crew and dig up any small incidents I could find. With the use of a little exaggeration, I could make sure our ghost had gotten up to lots of mischief.

I leaned back in my chair, tapping my pen against my chin as I surveyed the information laid out before me. All of these details were exploitable, but I needed to be cautious not to overstep any boundaries. After all, I wanted to win this competition, but not at the expense of my integrity.

"Hey, Remi," Linda called from the desk next to mine. "Any luck conjuring up that ghost?"

I'd sat next to Linda for years and she'd become a bit of a friend by default. She was nosy and loud but was a terrific journalist. She knew I'd been assigned this story, but per Caroline's instructions, she knew nothing about the competition between Dawn and me or that Mindy Blakedale was leaving Hollywood Exposé.

"Ha, very funny," I shot back, rolling my eyes. "But yeah, I've got some leads. Just trying to piece it all together."

"Good luck!" she replied with a hint of sarcasm. "You're gonna need it for that stinker of a story."

I sighed, knowing that my competition was fierce and the material I had to work with was flimsy. But there was no time for self-doubt. I needed to focus on creating an intriguing story and proving myself as the top contender for this promotion.

"Alright, ghost," I said, cracking my knuckles and returning to my research. "Let's see what other secrets you're hiding."

And with that, I dove back into the chaotic world of Ghost Parker and its band members, determined to craft an intriguing story behind the haunting rumors and earn my place as the face of Hollywood Exposé.

After a few hours of research, I glanced down at the notes I'd taken, filling up pages and pages of my new journal, as I attempted to piece together a story that would captivate readers and secure my promotion. But as the intimate details of each band member's life stared back at me, a gnawing unease began to take root in my chest. The question crept into my mind again: Was it right for me to exploit these people's lives for the sake of my career?

"Shit," I mumbled to myself. *You're just doing your job. It's not like you're making stuff up out of whole cloth.* But even as I tried to reassure myself, I couldn't shake the feeling that twisting real-life tragedies to fit my ghostly narrative was ... wrong somehow.

"Ugh, I need a break," I sighed, pushing away from my desk and heading toward the breakroom. Maybe a cup of coffee would clear my head and help me figure out how to proceed with my assignment.

As I poured myself a cup of liquid motivation, the door to the breakroom swung open, and in strutted Dawn, looking as smug as ever. My heart sank. Just what I needed: a face-off with my competition.

"Hey, Remi!" she chirped, pouring herself a cup of coffee as well. "How's that ghost story coming along?"

"Fine, thanks," I replied curtly, trying to hide my inner turmoil. The last thing I wanted was for her to sense any weakness.

"Really?" she asked, raising an eyebrow skeptically. "You know, you don't have to pretend with me. We're all friends here."

She was definitely not a friend of mine and I had no intention of giving her any ammunition to use against me. "It's coming along nicely. Better than I expected, actually."

Dawn's eyes narrowed as she took a sip of her coffee, studying me like I was an interesting specimen under a microscope. "Is that so? Just how much progress have you made on it? Found any juicy tidbits yet?"

"Actually, yes," I said, trying my best to sound confident despite the roiling emotions inside me. "I've uncovered quite a few interesting facts about the band members' lives."

"Really?" Dawn leaned against the counter, casually stirring her coffee. Her gaze never left mine, a predatory glint in her eyes. "Well, let's hear it then. What do you have?"

"Uh, well..." I hesitated, not wanting to reveal my hand to this snake. "I'm still working on piecing everything together, but it's really coming together nicely."

"Ah, I see." Dawn smirked, taking another sip of her coffee. "Well, I hate to break it to you, Remi, but while you're busy agonizing over your little ghost story, I've been digging up some serious dirt on our favorite love-to-hate-them, black sheep royals who live in our own backyard. Trust me, when this story hits, it's going to make huge waves. We're talking bombshells."

"Good for you," I said, clenching my fists to keep them from shaking. I didn't want to give Dawn the satisfaction of seeing how much her words affected me. She was as talented as she was vicious. If she had a good scoop, it would be hard to beat her.

"Of course, I suppose I should be worried about my competition," she continued, her voice dripping with insincere concern. "But honestly, Remi, you always struck me as a bit ... soft-hearted for this industry. Can you really stomach exploiting people's private lives for the sake of a sensational story?"

"Who says that's what I'm doing?" I retorted, anger bubbling up inside me. I knew she was playing mind games, trying to get under my skin, but I couldn't help but rise to the bait.

Dawn smirked, clearly enjoying herself. "Please, Remi. It's not like we're writing for *The New Yorker* here. We're in the business of selling gossip and scandal, and if you think you can succeed without getting your hands dirty, then you're even more naïve than I thought. But hey, you do you. Just don't come crying to me when you lose that promotion."

I could feel my resolve wavering, the temptation to give in to the cutthroat tactics that seemed to come so naturally to Dawn. "Thanks for the pep talk," I replied through gritted teeth, my heart pounding in my chest.

"Anytime, sweetheart," she said, tossing her empty coffee cup into the trash. "You've got to be ruthless in this industry and it looks like you just don't have what it takes."

"Ruthless, Dawn? There's a difference between being ruthless and being heartless. Something you wouldn't understand," I snapped, my patience wearing thin. "You might think exploiting people's pain is the way to succeed, but that's not how I operate."

"Is that so?" she retorted, her eyes narrowing. "Well, good luck with your sugar-coated fluff piece. You won't make a dent in this industry if you don't have the stomach for the real stories." Her voice was dripping with disdain.

I could feel my face grow hot as anger bubbled within me. "Real stories? Is that what you call digging into people's personal tragedies and airing them out without any regard for their feelings?" I shot back, my hands shaking slightly.

"Welcome to Hollywood Exposé, sweetheart," she said mockingly, tilting her head to the side. "Maybe you're just not cut out for it after all." She gave me an infuriating smirk, clearly enjoying the rise she was getting out of me.

My eyes narrowed. "Listen, Dawn," I said, trying to keep my voice steady. "I'm going to get this promotion because of my talent, not because I stooped to your level. And when I do, I'll know I did it the right way."

She laughed, a cold, patronizing sound that made my blood boil. "Oh, Remi, you're so naïve. But whatever helps you sleep at night, darling." With those parting words, she sauntered out of the break-room, leaving me to stew in my frustration and doubt.

I slumped against the counter, trying to catch my breath and regain control of my emotions. Was Dawn right? Was I too soft-hearted to make it in this industry? As much as I wanted to prove her wrong, I couldn't deny that the idea of exploiting Ghost Parker's personal tragedies for my own gain left a sour taste in my mouth.

"Damn it," I cursed, gripping my coffee cup so tightly that it threatened to crush under the pressure. I needed to find another angle, something that would allow me to stay true to myself while still delivering a story that would blow everyone away. It seemed near impossible.

"Alright, Dawn," I muttered, steeling myself for the battle ahead. "You want a fight? You've got one."

As I left the breakroom, her words echoed in my head. Was I willing to risk losing this promotion by sticking to my moral compass? I'd been burned before, trying to do what I thought was right. I hadn't just been burned, I'd lost the career that I'd loved. I absolutely was naïve.

Had I learned anything? Would my naivety hold me back and cause me to publish a puff piece that would lose the competition? Or would I dive into the murky waters of exploitation just to come out on top? Even my boss, Caroline, had warned me that I was going to have to fire on all cylinders to win this thing. If I held back too much, I was doomed.

I stormed back to my desk with the image of Dawn's smug smirk burned into my memory. My heart pounded in my chest, and my hands still trembled from our confrontation. I couldn't let her win, not like this.

I felt my resolve harden. Yes, she was right about one thing: this industry was cutthroat. We often made our bread and butter off of other people's misfortunes. If I thought I had the chops to make it in this industry, I had to prove it.

"Game on, Dawn," I whispered to myself, clenching my fists in determination. "Game on."

I stared at my notes once more, considering my options. And as the weight of my decision bore down on me, I realized that no matter what I chose, the consequences would haunt me long after the competition was over.

Chapter 6

Greyson

THE SALTY OCEAN BREEZE swept across my face as I pulled into the driveway of Talia's beach house. The last time I had been here was for Talia's baby shower, which had morphed into Knox's surprise birthday party — a bonfire celebration on the beach. Memories came flooding back; it was on this very beach where I had seen Ghost again, in all his enigmatic glory. His fingers danced effortlessly over the guitar strings, creating hypnotic melodies that mesmerized the gathered crowd. The fire illuminated his chiseled features and piercing blue eyes, highlighting just how handsome and captivating he was. His voice, smooth as velvet, carried the weight of unspoken emotion — a haunting siren's call that had stirred something deep within me.

I tried to stifle the feelings that surged through my chest, but each note only intensified the attraction that I knew he didn't return. Eventually, the pain became unbearable, and I had no choice but to distance myself from the scene, escaping further down the beach and into the darkness.

"Greyson!" Talia's voice snapped me back to the present as she flung open her front door, her warm smile a welcome relief. "You made it!"

"Of course I did. I couldn't think of a better way to spend my day off taping than to see how baby Zoe is doing," I replied, taking in the sight of her newfound motherly glow. In my hands, I held an adorable baby girl outfit, complete with a pretty pink tutu with hot pink edging and a stretchy baby headband with a matching flower.

"Another gift? You have to stop spoiling Zoe!" Talia admonished playfully, taking the outfit from me and holding it up to admire.

"Can't help it," I confessed, grinning sheepishly. "She's just too cute."

Talia sighed. "Tell me about it." She led me inside and fixed me a lemonade while we chatted. "How are you doing, Grey?"

Smiling, I brushed off any hint of the inner turmoil that had been plaguing me. "Ah, you know, the usual TV star life," I joked. "How's being a new mom treating you?"

"Exhausting, but worth every sleepless night," she replied, settling onto the couch with a soft groan. "You wouldn't believe some of the ridiculous things that have happened."

I sat next to her. "Try me," I challenged, genuinely eager to hear her stories.

"Alright, let's see..." She paused for a moment, recalling the chaos of her new life. "The other day, Ryder accidentally put Zoe's dirty diaper in the laundry hamper instead of the diaper pail. You can imagine the mess we found when we went to do laundry."

Imagining the disastrous scene in all its gruesome detail, I cringed. "Yikes!"

"Yep," Talia laughed, shaking her head. "But it's all part of the adventure, right?"

My nose wrinkled in protest. "If you say so." I allowed myself to get lost in the lighthearted banter. For a moment, my thoughts drifted away from Remi and Ghost and the complex web of emotions that had ensnared me.

"Speaking of adventures," Talia began, a mischievous glint in her eye, "you know what Ryder and I haven't been able to do since Zoe was born?"

I groaned, but couldn't suppress a smirk. "Please don't tell me you're about to launch into talk about your sex life."

She picked up the small pillow by her side and threw it at me. "Hey, I'm just saying, it's been five weeks. And I'm starting to get that itch again. The first few weeks, I didn't think I'd ever want to have sex again."

I grimaced theatrically. "Uh, if it's an itch you're feeling, you better check with the doctor. You might need some kind of cream."

"You're a funny guy," she deadpanned. "Think about it — could you imagine laying next to a hot guy like Ryder every night and not being able to have sex? But, it's fine, we've always been fans of oral, anyway." She winked, causing me to choke on my drink.

"Okay, I really didn't need to know that, thank you very much," I grimaced, trying to banish the mental image. "What did Knox call it at your wedding? Love at first lip lock? It's more like love at first 'lips locked on each other's genitalia'. You two are crazy."

"Can't deny it." She shrugged with a grin. "But enough about that. What I really want to know..."

Her voice trailed off as Ryder strode into the room, cradling Zoe in his arms. Ryder always looked hot with his fit body and his rumpled dark hair and thick eyelashes, but carrying the tiny baby girl, he somehow looked even hotter. It was no wonder Talia was still head over heels for him.

"Hey, Greyson." He glanced over at Talia. "She's had her bottle and been changed. Do you want me to keep her while Grey is here?"

"No, I'll take her." She stood up to take Zoe from his arms. "How about we take her on a walk around the neighborhood? I could use the fresh air."

"Sounds like a plan," I agreed and then helped her gather up the hundreds of items we'd need to take with us.

As we strolled along, pushing the baby carriage along the little slice of paradise where Talia lived, the sun casting warm rays on our faces, Talia turned her attention back to me.

"Grey, how are things going with Remi?" She glanced over at me, the breeze ruffling her long blonde hair.

I hesitated, weighing my words carefully. "Honestly, Talia, I was about to propose to her. I had the ring; I had the champagne chilled. But at the last minute, I backed out."

"Really? Why?" Concern flickered across her face.

"Because..." I sighed, struggling to put my feelings into words. "I still struggle with my attraction to men. And I'm not sure if it's fair to Remi. I love her, but I can't turn off my feelings for ... other people."

Talia listened intently, her eyes filled with understanding as she absorbed my confession. As we continued walking, we arrived at a small neighborhood park and settled down on a bench, the serene surroundings a stark contrast to the turmoil inside me. Baby Zoe slept peacefully in her stroller, oblivious to our conversation.

"Greyson," Talia began gently, "it's okay to feel confused and conflicted about your feelings. You're dealing with something that can be very difficult to navigate. And it's important to remember that you deserve love and happiness, just as much as anyone else."

Her words offered a small comfort, but the gnawing uncertainty still clawed at my insides. I knew I had some tough decisions ahead — not just for myself, but for Remi, as well.

The leaves rustled softly in the gentle breeze, a stark contrast to the fiery chaos of my thoughts. I knew I had to be honest with Talia — and myself — about the real reason behind my hesitation to propose to Remi.

"Truth is," I began, my voice barely above a whisper, "I've been thinking about breaking up with Remi."

Talia's eyes widened slightly, but her expression remained sympathetic. "You have? Why?"

I glanced down at my hands, ashamed to admit this out loud. "Remember how I told you I had that massive crush on Ghost? Well, it was a bit more than a crush."

The corners of her mouth turned down in a frown. "I thought you got over that? You said once you started dating Remi, all those feelings went away."

"That's what I wanted to happen. I really did, but I can't shake my feelings for Ghost, no matter how hard I try." I gazed out over the park and laughed bitterly. "And you know what's ironic? Remi just got an assignment to cover Ghost Parker's tour for Hollywood Exposé. She'll be traveling with them for months."

"Shit, that must be difficult for you," Talia said, her voice filled with genuine concern. "How do you feel about her being away and around Ghost?"

"Terrified, honestly," I admitted, my heart racing at the thought. "I trust Remi, but I don't know if I can handle her being so close to the one person I can't get out of my head. She'll be talking to him — interviewing him. It's very intimate, in a way. That's how she and I got so close, to begin with."

Talia stood up and adjusted the sun shade on the stroller. "Does she know? About Ghost?"

"No, she knows that I still have feelings for an unnamed man, but I've slightly downplayed my fucking obsession." My jaw tensed. "After I found out about her assignment, I thought about telling her that Ghost is that guy, but that might make things complicated. It might skew the way she interacts with him and mess up her assignment if she can't remain neutral. This particular assignment happens to be very important for her career."

"Keeping secrets can come back to bite you in the ass," she warned.

"Any relationship I have with Ghost is all in my head. He doesn't even like being in the same room as me. He's straight as an arrow, so it doesn't even matter, anyway. What good would it do to tell Remi?" The bitterness and pain in my voice were unmistakable.

Talia sighed, her gaze drifting toward the gently swaying trees. "Greyson, I wish I had some insight into Ghost for you, but he's always been mysterious, keeping his emotions under wraps. I don't think he is specifically avoiding you. There's just something tragic in his past — he hinted at it once — that holds him back."

"Maybe that's why I can't let go," I mused, the weight of my unspoken fears settling heavily on my chest. "I see his pain and loneliness and it draws me to him. It's like we're both struggling with our demons and somehow, that makes it impossible for me to truly move on."

"Grey, I think you need to be honest with yourself and Remi," Talia advised, her tone gentle but firm. "I think you did the right thing, postponing the marriage proposal for now. You need to sort out your feelings first. There's nothing wrong with that. Maybe both of you should take a break from your relationship during her assignment to work on yourselves. That would be one way to test if your love for each other is real."

"Maybe you're right," I agreed, my mind already racing with the possibilities. Although it terrified me, I knew that confronting my feelings was the only way to find the happiness and acceptance I craved. And maybe Remi and I could weather this storm together.

"Whatever you decide, Greyson," Talia added, giving my hand a reassuring squeeze, "remember that you deserve love and happiness, no matter who you choose or what path you take."

I nodded, grateful for her unwavering support. "Let's head back. I've got some thinking to do."

A stiff ocean breeze blew on occasion, but the warmth of the midday sun kept it from feeling too chilly. The rhythmic sound of baby Zoe's stroller wheels rolling across the sidewalk provided a soothing backdrop to our contemplative silence.

"Hey," Talia said, breaking the quiet. "I just want you to know that I'm always here for you. You can talk to me about anything, anytime."

"Thanks, Tal," I replied, feeling the warmth of gratitude wash over me. "I don't know what I'd do without you. You're the only one I can talk to about this stuff." Because I was a celebrity, I had to be very careful who I opened up to. I'd learned that the hard way.

She smiled, and I couldn't help but notice the way her eyes gleamed in the bright sunlight. "That's what friends are for, Greyson. And don't worry — I won't charge you for therapy. Yet." She winked playfully, and I chuckled at her lighthearted attempt to ease the tension.

"Deal," I agreed, laughing despite the turmoil bubbling beneath the surface. "But seriously, thank you. I'm going to take your advice to heart and really confront my feelings head-on. I've got to figure this out if I want to move on with Remi."

Talia nodded. "It's not an easy thing to do, figuring out all this complicated crap, but it's the only way to find true happiness. And you deserve that. Don't ever forget it."

As we approached the beach house, the lingering scent of saltwater filled my nostrils, and I could hear the distant squawking of gulls. I took a deep breath, letting the cool ocean breeze clear my mind and fortify my resolve.

"Alright," I said as I took one last peek at Zoe snuggled safely under her blankets. "I guess this is goodbye for now. Tell Ryder I said goodbye and good luck on the rest of the tour if I don't see him."

"Will do," Talia promised, pulling me into a fierce hug. "Take care of yourself, Grey. And remember: no matter how hard the road gets, you're never alone."

"Thanks, Tal," I murmured into her shoulder, feeling the comforting weight of her support. "I'll keep that in mind."

With one final squeeze, we released each other, and I turned to leave. As I walked toward my car, I knew what I had to do. Sometimes, the most difficult choices were the ones that ultimately led us to the right path — even if they seemed impossible at first. It wouldn't be easy, but I was taking the first steps toward a future where I could finally be true to myself.

And hopefully, Remi and I would find ourselves on the same path on the other side of this.

Chapter 7

Remi

I HESITATED OUTSIDE GREYSON'S West Hollywood home, my heart pounding in anticipation of seeing him. He'd asked me to come over to talk before we went out for dinner, and I couldn't help feeling apprehensive about what he wanted to talk about. I had an important work trip coming up tomorrow — a chance to dig up some dirt on the band that had been dominating my every thought — and I didn't want anything to distract me from it. I knew that Greyson wasn't excited about me going on tour with a rock band and that he didn't want me to be away for so long, but my career was just as important to me as his career was to him. This was the chance to prove myself.

Greyson lived in a beautiful Spanish hacienda-style house on a side road just off Sunset Boulevard. It looked like something straight out of a movie. The terracotta roof tiles contrasted against the white stucco walls, while vibrant bougainvillea vines crawled along the exterior, adding a pop of color. Despite its charm, I couldn't shake the feeling that tonight would be anything but idyllic.

I let myself in, making my way through the tastefully decorated interior full of sleek, modern furniture and eye-catching artwork. Greyson had always been one for aesthetics, and it showed in every aspect of his life, including his home. But what I loved best about his home was the backyard oasis. It was a tranquil retreat, complete with a sparkling pool, an outdoor kitchen, and cozy seating areas nestled among lush greenery. I headed straight to the backyard, hoping it would ease my troubled thoughts.

I wrapped myself in a green throw blanket and cuddled up on the sofa, waiting for Greyson to get home. My eyes fluttered shut as I listened to the water fountain gurgling somewhere behind me.

Sometimes it still felt surreal that I was dating Greyson Durant. He was a worldwide celebrity, adored by millions of fans, wealthy beyond imagination, and breathtakingly beautiful.

I'd been completely star-struck when I interviewed him. It had taken all of my willpower not to gush over him like a slobbering fan. He was even more gorgeous in person than on TV. He had a tall, muscular frame with broad shoulders, a flat stomach, and toned arms. His facial features were classically handsome: a strong jawline and deep, captivating blue eyes. His thick, dark hair that swept across his forehead was always stylishly tousled.

The first time I met him, during that very first interview, I was prepared for him to be an egomaniac. Instead, he was kind and down to earth. It was the first time I'd ever felt attracted to any of the celebrities I'd met, and I'd met lots of them due to my profession.

As I got to know him over the weeks of interviews and follow-up sessions, my attraction only grew deeper. His honesty about himself, his charm, and his intelligence all shined through. He was the entire package. When he admitted that he felt a connection with me, well, let's just say, it took me a long time to feel comfortable receiving his attention. I didn't feel worthy.

One of the things he said that he liked about me was that I treated him normally. He once told me that most of his fans expected him to be ruthless like his character on *Devious*, Colton Grimaldi, and it left them disappointed if he didn't act that way. He despaired that most of his life seemed like an act. But he was nothing like Colton. Deep down, he was a kind soul with a big heart.

If I had any doubts about dating a big Hollywood celebrity, they'd vanished over the holidays. Greyson and I had spent all our free time together, and he'd been wonderful with my mother and sister when they came to spend Christmas with me. He'd been a big hit with them and won them over effortlessly. Outside of the spotlight, Grey was an unpretentious and down-to-earth guy.

I heard some noise from inside the house and knew he must be home.

"Remi," Greyson greeted me with a smile as he walked into the backyard, moving with an innate air of confidence and sex appeal. He must have just arrived home from taping *Devious*, still wearing his effortlessly stylish wardrobe from the set. It still never ceased to amaze me how sexy he was every time I saw him.

He strode over to the couch and leaned down to give me a quick kiss.

I sat up and patted the couch cushions for him to sit next to me. "Hey, Grey," I replied, trying to stifle a yawn. "I almost fell asleep. Too many late nights doing research."

"So, you're leaving early tomorrow morning, right? How long will you be gone?" He sunk down on the couch next to me.

"Yep," I confirmed, taking a deep breath. "At least a week. It depends on what I find. I'm going to scout out the hometowns of some of Ghost Parker's members for my assignment. See if I can find any interesting stories from their pasts and do a little ghost hunting. And I have a few interviews lined up."

Greyson raised an eyebrow, his tone shifting from friendly to concerned. "Digging up dirt from the past, huh? I don't know, Rem. That seems kind of intrusive, don't you think?"

"What?" I bristled at his accusation, my defensiveness kicking in. "I'm just doing my job, Grey."

He placed his hand on my leg in a placating manner. "Look, I know you're ambitious and want to prove yourself, but sometimes I worry about how far you'll go for a story."

I crossed my arms. "Seriously? It's just research. I interviewed you and I did a damn fine job. My piece was fair and honest. I didn't exploit you or make you look bad. Why are you on my case about this?"

Greyson stared at me for a moment, his eyes searching mine before he finally spoke. "Do what you have to do, Remi. Just... be careful, okay? Don't let ambition steer you the wrong way."

I nodded, swallowing the lump in my throat. I knew Greyson cared about me, but the tension between us felt palpable. As much as I wanted to brush it off and enjoy our evening, I couldn't help wondering if there was more to his concern than he was letting on.

As the sun began to set, casting an orange glow over Greyson's backyard oasis, we sat in silence for a few minutes. The air was thick with unspoken thoughts and feelings, making it nearly impossible to enjoy the peaceful atmosphere.

"Remi, there's something I need to talk to you about," Greyson finally said, his voice soft and hesitant. I turned my attention toward him, my heart thudding in my chest, as I braced myself for whatever he had to say. "It's not easy for me to discuss this, but I think it's important that we talk about it."

"Okay," I whispered, encouraging him to continue.

He took a deep breath, running his fingers through his perfectly styled hair. "I've been struggling with my emotions lately. I don't want to keep anything from you, so ... here goes." He paused, gathering his courage before revealing his truth. "You know that I'm attracted to other men, and I told you about the one man I had deep feelings for. Well, as much as I've tried to ignore them, those feelings haven't gone away."

For a moment, I felt like the ground had given out beneath me. I blinked, trying to process the information as Greyson continued to pour his heart out. "I haven't acted on it, but I can't ignore these feelings any longer. It feels unfair to you, Remi."

"Grey," I started, my mind racing with questions and confusion, yet I couldn't find the right words to express them. "I thought you said that man didn't return those feelings? I don't understand. Why are you telling me this now?"

"Because I love you," he replied earnestly, his eyes pleading with mine. "But I need to figure this out, Remi. I need to do some soul-searching and come to terms with who I am."

His words struck me like a punch to the gut, and I could feel the tears threatening to spill over. "So, what does this mean for us?" I asked, my voice barely audible.

Greyson sighed. "I think we should take a break while you're away on assignment. We both have things we need to work through, and it might be best if we do it separately."

"Are you kidding me?" I scoffed, my heart aching with the realization that what he was suggesting might turn out to be anything but temporary. "You want to throw away everything we have over some man that doesn't even care about you?"

"Remi, please," he implored, his eyes filled with turmoil. "I don't want to hurt you any more than I already have. This isn't easy for me either. But I need to do this. I owe it to myself and to you."

My throat tightened, choking back the sob that threatened to escape. I couldn't bring myself to look at Greyson as I spoke. "No. We don't need to break up in order for you to figure this out."

"Remi, you know I love you, but my bisexuality is a part of me that I can't ignore any longer," Greyson explained, his voice wavering. "You deserve someone who is fully present in this relationship, and right now, I'm not."

I tried to keep my voice steady despite the tumultuous emotions churning inside me, but I could hear it rising in panic. "We've been through so much together. We can work through this, too. You don't have to push me away."

He sighed, running a hand through his hair in frustration. "I know how much you care, but I need to figure this out on my own. This isn't about pushing you away. It's about giving both of us the space we need to grow and understand ourselves better."

The conversation was quickly spiraling out of control, the tension between us nearly palpable. I felt a mixture of anger, hurt, and confusion. I waved my hands in agitation. "So, what are you going to do? Have sex with this guy you're lusting after and see if it's better than with me?"

Anger flared up in his eyes, but he immediately tempered it. "This isn't about fucking some guy, Remi. Yes, I'm attracted to men sexually, but I also develop deeper feelings of love for them. Before you, I don't think I ever really fell in love with a woman. But, I've fallen for men. I think it's a natural affinity, so I'm damn confused. And if I commit my life to you, I want to be damn sure my commitment is one hundred percent."

"I don't understand. I'm attracted to men, too. But when you love someone, you don't act on those feelings. Maybe this is just about commitment and has nothing to do with your sexuality." My voice cracked. My emotions were getting the best of me. "Or maybe it's me. Maybe you just don't love me enough."

"Remi, stop." He put his hands on my shoulders and forced me to look at him. "I've been in the spotlight my entire adult life, and I've had to hide my sexuality. Being a celebrity has prevented me from showing my true self to the world. I'm messed up, Rem. I just need some time to get it all straight."

Deep down, I knew he had a point. He was being honest and open with me. If I couldn't accept that, then I wasn't accepting him. Still, it was scary. Maybe some time apart would give him clarity, but maybe it would split us apart for good.

"Fine," I muttered, feeling defeated and upset. "Take your break. See other people if you want. Do whatever it is you need to do. But don't expect me to just wait around."

"Remi," he said softly, reaching out for my hand. I pulled away before he could touch me. "I hope you know that I never meant to hurt you."

"Save it, Greyson," I snapped, gathering my things as tears finally spilled over. "Just let me go."

With that, I jumped up from the sofa and ran inside his house, leaving behind the man I'd grown to love so desperately. I quickly gathered up my things and bolted for the front door. A sob gathered in my chest, but I swallowed it down.

I rushed out of Greyson's house, my heart feeling like lead in my chest. The cool evening air hit my face, a stark contrast to the heated exchange I had just left behind. My eyes stung with unshed tears, but

I refused to let them fall. Not here, not now.

"Remi," Greyson called after me, his voice strained and vulnerable.

I hesitated for a moment, wanting so desperately to turn back and throw myself into his arms. But I knew that would only prolong the inevitable. If I didn't give him this leeway to figure out his sexuality, it'd eventually be the end of us, anyway.

"Take care, Greyson," I murmured without looking back, my voice barely audible even to me.

I fumbled with my car keys, my hands trembling ever so slightly. As I got into my car, I couldn't help but glance up at Greyson's house one last time. The warm glow from his living room seemed to mock me, a cruel reminder of what I was leaving behind.

Driving away, I felt a deep sense of worry and uncertainty settle within me. What if this break changed everything between us? What if we couldn't find our way back to each other? The thought terrified me, but it was a possibility I had to prepare for.

"Dammit." I slammed my palm on the steering wheel, trying to shake off the heavy feeling that threatened to consume me. I'd always felt that Greyson was too good for me. Why would he settle for someone like me? I shouldn't be surprised he was having doubts.

As I drove down the busy streets of West Hollywood, my mind wandered to the wonderful Christmas I'd spent with Greyson. There was no denying the connection between us. He'd told me that it was the best Christmas break he'd ever had since he was a kid. My mother and sister had come out to visit me and they both loved him. Just two weeks ago, everything had been perfect. And now it was all in shambles.

Why did love have to be so damn complicated?

The city lights blurred past me as I continued to drive, lost in my thoughts. I would be away the next week conducting research for my story and then shortly after I came back, I'd be joining Ghost Parker on the second half of their tour. Between the tour and Greyson taping for his show, I wouldn't have gotten to see him all that much, anyway. Maybe now, I could put all my focus on creating a fantastic story and not be distracted by my love life. I didn't have much choice in the matter, so I'd have to make the best of it.

I'd be out ghost-hunting while Grey was soul-searching. Hopefully, we'd both find what we were looking for. I prayed that whatever lay ahead would lead me back to the man I loved.

Chapter 8

Ghost

THE SPOTLIGHT BATHED ME in its harsh, unforgiving glare as I sang my heart out to the frenzied crowd. The roar of their excitement filled the concert hall, a thunderous cacophony that made my pulse race with exhilaration. From my vantage point on stage, I could see the ocean of people losing themselves in the moment, swaying and dancing to the beat of our music.

"Come on!" I shouted into the microphone, urging the crowd to join me in the chorus. Their voices rose in unison, echoing mine as we sang together, feeding off each other's energy. It was intoxicating, the rush of adrenaline that coursed through my veins as I connected with every single person in that crowd. I felt like a god, commanding the emotions of thousands of souls with just the power of my voice.

I fucking lived for this — this electrifying high that only performing could bring. There was nothing else in the world that could compare to the raw intensity of it all, and I reveled in the knowledge that I was born for this, destined to captivate the masses with my talent.

"Thank you, Pennsylvania!" I called out, breathless from the exertion of putting everything I had into the performance. The music came to a climactic end, and the crowd erupted in deafening applause and cheers. Sweat poured down my face, my hair sticking to my forehead, but I didn't care — I was alive, more alive than I'd ever felt in a long time.

"Ghost!" I heard a few individual shouts among the roar of the crowd, their adulation fueling the fire within me. I lifted my chin, showing my gratitude and appreciation for their devotion. Then, with one final wave, I turned and walked off the stage, the cheers still ringing in my ears.

My chest heaved with every breath, the adrenaline still surging through my system as I took a moment to savor the aftermath. The high was unlike anything else, an addiction I could never break free from — not that I'd ever want to. This was my life, and I wouldn't trade it for the world.

Sid's grin was wide and uncontainable as he stepped beside me. "That was fucking awesome."

The exhaustion of the performance had yet to set in, but I knew it would soon. For now, though, I allowed myself to float on the euphoria that came from giving everything I had to that stage — to those fans who loved me as much as I loved them.

Knox clapped a hand on my shoulder. "Ghost, you killed it out there, mate."

I nodded, knowing full well that our combined efforts had made this night one to remember.

"Fuck, yeah. We all did," I agreed, the fire within me still burning strong. "Now let's go celebrate."

The dressing room buzzed with energy as we made our way inside, everyone still riding the high from the concert. Bash, our drummer, was already bouncing off the walls, his boundless energy still ready to be unleashed. "I need to find a chick, or make that two or three, and get this party started." He shook out his hands as if getting ready to step into a boxing ring.

"Easy there, Bash," Sid chuckled, shaking his head at his friend's antics. "You've got all night for that."

Bash grinned mischievously. "Speak for yourself, brother. I've got a lot of plans and no time to waste. Besides, I can't sleep all day like you jokers. I've got to get up early, so I can spend time with Kody."

"Alright, mates, let's just get cleaned up first," Knox suggested, wiping sweat from his brow as we all agreed and began preparing ourselves for the night ahead.

As I attempted to make my way to the showers, Trudy, our PR rep, stopped me with a hand on my arm. "Ghost, wait. There's someone you need to meet," she said, excitement evident in her voice.

Trudy was always shoving important people in my face at the most inopportune times. "Can't it wait until after I shower?" I asked, trying to disentangle myself from her grip. But Trudy was persistent.

"No, it can't," she insisted. "This is Remi Sutton. She's a feature writer at Hollywood Exposé, and she's going to be joining us on tour. She's doing a full media package on Ghost Parker. Trust me, this is huge."

"Okay, okay," I relented, extending my hand to greet her. "Nice to meet you, Remi."

My eyes flicked to the girl standing beside Trudy. She looked like the typical Hollywood Exposé anchor — young, sexy, with perfect hair and perfect makeup.

"Likewise," she replied, her handshake firm and confident.

Our eyes locked, her hand still in mine. I felt a rush of electricity, and all at once it was as if the world had disappeared around us. My breath caught in my throat and I found myself lost in the depths of her gaze, feeling an intense awareness that left me surprised and curious.

Something about her intrigued me, though I couldn't quite put my finger on it yet. I studied the girl before me, trying to ferret it out. She was definitely attractive, but so were many of the girls I met. Maybe it was something about the defiance burning in her eyes that was decidedly opposite from the friendly demeanor she presented that had me taking notice.

"Welcome to the madness," I said with a smirk, gesturing to the bustling activity occurring around the room. "I hope you're ready for one hell of a ride."

A glint of determination sparked in her eyes. "Trust me, I am."

"Great," I said, casting a glance over my shoulder at my awaiting shower. "Now, if you'll excuse me, I need to get cleaned up. We've got a party to attend."

"Of course," Remi nodded, stepping aside to let me pass. "I'll see you there."

As I hurried into the shower, my thoughts kept drifting back to Remi. I had a feeling in my gut that she wasn't here to do a fluff piece on the band. And it was obvious by her demeanor that she wasn't going to gush all over me like most other reporters did. She was here to dissect me and lay me bare to the world. I'd have to be careful around her. Maybe the odd energy I felt was merely my subconscious warning me to be cautious of this girl.

I stepped under the hot spray of water, thinking about the pretty reporter with the kissable lips. I had a hunch that getting to know her would be anything but boring.

Freshly showered and dressed in my usual attire of tight jeans and a form-fitting black shirt, I stepped back into the chaotic world I inhabited. The party was already in full swing, the air thick with the scent of booze, sweat, and lust. Music pulsed through the room, shaking the very foundations of the building.

The women far outnumbered the men, and most of them were dancing together with wild abandon, their bodies pressed tightly up against each other as they lost themselves to the rhythm. Shots were downed in rapid succession, while laughter and flirtatious banter filled the air. It was a decadent playground, and it felt like home.

I scanned the room for Remi, finally spotting her near the bar, looking a bit taken aback by the scene before her. She seemed out of place among the scantily clad women that postured for attention and the guys who eagerly lapped up their sexual antics.

"Ghost!" a voice called to me, drawing my gaze to a pair of barely dressed women who approached me with sultry smiles. "Come play with us," one of them purred, running a hand down my chest as she eyed me with a blatant invitation.

"Maybe later, ladies," I replied, attempting to sidestep them and make my way to Remi. But they persisted, clinging to my arms and whispering naughty suggestions into my ear, their words dripping with lust and indecent proposals. With a sigh, I resigned myself to the fact that it would take some time to extricate myself from their grasp.

When I finally managed to escape the clutches of my overzealous fans, I made my way to Remi, studying her more intently as I approached. She was even more beautiful up close — her long, silky dark hair cascading over her shoulders, framing an oval face with feminine features, the most striking of which was her dark brown eyes accentuated by long, sooty lashes. Her pretty pink lips begged to be tasted.

But it was her body that truly captivated me. She wasn't the stick-thin model type I was used to encountering; she had lush curves, a goddess among mortals. My eyes roamed over her form appreciatively, and I couldn't help but imagine the way those curves would feel pressed against me.

"Enjoying the party?" I asked as I finally reached her side, leaning against the bar casually.

"Uh, yeah," she replied, her eyes darting around the room again. "It's definitely ... something."

"Welcome to our world," I said with a grin. "I hope you can keep up."

She arched an eyebrow, her eyes finally meeting mine. "Is that a challenge?"

"Maybe," I replied, smirking. "I just think it's important for you to know what you're getting into. We're not all glitz and glamour. I'm not going to sugarcoat it, Remi. There's a dark and gritty side to rock and roll."

"Trust me, I know," she said, rolling her eyes. "I've been covering entertainment for years. But I have to admit, you guys take hedonism to a whole new level."

I choked back a laugh, not wanting to make her feel like I was mocking her. "Hedonism? You think this is hedonism? You haven't seen anything yet." I lifted my glass to her in a mock toast before taking a sip, never breaking eye contact. My attraction to her was undeniable, and I wanted her to feel it, too.

"Anyway, I'm really looking forward to interviewing you," she continued, her cheeks flushing slightly under my gaze. "Your songwriting is incredible, and I'd love to get a better understanding of your creative process."

She was either earnest and eager, or she was playing me as she tried to reel me in. "Ah, so you want to dig deep, huh?" I played along, leaning in closer. "Well, I promise to be an open book for you, Remi."

"Really?" Skepticism laced her voice. "Because from what I've heard, you're anything but."

"Everyone has their secrets," I admitted with a shrug. Then, I turned the full power of my smile on her. "But if there's anyone who can crack the mystery, I'm sure it's you."

I could sense her reluctance, maybe even a touch of shyness, but I also knew she couldn't deny the chemistry between us. It was electric, and I was determined to explore it further.

"Only time will tell, Ghost," Remi finally said, her lips curling into a smile. "But I won't let you off easy."

Smirking, I replied, "I wouldn't expect anything less. Shall we start now?" I stepped closer to her and ran my finger lightly down her arm, feeling a thrill as she shivered at my touch. "I'm sure there's a lot you'd like to learn about me."

My attention was suddenly pulled away from Remi as a group of overeager fans swarmed us. I could see the disappointment in her eyes, but the reality of my life was never far away. I tried to divide my attention between Remi and the groupies, but it was impossible to ignore their persistence.

"Ghost, can we get a picture with you?" one of the women asked, her hand already on my arm.

"Of course," I said with a tight smile, trying to maintain some semblance of politeness. As I posed for photos, I glanced over at Remi, feeling a pang of guilt, but when I saw her scowling at me, something in me rebelled. I hadn't done anything wrong, but it was like she'd passed judgment on me and found me lacking. And I didn't like it.

Sure, one of the girls had gotten a bit handsy and was fondling my dick through my pants. Was I supposed to make a big scene about it? Fuck, no. In fact, it felt good. I downed the rest of my drink in one gulp. Maybe I wanted to prove that I could have anyone I wanted, or maybe I just wanted to make Remi jealous. She was a little too uptight for me, anyway.

Whatever the fuck it was, I allowed another woman to pull me into a dark corner of the room, knowing full well what she was offering.

"God, I've been dying to do this," she whispered breathlessly as she dropped to her knees, eagerly unzipping my pants. My cock was instantly hard as I thought about Remi's plump lips wrapped around me instead of this girl's. I tried to remain casual, but fuck, it felt good getting my cock sucked while Remi watched, not able to conceal her wide-eyed shock.

Our eyes met across the room and then she turned away, embarrassment and anger evident on her face. She was definitely different from most of the girls I knew, but I didn't actually want to piss her off. She was with the media, after all. I didn't give a shit if she reported about my partying lifestyle, but there were things in my past that I'd rather have left alone. It was best to stay on her good side.

Once the deed was done, I quickly fixed my pants and sought out Remi, determined to patch over any hurt feelings or embarrassment I'd caused her, for my own good. Any way she presently judged me was fine. I just didn't want my past dredged up for public consumption.

She'd retreated to the other side of the room where she was talking with Trudy, her back to me. I grabbed a fresh drink and then sidled up to them. Trudy gave me a warning glare and then strategically excused herself. I'm sure she thought it was in our best interest if I made nice with the reporter.

I gave Remi a sly smile. "Where were we? Sorry about that, I got side-tracked."

Her voice was cold and distant. "Did you do that for my benefit?"

"For my own benefit," I answered honestly, trying to gauge her reaction. "But if you got off watching, I'm fine with that."

"That's not what I meant," Remi snapped, clearly hurt by my actions. "I want to know who you really are, not the shallow playboy image you project."

"This is exactly who I am," I challenged. "Take it or leave it."

She chewed on her lip, studying me as if I were some exotic new specimen of bug. "I don't believe that. This is just an act you put on."

"I'm sorry to disappoint you, sweetheart." I chuckled cruelly. "I'm a shallow bastard and this is my playground."

She glanced around the room, taking in the rowdy party that had descended into a chaotic whirlwind with people dancing, grinding, drinking, and getting high while music blared from the speakers. A good number of the women were now topless and sexual activities were happening in plain sight. It was still a few steps away from a full-blown drunken orgy, but I could see how she might call it hedonistic.

I grabbed her hand to distract her. "Come on, Remi, let's grab a drink and talk," I suggested, leading her toward the makeshift bar at the back of the room.

Bash called out to me as we passed by. He stumbled over to us, his arm slung around the waist of a petite blonde. "You've gotta try this. It's a peanut butter and jelly shot."

"Maybe later, Bash," I replied, trying to keep my focus on Remi. Her dark eyes were wide, taking in the debauchery surrounding us, as though she'd never seen anything like it before. At that moment, she looked so innocent and vulnerable, and I couldn't help but feel an overwhelming desire to protect her.

"Suit yourself, bro." Bash's eyes shrewdly swept over Remi and then laughed to himself before disappearing back into the crowd with the blonde girl.

Still clutching her blue journal in her hand, she accepted the drink

I handed her, but I noticed that she didn't take a sip. I studied her while I swallowed a large mouthful of my own drink. She was fidgeting slightly, clearly uncomfortable, whether it was the party or my company I didn't know.

I leaned in close to her ear. "Relax, this is a party."

She glanced up at me and then took a small sip of her drink before putting it down on the makeshift bar.

"I'm here to work," she said matter-of-factly. "Not party."

I cocked an eyebrow. "Are you always working? Or do you let yourself have fun once in a while? That's why you're here, isn't it? To get the full experience of the band and our lifestyle?"

The bright lighting of the room bathed the party that was in full swing behind us in a gritty reality that showcased the ugliness of overindulgence and excess. My gaze remained fixed on Remi, her face a picture of determination amidst the chaos. It was amusing to see her trying so hard to maintain her professional composure.

"I'm just here to do my job," she replied firmly, though her cheeks betrayed her by flushing a deep shade of pink.

"Tell me, Remi," I said, leaning in closer, "what is it that you really want to know about me?" I watched her eyes flicker with uncertainty, sensing her struggle to balance her curiosity with her duty as a reporter.

She looked down at the notebook clutched in her hands, a look of concentration on her face. "I'm curious about the music you make," she said, her voice barely audible over the noise surrounding us. "Where do you think your music fits in relation to other classics in rock history?

"Is that all you're interested in? The art, not the artist?" I grinned wickedly, taking a step closer, allowing the chaos of the room to wrap around us like a shroud.

She hesitated for a moment, her professionalism wavering. "Well, I suppose ... I mean, yes, of course."

"Ah, but I think there's more to it than that." My hand brushed against hers, causing her to flinch slightly. She was intriguing, and I wanted to peel back the layers of her polished exterior to find the woman beneath. I could sense the vulnerability she tried so hard to hide.

"Ghost, I—" she stammered, clearly affected by my presence. Knocking her off her game and keeping her off-balance was amusing, a distraction from the emptiness that haunted me. It was a dangerous dance we were both participating in, willingly or not."My readers want to know about the man behind the music, too. Not the partying rockstar, but the real man."

She gazed up at me so earnestly, I hated to disappoint her, but she needed to know she was playing with fire.

"I'm afraid that's something you'll never know," I said, my voice low and husky.

I leaned in, running my fingers lightly across her jawline before brushing my lips against hers — just a whisper of a kiss. She let out a soft gasp at the contact.

"Relax, Remi," I whispered, my breath hot against her ear. "I don't bite ... unless you ask me to." Her quick intake of breath was all the answer I needed.

She reached for her drink and took a long sip. "I'm just trying to do my job."

"Very well," I relented, stepping back and allowing her some space to breathe. Her eyes searched mine, a mix of relief and disappointment clouding her expression. "But remember, Remi, you're the one who wanted to know more about me. You might not like what you find out."

Suddenly, the clamor of the party wrapped around me like a suffocating embrace. The air was thick with the scent of sweat and alcohol, the harsh lighting doing nothing to hide the depravity around us from Remi, as she struggled to maintain her aura of composure and professionalism.

"Tell me, Ghost," Remi began, her eyes locked onto mine, as if trying to physically reset our relationship. "What sparked your interest in music?"

"Ah," I smirked, relishing the opportunity to ruffle her feathers. "You mean what inspired my descent into this chaos?" I gestured to the party-goers around us, their bodies undulating to the pounding bass of the music.

She flipped open her notebook and slid the pen out of its holder. "Chaos ... Interesting choice of words," she murmured, scribbling something down in her notepad. "So, would you say music is an escape for you?"

"Perhaps," I replied, inching closer to her. "Or maybe it's the only way I can truly express myself." I reached out and brushed a stray strand of hair from her face, feeling the heat rise in her cheeks. It was all too easy.

"Right." she bit her bottom lip. Professionalism seemed to be slipping from her grasp. "What about your past? Does that influence your music at all?"

"Ah, now we're getting personal," I said, watching her struggle to maintain control. "Yes, my past affects my music. It's shaped who I am today."

"Can you elaborate on that?" she asked, eyes wide with anticipation.

"Isn't that true of everybody? Doesn't their past help form who they are?" I asked, my voice low and dangerous. "How about you? Has your past affected how you do your job?"

Her breath hitched, and I could see the flicker of uncertainty in her eyes. But she quickly regained her composure and replied, "I'm here to interview you, Ghost."

"Of course," I said, backing off for now. "Well, let's just say that trauma has a way of changing a person."

"Trauma?" she echoed, her pen poised above her notepad.

I flashed her a cryptic smile. "Let's leave it at that for now," I replied, enjoying the way her curiosity gnawed at her. There was something undeniably thrilling about keeping her hanging on my every word.

"Alright," she said reluctantly, clearly wanting more but knowing better than to push too far. "Let's talk about your band. How did Ghost Parker come together?"

"Destiny, perhaps," I mused, allowing myself a moment of vulnerability. "We were all broken souls seeking solace in the chaos of music."

Her professionalism was momentarily forgotten as she looked at me with newfound admiration. "Beautifully put," she whispered.

"Thank you," I replied, my voice laced with darkness. "But beauty often hides the most sinister secrets."

Her eyes widened at my words, and for a fleeting moment, I allowed myself to become lost in their depths. A shiver ran down my spine, and I knew that this game of cat and mouse had only just begun.

As our conversation continued, I couldn't help but feel my attraction to Remi intensify. There was something about her — her fiery spirit, her intellect, her determination — that drew me in like a moth to a flame. And as I looked into those deep brown eyes, I vowed to myself that I would break through her professional defenses before she left the tour.

There was no doubt that I wanted to fuck her as much as she wanted it, too. But more than that, I wanted to know her, to understand what made her tick. Because for the first time in a long while, I had found someone who challenged me, someone who made me feel alive.

And I wasn't about to let that slip through my fingers.

Chapter 9

Remi

This was it. I was officially on tour with my rock band. Nothing could have prepared me for how surreal and exhilarating it would feel. If I'd gotten this revved up by the guys by watching from afar, I wondered what it would be like to meet them all, up close and personal. Especially Ghost.

From the moment I first clapped eyes on him, I'd been spellbound by Ghost. Standing in the wings, I watched Johnny 'Ghost' Parker on stage, completely captivated by his raw talent. The way he commanded the audience's attention was nothing short of mesmerizing. With each note, his voice seemed to wrap around my heart, pulling me deeper under his spell. I couldn't help but be reminded of Greyson, and how his own remarkable charisma had once pulled me in just as easily.

I had read online about his supposed mesmerizing personality, but nothing could have prepared me for the reality of Ghost. He seemed to absorb all the energy from his fans and project it back a hundredfold. His passion clung to him almost like a mystic energy vibrating around him. My breath quickened, and I shivered with amazement as I watched the remarkable performance; it was something that felt truly special.

Ghost held the microphone like it was an extension of himself, his lips brushing against it as he belted out lyrics that spoke of love, loss, and pain. The passion with which he sang was palpable, every word resonating deep within me. The raw emotion in his voice made my skin tingle and my breath catch in my throat.

Around me, crew members worked diligently, their faces bathed in the dim glow of the stage lights. But my focus never wavered from Ghost. His eyes, intense and piercing, seemed to search the crowd for something — or someone — unseen. It was as if he were calling out, demanding to be heard, to be understood.

His voice echoed through the arena, powerful and raw, sending shivers down my spine. Sweat dripped from his brow as he belted out every note with an intensity that made it impossible to look away. As the song reached its crescendo, Ghost threw his head back, a vein in his neck throbbing as he poured his soul into the final notes. The crowd roared their approval, but all I could hear was the sound of my heartbeat pounding in my ears. At that moment, I knew I was in trouble. He was unlike anyone I'd ever encountered before, and the attraction I felt toward him both thrilled and terrified me.

My heart thumped wildly with excitement. It was only my first day on tour with Ghost and his band, and I was already entranced by his performance.

"Remi," Trudy called, tapping me on the shoulder. "Come with me. I'll introduce you to Ghost."

She led me back through the winding backstage maze. It gave me a few moments to compose myself, which I desperately needed. It was hardly professional to be salivating over the lead singer.

Excited anticipation thrummed through my body. I was about to meet the boys of Ghost Parker, including the sexy lead singer, Ghost. We waited a few moments, and then I heard the band approaching before I saw them. The members of Ghost Parker were making a racket, obviously still pretty pumped up from their performance. I glanced over at the guys as they came into view, but my eyes immediately sought out Ghost.

I took a moment to fully absorb his appearance. He was tall, with broad shoulders and a muscular physique. His blond hair was slightly disheveled and still damp from his shower. He wore a tight black T-shirt that showcased his toned arms and chest. His chiseled jawline and piercing blue eyes only added to his magnetic charm, which seemed to pull everyone in his vicinity into his orbit. There was no point in denying it. He was exceedingly handsome. My stomach fluttered with butterflies, and I struggled to find my voice as I stared at him.

The guys in the band paid us little attention, but Trudy stopped Ghost as he was passing by. She introduced us and I wasn't sure what I said. As soon as Ghost turned his attention to me, I was lost. His stunning blue eyes seemed to hold a thousand secrets, and I found myself yearning to unlock every one of them.

He was gone so quickly, I had to shake myself. I was breathless from our encounter, and my fingers still tingled where he'd touched me. I could barely listen as Trudy explained to me that she had some post-concert business, but that I should feel free to grab food or drinks. People would slowly trickle in and the after-party would be in full swing by the time the band members finished with their post-concert business. She assured me that she would make sure I met all the band members then.

Trudy left me and already the room was filling up with women who were looking me over. They were assessing the competition, but then quickly dismissed me when they saw how I was dressed compared to them. They had come to attract male attention; I had come to be professional. I had dressed attractively, but I wasn't showing tons of skin.

The atmosphere in the room grew wilder by the minute. Soon, bass-heavy music pulsed through the air, making it hard to think. Alcohol was flowing. Illicit drugs were being passed around. Of course, I'd been around this type of scene at some Hollywood parties I'd attended with Greyson, but those parties had a thin veneer of class to them — at least they pretended to — despite the outrageous behavior. Here, everything seemed ten times seedier. The atmosphere was much more raucous, as partiers flaunted their wild sides and celebrated with reckless abandon.

Bodies writhed together on the makeshift dance floor, some barely dressed, others adorned in various stages of undress. Empty bottles began to decorate every surface of the room, while people laughed and yelled over the music, their inhibitions long forgotten.

I remained as unobtrusive as I could as I stood in a corner waiting for the band to make their appearance. The first guy I saw was the drummer. He was easy to pick out because swarms of girls surrounded him the moment he showed up. I decided to introduce myself before he got too involved in the party.

"Hey," I said hesitantly as I approached him. "I'm Remi, the reporter who's going to be on tour with you guys."

"Ah, Remi!" Bash exclaimed with a friendly smile. He was a tall man with dark, messy hair and a mischievous glint in his stunning green eyes. "Nice to meet you. Trudy mentioned you'd be joining us."

I didn't have much more of a chance to talk to him before some girls teamed up to capture his attention. I stood there awkwardly for a moment before I backed away.

As I ventured further into the chaos, my eyes locked on Ryder, the rhythm guitarist. He stood near the bar, nursing a drink while chatting with a few fans. I made my way over to him, hoping to strike up a conversation without revealing too much about the research I'd conducted on him prior to joining the tour.

"Hi, Ryder," I greeted, forcing a smile as I extended my hand. "I'm Remi."

"Hey, Remi," he replied, shaking my hand with a firm grip, calloused from years of strumming guitar strings. "Welcome to the circus."

"Thanks," I laughed nervously, trying to keep it light as we exchanged small talk.

I scanned the room, but I didn't see Ghost anywhere. "Congratulations on the great show tonight," I told Ryder, forcing my attention back to him. "You guys really know how to bring the house down."

He tipped his drink in salute. "We do our best."

I squeezed my notebook tight, thinking about all the research it contained about Ryder. "Speaking of congratulations, congrats on the new baby. It must be tough to be on tour right now without your wife and your daughter."

His face lit up as he talked about his daughter. "Yeah, Zoe is just amazing. I can't believe how much having her has changed my life and my priorities. But, yeah, it's tough leaving them behind. I really miss them both. I keep in touch as much as I can, but it's not the same."

"Ryder, didn't you grow up in Ohio?" I asked casually, hoping to gather more information without exposing my intentions.

He took a sip of his drink. "Born and raised. Why do you ask?"

"Oh, just curious," I lied, feigning a casual smile while my mind raced with the details I had uncovered during my visit to his hometown. I needed to be careful not to reveal too much too soon; playing this game required finesse and subtlety.

As the party raged on with no sign of Ghost, I excused myself from Ryder and made my way over to Sidney, the bass player. He was chatting with a gorgeous woman, who I assumed was his wife.

"Hi, Sidney," I greeted him, offering a warm smile. "I'm Remi. I'm writing a piece on you guys for Hollywood Exposé. I heard you just got married?"

"Hey, Remi," he replied, his arm wrapping protectively around the woman at his side. "Yeah, this is my wife, Kaylie."

"Nice to meet you, Kaylie," I said, shaking her hand. It occurred to me that she was Bash's little sister, but I didn't want to mention it just yet. I would definitely want to interview her, though. She might be able to give me good insight into both men, her husband and her brother.

"Likewise," she replied sweetly.

As we continued our conversation, Knox, the lead guitarist, joined us. His presence brought yet another dynamic to the group, and I tried to keep my composure as I studied him. I recalled that years ago, he had been engaged and his fiancée had died in a car crash. The tragedy left an indelible mark on him, one that I hoped to question him more about at a later date.

"Hey, Knox," I greeted him with a smile, "I'm Remi."

He gave me a playful nudge. "Well, if it isn't the newest member of the crew. I heard you were tagging along to cause us all sorts of trouble."

His Scottish accent was so sexy it could melt the panties off any woman. I tried to keep my cool and not swoon whenever he spoke.

"I promise to keep the trouble to a minimum," I joked, trying to match his playful tone.

Sid and Knox were friendly and hilarious as they joked around, a stark contrast to the intense energy I felt from Ghost.

As the minutes flew by, the drinks kept flowing and the group grew more relaxed. I found myself laughing and chatting with the guys from the band. Every single member of the band was attractive and everyone had been welcoming to me, but only one man had fully captured my attention and left me waiting in suspense for his arrival. I had to bite my tongue not to ask them where he was.

Growing edgy, I excused myself and wove my way through the throngs of people toward the bar. I desperately needed a drink. Nursing my drink, I took in the wild sight before me.

I watched as women, clad in barely-there outfits, threw themselves at the band members, vying for attention and a chance to share a moment, however fleeting, with these rock gods. Others snorted lines of white powder off glass tables, their eyes wild with reckless abandon, while others raised shot glasses high into the air before pouring the liquid down their throats.

Even as I took in the debauchery around me, my thoughts were never far from Ghost, and the undeniable chemistry that had sparked between us at our brief meeting. I couldn't help but feel both excited and terrified at the prospect of what might unfold during my time on tour with him. And though I knew I needed to maintain my professionalism, there was an ever-growing part of me that wanted nothing more than to lose myself in the depths of his dark, mysterious world.

I couldn't help but feel disloyal to Greyson, even though he'd broken up with me. I'd spent my entire week traveling the country, researching the pre-band lives of Ghost Parker, hoping that Grey would contact me. When I got back to L.A. I was sure he'd call me before I left to join the tour. But since that horrible day, there'd not been a single word from Greyson, and that hurt.

But I had no intention of giving up on him. I loved him. That's why I needed to shake off the little celebrity crush I felt for Ghost. It would only get in the way of my story, anyway. My focus needed to be on getting information and not partying. I'd do my job and get back to Greyson so I could focus on fixing our relationship. I still loved him and he loved me, despite his confused feelings about his sexuality. After he'd repressed them for so long, it was no wonder they were tangled up inside him.

Tapping on the soft leather cover of my research notebook reminded me why I needed to get back into the center of the party and see if I could meet any of the crew that may have been on Ghost Parker tours in the past. My top priority was to find the ghost and steering the conversations with the crew would be easier when alcohol had loosened their tongues.

I felt him before I saw him. It was like his presence caused a ripple in the universe that I felt deep in my soul. My heart sped up as I scanned the room. It didn't take long to spot him. He stood across the room, surrounded by adoring fans who seemed eager to bask in his presence. His damp hair clung to his forehead, his black shirt clinging to his toned torso as if it were painted on. My heart raced at the sight of him, and I couldn't tear my eyes away.

He moved through the crowd, charming everyone in his path. He was like a magnet, drawing people to him effortlessly, and I found myself caught in his pull. I knew I needed to focus on my assignment, but there was something about him that made it almost impossible to resist.

As if sensing my gaze, he glanced over at me, his eyes smoldering with a dark intensity that sent shivers down my spine. I watched as he weaved his way through the party, finally stopping in front of me. The air seemed to crackle with electricity as he stood there, a wicked grin on his lips.

"Enjoying the party?" he drawled, his voice low and smooth like velvet, wrapping itself around me and pulling me closer.

I was face-to-face with the man who'd just stolen my breath and left me utterly spellbound. And as I looked into Ghost's stormy eyes, my heart skipped a beat. The intensity I felt in them sent butterflies into a frenzied dance in my stomach, and I found myself struggling to find words. Trying to keep my voice steady, an answer to his simple question spilled out in a breathless rush. My heart hammered in my chest, and a warmth spread through me as I took in his chiseled features and dangerous aura. I knew I should be on guard, but I couldn't help but feel drawn to him.

I tried to strike a casual air as we chatted, but I was anything but as I redirected his flirty remarks and attempted to keep the conversation professional. When Ghost laughed softly at one of my remarks, the sound made my knees weak.

An intense wave of déjà vu swept over me — this was exactly how I'd felt when I first met Greyson. The certain realization that I was extremely sexually attracted to Ghost filled me with guilt. What was wrong with me? I loved Grey, but there was an intensity in Ghost's gaze that I couldn't ignore, and it sent shivers of lust down my spine. I could practically feel the heat radiating between us, and a part of me ached to get closer to him.

Ghost was an enigma to me, and I wanted nothing more than to peel back the layers and uncover what he was hiding. As we spoke, fans and groupies constantly swarmed around him, attempting to steal his attention. He brushed them off politely, but it was clear he was growing increasingly irritated by the interruptions.

Just as our conversation began to flow more naturally, a woman in a slinky dress appeared and pulled Ghost away from me. Her hands were possessive as they trailed over his body. My stomach churned with unease as she led him to a dim corner of the room, not bothering to hide their actions from the partygoers.

The sight of her on her knees before him, pleasuring him so brazenly, filled me with a mixture of hurt and disgust. As if sensing my gaze, Ghost glanced over at me, his eyes cold and indifferent. It was clear he didn't care that I was watching, and it stung more than I cared to admit. That look was like a slap in the face, and I suddenly felt very out of place in this wild scene that unfolded around me.

I felt like I had been plunged into a world I didn't belong in, the debauchery around me suffocating and foreign. How could I ever hope to navigate this treacherous landscape and keep my heart intact?

I turned away from the ugly scene, needing to escape. As I walked away, losing myself in the crowd, I couldn't shake the feeling that I was both drawn to and repulsed by Ghost — a dangerous combination.

The pounding bass of the music vibrated in my chest as I stood there, reeling from the events that had just unfolded. Ghost's blatant disregard for my presence left a bitter taste in my mouth, and the sea of sweaty bodies only made me feel more out of place. I tried to ignore the carnal acts happening in every corner of the room and focus on my assignment, but it was getting increasingly difficult. The air was thick with the scent of sweat, alcohol, and lust, and it was making it hard to breathe.

Trudy must have noticed me floundering. "Remi!" She shouted above the noise, waving me over. "Do you want a drink?"

"Thanks, but I'm good for now," I replied, forcing a smile. As much as I wanted to be anywhere but here, I knew I couldn't leave. Not when there was a story to be uncovered, secrets to reveal. I joined Trudy's small circle of friends. "This is quite a party."

As I continued talking with Trudy, I glanced around the room, searching for Ghost. He must have finished with the woman because I spotted him laughing with a group of fans. He must have sensed my scrutiny because our eyes locked from across the room, tripping my pulse.

His gaze held a magnetic pull that I found impossible to resist, despite the gnawing guilt and sense of shame in the pit of my stomach. The chemistry between us was palpable, and I knew that giving in to it would be a monumental mistake. And yet, I couldn't help but wonder what it would feel like to taste his lips, to feel his strong arms wrapped around me. I found myself fascinated by Ghost, drawn in by the enigmatic aura that surrounded him. My body tingled with arousal, a burning desire that threatened to consume me, and I fought against the urge to surrender to it. It was exhilarating and terrifying at the same time.

I forced myself to look away and rejoin the conversation with Trudy. She was talking about a big snowstorm that was supposed to come up the east coast. She was looking forward to seeing snow as the tour had not encountered any so far.

"Where were we? Sorry about that, I got side-tracked." Ghost's voice, low and seductive, suddenly cut through the surrounding chaos, and I looked up to find him standing next to me, his earlier liaison seemingly forgotten. Despite my feelings of hurt, my pulse raced, and the air around us crackled with electricity. Our eyes locked again, and I felt myself falling deeper into the abyss, powerless to resist the allure of his dark, enigmatic world.

I struggled to maintain my composure in the face of his magnetic charm. "Did you do that for my benefit?" He knew what I meant.

Ghost leaned closer, his breath hot against my ear as he whispered, "For my own benefit. But if you got off watching, I'm fine with that."

His voice was a caress that entwined itself around my senses and sent a shiver down my spine, and I knew I was playing with fire. But as the party raged on around us and the darkness within Ghost beckoned me closer, I found myself powerless to resist the pull. Despite my misgivings and the warning bell clamoring in my head, Ghost managed to charm his way back into my good graces.

I told myself I was merely remaining non-judgemental and professional for the sake of my story, but I was deluding myself. Ghost pulled me over to the bar in the back of the room, where it was a little less hectic. To my surprise, we had a long talk about music and he opened up to me and allowed me to delve a little deeper. It was precisely the kind of material I needed from him. I just had to dodge the flirtations that came with it. He probably acted this way with all the women he talked to. Only I would be naïve enough to take it to heart.

Taking a sip of my drink, I finally felt like I was getting my sea legs at this party. Until I noticed the scene over Ghost's shoulder. A bald man with a goatee, who was loaded up with muscles and tattoos, was pulling up a woman's skirt. The woman was wearing nothing under the skirt, her bare ass jutting out in offering as she leaned her palms against the wall. And now the guy was pulling his dick out of his pants. My God, he was going to fuck her five feet away from us.

Ghost must have seen the distress on my face because he turned around to see what had caught my attention. A playful smile tugged at the corners of his lips. "You like to watch, huh?"

The man started pushing into her, and I frowned with disgust. "I can't help it. They're doing it practically in my face."

"Ah, you're too innocent for this scene, sweetheart," he teased, his fingers lightly brushing against my arm, sending shivers down my spine. "But maybe I can corrupt you just a little."

"Thanks, but I think I'll pass," I retorted, trying to sound lighthearted. The truth was, I was dangerously close to giving in to my desires for him. Greyson's recent breakup had left me vulnerable, but I didn't want to become another one of Ghost's conquests. "What they're doing cheapens the act."

"They're just having fun," he insisted, his eyes dancing with mischief. "Live a little, Remi. What's the worst that could happen?"

His voice was low and rich, sending shivers down my spine. The way he said my name was intoxicating, and I found myself wanting more — more of him, more of this dangerous closeness that had me teetering on the edge of something forbidden.

I hesitated, wrestling with the conflicting emotions churning inside me. I was consumed by the undeniable attraction I felt for Ghost, and I knew how dangerously close I was to losing control of myself. With Greyson's recent breakup still fresh in my mind, it seemed inevitable that I would seek solace in the arms of someone like Ghost — someone who could make me forget, if only for a moment. But I couldn't let that happen; I had a job to do, a story to write, and giving in to lust would only cloud my judgment.

"Ghost, I..." I began, searching for the right words. "I'm here for a reason, and I need to stay focused on that."

"Ah, the assignment," he said with a knowing smirk. "Well, if you change your mind, I'll be around." His gaze lingered on me for a moment longer, but there was a flicker of something else — regret, maybe? — before he turned back into the fray of the party, leaving me breathless and conflicted.

I watched him go, my heart pounding in my chest. It took every ounce of willpower I had not to follow him, but I knew I had to stand strong. For now, at least, I had to keep my distance from the enigmatic rockstar who had managed to captivate me so completely.

The rest of the party seemed so flat and uninteresting without Ghost at my side. I couldn't keep my eyes off him as he moved through the crowd. My heartbeat quickened at the sight of him emerging from a throng of adoring fans. He looked like a god among mortals, with his golden hair tousled just enough to frame his chiseled features, and his tattoos peeking out from beneath his sleeves, hinting at a hidden wildness beneath the surface. His eyes held a smoldering intensity that seemed to pierce through me, holding secrets I was desperate to uncover.

When he wrapped his arm around a pretty woman in a skimpy dress, a pang of jealousy shot through me. It was as if he'd forgotten me. Not once had he looked over.

I stood up, knowing I had to get out of there. This inexplicable attraction to Ghost was going to get me into trouble. Even if it was for the assignment, getting closer to Ghost was dangerous. If I crossed a line and started having real feelings for him, it could jeopardize not only my assignment but also my ability to maintain control over my own desires.

I felt the darkness within me yearn for his touch, hungry for the consuming passion that seemed to radiate from his very being. Memories of Greyson flitted through my mind, of the magnetic pull I had felt toward him, but the attraction with Ghost was different — more raw, more primal. And with that realization came a wave of guilt.

What was I doing? My mind raced with thoughts of him, of Greyson, and of the guilt that threatened to consume me as I made my way out of the party. I knew that falling for Ghost was a mistake, one that could cost me everything. But as I ran away, part of me couldn't help but wonder if it was a risk worth taking.

Chapter 10

Ghost

IT HAD BEEN A few days since Remi joined us on tour, and I couldn't help but notice her constantly watching me. Her eyes seemed to brand me whenever I was on stage, yet she always kept her distance. Damn, that woman knew how to play it cool. But the more she ignored me, the more I craved her attention.

I decided it was time to break through that professional barrier of hers and taste some of the passion I could see burning in her eyes. But first I had to find her. She was more elusive than a unicorn. The opportunity presented itself when I found her interviewing Ryder a few hours before sound check.

"Ryder, can you tell me about the challenges you've faced growing up? How did they shape your music?" Remi asked, flipping through her notebook with a seriousness that was almost intimidating.

Ryder squirmed in his seat, visibly uncomfortable with the question. He wasn't one to share much about his personal life, let alone with a reporter. "Well, you know, every musician has their own struggles," he said evasively. "I guess mine just made me more focused on my art."

Remi pressed on, relentless in her pursuit of the truth. "What about your family? Did they support your music career?"

"Uhm, yeah, sure," Ryder replied, his voice strained as he tried to maintain his composure. I could see he was struggling to be open and honest, yet to keep certain things private. It wasn't like him to be so guarded, and I couldn't stand by and watch any longer.

"Hey, Ryder," I called out, striding over to them with purpose. "There's a band meeting happening right now. We need you there, man."

Ryder looked relieved while Remi raised an eyebrow, clearly not convinced by my sudden interruption. "Really, Ghost? Right now?"

"Yeah, sorry," I said, giving her an apologetic grin. "Band business, you understand."

"Of course," she replied with a tight smile, her eyes narrowing as if trying to read my thoughts. But she couldn't do anything about it and reluctantly closed her notebook. "I guess we'll have to finish this interview later, Ryder."

"Sure thing," he said, practically leaping out of his chair. "Thanks for understanding, Remi."

As we left the room, I couldn't help but feel a sense of victory. Sooner or later, she'd have to stop ignoring me. It was past time to get to know the real Remi, beyond her professional facade. And maybe, I'd finally taste that passion I'd been craving.

Later that night, after the concert, I found myself surrounded by the raucous laughter and clinking glasses of our post-show party. We were in the dimly lit arena, planning to go out to a club after some drinks.

Remi, her dark hair cascading down her back like a raven waterfall, stood near the bar, making notes in her ever-present notebook. My cock stirred at the sight of her beauty. She didn't flaunt herself like other girls I met on the tour, but I could tell that beneath her clothes lurked a paradise just waiting to be explored.

"Hey, Remi," I said, sliding up beside her, inhaling the sweet scent of flowers that hung in the air around her. "Why don't you take a break from work and have some fun? You're at a rock star party, for crying out loud."

She looked at me skeptically, her pen hovering over her notebook. "I'm here to do a job, Ghost. Not to party."

"Come on," I insisted, signaling the guy who was mixing some drinks. "One drink won't kill you."

Her gaze met mine with hesitance, but she finally nodded, a small smile playing on her lips. The guy, probably one of the crew, handed her a glass filled with an amber liquid.

"Thanks," she said softly, taking a sip of her drink. The air around us felt charged, as if we were both walking on a tightrope strung between desire and restraint.

The drink seemed to loosen her up and, before it was finished, our banter flowed easily, filled with playful jabs and witty comebacks. Remi was smart and personable when she let herself relax. I'd seen her that way with other people, but she always seemed to keep her guard up around me. I could feel the connection between us growing and it felt good to see her smile, to catch a glimpse of the woman beneath the professional exterior.

Just as I was starting to feel we were making progress, Trudy, our manager, came over with an insistent expression. "Ghost, there's a VIP here who wants to meet you. Can I steal you away for a moment?"

"Sure, Trudy," I sighed, shooting Remi an apologetic glance as

Trudy pulled me away. "Save my spot, will you?"

"Go ahead, Mr. Rockstar," she teased, rolling her eyes. "Don't keep your adoring fans waiting."

The VIP turned out to be some awkward, stuffy dude with his teenage daughter, who seemed to have swallowed her tongue. I stumbled through several minutes of conversation, signed an autograph, and took a selfie before I could escape.

The gathering had grown wilder as I talked with the VIPs, who were quickly ushered away by Trudy. I looked around, noticing that the road crew had joined the party. As I searched for Remi in the rowdy crowd, I couldn't shake the feeling that something was off. My instincts were screaming at me to keep an eye on her since one drink had already made her tipsy. I knew she could handle herself, but my protective nature was getting the better of me.

I finally spotted Remi, cornered by a burly guy from the crew, his imposing figure looming over her. She looked uncomfortable, her eyes darting around for an escape route. Without hesitation, I pushed through the crowd, positioning myself between them.

"Hey, man," I said, my voice cold and hard. " I think it's time for you to leave her alone."

The guy scowled but backed off, especially when he saw who he was dealing with. Remi looked at me with a mix of relief and gratitude. Her eyes were wide, and her breathing was shallow, betraying her unease.

"Thanks," she murmured. "I think I'm done for the night. I'll just head back to my tour bus."

"Let me walk you there," I insisted, not willing to let her go alone after what had just happened. She hesitated for a moment before nodding in agreement.

"Fine," she agreed, clearly shaken by the encounter.

As we walked through the cool night air, I couldn't help but feel a sense of responsibility for her well-being. It was a new feeling; I'd never really felt so protective of someone before, especially a woman I barely knew.

"Hey, why don't you come on my tour bus for a bit?" I suggested, trying to keep my voice casual. "We never get a chance to talk without someone interrupting."

My heart thundered in my chest, waiting for her answer, and I wondered if she could feel the magnetic pull between us as strongly as I did.

Remi looked hesitant but intrigued. She held up her blue journal. "Should I be taking notes, then?" she joked, attempting to hide her uncertainty.

"Strictly off the record," I assured her, flashing a grin. "This is purely personal. No work allowed."

She raised an eyebrow skeptically. "Are you sure your adoring fans won't miss you at the party?"

"Trust me, they'll survive," I replied, gesturing toward my bus. She hesitated for a moment longer before finally nodding in agreement. We walked together, the darkness enveloping us as we stepped deeper into the night and away from the chaos of the party.

I led her to the bus that I shared with Knox and Ryder, which I knew would be empty. One of the security guards who remained outside the venues to guard the buses and trailers took note of us. I also knew that Bishop was probably following behind us, but I didn't want to bother Remi with all that.

I pressed the button to open the bus door from the outside and gestured for Remi to head inside. She stopped, and I held my breath, wondering if she'd actually get on. For a moment, we just stood there, staring into each other's eyes, the world around us fading into oblivion.

After an obvious hesitation, she sighed and then climbed onto the bus. It was dimly lit, creating an intimate atmosphere that had been absent from the raucous party we'd left behind.

"Have a seat," I said, gesturing to the couch while I grabbed us both a drink from the fridge. Handing her a beer bottle, I took a sip of my own, savoring the cool liquid before diving into conversation.

Remi took a seat on one of the plush couches, her fingers nervously drumming against her thigh. I sat down across from her, leaning back and trying to exude an air of relaxation.

"So, tell me about life outside of work, Remi. What do you like to do when you're not chasing after rock stars?"

She raised an eyebrow, clearly wary of opening up too much. "I don't know, Ghost. That seems awfully personal." Her gaze flickered between me and the door as if contemplating an escape route.

"Ah, but that's the point," I countered, flashing her a disarming smile. "It's part of my therapy, you see. I'm required to interview every woman I meet for at least fifteen minutes."

"Really?" she questioned, squinting at me suspiciously. "I didn't realize therapy could be so entertaining."

"Only when it involves beautiful women," I quipped, feeling a thrill at the blush that crept up her cheeks.

A small smile tugged at the corner of her lips, her shoulders losing some of their tension. We sat there in silence for a moment, the weight of our unspoken thoughts pressing down on us.

"Ghost," she began, her voice soft and tentative. "Why did you really bring me in here?"

"Because I want to get to know you, Remi," I answered honestly. "You're not like the other people who hang around the band. You're intelligent, perceptive, and I can't help but feel drawn to you."

My heart pounded as I laid my feelings bare, leaving myself vulnerable in a way I hadn't been in years. The darkness outside the bus seemed to close in on us, amplifying the intimacy of our conversation. Remi's eyes widened, her breath catching as she processed my words.

"Ghost," she whispered, her voice trembling with uncertainty. "I don't know what to say."

"Then let's just talk," I urged, desperate to break through her hesitation. "Tell me something about yourself, anything at all."

"Fine," she relented, taking a deep breath. "But after that, it's your turn."

Remi took a deep breath and began to share bits and pieces of her life outside of work. She loved photography, hiking, and had a weakness for political thrillers. As she spoke, I found myself genuinely intrigued by this woman who was so determined to maintain a professional facade but had a depth to her that I hadn't expected.

"Alright, your turn," she said, finishing her drink and crossing her arms. "What does the mysterious Ghost do when he's not rocking out on stage?"

I stretched out my long legs. "Hmm. Let's see. I'm usually writing lyrics or playing guitar."

She tucked her silky hair behind her ear. "That doesn't count. Give me something non-music related."

I thought for a moment while I got us two new drinks. "Well, I like to work out. I've been going to this rock-climbing gym near my place in L.A., but sometimes I get recognized. I'm hoping to get good enough where I can do some real climbing outdoors."

"I can tell you work out. You must need a lot of stamina ... to perform, uh, on stage." Even in the dim light, I could see the blush staining her cheek. It was cute.

"Yes, I've got a lot of stamina." I winked at her. "I can perform all night long."

She looked down at her hands clenched in her lap. "What else do you do for fun?"

I ticked off a few items with my fingers. "I'm pretty decent at poker. Let's see, I like to go snowboarding and kayaking. Lately, I've been learning all I can about investing. I've been taking some internet classes."

"Wow," she murmured, clearly impressed. "I never would have guessed that about you, Ghost."

As our conversation continued, I felt the barriers between us slowly crumbling. The more we revealed about ourselves, the more I found myself drawn to this enigmatic woman who had entered my life so unexpectedly. And for the first time in a long while, I began to hope that perhaps there was a chance for a meaningful connection beyond the bright lights and deafening noise of the stage.

Despite doing dozens of 15-minute interviews over the years at Maggie's behest, I've never felt more comfortable talking to another person. I didn't feel adrift and so disconnected from Remi like I normally did. Usually, other people seemed like utter alien beings that I had trouble relating to. With Remi, it felt like we actually connected.

Maybe the recent breakthroughs I'd had in therapy had opened me up, allowing me to let other people in. It was an interesting thought, something I was sure to discuss with Maggie the next time I spoke with her.

Despite my attempts to keep the conversation light, I could sense that there was something weighing on Remi's mind when her eyes began to sparkle with unshed tears. As far as I could tell, she'd had only three drinks tonight, but I had a hunch that she didn't have much of a tolerance for alcohol. She grew introspective and seemed sad.

"What's wrong?" I asked gently.

She hesitated, as if she were grappling with whether to share her thoughts or not. Finally, she sighed and said, "You know, my boyfriend recently broke up with me. We used to share everything with each other all the time. I really miss him."

"Ah," I said, nodding in understanding, even as a bolt of jealousy sliced through me. "I do understand, Remi. Breakups are never easy, no matter the circumstances."

Her voice was barely audible in the quiet space. "He said he loved me, but ... I don't know. He has feelings for someone else, too." The vulnerability in her words sent a pang through my chest. I could see how much this confession cost her, and the pain behind those beautiful eyes tore at me.

I reached out and put my hand on her arm, offering comfort. "That must be tough for you."

"Yeah..." she murmured, her fingers twisting anxiously. "But it's over, and I need to focus on my assignment. This is supposed to be an interview, isn't it? Let's get back to business."

"Remi," I said softly, reaching out to touch her arm. "It's okay to hurt. It's okay to feel conflicted about it. You don't have to shut down and bury yourself in work."

Her eyes met mine, the shimmer of unshed tears betraying her emotional turmoil. As our gazes locked, an undeniable electricity surged between us. The air crackled with tension, a mutual longing we couldn't deny.

"Ghost," she whispered, her voice thick with emotion. And then, without warning, Remi lunged forward and kissed me, her lips crashing against mine with a ferocity that took my breath away.

Caught off guard, I tensed momentarily before surrendering to the kiss, allowing myself to be swept up in the whirlwind of passion that ignited between us. Her hands gripped my shirt, pulling me closer as her tongue danced with mine, her breath hot and urgent against my skin.

My senses were overwhelmed — the taste of her, the scent of her hair, the warmth of her body pressed against mine. My heart raced as I returned her passion, my hands tangling in her hair, pulling her closer.

Her lips felt like wildfire, igniting every nerve in my body as they moved against mine. My hands instinctively found their way to her hips, anchoring myself in the storm that was Remi Sutton. As our mouths explored one another, I could taste the raw vulnerability she'd shown just moments before, now mixed with a fierce desperation that resonated within me. It was unlike any kiss I'd experienced before — a tumultuous blend of desire and anguish, passion and pain.

Her fingers dug into my shoulders, as if she were trying to hold on to something solid amidst the emotional whirlwind we'd created. Our tongues tangled together, exploring and teasing, leaving no doubt that this was more than just a simple kiss — it was a declaration of need, a desperate grasp for understanding and solace in each other's arms.

My heart raced, pounding in my chest like a drum solo at a rock concert. I could feel the heat and urgency of desire radiating through me, and my muscles tensed with anticipation as my cock throbbed with desperate need. While part of me questioned the suddenness of this intense connection, another part reveled in it, embracing the chaos that Remi brought into my carefully constructed world.

"Ghost," she moaned between kisses, and I could hear the vulnerability in her voice, the desperate need for something more.

For a moment, we were lost in each other, caught in the whirlwind of desire and anguish that fueled our connection. Our kiss deepened as she thrust against my hard cock. Fuck, I wanted nothing more than to sink into her sweet surrender.

"Wait," I gasped, gently pulling away from her. "Are you sure about this?"

As quickly as it had begun, the moment shattered. Remi's eyes flew open, her breath hitching as she suddenly pulled away from me. Her eyes had a wild, haunted look as she stared back at me, reality slowly seeping back in. The spell was broken, and she seemed to shrink away from me, as if horrified by what had just transpired between us.

"Ghost, I — I'm so sorry," she stammered, her voice barely audible over the sound of my own ragged breathing. Tears welled up in her eyes. "I shouldn't have done that. I don't know what came over me."

Before I could say anything, she turned and fled the tour bus, leaving me standing there, my heart pounding and my mind reeling.

The silence that settled around me was deafening, a stark reminder of the emptiness left in her wake. I stood there, stunned by the turn of events, my chest still heaving as I tried to make sense of what had just happened. The kiss — that wild, incredible, earth-shattering kiss — had proved to me that Remi and I shared something far beyond a casual physical attraction. It was a connection that I'd never felt before.

But how could I pursue this connection when she'd fled so suddenly, leaving me with nothing more than the memory of her taste on my lips and the haunting look in her eyes? My mind raced with questions and doubts, but one thing was certain — Remi and I were meant for something more than just a fleeting moment of passion.

Chapter 11

Remi

I SAT ON THE edge of the couch, nervously flipping through my notes in preparation for my interview with Ghost. I was in his suite at the hotel, and I couldn't help but feel a little overwhelmed. I'd been avoiding being alone with him ever since that kiss nearly a week ago.

The kiss had left me reeling. It had been so spectacular, shaking me to my core, that I'd become utterly lost in it. At that moment, I had forgotten everything: my professionalism, my assignment, and my commitment to Greyson. Even though Grey and I were on a break, the kiss still burned in my mind like a betrayal to him.

Since then, I'd kept my distance from Ghost because of how my body reacted so wantonly, and that scared me. It made me doubt myself. I'd gotten a taste of something so amazing that I wasn't sure I could stop myself from indulging in more. I was drawn to Ghost's alluring presence; he was a constant temptation, and I felt different around him; more alive, more vital, more everything. His presence gave me the same feelings of excitement and adventure I got when I was with Greyson.

Just thinking that in my head made me feel guilty. What did it mean? Was my love for Greyson not real? I'd never felt this way around other men before.

I'd told Grey that you could be attracted to other people, but would never act on it if you were truly in love. He seemed to be struggling with that and I hadn't been able to understand it. Ironically, I understood it more now. I was acting the opposite of what I'd preached and had admonished Grey for.

And yet, my feelings for Grey hadn't changed. I knew in my heart that I still loved him. It was so complicated that I couldn't work it out in my head because there was no doubt that I also wanted to be with Ghost. The confusion in my head ran around in circles, never resolving.

So, I had stayed away from Ghost, but the attraction had only grown more intense. As much as I tried to convince myself that those feelings were merely a rebound effect from my separation with Grey, I knew that these feelings for Ghost were something deeper than I wanted to admit.

Ghost and I hadn't spoken much in the past week, but the tension between us was palpable. While avoiding Ghost, I'd gotten much closer to the other band members and even some of the crew. Part of that came from living on the road in close contact. It wasn't always easy in the cramped quarters — only staying in hotels on occasion — but there was a camaraderie in the group that was easy to fall into. I'd been accepted by the friendly bunch and had grown to appreciate them as individuals.

The guys in the band either seemed to be sleeping, working, or partying, with not a lot of time in between. But I'd caught some of their free time interviewing them, eating meals with them, and just hanging out until I'd gotten to know each of them better. They were starting to feel more like real friends than subjects of my work assignment.

Within minutes, I would conduct my most important interview. There were some candidates for my ghost that could work, but attaching the ghost to the lead singer of Ghost Parker would be infinitely better.

My heart raced as my eyes darted across the pages, taking in the background information I had painstakingly dug up. I knew Ghost's past was a sensitive topic, especially since he'd mentioned therapy during one of our previous conversations. Shit. I tapped my pen on my journal. I couldn't let my confusing feelings for him cloud this interview. I needed to focus.

My growing feelings for him were becoming a problem in more than one way; they were certainly interfering with my professional judgment. Night after night, I watched him on stage, captivated by his charisma and talent. His presence was magnetic, drawing me in closer than I ever intended to get. The attraction was so strong that it had even begun to infiltrate my dreams.

Just last night, I dreamt that I was backstage, watching as he performed under the dim lights. His deep, wicked baritone sent shivers down my spine as he sang lyrics filled with raw passion. In the dream, he locked eyes with me, pulling me into his embrace before claiming my lips in a searing kiss that left me breathless. I awoke alone, flushed and craving more of him.

Shaking off the memory of the dream, I took a deep breath and steadied my nerves, determined to keep my personal feelings from clouding my judgment. I glanced over the questions I had prepared for the interview, debating whether to ask about his past. It felt intrusive, but I couldn't deny that it was relevant to the music he created. And maybe his past would conjure up just the ghost I needed for this assignment.

"Ready when you are, sweetheart," Ghost's voice interrupted my thoughts, causing me to jump slightly. He leaned against the doorframe, dressed in black jeans and a tight-fitting blue shirt that showed off his toned muscles. His smoldering gaze met mine, and I felt my resolve waver.

"Okay," I said, taking another deep breath. "Let's get started."

Without another word, he crossed the room and then sat down in an armchair to my left, waiting for my first question.

I began the interview with an easy one. "How did you get your nickname, Ghost?"

He'd been asked that question many times before, and I didn't expect an answer any different from what he'd told reporters before, but I felt I had to ask. Maybe I'd get some nugget that dovetailed nicely with the secret story I was working on molding.

He paused for a moment, then looked me in the eye. "It's a long story," he said with a slight smirk, his voice low and raspy.

I felt my heart racing as I leaned in closer to hear what he had to say. He ran his fingers through his hair and chuckled softly. "The truth is, it started with my friends in high school," he began.

He went on to explain that when he was younger, his friends used to tease him about his ability to disappear without anyone noticing. They started calling him Ghost, and it stuck.

He'd given me the standard answer, but something made me want to dig a little deeper. "Did you feel that you needed to be able to disappear sometimes?"

He shifted in his seat and rubbed the back of his neck. "No, I just left when I got bored, that's all. My friends weren't that observant, I guess."

I nodded. It felt like there was something there, but it didn't seem like something I needed for my story, so I pressed on. "So, I noticed you have a record — that you've been convicted in several cases of disorderly conduct. Can you talk a bit about that?"

Ghost's eyes narrowed, but he smoothly evaded the question. "You know, Remi, we all have moments in our lives when we lose control. It's part of being human, isn't it? But what really matters is how we learn and grow from those experiences."

"Fair enough," I continued, undeterred. "What about your family life? How has that influenced your music?"

His brow furrowed, and he bit his lip as if to hold back a sharp retort before answering with a clipped voice, "My family life has nothing to do with my music, Remi. This interview is supposed to be about my art and my career, not digging up skeletons from my closet."

"Actually, Ghost, your past is relevant to the music you create," I argued, trying to maintain my professional composure. "Your fans want to know about the real you, and they'll be on your side if you open up to them. Don't you think they deserve that much?"

He crossed his arms defensively, his jaw clenched tight. He was shutting down, refusing to answer my questions. But I couldn't let this opportunity slip away, so I decided to push him further. This answer to the next question could be the entire key to my story.

"Did the suicide of your stepbrother, Adam Locke, affect your music?" I asked, wondering if I had crossed a line.

A flicker of intense sadness passed across his face, and I knew I'd hurt him deeply with the question. Within seconds, his expression shifted from shock and hurt to smoldering anger as his jaw set and his eyes narrowed.

The room seemed to freeze as Ghost's piercing gaze bore into me.

All the warmth drained from his face, replaced by a cold fury that sent chills down my spine. I knew I'd gone too far, but there was no turning back now.

"Who the hell do you think you are?" Ghost exploded, his voice barely contained. "Where did you even find out about Adam? You have no business digging into my life like that!"

His temper was a force to be reckoned with, and I suddenly felt very small in the lavish hotel suite. My heart pounded in my chest as I tried to formulate a response, but he didn't give me the chance.

"Interview's over." Ghost stormed out of the room, slamming the door behind him. The sound echoed through my ears, leaving me trembling in its wake.

I'd tried so hard not to allow my professional judgment to be clouded by my growing feelings for Ghost that I'd gone too far in the opposite direction and lost my sense of compassion in the pursuit of the story.

"Damn it," I whispered to myself, running a hand over my face. I knew I needed to find Ghost and apologize, try to salvage what was left of our relationship — both personal and professional. For the next hour, I searched the hotel, knocked on his bandmates' doors, and even checked the bar and lounge areas, but there was no sign of him.

The weight of my actions settled heavily on my shoulders as I realized that Ghost was nowhere to be found. What had I done? Had I just ruined everything between us because I let my desire to write a sensational story get the better of me?

I sighed deeply, knowing that I had to face the consequences of my choices. All I could do now was hope that Ghost would eventually be willing to hear me out and give me a chance to make amends. With each step I took through the hotel, my guilt grew heavier.

I returned to his hotel suite, hoping he might have come back. The door was still closed, and when I knocked hesitantly, there was no response. My heart sank even further, but I couldn't just give up. I sent him a text message, apologizing for my actions and asking if we could talk.

Time seemed to crawl by as I waited in the hallway outside his room. Each passing minute felt like an eternity, my thoughts consumed with regret and worry. When he didn't return my text, I headed back to my hotel room. Sound check was in a couple of hours and I decided I would go, just to apologize before his show.

When I arrived at the venue, I spotted him immediately. He was standing on stage, leaning on the mic stand, but something was off. His movements were uncoordinated and sluggish, his eyes glazed over — he was visibly drunk.

"Hey, mate, just take it easy," Knox said, trying to steady Ghost as he stumbled forward. "We'll help you sober up before the show."

Watching from a distance, my heart clenched with guilt. This was all my fault. I had pushed him too far, and now he was hurting. He obviously had a lot of unresolved feelings about his stepbrother's death, and I'd just callously opened those wounds up again. As much as I wanted to rush to his side and apologize, I knew that now wasn't the right time. Instead, I retreated to the VIP section to watch the concert unfold.

Despite his intoxication, Ghost managed to perform — his raw talent shining through, even in his compromised state. The crowd went wild as he sang, seemingly oblivious to the turmoil simmering beneath his magnetic persona.

His uncharacteristic aggression, however, didn't go unnoticed. Midway through the concert, Ghost kicked over his mic stand in a fit of anger, sending it crashing to the floor. The audience cheered wildly, their eyes glued to the spectacle unfolding before them.

"Here's a song called *Poison*," he announced, his voice dripping with venom as he glared into the crowd. "Dedicated to a reporter I like to call Little Miss Fake News." My stomach twisted into knots, realizing he was talking about me. I had found some information that he'd kept locked away and he was using the only outlet he had to express his pain — his music.

From the VIP section, I watched helplessly as Ghost continued to perform, each note breaking my heart a little more. I knew I had gone too far, and now the consequences were playing out for all to see. The guilt weighed heavily on me, like an anchor around my neck, dragging me down into a sea of regret.

Between songs, I could see Ghost chugging from a bottle, his bandmates trying their best to intervene and sober him up. But there was no stopping him now. He was a man on a mission, using the alcohol to numb the pain I had inadvertently caused.

As the concert drew to a close, the crowd continued to cheer and scream for more, but their adoration was tainted by the knowledge that I had done this to him. My foolishness had driven Ghost to the brink, and it was all because I put my ambition over decency.

"Thank you, goodnight!" Ghost shouted into the microphone as the final chords of the encore rang out. He stumbled offstage, the weight of his pain and intoxication finally catching up with him.

At that moment, I knew I couldn't just stand there in the VIP section any longer. It was time to face the music, so to speak, and try to make amends for my actions. I had to find Ghost and apologize, even if it meant putting my heart on the line.

After the concert, I watched as Knox and Ryder half-carried, half-dragged Ghost back to the tour bus. His body seemed to sway and stumble, a testament to the copious amounts of alcohol he'd consumed earlier. They were clearly worried about him, just as I was.

"Hey," I called out, jogging over to them. "Can I talk to him for a minute?"

Knox raised an eyebrow, skeptical of my intentions, but eventually sighed and stepped aside, allowing me access to the sanctuary where they hid away their wounded star.

"Fine, but don't take too long," he warned, casting a wary glance at Ghost before turning away.

"Thanks," I murmured, stepping up into the cramped space.

Ghost was slumped on one of the couches, his eyes red-rimmed and unfocused. He looked so vulnerable, so broken. It tugged at something deep within me, stirring a protective instinct I didn't know I had. He glanced up when he heard me approaching, his face contorting with anger.

"What the hell do you want?" he demanded, his words slurred slightly.

I sat down across from him. "Ghost, please," I pleaded, "I just want to talk."

"About what? How you fucked everything up?" He sneered, looking away from me.

"Actually, yes," I said softly. "But first, I want to tell you about something that happened to me a few years ago."

"Go away," he mumbled, trying to turn away from me. But I persisted, the desperation and sincerity in my voice impossible for even him to ignore."Please, Ghost. You need to hear this. I ... I want to explain."

He frowned but didn't object, so I took a deep breath and began my story. "I may be just an entertainment reporter, but I take my craft very seriously. I'm a journalist first. Entertainment reporters are looked down on by many — they're deemed not important — as people who produce fanciful, dumbed-down fluff. 'Real' journalists tend to look down their noses at journalists like me as the ones providing entertainment to pacify the unwashed masses, while the smart people do the real work. And some of that is true and maybe I take my work too seriously, but I don't offer up gushing profiles of artists; I like to offer deep and meaningful insights to my readers."

"Great," his voice dripped with sarcasm. "What's your point?"

"I just want you to understand why I dig deep. It's not for the sake of a sensationalist story. I do it to get the best story." I paused for a moment. Did I even believe my own words? That may have been true in the past, but this promotion competition was definitely testing the limits of my ethics. I leaned forward. "I want to help people. I want to show your fans the real you. That includes all the scabs and the pain along with the good. People can relate to that, Ghost."

He scoffed at my reasoning, his voice biting and derisive. "So, I'm supposed to believe your motives are pure?"

I pursed my lips, trying to explain myself. "My first love has always been investigative journalism, but that's gone now, so I try to bring a little piece of that to entertainment journalism. Researching is in my blood and I always want to write the best story, no matter the subject. I'm sorry I pushed it too far."

He disregarded my apology and latched on to the piece of my past that I'd inadvertently revealed. "What do you mean that's gone now? What happened to it?"

I sighed, realizing that I owed him the truth. "Before I became an entertainment journalist, I was an investigative reporter," I began, swallowing hard. "I dug up dirt on powerful people, exposed their lies and corruption. But one day, I went after the wrong politician. He destroyed my career — I was fired, blacklisted, and even received death threats."

Ghost's gaze darkened. I wasn't sure what he was thinking, but I knew I had to finish the story.

"Everything I'd worked for was gone. I thought it was over, but I clawed my way back into a different field of journalism. That's why I'm here with you now." I paused, searching his face for any sign of understanding.

He lifted his chin in defiance, his eyes never leaving mine as he slowly scrubbed the denim fabric of his jeans with the palms of his hands as if trying to wipe away an unpleasant memory. "Is your sad story supposed to make it all better? That dragging my stepbrother's suicide into the public entertainment story is somehow okay?"

"Look, digging into your past is part of my job," I admitted, my voice wavering. "But I let my ambition get the better of me and went too far. And I'm so, so sorry for hurting you."

He stared at me for a long moment, his eyes filled with a mixture of anger and pain. Finally, he sighed and rubbed a hand over his face. "You shouldn't have done it, Remi. You crossed a line. I thought you were a friend."

"I know," I whispered, my heart aching with regret. "But I can't change what's already happened. All I can do now is try to make it right."

He stared at me for a long moment, his stormy eyes searching for any hint of deception or malice.

"Make it right?" He scoffed, shaking his head. "How are you going to do that?"

I reached out to place my hand on his arm. "We start by being honest with each other," I replied. "Talk to me. I understand how hurt you are. Don't shut me out."

"You don't know anything about me," he spit out bitterly, wrapping himself in despair. "You can't possibly understand."

"Ghost, please—" I tried one last time, reaching out for him, but he recoiled from my touch as if it burned him.

He closed his eyes, shutting me out completely. "I thought you were different. Just leave me alone," he whispered, the words barely audible above the sound of my aching heart.

As I left the bus, feeling more defeated than ever before, I couldn't shake the image of Ghost huddled in on himself, drowning in pain and despair.

Chapter 12

Greyson

THE HOLLYWOOD ELITE SWIRLED around me like champagne bubbles in a crystal flute. The producer's mansion shimmered with the glint of chandeliers and the dazzle of designer gowns. Laughter and clinking glasses filled the air as guests mingled, exchanging pleasantries and business cards.

"Greyson, darling! So good to see you," a voice trilled as yet another actress draped herself on my arm. It had been hours since I arrived, and I couldn't get a minute's peace. My cheeks ached from forcing smiles, and my mind longed for an escape from the insipid conversations.

"Hello, Alexis," I replied, trying to mask my boredom. She was a well-known actress from a daytime soap, her perfectly coiffed hair and sparkling eyes betraying none of the desperation that clung to her like perfume.

"Isn't this party just fabulous?" she purred, sidling closer. Her fingers grazed my arm, sending an unwelcome shiver down my spine. "It's been too long since we last caught up, Greyson. You know, I've always thought there was something ... electric between us."

I struggled to keep my face neutral, my thoughts drifting to Remi. Breaking up with her had been a stupid idea. It wasn't Alexis's fault, but her advances only reminded me of what I'd lost. I wanted nothing more than to contact Remi, to see how she was doing, but pride held me back.

"Electric, huh?" I quipped, raising an eyebrow. "Must be all that hairspray."

Her laughter tinkled, like breaking glass. As she leaned in even closer, I spotted Jonas Steel, my ex-lover, across the room. Our eyes met for a brief moment before he looked away, leaving me feeling exposed and vulnerable.

"Greyson, are you listening?" Alexis asked, her voice rising with annoyance. I realized I hadn't heard a word she'd said.

"Sorry, Alexis," I said, extricating myself from her grip. "I just remembered that I have an urgent call to make."

"Fine," she huffed, tossing her hair as she stalked away in search of more attentive prey.

As I retreated to a quieter corner of the party, my thoughts tumbled like dominos, one after the other, Remi, Jonas, Ghost. I'd longed to find love, finally found it, and then thrown it away because I didn't trust it enough. My heart ached with the weight of it all, and I knew I couldn't keep running from the truth. I needed to confront my feelings for both Remi and Ghost, and find closure once and for all.

Jonas approached me with a confident stride, his eyes never leaving mine. He was striking in a way that felt unreal, like something out of a fantasy. Only Hollywood could produce someone so effortlessly attractive.

"Greyson," he said smoothly, a hint of a smile playing on his lips. "I saw Alexis hitting on you earlier. I knew you wouldn't be interested in what she had to offer."

"Jonas," I replied, trying to keep my voice even. "What brings you here? Besides the free booze and beautiful people?"

He laughed, a low and sultry sound that sent shivers down my spine, despite my best efforts to remain unaffected. "You know me too well," he said, leaning in closer. His hand brushed against my arm in a suggestive touch, sending a wave of memories crashing down on me — memories of passion, desire, and nights spent tangled together.

"Grey," Jonas murmured, his breath warm on my ear. "It's been a long time since we've had some fun together. Why don't we pick up where we left off?"

For a moment, I hesitated. I hadn't had sex since Remi left, and the loneliness gnawed at me like a relentless hunger. But as the ghost of her touch lingered on my skin, I knew that I couldn't betray my heart any longer.

"Jonas," I said firmly, pulling away from him. "I can't do this. There's someone else. I'm sorry."

His eyes flashed with hurt and he stared at me for a long moment before finally giving a brief nod of understanding. He walked away without another word. I felt a pang of guilt, but I remained resolute in my decision.

Desperate for a distraction, I tried mingling with the other guests. Their laughter and chatter did little to fill the emptiness inside me. My thoughts kept returning to Remi, her warmth and understanding, the way she'd made me feel alive for the first time in years.

Feeling suffocated by the sea of people and noise, I retreated to a quiet corner of the party. As I leaned against the wall, I closed my eyes and took a deep breath, trying to steady myself. My heart still felt heavy with regret for ending things with Remi, but I couldn't deny the lingering feelings for Ghost that haunted me.

My mind raced as I considered my options. I knew that seeing them both in person was the only way to truly confront my emotions and find closure. The thought terrified me, but I also yearned for the chance to make sense of the tangled web of my heart.

With newfound determination, I pulled out my phone and sent Remi a text message, asking if we could meet up at an upcoming concert where Ghost Parker would be performing. If I was going to face this head-on, they both needed to be there.

To my surprise, Remi responded right away by calling me on a video call. Her photo filled the screen, and my heart skipped a beat at the sight of her. Swallowing my nerves, I stepped away from the party and searched for a quiet place to talk.

I stepped through the French doors onto the stone patio, feeling the cool night air brush against my skin as I searched for a quiet place to talk with Remi. The party's laughter and chatter seemed muted now, leaving me alone with my thoughts and nerves. I tapped the answer button on my phone and took in her beautiful face on my screen.

"Hey," she said softly, her eyes searching my face for any sign of what I was feeling. "It's good to see you, Grey."

"Hey, Remi," I replied, trying to keep my voice steady. "I didn't expect you to call so soon. I thought you'd be asleep now. It's got to be after midnight there, but I guess there are a lot of late nights when you're covering rock stars."

She gave me a small smile. "No, I'm still up. Things aren't going so great with my assignment right now, so I'm trying to work it out. How about you? You're outside somewhere? And you're dressed up."

A few couples had spilled outside the party to get some air, so I kept walking to find a more private place to talk. "Yes, I'm at a party in the

Hollywood Hills. The view is gorgeous out here."

"My view is not as nice." She swept her phone around so I could see the cramped space she was in. "I'm in a bunk on the bus. Home sweet home for now."

"Are you with the band?" I couldn't help but wonder if Ghost slept within a few feet of her.

She was busy pulling the curtain to her bunk closed as she talked. "No, I'm on a bus with some of the staff that keeps the show running smoothly. The band has two buses that they use for themselves and their families. They're more luxurious than my bus."

I walked down a path filled with scrubby bushes until I found a little alcove with a bench. I sat down and focused on Remi. "You mentioned things aren't going well there?"

She settled back against her pillow, her dark hair fanning out around her face. God, I missed seeing her like that in my bed. "Nothing I can't handle. Anyway, your text caught me by surprise, and I figured we should talk about it. You want to come here?"

"Yes," I nodded, taking another deep breath. "I, uh, I've been doing a lot of thinking lately, and I realized that I need to see you in person. I said a lot of things before you left, but I don't think I explained myself very well and I didn't listen to what you were saying very well."

Remi studied me for a moment before responding, her expression unreadable. "I can understand that, Grey. You caught me a bit off guard that day and my emotions were a bit too tangled up to understand what you were telling me."

"I take the blame for that. I really went about it all wrong," I admitted, rubbing the back of my neck. "So, would it be okay if we met up at one of the Ghost Parker concerts?"

"Of course," she said without hesitation. "You know I'll always be here for you, Grey. No matter what."

"Thank you, Remi. That means a lot to me." A wave of relief washed over me, but growing anxiety quickly replaced it. As excited as I was to see Remi again, I couldn't ignore the jolt that ran through me at the thought of seeing Ghost again. "I can fly out to wherever you are on the tour this weekend. What do you think?"

"Then come to the Boston concert on Saturday," she said, her voice filled with excitement. "I'll have Trudy hook you up with a VIP pass. I'll text you the details tomorrow."

"Sounds good," I confirmed, my heart pounding in my chest, feeling a rush of anticipation at the thought of seeing her again.

We chatted a bit more about the tour, her life on the road, and what had been happening with me since we'd last spoken. As our conversation continued, she mentioned Ghost casually a few times. Of course, she had gotten to know him while she was writing a story about him and his band, but it made me realize that I needed to be completely truthful with her that the man I had feelings for was Ghost. If we were going to have any chance of moving forward, she deserved to know everything, no matter how uncomfortable it made me feel.

"Remi, there's something I need to talk to you about when I see you," I confessed, my throat tightening with anxiety.

Her expression shifted to concern. "Is it about your unresolved feelings for someone else?" she guessed.

I nodded, impressed by her intuition. "Partly, yes, but it's mostly about us."

"Alright," she agreed, her eyes searching mine through the screen. "We'll talk about it in Boston. Just promise me one thing, Grey?"

"Anything," I vowed, desperate to show her that I was committed to rebuilding our relationship.

"Be honest with me," she implored. "No more secrets or half-truths. If we're going to figure this out, no matter how it turns out, we need to be completely open with each other."

I took a deep breath, feeling a mingling of hope and nerves. "I promise, Remi," I assured her. "No more secrets."

A warm smile spread across her features. "Good," she said. "I can't wait to see you on Saturday, Greyson."

I couldn't help but return her smile. "Me too. I've missed you, Rem."

"Missed you too," she admitted softly, her eyes shining with sincerity. It felt like a balm to my soul, knowing that she still cared.

"Okay, see you then," I told her, trying not to grin crazily like a complete fool. "Take care, Remi."

"You too, Grey," she said before ending the call.

As I stared out at the glittering cityscape, I felt a strange mix of emotions swirling within me. Excitement pulsed through my veins at the thought of seeing Remi again, but I couldn't deny that I was also looking forward to seeing Ghost. The upcoming confrontation terrified me, but I knew it was necessary if I wanted to find closure and move forward.

I returned inside to the party, my emotions swirling inside me like a hurricane, a chaotic mix of hope, nerves, and longing. The chatter and laughter around me seemed distant as if I were underwater. The opulent decorations and twinkling lights blurred together, my mind preoccupied with the decision I had made.

I gravitated toward a quiet corner of the party, away from the glitz and glamour. As I settled into a plush, oversized chair, I stared into the depths of my nearly empty wine glass, the remnants swirling in slow circles. My thoughts raced, a disorienting blend of anxiety and anticipation.

"Greyson Durant, lost in thought?" A familiar voice teased, snapping me out of my reverie. I looked up to find my close friend, Lucy, who was a series regular on *Devious*, standing before me with a playful smile.

I stood to deposit a kiss on each of her cheeks. "Lucy, good to see you," I greeted, trying to shake off my introspection. "Just needed a moment to myself."

"Understandable," she said, taking a seat in a nearby chair. "These parties can be so much after a while."

Nodding in agreement, I finished off my wine, the rich flavor doing little to alleviate my anxiety. "So, what's going on with you?" I asked, attempting to shift the focus away from myself.

"Oh, you know," Lucy began, complaining about her latest boyfriend and the drama that came with him. As much as I tried to listen, my thoughts kept drifting back to Remi and Ghost.

Lucy must have noticed my preoccupation. "Grey, are you okay?"

"Actually, I've been thinking about Remi," I confessed, not wanting to keep my friend in the dark.

"Really? Why is she on your mind?"

"I realized how much I miss her, and I regret ending our relationship." Pausing, I hesitated before continuing, "But at the same time, I can't deny that I still have lingering feelings for someone else."

Lucy studied me for a moment, her expression thoughtful. "You know, Grey, sometimes the only way to move forward is to confront your emotions head-on."

"You're right," I agreed, mulling over her words. "In fact, I just spoke with Remi, asking if we could meet up this weekend."

"Good for you, Grey," Lucy encouraged, giving my hand a reassuring squeeze. "I think it's important that you face these feelings and find closure, whatever that may look like for you."

"Thanks, Lucy," I replied, appreciating her support. "I just hope I'm making the right decision."

"Only time will tell," she said with a small smile. "But remember, you shouldn't have to twist yourself into a pretzel to make it work. Remi should accept and appreciate you for who you really are. You shouldn't have to change your nature to satisfy her idea of what the relationship should be."

I froze. "What do you mean? Remi's not trying to change me."

"Isn't she?" She cocked her brow enigmatically. "I always thought Remi would have trouble keeping a man like you satisfied."

My face felt hot, my fists clenched at my sides as I glared at her, fighting the urge to raise my voice. My jaw clenched as I asked her each question with a sharpness that hinted at accusation. "A man like me? What are you talking about, Lucy?"

"Don't get all defensive, Grey." Her lower lip jutted out in a pout. "You're a man of many persuasions and needs. Someone like Remi might be too close-minded to see that."

I held back a sharp retort and modulated my voice. "Remi isn't close-minded. She has always accepted who I am and supported me."

"Well then, that's terrific." Her tinkling laughter held a note of phoniness. I'd been front and center to her acting skills on set over the years, so I could easily spot her putting on an act now.

Lifting my empty wine glass, I said, "I could use a refill. Care to join me?"

"Absolutely, darling." She rose and waited for me.

Together, we rejoined the festivities. I used all my own acting skills to feign having a good time, but my thoughts never strayed far from Remi and how I could resolve my confused feelings.

An hour later, I made my exit. With one last glance at the opulent party behind me, I stepped out into the cool night air, pulling my jacket tighter around me. The sounds of laughter and clinking glasses faded as I walked down the producer's lavish driveway, my mind racing with thoughts of Remi and Ghost and what awaited me in Boston — a confrontation of emotions, a chance at closure, and the hope of finding real happiness amidst the chaos. It was time to lay all my cards on the table, for better or worse.

Chapter 13

Ghost

THE ROAR OF THE crowd still echoed in my ears as I stumbled offstage, sweat and adrenaline coursing through my veins. I'd managed to stay mostly sober for this show, at Knox's insistence, but now that it was over, my self-restraint evaporated like morning fog under the sun. Snatching a bottle of whiskey from our dressing room, I carried it with me into the shower, gulping down mouthfuls between lathering up and washing off the grime.

"Ghost, you ready?" Knox called through the door, impatient to get to the after-party. "We got people waiting."

"Coming," I hollered back, finishing off the last swig before stepping out of the shower and wrapping a towel around my waist. The meet and greet was a blur of faces and eager fans, their awestruck gazes only fueling my need to keep the party going. We hit the club with an entourage in tow, ready to tear the night apart.

As we claimed our spot near the bar, I saw Remi in my peripheral vision watching me closely. Her eyes were hard and focused, locked onto me with an unreadable intensity. But tonight wasn't about her; it was about losing myself in the chaos. I pretended not to see her and turned my attention to the bartender, ordering round after round of shots for the group.

"Ghost, man, you should slow down," Sidney warned, his voice barely audible over the pounding beat of the music. But his concern only spurred me on, pushing me deeper into the swirling tide of alcohol and drugs that had become my solace.

"Fuck it," I slurred, grabbing a handful of pills someone had handed me and tossing them back without a second thought. My vision swam, and the world tilted on its axis, but I kept dancing and drinking like a man possessed.

"Ghost, stop!" I heard a woman's voice shouting above the din, but it felt distant, like a memory that refused to surface. The next thing I knew, I was climbing onto the bar, knocking over bottles and glasses in my frenzied state.

Bishop, my security guy, usually unflappable, grabbed at my arm with a scowl. "Get down, man!" But his anger barely registered as I shoved him away, too wasted to care about the consequences.

"Fuck you all!" I screamed into the night, my voice cracking with desperation. "I'm fucking invincible!"

"Dammit, Ghost, you daft, bloody bampot," Knox hissed, helping Bishop drag me off the bar before I could do any more damage. I could see the flash of cameras capturing my unraveling for the world to witness. Yet, somehow, it didn't matter. All that mattered was the momentary oblivion that numbed the pain gnawing at my soul.

"Fuck 'em all," I slurred, swaying on my feet as we exited the club. An image of Remi's face flickered in my mind, her eyes wide with concern or maybe judgment. Hell, she was probably thrilled that I was giving her such salacious material for her article. No doubt it dovetailed nicely with the lurid details from my past. I let out a maniacal chuckle as I spiraled further and further into darkness.

♪♪♩♩

Sunlight streamed through the tour bus window, assaulting my eyes and intensifying the pounding in my head. I groaned, pulling a pillow over my face to block out the light. My body felt like it had been hit by a truck, and every noise seemed to reverberate through my skull.

"Hey, mate," Knox's voice broke through the haze of pain as he pulled open the door to the back bedroom. "You okay?"

"Does it look like I'm okay?" I snapped, lifting the pillow just enough to glare at him. But my anger quickly dissipated as I saw the genuine concern etched on his features.

"Sorry," I mumbled, letting the pillow fall back over my face. "I'm just... Yeah, I feel like shit."

Knox sat down beside me, his weight causing the mattress to dip. "Last night got pretty wild, yeah? What's going on with you?"

"Wild" was an understatement, but I didn't have the energy to argue. Instead, I hesitated before finally admitting, "Looks like a part of my past is coming back to haunt me."

"Fuck, I know how that is." He drew in a ragged breath. "All that shit with Aila weighed me down for years until I finally confronted it head-on. Ignoring it didn't really work. You know that you were the one who helped me realize it. Maybe you need to deal with it once and for all. I don't know much about your past, mate. You've never shared it with me, so my advice might be total shite."

I sat up and ran a hand through my unruly hair. Knox had dealt with some weighty matters from his past, his fiancee's death and his feelings of guilt and responsibility for it. My past seemed darker and more lurid. Shameful. I hadn't even been able to tell Maggie about all of it yet.

Knox was the best friend I had, and I knew implicitly that I could trust him. Part of connecting with people was letting them in, and I desperately needed someone on my side. I'd tell him at least some of it.

It took a moment, but eventually, the words spilled forth. "My dad... He was abusive, man. To me and my stepbrother. And my stepbrother, he... he couldn't take it anymore. He killed himself." The words felt heavy, like stones dropping into a still pond, the ripples of emotion threatening to pull me under.

Knox's face drained of color and his mouth hung open as he breathed a single word. "Fuck." He stared at me with wide eyes full of concern and sympathy. His voice cracked when he spoke again, "Ghost, I had no idea... I'm so sorry."

"Remi found out," I continued, the dread mounting in my chest. "I don't know how, but she knows everything. If she publishes this, for the world to salivate over... I don't think I can handle it."

Knox's hand landed on my shoulder, his grip firm and reassuring. "Look, mate, you need help dealing with this. You should probably tell Trudy. If it's going to come out, find out how to get ahead of it all. And you should really talk to Maggie. She'll help you manage your emotions. It's going to stir up a lot of nasty shite for you."

I sighed, knowing he was right, but not wanting to admit it. Just thinking back to those years had sent me spiraling. Having it broadcast to the world would crush me under the weight of all the humiliation and shame. "Yeah, maybe I'll call Maggie," I conceded, the weight of the situation settling over me like a wet blanket.

"Trust me, Ghost," Knox encouraged, squeezing my shoulder before standing up. "You don't have to face this alone. If you need anything, just ask. Even if it's just to talk, yeah? I'm a bloody good listener even if my advice is shite."

As he walked away, leaving me to my thoughts, I couldn't help but feel grateful for his unwavering support. It didn't make the situation any easier, but at least I knew I wasn't completely on my own.

After I took a quick shower and had a bite to eat, I went back to the small bedroom, which rotated between me, Ryder, and Knox. I stared at the phone in my hand, the number for Maggie already typed in. Taking a deep breath to steady myself, I hit the call button and listened as it rang. A moment later, her familiar voice answered.

"Hey, Ghost," Maggie greeted warmly. "What's going on?"

"Uh, hey Maggie," I started, my voice uncharacteristically shaky. "I... I need some advice."

"Of course," she replied, her tone shifting to one of attentive concern. "What's been happening?"

I recounted the recent events with Remi, my spiral, and the fear that gripped me at the thought of my past being exposed. As I spoke, I could tell Maggie was listening carefully, taking in every detail.

"Ghost," she said softly once I had finished, "you need to confront your feelings about your past. It's time. It's clear that it's affecting your present more than you realize."

"Easy for you to say." My hands were clenched into tight fists. "But how am I supposed to do that?"

Her voice was calm and steady. "Remember the four steps we were working on? Acceptance, Analysis, Action, and Forgiveness?"

I rubbed at my aching temples. "Yeah. How does that fit in?"

"You said Remi knows about your stepbrother's suicide? And possibly the abuse? Well, I think you should give Remi a quote to print.

Something generic, along the lines of..." Maggie paused for a moment to collect her thoughts, "Of course, it affects my music. Tragic things in our past shape who we are as people. It's what we do with those tragedies that can make all the difference. And I choose to ... I don't know if you want to mention your charitable giving or not, but it does say a lot about you Ghost. You're a very generous man."

I turned the idea over in my head. Could I do that? "So, I should just go along with it? Let her expose my past for the world to see and to judge? To pick apart my brother's suicide like it's the latest scandalous gossip?"

"It might be sensationalized by some, but that just reflects negatively on them. You can remain above all that." I could hear her pen tapping on her desk in the background. "Obviously, your PR people can help you craft a better quote than the one I just made up. But Ghost, this is part of acceptance. As terrible as it all was, it happened."

My throat tightened at the thought of exposing myself, the rawness of my emotions leaving me feeling vulnerable. "There's other stuff, stuff I haven't told you about, that I'm more ashamed of. If that ever got out..."

"Do you think you're ready to tell me?" she asked quietly.

I closed my eyes. "Yeah. I think so. I'm tired of holding this all inside."

She said nothing for several moments. "I'd prefer to have that conversation in person. Can you wait until the end of your tour? Or do you feel it's more pressing?"

"You wouldn't be asking me that if you saw me last night." I was only half-joking.

She sighed. "That's what I thought."

I told Maggie that I would check in with the tour manager and find a spot in my schedule that would work. It wouldn't be cheap to have

Maggie come to see me for a few hours, but it would be worth every penny.

"Ghost, remember that you're not alone in this," Maggie reminded me gently. "You have people who care about you and want to help. Don't be afraid to lean on them."

"Thanks, Maggie," I said, already feeling better after talking to her.

She was upbeat and friendly as she ended our conversation. "Call me if you need anything else, or if you just want to talk, okay? Take care, Ghost."

"Will do," I promised, ending the call and letting out a heavy breath. The road ahead was going to be far from easy, but with Maggie's guidance and the support of my friends, maybe I could find a way through this tangled mess. And, for the first time, I felt like I needed to unburden myself.

I knew I had to confront Remi about what she knew and possibly give her a quote, but the thought of baring my soul to her was terrifying. Still, deep down, I knew it was necessary. My secrets couldn't remain hidden forever, and dealing with them head-on was the only way to regain control over my life.

Stepping out of the room, I saw Knox and Ryder lounging on the couch, watching TV. I grabbed a drink from the refrigerator, lost in thought.

Suddenly, the tour bus door swung open with a loud creak. Trudy burst in, her eyes sparkling with excitement, and a grin stretched across her face.

"Guys!" she exclaimed, looking around at us. "You won't believe who just confirmed they're coming to our Boston show!"

"Who?" I asked, my curiosity piqued despite the emotional whirlwind I was dealing with.

"Greyson Durant!" Trudy nearly shrieked, bouncing on her toes.

"Can you believe it? Greyson freaking Durant is going to be at our concert!"

A wave of conflicting emotions washed over me, leaving me feeling more disoriented than ever. Of all people, it had to be him? Fuck.

"Wow, that's ... great," I managed, forcing a smile onto my face even though my stomach twisted into knots. "Boston's gonna be quite the show, then."

Trudy was grinning like a kid on Christmas morning. "This is going to be epic! I can't believe I get to meet him."

As I watched her celebrate, I couldn't help but feel a strange sense of dread settling in the pit of my stomach. The thought of Greyson being there — seeing me perform, watching me from the shadows — made my heart race and my palms sweat. There was something about him that unnerved me. I didn't want him around me, especially now when I was dealing with so much shit from my past.

It made no sense. I had barely spoken two words to the man since I'd met him years ago, and yet his presence loomed large over me. Why did he have such an effect on me? Was it just jealousy of his fame? I really didn't think so. It was something deeper, more primal.

"You okay, Ghost?" Knox asked, snapping me out of my introspection.

"Yeah," I lied, rubbing the back of my neck. "Just ... wondering why he's coming, I guess."

He shrugged, clapping me on the shoulder. "Maybe he just wants to see a show? He's a cool bloke. We'll have to show him how rock stars party when he's here."

"Totally," I agreed, nodding my head as if I was on board with the excitement. But inside, I knew that Greyson's arrival would only complicate an already tangled web of emotions, and I couldn't shake the feeling that I was standing on the edge of something monumental, maybe even something catastrophic.

But for better or worse, there was no turning back now. The cards had been dealt, and it was time to face whatever hand fate had in store for me.

Chapter 14

Remi

I STEPPED INTO THE hotel's dining area, the smell of freshly brewed coffee and sizzling bacon filling the air, as I joined the band members and their families for breakfast. My heart raced with excitement, but my stomach twisted in knots of apprehension as I became more involved in their lives. I was starting to think of them more as friends than as the subjects of my reporting. It was hard to stay neutral when the logistics of the tour pushed us all so close together.

My first taste of life on the road — living on the cramped tour bus with Trudy being the only other female on board, moving from city to city, living out of suitcases, and nonstop partying. It was exhilarating, but it was starting to feel like a grind.

Kaylie scooted over to make room for me at the table. "Morning, Remi!" Kaylie greeted me warmly, her eyes sparkling with enthusiasm.

"Morning," I replied, taking a seat next to her. Sid sat on her other side, his arm casually draped around her shoulders.

"Remi, you have to hear this," Kaylie said, leaning in closer. She sipped her coffee before continuing, "Sid got locked out of our hotel room this morning wearing nothing but a towel! I couldn't hear him banging on the door because I was in the shower. A maid had to let him in." Her laughter filled the air, drawing smiles from everyone around us.

"Hey, it wasn't my fault!" Sid retorted as he stabbed a piece of bacon with his fork. "The door slammed shut when I went to grab the newspaper."

Kaylie launched into stories about her life with Sid, sharing their experiences on the road and giving me a glimpse into the challenges and joys of being part of a rock band's family. "When we first started dating," she began, smiling sweetly as she reminisced, "Sid would call me every night from a different city. It was sweet but also kind of crazy trying to keep up with his schedule."

"Tell me about it," I said, nodding in agreement. "But it must be exciting too, right?"

"Definitely," she confirmed, her eyes lighting up. "Every day is a new adventure."

As we continued eating, I asked Bash about the challenges of being a single dad on the road.

He took a bite of his pancakes. "It's tough, you know," he admitted. "Juggling music and raising a child isn't easy, but we make it work. I try to bring him along whenever I can, and when I can't, my sister helps out."

"Family is everything," Kaylie chimed in, squeezing Sid's hand.

The conversation flowed naturally as we shared stories and laughter, the camaraderie at the table unmistakable. As I looked around at these people who had welcomed me into their world, I couldn't help but feel a sense of belonging. Despite the hardships and chaos of life on the road, there was an undeniable bond between them — a family forged not by blood, but by shared experiences and unwavering loyalty. That was the kind of thing I wanted to highlight in my story.

I scooped up a forkful of scrambled eggs and turned to Ryder, who was on my other side. "Ryder, what's your favorite band, aside from Ghost Parker, obviously?" I asked, wanting to learn more about him.

"Ah, that's a tough one," he said, scratching his chin thoughtfully. "You can't beat the classics, Led Zeppelin, The Rolling Stones, Pink Floyd ... man, I wish I could've been around to see those shows."

"Right?" I agreed, laughing. "I'm pretty sure I was born in the wrong decade."

Ryder chuckled before taking a sip of his coffee. "But hey, at least we still have some great bands today. What's your favorite concert you've been to?"

I paused to think. "It's hard to choose, but I think seeing Coldplay live was awesome. So was Imagine Dragons."

"Hmmm." He nodded. "Favorite band?"

"Besides you guys?" I joked, earning a chuckle from him. "Hmm, probably Arctic Monkeys. Alex Turner's lyrics are so raw and honest; they always get me."

Ryder nodded approvingly. "I bet Talia would love them too if she could remember the lyrics correctly," he laughed, referring to his wife. "She's notorious for butchering songs."

"Really? That sounds hilarious!" I exclaimed, trying to picture Talia singing off-key.

"Trust me, it is," he said with a fond smile. "She has this uncanny ability to turn any song into a comedy routine. It's a talent, really."

"Speaking of Talia," I mentioned casually. "She's friends with Greyson Durant, right? I ... I used to date him."

Ryder's eyes widened in surprise. "Wait, you dated Greyson? That explains why he's coming to our show on Saturday. We couldn't figure out why he suddenly wanted to see a show and in Boston at that."

I took a sip of my orange juice to hide my blush. I felt a bit self-conscious, but also oddly proud that my connection to Greyson was the reason for his interest in the band. "Who knows? Maybe he just wants to see you guys rock out."

"Or maybe he misses you," Kaylie suggested with a playful wink.

Before I could respond, Bash's toddler son, Kody, waddled over to me and tugged on my pant leg. I looked down at his big, innocent eyes and couldn't help but smile. "Hey there, little man. What's up?"

"Up, up!" Kody demanded, reaching his tiny arms toward me. I couldn't help but smile at the adorable little boy.

I glanced at Bash for permission before scooping him onto my lap.

"Looks like you've made a new friend," Ryder teased.

He immediately snuggled into me as if we'd known each other for years. It was then that I realized just how much being accepted and welcomed by the band's inner circle, even by its youngest member.

Kody was playing with the ends of my hair as Knox told a story about a practical joke Sid and Bash had once played on him. The laughter around the table quieted as we turned to see Ghost stumbling in, looking disheveled and distant, with dark circles under his eyes.

"Morning, sunshine," Bash greeted him with a smirk, though concern laced his tone.

Ghost mumbled something unintelligible, rubbing his temples as he surveyed the room. His eyes locked onto mine for a brief moment, and I could see the unease lingering behind them.

"Uh, I forgot something in my room," Ghost muttered lamely, turning on his heel and retreating back down the hallway.

Knox called after him, "Wait up, Ghost." He exchanged worried looks with the rest of the band before excusing himself to follow Ghost.

"Is he okay?" I asked quietly, as if voicing my concern might shatter the delicate balance of the morning.

Ryder sighed, running a hand through his hair. "He's been ... off lately. We're all worried about him, but he keeps pushing us away."

"Seems like Knox is trying to help, though," I observed, glancing at the door again.

"Knox is probably the only one who can get through to him right now," Sid admitted, taking a long sip of his coffee.

As breakfast came to an end, my thoughts kept drifting back to Ghost. Despite the laughter and camaraderie around the table, I couldn't shake the feeling that something was terribly wrong. I wanted to talk to him, to help in any way I could, but he remained elusive all day.

I decided not to go to sound check, fearing my presence might upset Ghost before the concert. Instead, I retreated to my hotel room, immersing myself in research and notes as I tried to come up with a new angle for my story — one that wouldn't exploit or hurt anyone involved.

After what felt like hours of fruitless brainstorming, I threw myself onto the bed in frustration. A mental image of Ghost haunted me, his disheveled state at breakfast a stark reminder of the pain hiding beneath the surface of his enigmatic persona. My heart ached for him, and I knew I couldn't betray his trust by using his story for my own gain. I wasn't willing to hurt him or the band for the sake of my career. They had all welcomed me into their inner circle, and I owed them better than that.

♫♫♪♩♩

The concert was electric. Ghost's raw energy and charisma filled the arena as he commanded the stage, pouring out his soul with every note. Despite my lingering concern for him, I couldn't help but be swept away by the magic of the performance.

But after the final encore, things took a dark turn. With each drink Ghost consumed at the after-party, he grew louder and more reckless, flirting shamelessly with anything that moved. My heart clenched at the sight of him spiraling out of control, the pain I'd seen in his eyes earlier that day now buried beneath a thick layer of bravado and alcohol.

"Hey, Knox," I said, approaching him with a worried look. "Do you think we should get him out of here?"

"Way ahead of you," he replied, nodding at Bishop, Ghost's towering security guard.

Bishop took hold of Ghost's arm. "Come on, Ghost. We should get you back to the hotel before things get out of hand."

Together, Bishop and Knox began maneuvering him through the crowd toward the exit.

"Fine!" Ghost growled, finally surrendering to their persistence with a scowl. "But I'm not done partying!"

"Of course not," Knox muttered sarcastically. Worried about him, I fell into step beside them, determined to offer whatever support I could.

"Remi," Knox said, glancing back at me as he reached the door. "I'm not sure you should come."

I hesitated for a moment. "I just want to make sure he's okay."

Outside, a car was waiting. I shivered in the cool night air as Bishop and Knox wrangled Ghost into the back seat of the car.

Knox closed the door and then saw me standing there. "Go back to the party. He'll be fine. I'll make sure."

"Is he upset with me?" I blurted out.

Knox sunk his hands into his pockets and rocked back on his heels. "I'm not going to talk to you, Remi. You're a reporter and this is private. You could really damage him with what you report."

If Ghost was acting this way because of me, I had to know. "Is this about his step-brother? I'm so sorry I asked him about that. I'm not going to mention it at all in the media package. I don't want to hurt him; I don't want to hurt any of you."

Knox's voice was thick with concern. "Ghost is terrified that you're going to dig up his past and publish all the dark stuff about him. He thinks you're just another vulture waiting to pick at his scars for a juicy story."

"God, no," I breathed, appalled by the idea. "That's not what I want at all. I'm here to write about the band, not hurt him or anyone else."

And I wasn't. Not now. My stomach churned with disgust and shame at how close I'd come to doing exactly that. Even if I'd felt conflicted, I'd still been digging into the band's past to see if I could uncover a ghost no matter what kind of pain that ghost unearthed for the band.

Knox wavered with uncertainty. Finally, he replied, "Good, because he doesn't need any more pain in his life."

"Let me go with you." My resolve hardened. "I want to assure him that I would never betray him like that."

The car ride back to the hotel was filled with an oppressive silence, broken only by Ghost's shallow breaths as he lay slumped in the back seat, his head resting against the window. I couldn't help but watch him, my heart aching at the sight of this once vibrant man reduced to a shell of his former self.

The tension in the air was palpable as we pulled up to the hotel. Knox and Bishop managed to hoist Ghost out of the car, his limbs limp and heavy. They half-carried, half-dragged him to his room, trying their best not to draw attention from any curious onlookers. Ghost groaned as they eased him onto the bed, his body limp and vulnerable.

"Let's try to sober him up," Knox suggested, grabbing a bottle of water from the minibar. "Remi, can you help me sit him up?"

"Sure," I said, moving to Ghost's side and gently lifting his upper body. Together, Knox and I worked on getting him to drink some water, his hazy eyes staring blankly ahead.

Bishop was frowning. "He didn't drink that much alcohol. I was watching."

"Valium," Ghost mumbled.

Knox exchanged a worried look with Bishop. "Ah, Christ. You shouldn't mix that shite with alcohol, mate. How many did you take?"

Ghost grabbed the water bottle out of Knox's hand. His eyes blinked open. "Just two. And it's fucking starting to wear off. I can feel the anxiety returning." He turned his head to look directly at me. "Or maybe it's just the company."

I tensed up. "Ghost, I want you to know that I'm not here to hurt you. I promise. I'm not going to publish any of that stuff about your step-brother."

He pushed away from me, sitting up on his own. "I need to talk to Remi alone."

Knox hesitated for a moment before nodding to Bishop. "Alright, I'll be right down the hall. Call me if you need me."

With that, they left the room, leaving me alone with a half-drunk Ghost. My heart pounded as I took a deep breath, preparing myself

HOW TO CATCH A ROCKSTAR 165

for what might come next.

"Ghost," I began, my voice steady. "I'm so sorry you're hurting because of me. I swear to you, I won't use your past against you. That's not why I'm here. I care about you. I'd never hurt you like that. Please believe me."

He stared at me for a moment, then nodded, his expression clouded with pain. "You should know the truth, then," he murmured, his voice barely audible. "My mother left my father when I was young. He met Adam's mom, and she ran off too, leaving Adam behind. My dad raised us on his own, but he turned to alcohol. He was an abusive drunk."

I held my breath, my chest tightening as I listened. I knew this story didn't have a happy ending.

"Things got so horrible that Adam couldn't take it anymore. I think back now — if only we'd just run away when things got bad with my dad." Ghost was staring off into space as he recounted the horrors. "But we took the fucking abuse. Day after day. Until one day, I found Adam hanging in his bedroom."

"My God, I'm so sorry you went through that." I couldn't hold back my tears as I reached for his hand, gripping it tightly. The horror of his past washed over me like a cold wave.

His eyes glittered with anger. "I have to accept it and forgive myself so that I can begin healing. But I'll never forgive my bastard of a father."

I swiped at my tears. "There's a quote that goes something like this: forgiving is not forgetting. It's remembering, but letting it go."

He pulled his hand away from mine. "Yes, Maggie told me something like that."

I wondered who Maggie was, but I didn't say anything. After a minute of silence, Ghost spoke again. "I'll give you a sound bite about

Adam that you can use for your story."

My heart sank. "I told you I'm not going to use that. I meant it, Ghost."

He stared straight ahead. "It doesn't matter. I have to accept that it happened."

I didn't know what to say. As we sat in silence, I couldn't help but feel the weight of Ghost's pain. It was a palpable thing, heavy and suffocating. I wanted to reach out to him, to comfort him in some way, but I knew better than to try.

After a few minutes, Ghost spoke again." Adam and I," his voice cracked. "We were sexually abused by my father's friends for money when we were just kids."

As Ghost's words echoed through the room, a raging storm of emotions surged through me. An intense wave of horror and anguish surged through my veins, making me nauseous. Every nerve in my body screamed in agony for the unbearable pain he was suffering.

My stomach churned as I tried to process the atrocities Ghost had just recounted. No words could possibly express the heartbreak I felt for him at that moment, but I knew I had to try. "No one should ever have to go through that," I whispered, choking back the tears that threatened to spill once again.

His haunted eyes met mine — my only thought was to protect him from any further pain. He looked so vulnerable, his eyes were full of raw emotion that tugged at my heartstrings.

I reached out to him, my hand shaking slightly as it brushed against his cheek. He flinched at the contact but didn't pull away. "I'm so sorry, Ghost. I wish I could take away all the hurt and pain you've been through, but I can't. All I can do is to be here for you, if you'll let me."

Ghost's expression softened, his eyes searching mine as if trying to find the answer to a question he wasn't sure how to ask.

I would do anything I could to help him face and overcome the darkness of his past. There were demons lurking beneath Ghost's surface — as evidenced by his self-destructive behavior — that threatened to consume him whole, and now I knew where they came from. He'd been battling them for years, and deep inside, I knew it wasn't going to be an easy fight.

I pulled my hand back slowly. "You should get some rest. We can talk in the morning if you'd like."

As I stood to leave, he reached out and caught my hand. "Please don't go," he whispered. "I don't want to be alone right now."

My heart ached for him, and I couldn't bring myself to walk away. Instead, I sat back down beside him on the edge of the bed, our fingers entwined.

Chapter 15

Remi

WE SAT IN SILENCE for a while, just holding hands and breathing in unison. Gradually, the space between us seemed to shrink, and I found myself leaning into him. His warmth was a comfort, a balm against the horrors he had just shared.

As we settled onto the bed, our bodies naturally gravitated toward each other. The warmth of his skin radiated against mine, comforting in its familiarity.

"Do you want to talk about it?" I asked tentatively.

He turned onto his side so that he was facing me. "No, I want to forget about it."

He reached out and brushed his thumb across my lips, a gentle caress that caused a fluttering in my stomach and an answering response between my legs. His eyes were dark and glazed with passion as he looked into mine, and I knew what he wanted.

He watched quietly as a million thoughts raced through my head.

Grey was coming to visit in two days, and things between us were still unresolved. Every rational part of me knew that having sex with Ghost was a bad idea, but for all I knew, Grey could be coming to end things between us for good.

I couldn't deny that I wanted to have sex with Ghost. From the moment I'd first set eyes on him while he was performing up on stage, I'd felt a deep stirring of arousal. I probably felt the same way as any other female that watched him perform, but I was the lucky one who had gotten to know him beyond the music. I got a peek behind the stage persona at the beautiful yet damaged soul.

It was confusing because I was sure that I still loved Greyson. If I could salvage my relationship with him, I would, in a heartbeat, but I'd take my pleasure with Ghost in the meantime. I didn't delude myself into thinking Ghost was offering anything more than a night, but I wasn't going to pass up the chance to be with him. I felt a deep connection to him and no matter how wrong it was, it felt right.

I closed my eyes, pushing Grey out of my thoughts. This was pure insanity, but I was following my heart as much as my hormones.

I don't know how Ghost knew the exact moment I'd made my decision, but he did. He leaned in to kiss me softly on the lips. The flutters dancing in my stomach turned into a butterfly mutiny. The kiss was soft and gentle, sending waves of pleasure through me, to the very depths of my being. I felt a deep, pulsing ache between my legs as desire seeped into every nerve ending and I knew then that I was lost.

His lips were tentative at first, a slow exploration of newfound intimacy. As the seconds passed, however, the heat between us began to build, and the gentle pressure of his mouth against mine intensified.

I moaned as our kiss grew even more passionate. My skin tingled with desire and heat pooled deep in my belly. His powerful arms wrapped around me, pulling me flush against him as his tongue explored my mouth. The feel of his strong, lean body pressed against mine sent shivers down my spine and made my inner muscles tighten with anticipation.

My fingers tangled in his hair, tugging gently as I surrendered to the desire that surged through me. Finally, with a deep breath, Ghost pulled away from me just enough so that we could look into each other's eyes again. I'd never seen such intensity in his gaze before, and it made my heart skip a beat. He cupped my face in his hands and looked at me a moment before whispering, "Remi."

I had enough sanity to wonder briefly if he was using sex to block out the pain of his past, but it really wouldn't matter to me if he was. I was too far gone.

The rest of the world fell away, leaving only Ghost and me in a cocoon of desire and potent sensuality. I felt emboldened by the connection we shared. My hands boldly slipped under his T-shirt, raising it up so I could explore. His chest was smooth and firm beneath my fingertips, and a hum of appreciation escaped from deep within my throat when my lips touched his skin.

That was all the signal he needed. His hands moved deftly, unbuttoning and peeling away the layers of clothing that separated us until we were both completely bare. The sight of him in all his chiseled, tattooed glory nearly stole my breath away, but it was the hunger in his eyes that truly undid me.

"Remi," he growled, his lips trailing a path down my throat to my collarbone. "You're so beautiful."

His words sent shivers down my spine and I could feel myself growing more aroused by the second. His tongue traced circles against my skin as his hands traveled lower, eliciting gasps from me with each touch.

We explored each other hungrily, our bodies pressed tightly together as if we were one. Each touch was more electric than the last and I felt myself losing all sense of time and space.

His hands moved lower, cupping my ass in an intimate embrace as he pushed himself further against me. With one swift move, he had me pinned against the mattress as we both surrendered to the passionate desire between us.

My skin was on fire everywhere he touched, and his lips trailed kisses along my neck, sending shivers down my spine. He slowly inched down until he came to my breasts. He circled a tongue around one nipple and then the next, and I shuddered as I felt them tingle and swell in response. When his teeth nipped lightly at my hardened flesh, it was like being struck by lightning. A jolt of pleasure cascaded straight to my pussy.

My fingernails dug into his shoulders as pleasure flooded my senses. His hand slid between my legs, fingers teasing and tantalizing my most sensitive spots. With each dip, swirl, and stroke of his skilled digits, I felt myself getting closer and closer to the edge.

"You're so wet," he rasped before plunging his fingers inside me and fucking my pussy with a fierce intensity that left me trembling. His thrusts were relentless as he pushed me closer to an intense orgasmic bliss.

"Please, Ghost," I groaned, not entirely sure what I was begging for, only knowing that I needed to feel him closer.

His thumb found my clit and rubbed it in slow, teasing strokes until my hips were chasing his every stroke. "I could slide my dick inside you right now, but I want to taste that pussy first."

"Yes," I hissed. My inner muscles clenched at his words. Oh my God, I wanted everything he could give me.

He trailed his lips along my stomach, my thighs quivering in anticipation of what was to come. His gentle nibbles all over my body sent waves of heat running through me, igniting a fire deep inside. He worshipped my body, kissing and caressing a trail downward until he reached the apex of my thighs.

His broad shoulders pushed apart my legs, exposing my most intimate parts to him. He hovered over my searing center with his soft mouth and the surge of pleasure that followed was so intense, I could barely contain myself. With each flick of his tongue, the waves grew stronger and stronger. He expertly teased and tormented me until I was straining and writhing against him, forcing him to hold me still while he explored every inch of me, devouring me with his skilled lips.

His skin was hot and slick with sweat, and his breath came in quick gasps as he explored every inch of my intimate flesh with his mouth. A single finger slid inside me, probing gently and then more urgently, until I felt a familiar surge of pleasure. He knew just where to touch and how, and soon we were both lost in the exquisite sensation.

His tongue attacked my clit while his fingers pumped in and out of me, mercilessly pressing against my G-spot until I thought I'd explode. I felt the orgasm building as wave after wave of pleasure coursed through me, and I was powerless to resist. The sudden spasm that shook me came like a shock of electricity, rushed through my core, and radiated outwards in waves of bliss. With a final surge, the orgasm hit me like a tidal wave and I screamed out in bliss as my body shook from the intensity of it.

He stayed buried between my legs as I rode out the powerful orgasm. My hands fisted the bedsheets until the spasms stopped.

Ghost slowly kissed up my body, lingering on each inch before finally reaching my lips. I could taste myself on his lips, and it only made me more excited. We kissed passionately for several moments before he pulled away and looked into my eyes, smiling mischievously.

"I want to watch you suck me off and then lay back and watch you ride my dick."

I laughed. "You're a closet romantic, huh?"

The cloud of despair that had haunted his eyes had lifted. He used his lips and teeth to brush against my ear, the roughness of his stubble tickling my neck. Soon I was breathing heavily and pleasure started to stir in my body.

My hands slid over the smooth skin of his back, pulling him closer to me. His arousal pressed into my thigh, hard and insistent, promising everything I desired. I arched my hips into it, relishing the tremor that rippled through his body.

I wanted him; I wanted to make him mindless with need. Wrapping a leg around his back to trap him to me, I pulled him in for another kiss.

The intensity of our kiss was like a drug, intoxicating me and making me feel alive in ways I hadn't before. He rolled us over until I was lying on top of him. His fingers ran down my back, tracing every curve until they reached the small of my back. He pressed me even closer to him as his tongue swept across mine and I could feel his heart beating against mine.

I reluctantly tore myself from his lips, dying to explore his cock with my mouth. Kneeling between his legs, I ran my hands up and down his thighs before I looked up and met his eyes, full of anticipation. He was reclining back with complete confidence, hands resting behind his head as he watched me with rapt attention.

I slowly lowered my lips down the length of his shaft, taking my time to enjoy the feel of his silky skin. I licked around the head of his cock with my tongue, grazing it ever so gently with my teeth. He groaned, and I felt his cock twitching in my hand.

Every movement sent sparks of pleasure through me that made me crave more. As I worked him deeper, my hands moved to cup the heavy weight of his balls. A low moan and slight thrust of his hips told me how much he appreciated what I was doing.

I swirled my tongue around the tip with each pass as I took him deeper and sucked harder. I knew he was getting closer to the edge when he made a pained sound and thrust his hips forward in an attempt to get even deeper. I almost gagged as he pressed deep against the back of my throat, but I managed to keep up the frenetic pace.

When he reached down and stopped me, I crawled back up the bed and straddled him. Once more, I felt his cock against me, hot and pulsing against my pussy. I reached down and grasped him. "I want you inside me."

"Fuck, I want to be inside you, bunny." His voice was hoarse and his eyes were dark with lust. "Ride me hard."

I rubbed his dick back and forth against my slit, relishing the way he was watching me with hooded eyes before I impaled myself on it.

"Goddamn, that feels good," he ground out as clenched his teeth. I braced my arms on his chest for leverage as I moved up and down. He ran his hands up my thighs and back up to my breasts, where he ran his thumbs over the hardened peaks of my nipples, causing a surge of pleasure that made me clench against his cock.

He moaned. "Feels so... Oh, fuck. Condom."

I was so far gone in a sexual stupor that the words didn't sink in at first. "Oh, shit."

Scrambling, I yanked myself off him awkwardly and tumbled over onto my side.

"How could I forget that?" I shook my head in disbelief.

Ghost sat up and leaned to his left so he could rummage through the drawer in his nightstand. Within seconds, he'd found a condom and rolled it on before pulling me into his lap. "It's okay, bunny."

HOW TO CATCH A ROCKSTAR

I was shaken by having forgotten something so essential, but with one kiss, the flame of desire was again burning me up. It didn't take Ghost long to make me forget all about my lapse of judgment. Every inch of my body throbbed with desire, and I desperately needed him back inside me.

Ghost flipped me onto my stomach and held me down while he placed kisses on the back of my neck, raking his lips over my skin and sending shivers up and down my spine. While his hands roamed my body, caressing me here, stroking me there, he placed a pillow under my hips.

Suddenly, he was entering me from behind. I moaned in pleasure as his thick cock stretched my insides and filled me completely. His thrusts were deep and unrelenting as he drove us both toward the ultimate climax.

I couldn't get enough of him — the feel of his hard body pressed against mine as he moved inside me, the way his hands roamed my body, learning every inch and curve with each stroke.

His hand skimmed down my thigh and raised my knee, propping me up so he could drive into me deeper. When his arm slid around my waist and his fingers found my clit, I detonated.

My hands fisted the bedsheets as I cried out in ecstasy, my orgasm ripping through me and quickly reaching its peak. Ghost was right behind me. A few thrusts later, he was grunting with his own release. I trembled as wave after wave of pleasure washed over me, temporarily suspending all thought and awareness until I felt like I was floating in a sea of bliss.

As the last vestiges of pleasure subsided, Ghost shuddered above me one final time before collapsing onto the bed beside me. Eventually, our breathing returned to normal, and I turned to him. He wrapped me in his arms tightly, holding onto me like he'd never let go.

As I lay there in his arms, the warmth of his embrace surrounding me like a blanket, I knew that this moment would stay with me forever. It had been beautiful and no matter what happened, I'd never regret it.

A few minutes later, I felt Ghost slipping away to take care of the condom, but I was close to dozing off. I briefly thought about getting up and returning to my hotel room, but then Ghost's warm body was pressing up to mine again and all those thoughts flew out the window.

Chapter 16

Ghost

THE FIRST RAYS OF sunlight pierced through the crack in the curtains, casting a bright beam of light across the darkened hotel room. I stirred, feeling the warmth of soft curves pressed against me, and quickly remembered that it was Remi in my bed. Our bodies were entangled; I could feel the soft tickle of her breath on my chest where her cheek rested. The faint musky scent of sex lingered in the air and mixed with the soft floral fragrance of her shampoo.

The smell was a potent reminder of the incredible sex we'd had last night. My heart started thumping in my chest. My cock was hard and throbbing, but as much as my body wanted to fuck Remi right this second, my mind was racing faster than my heart.

I needed to think because something odd was happening. I was feeling something foreign right this very second. My immediate thought was to take a Valium and shut those feelings down, but even though having odd feelings was scary and made me feel out of control, surprisingly, they didn't seem dark or negative.

In fact, I think I felt happy. I'd been living in numbness for so long that it was hard to process what the fuck this feeling was when the veil lifted for a moment. Fuck, that was sad.

I stayed perfectly still, hoping it wouldn't fade away until I could analyze it further. It had started with the sex last night. While I'd felt a spark of something between Remi and me since the first time we met, this experience was different — passionate and emotionally charged. It was as if the numbness that usually blanketed my life was gone, replaced with an intense connection to her.

Besides performing on stage, sex was the only thing that broke through that numbness for me. It was probably just a release of hormones, but for a few seconds, I felt something good.

Last night with Remi was different. Instead of dispassionately observing myself having sex as if from afar, going through the steps until I got my reward, it felt like I was actually present and feeling everything while it happened. It was completely different, and the difference was everything. I wanted to nudge Remi awake and have sex again, to see if it was real or if it had been some weird delusion.

I smiled to myself. Hell, I was even jonesing to call Maggie and tell her I might have had a breakthrough. For the first time, I didn't feel numb during sex. A live wire of pleasure and emotion coursed through me with every touch of Remi's skin. What was it about her that broke through the walls I'd built?

I'd been in therapy for years with Maggie. She'd drilled so much into my head about recovery from trauma that I could probably write a self-help book. The problem was that I hadn't truly embraced any of the advice. My preferred method of dealing with it was to ignore it, but that didn't always work.

Emotional blunting, Maggie called it. It had been my way of coping with the trauma as a child and it had carried over into my everyday life, creating a sense of emptiness and disconnect from the rest of the world. But that numbness had been far better than all the other crushing shit that I felt — like anxiety, helplessness, confusion, and even anger mixed in with a touch of guilt about Adam.

Maggie told me over and over that accepting what happened to me was the first step to healing. I always thought I'd accepted it, but if I hadn't actually told her the whole story after years of therapy, maybe I hadn't really acknowledged or accepted it. I'd kept the sexual abuse locked inside me like a vault until I'd opened up to Remi last night.

Suddenly, I was feeling different. Could it really be that easy? There was no way, but the Valium I'd taken had cleared my system and yet I didn't have that weight of dread clinging to me as I thought about my past. I wasn't drowning in anxiety.

I thought back to some of my sessions with Maggie. She'd told me that keeping trauma a secret could reinforce the feeling of shame that was associated with it. By simply retelling the story, distress was lessened and we could begin to process or make sense of a senseless event. What the fuck? I felt like I was actually starting to process shit right this second, for the first time ever.

No matter how long this weird sensation lasted, it was definitely a breakthrough of sorts. I was a completely fucked up guy, and no one knew that better than me. I used drugs, alcohol, and casual sex to suppress shit. I hid from the world at the same time that I performed on stage for everyone to see. For years, I couldn't even tell my trusted therapist about what happened to me. Then, I blurted it out to Remi, a reporter no less? Christ. But I couldn't deny it had changed something.

I'd finally told someone my secret, and she didn't go running from me in horror. She didn't call me stupid for taking the abuse. I'd always been extremely ashamed of what happened. I knew it wasn't my fault — I was just a kid — but there always existed that kernel of doubt that I could have done something more to stop it. Believing that if I never told anyone, then I'd never have to feel ashamed because no one would ever know. Yet, I'd revealed my secret, and the wave of shame never came. I dug deep, probing to see if it was lurking beneath the surface, ready to kneecap me at the worst possible moment, but I couldn't detect it.

I propped myself up on my elbow, studying Remi's peaceful face as she slept. Her long lashes rested gently on her cheeks, and her lips were slightly parted, revealing a hint of a smile. I wondered if merely just revealing my dark secret to Remi made me feel a stronger connection to her or if there was something special about her. My heart stuttered at the notion, a rare moment of vulnerability and connection washing over me.

"Hey, beautiful," I whispered, brushing a stray strand of hair from her forehead. She didn't stir, but the smile on her lips deepened ever so slightly. I couldn't help but grin in response; even in her sleep, she had this inexplicable hold on me.

I continued to observe her, my mind drifting back to the night we shared. A night where she'd seen the real me and accepted it — something I hadn't experienced in a very long time. It was as if Remi had unlocked a door within me, and I wasn't quite sure how to handle the emotions that flooded through.

She murmured in her sleep, snuggling closer to me. I tightened my embrace around her, waiting for this strange, happy feeling to dissipate.

The sound of Remi's breathing shifted, and I sensed the change in her consciousness even before her eyes fluttered open. For a moment, she gazed at me with a tender expression that made my chest ache.

Then I watched as a guarded wariness seeped into her eyes. "Good morning."

I was tense — fearing her reaction and unsure how I should act. My emotions were raw. Just feeling anything at all felt strange. They felt like a new pair of shoes — stiff and uncomfortable. "Hey, Remi."

She slowly pulled out of my arms. "Wow, this is ... I'll just grab my things and get out of your hair."

I let her go, immediately missing the feeling of her skin against mine. "No hurry."

She sat up stiffly, dragging the sheets up to cover herself. I knew a gentleman would look away, but I certainly wasn't about to.

Her phone buzzed on the nightstand. Biting her lip, she leaned over to grab it, carefully keeping the covers gathered around her. Her eyes went wide as she read the message, the color draining from her face. When she looked at me again, her eyes were shuttered.

As she scrambled out of bed, the sheets fell away, leaving her exposed, but she didn't seem to care. Her gaze darted around the room as if searching for an escape route. "I'm sorry, I shouldn't have — this was a mistake."

I sat up, frowning. "Remi, wait. What's going on?"

"Nothing." She yanked on her clothes with jerky movements, not meeting my eyes. "I have to go. Just forget this ever happened."

Panic rose in my chest at the thought of her regretting what we'd shared. I couldn't lose what I'd found with her, this glimmer of feeling that made me feel alive again.

I caught her wrist before she could flee. "Please don't do this." My voice came out rough with emotion I couldn't hide.

She froze, lips parting. For a breathless moment, I thought she might stay.

Then she pulled away with a sob. "I'm sorry," she whispered. "I can't."

The door clicked shut behind her, and I was alone with these confusing feelings. But this time, I didn't have the numbness to hide behind.

My heart thudded in my chest as I stared at the empty space in the bed where Remi had lain just minutes before. My skin still tingled from her touch, but she was gone — fleeing from me as if I were some kind of monster.

Feeling confused and hurt, I dragged myself out of bed and stumbled into the bathroom, turning on the shower to scalding hot. As the steam filled the small room, fogging the glass walls of the shower, I stepped under the punishing spray, hoping it would wash away the ache inside me. The water pummeled my skin, but it couldn't erase the memory of Remi's body entwined with mine or the connection I'd experienced with her. The events of last night replayed in my mind.

Remi's warmth in my arms, her soft gasps and moans. The way she'd clung to me afterward like she never wanted to let go. Now those memories were tainted by her hasty retreat, the panic in her eyes as she fled from me.

I leaned against the cold tile wall, letting the water cascade over me as I tried to process the events of the night and my confusing feelings for her. What had happened between us wasn't just a casual hookup — it had been intimate, raw, and real. And yet, she'd run from it like it meant nothing.

With a groan, I turned off the shower and wrapped a towel around my waist, feeling more lost than ever. I dressed quickly, trying not to dwell on the fact that Remi had done the same thing in this very room not long ago — her eyes full of regret.

After I dressed, I grabbed my bottle of pills and sat down on the edge of the bed. Taking Valium would take the edge of anxiety off. It would help blunt these confusing feelings I was dealing with, but I didn't want to remain numb anymore, whether it was induced by pills or not. I didn't want to constantly run and hide. I needed to face everything head-on. Maybe I was finally strong enough.

Making my decision, I put away my pills and reluctantly made my way downstairs to the hotel restaurant. The scent of freshly brewed coffee and bacon filled the air as I entered the dining area. I spotted a few of my bandmates gathered around a table. Their laughter echoed through the room, but it did little to lift my spirits as I made my way over to them.

"Hey, Ghost," Knox greeted me with a grin, gesturing for me to join them. "Are you feeling any better? You were a wee bit dodgy last night."

Sid glanced up from his plate of scrambled eggs. "Yeah, you were pretty fucked up. Is everything okay?"

Everyone was watching me intently as I sat down at the table next to Knox. "Yeah, I'm fine."

Luckily, our tour manager, Darren, who was sitting at the other end of the table, ended the conversation. "Where is Ryder?" He glanced at his watch. "Well, I don't have time to wait any longer. Busses are pulling out in 90 minutes. We're heading to Boston where you'll have a few interviews before soundcheck. Make sure Ryder gets on that bus."

Darren placed his napkin on the table, stood up, and then left. Everyone shrugged and then resumed eating.

The conversation around the table shifted to lighter topics, but it was all just background noise to me. My thoughts kept drifting back to Remi, her panicked expression when she woke up beside me, and the way she fled the room like her life depended on it.

Knox leaned in to talk and kept his voice low so the others wouldn't hear. "Anything you wanna talk about?"

"Maybe later," I answered, not wanting to go into details just yet.

I ordered breakfast and then let the conversation flowing around the table distract me while I ate. After everyone had finished their breakfast, they started to leave, except for Knox, who stayed seated long after his plate was empty.

When it was just the two of us left, he tilted his chair back and watched me picking at my food. "Alright, let's have it then."

"Uh, yeah," I replied, rubbing a hand over my face. "Just ... a lot fucking happened last night."

He glanced around the room to make sure no one could overhear us before he spoke, his voice filled with concern. "You mixed Valium and alcohol last night. I know it's not the first time, but you were a mess, mate. I was worried."

Sighing, I ran a hand through my hair. The memories of last night were hazy, but the feeling of despair still lingered. "I know, Knox. I was in a bad place, thinking about my past and what would happen if it got out to the public. But ... I talked it over with Remi."

His eyes narrowed, worry etched on his face. "You wanted to be alone with her. She seemed genuinely worried about you last night. I hope she's not playing us both."

"She's not. She promised not to publish any harmful information about me." I took a deep breath. "I feel relieved, like a weight has been lifted."

Knox relaxed slightly, but his eyes still held a flicker of doubt. "You sure you can trust her? She's a reporter."

"Trust me, Knox, she's different." I insisted, recalling the compassion I'd felt from her when I confided my horrible secrets.

Knox looked at me skeptically, but he didn't press the issue any further. "Alright then," he said with a nod. "That's good news, but you don't seem yourself. What else aren't you telling me?"

I took a deep breath, feeling the weight of everything that had transpired between Remi and me. I debated whether to confide in Knox, but ultimately decided that I needed someone to talk to.

"Knox, there's something dark in my past besides my stepbrother's suicide that I need to tell you. I feel like I'm ready to open up about some shit."

He nodded for me to continue. I looked around the room before standing up from the table. "Can we go for a walk? I think it would be easier for me to talk if we were alone and outside."

Knox grabbed his coat off of the back of his chair and stood up. "Yeah, let's go get some fresh air."

We stepped out of the hotel into an icy winter day and began walking along a path that meandered through the dormant landscaping. There wasn't a soul in sight except for the occasional cars passing in the distance.

I jammed my hands into my pockets. It was bitterly cold, but I didn't really feel it. We walked on in silence for a while before I finally figured out how to tell him, speaking slowly at first as if I were cautiously testing out the waters.

"My dad, he was a horrible man. I told you about how he got drunk and beat me and Adam. But, I didn't tell you..." I swallowed hard. "Something I've kept secret. Because it's so vile. It's shameful." I squeezed my eyes shut and continued, "Not only did he physically abuse my brother and me, but he also took money from men and allowed them to ... do stuff to us. We were sexually abused. That's why my stepbrother killed himself. He couldn't take it anymore."

Knox stopped in his tracks, his face filled with horror. He looked at me with such sadness that I could feel tears pricking at the corner of my eyes. "Fuck," he said softly, pulling me into a hug and thumping my back. "I'm so sorry. I had no idea…"

I let out a long breath, relieved that he hadn't recoiled in disgust. "Dude, I haven't even told Maggie yet. It's been festering inside me, but after I told Remi, I don't know — I feel different. Better. Like all Maggie's psychobabble about acknowledging it might be true."

He stepped away from me. This time, I could clearly see the unease on his face. "Wait. You told Remi? About everything?"

"Yeah," I said, my voice catching in my throat. "There's something about her. She's easy to talk to."

"That's because she's a reporter." He dragged a hand through his hair. "Fuck! What if she makes this public? Why wouldn't she? It would be one bloody brilliant scoop for her."

I shook my head, trying to calm him down. "She said she wouldn't. I trust her."

He raised an eyebrow and shot me a patronizing smirk as if he knew something I did not. It was clear that he thought I was a gullible fool. "It's her job to act like our friend and gain our trust. I knew I shouldn't have left you alone with her when you were so out of your mind. Fuck, mate, I know she seems like a nice girl, but I've got a bad feeling about this. When she interviewed me, she was asking about Aila. She's been digging into our shit, Ghost."

A hint of unease settled over me. "It's not like that. There's something between us. A connection." I swallowed hard and then let out a heavy sigh. "I fucked her last night."

Knox's mouth dropped open. "Fuck me! Tell me you didn't."

"This morning, she completely freaked out and ran out of the room. I haven't seen her since," I admitted.

His gaze pierced through me. "Maybe she realized that it's highly unprofessional to have sex with you?"

I inhaled deeply, catching a hint of wood smoke in the air. "I don't know, but I'm going to find out. I'm not going to let her run away so easily."

"Just remember that she's a reporter. You've got to be careful. She might be playing you."

After a brief pause, Knox hesitated, biting his lip as if weighing whether to say something. "There's something else you should know, Ghost..."

I waited for him to continue. When he didn't, I stopped walking. "Go on," I urged.

"Look, I don't want to add fuel to the fire, but I think it's important for you to have all the facts," he said cautiously. "Remi was dating someone before she came on our tour. It's someone we know."

My heart was thudding in my chest. "Who?"

"Greyson," Knox replied, his eyes searching mine for any sign of recognition.

"Greyson?" I echoed, my voice barely above a whisper. The words hung in the air like a storm cloud.

Knox nodded, his brow furrowed with concern as he watched my reaction. "Yeah, mate. Apparently, they were pretty serious."

I blinked with surprise. "Greyson? As in the actor Greyson? Talia's friend?" I couldn't quite believe my ears. Panic gnawed at the edges of my heart, and jealousy burned like acid in my veins. A whirlwind of emotions battered me from every angle, leaving me feeling disoriented and raw.

"Yeah," Knox confirmed. "He's coming to our show tonight to see her."

My mind whirled, trying to put it together. "When she first came on tour, she told me she had a boyfriend, but that he broke up with her."

Knox slapped me on the shoulder. "Well, he's clearly not through with her if he's coming to Boston to see her."

"I never liked that guy," I mumbled under my breath.

I didn't like how he was always trying to be the center of attention and how his fame seemed to go to his head. And I couldn't help but feel a pang of jealousy when he'd come over and everyone had lit up in his presence.

"Greyson?" Knox raised an eyebrow. "He's a decent chap for such a huge celebrity."

I couldn't really argue with that. The guy was a huge celebrity, attracting attention and adoration wherever he went, and he'd always been nice to my friends. He'd even tried being friendly to me, but I didn't like him.

He set my nerves pinging. It was as if he could see right through me to what I was thinking. Even though I fought it, there was something about him that made me pay attention — almost to the point of obsession. I resented it; I chalked it up to envy of his success and mega-stardom. But, in the sea of apathy that surrounded me, he triggered strong emotions. It had always made me uneasy, so I kept my distance from him.

"Ghost, forget about Greyson. Just focus on the show tonight, alright?" Knox advised, placing a steadying hand on my shoulder. "You can't control what Remi does, but you can control your performance on stage. That's what matters right now."

"Right," I agreed, even though deep down, the storm of emotions brewing inside me threatened to consume me whole.

Knox looked at the time on his phone. "We've got to get onto the bus soon. On the way to Boston, I think you should call Maggie and talk to her. You're working through a lot. You've been carrying some heavy baggage around for a long time. It's a lot to process. Keeping it all inside will slowly destroy you. Trust me, I know."

I remembered the day, not too long ago, when Knox decided he was going to quit the band because he thought I'd betrayed him. He'd gotten drunk off his ass and finally confessed all the dark secrets that were weighing on his soul due to his fiancee's death.

"You're hitting me with the baggage metaphor?"

Knox grinned. "Yep. What was it? You've got to unpack it, fold it up, and put it in drawers — or some shite like that."

I scoffed at his bungled quote. "Christ. It was a lot better when I said it."

We turned around and headed back toward the hotel entrance. "You're the wordsmith. Anyway, it worked, mate. 'You've got to let go of the past and start looking to the future.' I remember you telling me that just before you gave me Maggie's number when I was holding onto all that grief and guilt about Aila's death."

I rubbed my hands together to warm them up as we stepped into the lobby. I would definitely call Maggie, but strangely, suddenly the past was the last thing on my mind.

My thoughts were consumed with the knowledge that Remi and Greyson had been an item, and now he was coming to the concert tonight, perhaps hoping to lure her into his arms. But she'd spent the night wrapped up in mine.

The thought of facing both Remi and Greyson at tonight's concert loomed over me like an insurmountable mountain, leaving my stomach tied in knots. I had the incredible urge to pop a pill and make it all go away.

Knox was right; I needed to talk to Maggie before I did anything stupid. I took a deep breath, trying to center myself. But beneath the surface, I could feel the storm brewing — jealousy, betrayal, hurt, and anger swirling together like a hurricane waiting to make landfall. I was far from the safety of numbness.

Chapter 17

Greyson

THE CITY LIGHTS OF Boston blurred past the tinted windows of the sleek black car that carried me through the bustling streets. I had just arrived from L.A., feeling a pull of fatigue after taping for *Devious* all morning, followed by a day's worth of travel. My heart raced as I checked my watch, realizing that with the time difference, I wouldn't make it to the concert before the show started. I'd come here to see Remi, but the thought of seeing Ghost again sent shivers down my spine, a mix of excited anticipation and nervous tension.

"Almost there, Mr. Durant," the driver said, his voice calm and professional. I nodded, grateful for the distraction from my racing thoughts.

"Thank you," I replied, my mind wandering back to the reason for my visit. Was it possible that seeing Ghost and Remi together could finally help me resolve my tangled emotions? My love for Remi was undeniable, but the overwhelming attraction I felt for Ghost refused to fade even though he didn't return my feelings.

The car pulled up to the stadium, the low rumble of bass echoing in the distance as fans screamed and cheered. My stomach churned with a mix of envy and anxiety. Performing in front of people was indescribable; I longed to be on that stage with Ghost, sharing in the electrifying energy of the crowd. Despite my fame, I knew I would always be an outsider looking in when it came to Ghost's world.

I clenched my fists, trying to keep my emotions in check as the driver opened the door for me. Stepping out into the cool night, I breathed in the air, scented with a mix of gasoline, sweat, and the faint aroma of food vendors. It grounded me and reminded me that I was here, in the present, about to face the very people who had been consuming my thoughts for so long.

"Mr. Durant, this way please," a security guard motioned for me to follow him towards the VIP entrance. Screams and cheers echoed from inside, the crowd going wild as the opening act finished their set. My heart pounded in my chest, each step bringing me closer to confronting the feelings I had tried so hard to suppress. I hoped that whatever happened tonight would bring me clarity and peace. The thought of continuing to live with this uncertainty was unbearable.

The guard swiped a key card through a door marked 'VIP Entrance,' and then ushered me inside.

"Right this way, Mr. Durant," the guard said, his words barely audible over the din of the crowd. We headed down a hall and toward a discreet door marked which was also locked. And that's where I saw her — Trudy, Ghost Parker's PR rep, waiting for me with an eager smile.

A woman with a platinum blonde pixie haircut with pink steaks in it waved enthusiastically, rushing over to meet me.

"Mr. Durant, it's such an honor to meet you! I'm Trudy, the PR representative for Ghost Parker." She gushed, shaking my hand vigorously. "I'm a huge fan of your show, and I've been following your career since the beginning."

"Thank you, Trudy. And please, call me Greyson." I smiled, hoping to calm her obvious excitement. "It's always nice to meet someone who appreciates my work."

She beamed, clearly thrilled by my response. Her professionalism wavered as she hesitated for a moment before blurting out, "Do you think ... would it be okay if we took a selfie together?"

"Of course," I agreed, putting on my best celebrity smile as she fumbled with her phone, positioning it just right to capture the moment.

As the flash went off, I couldn't help but wonder how many more times I'd have to plaster on that smile tonight.

"Thank you so much, Greyson!" Trudy exclaimed, her face flushed with excitement. "I promise I won't take up any more of your time. Here is your backstage pass. I'll walk you to the VIP section or you could watch from the wings. Whatever you prefer. Ghost Parker's set will begin in about 20 minutes."

I took the pass from Trudy. "I was supposed to meet Remi Sutton here. Would you be able to help me find her?"

She nodded eagerly. "Of course! Remi would have come with me to meet you, but she's tied up with a photographer from Hollywood Exposé right now. I'm sure she'll join you as soon as she can. I can take you to the perfect spot to watch the band while you wait for her."

"Thank you." I placed a hand on her arm and her entire body visibly shuddered. Suppressing a laugh, I removed my hand. My fame always elicited strange reactions from fans. "Lead the way."

We walked together toward the heart of the stadium. I could feel the energy of the unseen crowd pressing in around us, stoking the fires of my anticipation. Ghost Parker's spellbound throng was waiting, and so was I — ready to confront the feelings that had long lain dormant, ready to embrace whatever fate had in store. My thoughts raced, flickering between the need to see Remi's warm smile and the enigmatic allure of Ghost.

"The band would love for you to join them after the show." She slid me a hopeful glance. "They're heading to one of Boston's hottest nightclubs, District 10. Security has been set up, and they assured me that they were well prepared to accommodate your needs should you join us."

Talking to Remi was my first priority, but I wouldn't mind the chance to hang out with the band. "We'll see, Trudy. Thanks for the invite."

"It's my pleasure."

The backstage area bustled with activity. We sidestepped several crew members rushing around, dodging the ordered chaos of cables and equipment scattered everywhere. "I'll let Remi know you're here. If you need anything else, please let me know. Enjoy the show!" She grinned and hurried off, no doubt to post our picture on social media.

I stood in the shadows watching the crew preparing for the show, fiddling with the technical-looking equipment, and instrument techs passing by handling various guitars. No one noticed my presence; they were so busy.

I recognized Ryder's voice first and then I heard a response to Ryder in a distinctly Scottish accent. That was Knox. The band was heading this way. Nerves had me rooted to my spot in the corner. I stood in the wings, my pulse racing, as the band gathered in a huddle — their apparent ritual before each show.

Ghost was blocked from my sight by the others, but his distinct voice carried over the din of the crowd. "Ride or die."

They all echoed the phrase before breaking apart and heading onto the stage. The cheers were deafening as Bash stepped on to stage first, followed by Sidney clutching his bass guitar.

Just before Ghost strode onto the stage, he turned and locked eyes with me. A shiver ran down my spine at the intensity of his gaze. In that fleeting moment, a thousand unspoken words passed between us that set my blood aflame.

Then he was gone, the crowd swallowing him whole. I leaned against the wall, my knees weak, and watched as he dominated the stage. The way he moved, utterly uninhibited, stirred something primal in me. His voice was sex and sin wrapped in a single, raspy note.

I was captivated, possessed, and owned in both body and soul. No one had ever affected me the way he did. As much as I'd hoped my strange obsession had faded over time, there was no denying that it was as strong as ever.

Ghost prowled across the stage, a predator on the hunt, scanning the crowd until he turned his head, his gaze locking onto mine again. A slow, knowing sneer spread across his lips and my heart stuttered.

I was lost, willingly drowning in him, with no desire to break the surface. At that moment, I knew nothing would ever be the same. I had stepped into the inferno willingly, eager to be consumed by the flames. There was no turning back.

Ghost had me, heart, body, and soul. The only question was — what was I going to do about it?

"Greyson!" a familiar voice called out from behind me. I turned to see Remi, her eyes devouring me from head to toe before she caught herself. A smile tugged at the corner of my lips. It was so good to see her again.

The dim light in the wings cast an ethereal glow on Remi as she joined me to watch the concert. My heart quickened, and I felt a surge of desire course through me as we exchanged overly polite greetings.

"Hey," I managed to croak out, swallowing hard.

"Hi," she replied, shifting nervously from foot to foot. The familiar scent of her perfume enveloped me, intoxicating my senses and setting my skin aflame with longing.

Her hesitant smile was like a dagger to my chest, reminding me of how much I'd messed up our last parting.

As Ghost Parker transitioned into a new song, I couldn't help but steal glances at Remi, watching the way her dark eyes sparkled in the low light, reflecting the passion that burned within her. Each stolen glance intensified the magnetic pull I felt toward her, and I fought the urge to reach out and touch her silky skin.

My attention shifted back and forth between the stage and Remi, torn between two powerful forces that seemed to be tearing me apart. Ghost's raw, primal energy onstage captivated me, igniting a fire deep within me that I couldn't quite understand. How could I love Remi so deeply, yet still be drawn to this enigmatic man who haunted my thoughts?

"Ghost is incredible, isn't he?" Remi murmured, her voice barely audible above the roaring crowd.

I nodded, unable to form words, feeling the weight of my conflicting emotions. As if sensing my turmoil, Remi looked up at me, her eyes searching mine for answers. But all I could offer her was a weak, apologetic smile, knowing that my heart was torn between her and the mysterious rock star who continued to bewitch me.

"Greyson, are you okay?" she asked tentatively, her concern evident in her furrowed brow.

"Yeah, I'm just glad to see you. I missed you." The knot in my stomach tightened as I forced myself to look away from Ghost. I knew

I had to be truthful with her about my feelings.

"Let's just enjoy the show," I suggested, trying to focus on the music that pulsed through the air like a lifeline. But even as the concert reached its crescendo, and the crowd screamed for more, I could feel the oppressive weight of my feelings for both Remi and Ghost crushing me, leaving me gasping for air.

As the final notes faded into the night, I found myself haunted by the question that had been plaguing me for weeks: How could I make a commitment to the woman I loved when Ghost stirred something dark and dangerous within me? The answer eluded me, slipping away like a shadow in the darkness, as my heart continued to be pulled in two impossible directions.

I needed to face reality. Ghost was simply a mad obsession, never destined to be, and Remi was my future. I had to be honest with her and see if she could live with it. If not, I would have to let her go, too. I knew that would leave me shattered, but despite the storm of worry raging inside me, I had no choice.

Remi led me away toward the green room so we could get out of the way of the bustling crew. I usually felt at home backstage — it was not unlike the set of *Devious* where the constant activity with the support staff made sure everything ran smoothly, but this was Ghost's domain and I was an interloper here.

We entered a large room that had several tables against the wall filled with a variety of catered food. It seemed awfully late to be eating, but what did I know?

"This is where everyone will hang out waiting for the band to shower and do their meet and greets or interviews. It can get kind of racy, especially when the groupies show up." She bit her lip tentatively. "But the band is going out to a club tonight. We can go if you want? Trudy tripled the security for you. In case you want to go."

I finally got to see her in the light. Remi had glossy black hair that cascaded down her back; sometimes it was shiny and straight, but tonight it held sexy, loose waves. Her curves were mouthwatering and her gaze was dark, mysterious, and inviting. Her luscious lips were a fiery red like they were made to be kissed. She was absolutely stunning, but faint lines of fatigue and apprehension were etched across her features. Had I caused that or was it something else? She had hinted that her job wasn't going that well.

I needed to get Remi alone so I could talk to her about everything. "I came here to talk to you. Unless you need to go to the party for your work?"

She didn't have a chance to answer because a man carrying a camera and wearing a lanyard that read 'media pass' entered the room and made a beeline straight toward us.

"Remi, I need you for a few minutes to go over the shoot list."

She turned to me with a frown. "I'm sorry. I only have a photographer for two shows, so I have to make sure I get everything. Will you be okay for a couple of minutes?"

I didn't want to interfere with her job. "Sure, take your time. I'll be here waiting for you."

A few women entered the room as Remi left with the photographer. They headed for a bar in the corner, getting drinks and shooting furtive glances my way. I sighed. I was probably only a few minutes from being recognized, but I didn't want to leave until Remi was back.

I made my way closer to the exit, in case I needed to make a hasty escape, and leaned up against the wall. The long day of work and then cross-country travel was wearing on me. Seeing Ghost had not cleared up anything for me. I'd been hoping my attraction for him had gone away or at least faded, which would have made everything so much easier.

A surge of people, accompanied by what looked like band members from the opening act, crowded into the room. Music started blasting and alcohol started flowing. It only made me feel more tired.

Suddenly, the hairs on my arm stood up. Searching for him, my eyes swept across the room. A bolt of heat shot through me at the sight of him, his broad shoulders accentuated by a tight black T-shirt, and long legs clad in worn jeans. Unruly blond hair fell over his forehead, barely hiding the piercing azure of his eyes. The memory of his gaze holding mine, those full lips pouty as he got his dick sucked off while I watched, had haunted my dreams for years.

I swallowed hard as he pushed off the doorframe and sauntered over, raw masculinity and predatory grace in every step. The heady scent of leather and spice enveloped me, fraying the last remnants of my restraint.

"Greyson. What are you doing here?" His voice was a low rasp, sending a shiver down my spine.

His eyes raked over me, lingering on the exposed skin of my neck and chest. Heat pooled in my groin under the intensity of his gaze. I struggled to form a coherent thought, drunk on his proximity and the promise of forbidden pleasure.

"I — I needed to see Remi," I managed.

"Is that so?" His voice was low with suspicion. "I thought you broke up with her?"

A flush crept up my cheeks as he moved closer, caging me against the wall with his arms. My heart thundered in my chest, a heady mixture of arousal, apprehension, and anger swirling in my veins. Anger at him for reducing me to a quivering wreck with just one look. At myself for craving his touch, even after he shot me a look of blistering disdain.

"Leave Remi alone." His breath ghosted over my lips, soft yet commanding. He was a mass of intense emotion and restless power,

HOW TO CATCH A ROCKSTAR

practically vibrating with a fierce energy that threatened to consume me.

Fuck. My dick was straining against the zipper of my jeans. If Ghost leaned forward another inch, I'd probably come in my pants.

I swallowed hard, struggling to form a coherent thought under the intensity of his gaze. "If Remi wants—"

The words died in my throat as he leaned in, brushing my neck as he spoke. "Stay the fuck away from her."

A soft moan escaped my lips. At that moment, I wanted nothing more than to drown in him, to lose myself in the searing heat and mindless pleasure only he could give me. But his words slowly sunk in and sparked my anger.

I placed my palms on his chest, intent on pushing him away and trying to ignore how firm the muscles beneath his shirt felt. "Mind your own fucking business."

Our eyes remained locked on each other, sizzling with the heat of our emotions. I pushed him away with a hard shove.

Luckily, that was when Knox stepped in, calmly breaking up the fight with a gentle touch on both of our arms. He leaned into Ghost, but I heard him say, "Take it easy, mate. Cameras are out."

I looked around and noticed that our encounter had caught the attention of the crowd and several cell phones were pointed in our direction. I took a deep breath, trying to calm myself down.

Ghost gave me one last smoldering glance before turning to Knox and nodding. He stepped back and held his hands up in surrender. "Alright, alright...."

Ryder joined our small circle, sticking out his hand for a shake. "Grey, what are you doing here? I heard you were coming, but Talia didn't know anything about it. She's jealous."

At least one person seemed happy to see me. I shook Ryder's hand.

"It was a last-minute thing. How's Zoe doing?"

Ryder answered, but I was only half listening. Ghost stood rigidly, his face a mask of rage and disgust as he stared at me with burning intensity. The hatred in his eyes was like a physical force pushing against me.

"Are you coming to the party? It should be a good time." Ryder seemed oblivious to Ghost's animosity or the groups of women circling closer, as if ready to ambush us.

A woman in a barely there silver dress brushed up against my arm. I took a step away from her. "I'm not sure. It depends on what Remi wants to do."

"What's going on with you two? I was surprised when she said you two used to date. Small world, huh?" Ryder took a pull from his beer bottle.

"Yes." I saw Remi enter the room and look for me. "Speaking of Remi, here she comes."

She subtly nudged the woman in the silver dress away so she could stand next to me. My back was to Ghost so that I could talk to Remi, but I could still feel him bristling behind me.

"I hope you don't mind, but I have to go to the party. Larry needs more candid shots of the band, but once he gets what he needs, we can leave. We can find a quiet place to talk."

"Okay," I reluctantly agreed.

I really wanted to get away from Ghost and his extreme hatred for me. He'd always hated me, but this time the emotions felt deeper. It added a cruel twist of irony to the whole situation. And from the confrontation we'd just had, somehow Remi was involved in his hatred. The night just kept getting worse.

"C'mon. Trudy's waiting in the car for us. Larry needs to scope out the place before the band gets there." She grabbed my arm. "Don't worry, she has security for you. And, just a fair warning, she's fangirling all over you."

Chapter 18

Ghost

I SLAMMED THE GLASS down on the bar, the amber liquid sloshing over the rim. The burn in my throat did nothing to dull the ache in my chest.

Greyson's arm wrapped around Remi, pulling her close to his body, his smile brighter than the lights overhead. The way he gazed at her like she was the only thing in the world that mattered...

I gripped the glass until my knuckles turned white, gritting my teeth against the surge of emotion. Jealousy. Possession. A desperate, clawing need to stake my claim.

The thought of Remi with him twisted my gut into knots. I couldn't get her face out of my mind, those gorgeous eyes staring up at me as I sunk inside her. The sounds she made, the way she arched into my touch...

"Another," I growled at one of the roadies, who was mixing drinks, shoving my glass forward.

Remi was gazing up at Greyson like he was a goddamn superhero, and then he pulled her into his arms. Greyson turned and caught my eye from across the room, probably to rub it in my face. I looked away, jaw clenched, and knocked back the drink in one burning gulp.

You're mine, bunny. I don't care who else you fuck, but you'll always be mine.

The thought should have scared me. Commitment wasn't my thing; possession had no place in my world. But the primal, possessive urge ravaging my thoughts refused to be ignored.

I wondered what Greyson would say if he knew I'd fucked his girl. Not his girl — his ex-girlfriend.

Fuck, I was burning with jealousy. I turned away from the sight of them and turned my attention to the two girls who'd been trying to talk to me. Maybe I'd let them take my mind off everything.

I felt the heat radiating from the bodies of the two women as they pressed closer to me, their sultry smiles and inviting eyes leaving no doubt about their intentions. The scent of their perfume mingled with the smoky air of the bar, creating a heady cocktail that threatened to intoxicate me even more than the whiskey I'd been nursing all night.

"Hey Ghost," Knox called out as he approached our little group, his brown eyes filled with concern. "We're heading to the limo now. Time to hit the nightclub."

"Sounds good," I replied, my gaze never leaving the women. With a sly grin, I added, "Why don't you ladies join us?" Their enthusiastic agreement sent a thrill down my spine, igniting a fire that had been smoldering deep within me for far too long.

As we filed out of the bar, I couldn't help but notice that Greyson and Remi were nowhere to be seen. A flicker of anxiety passed through me, but I quickly pushed it aside — tonight was about forgetting, not dwelling on those two.

Inside the limo, I settled myself between the two women, their warm flesh pressing against me from both sides. I took a long swig from the bottle of champagne the blonde girl handed me, feeling the carbonation tickle my throat as I drank. Across from us, Knox and Ryder watched me with a mix of amusement and concern.

"Slow down, man," Knox cautioned me, his words barely audible over the thumping bass of the music playing in the limo. I ignored him, taking another gulp of champagne while my hands began to roam over the curves of the women beside me.

As one of them leaned in to whisper something in my ear, her hand sliding up my leg, my thoughts strayed to Remi again. Where was she? And why did it matter so much? I'd shared my bed with countless women over the years, but there was something about her that had gotten under my skin.

"Ghost," Ryder's voice cut through my thoughts. "You okay, mate?"

"Fine," I snapped, forcing myself to focus on the women and the pleasure they offered, but the nagging sensation remained.

As I took another swig of champagne, the bubbles danced on my tongue and Knox's voice broke through the haze. "Ghost, you need to slow down your partying. Remember last night?"

How could I fucking forget? "Where's Remi?" I asked, ignoring his advice as guzzled more champagne.

Knox's eyes narrowed slightly. "Already at the club."

"I hope Greyson isn't there," I muttered under my breath, feeling a surge of irritation at the thought of him.

"What's wrong with Greyson?" Ryder piped up, sensing the tension between us.

"Nothing," I bit out, resisting the urge to vent my frustrations about the man who had wormed his way into my life — and possibly Remi's heart. "I just hate that asshole."

Ryder defended him, clearly not understanding the depths of my hatred for the TV star. "Greyson's a good guy."

"Are you worried Remi will get back together with him or something?" Knox asked, his voice laced with concern. His question hit too close to home, making me squirm in discomfort.

"I don't give a fuck what they do," I retorted, turning my attention back to the women flanking me. Their eager hands roamed over my body, but all I could think about was Remi — how she felt pressed against me, her soft sighs and moans as we'd moved together.

And Greyson. Of course, Remi would be interested in him. He was perfect. He had sex appeal, fame, and fortune. Hell, I'd fuck him if I were a woman.

"Ghost," Ryder persisted, leaning forward with genuine curiosity. "Is something going on with you and Remi?"

"Drop it," I snapped, my patience wearing thin. I wanted to lose myself in the pleasure these women offered, not discuss the tangled web of emotions that seemed to choke me whenever Remi's name was mentioned.

As if to prove my point, I leaned in and captured one of the women's lips in a searing kiss, my hands sliding down her back to grip her hips. I ignored the questioning gazes from Knox and Ryder, determined to forget about Remi, Greyson, and everything else that threatened to consume me.

One of the women grew bolder. She knelt down between my knees and within moments had my dick out and in her mouth. I closed my eyes, sunk my hands in her hair, and tried to get lost in the carnal pleasures, but all I could imagine were the lips of a certain TV star sucking me off. Fuck me.

Despite the girl's fervent efforts, she couldn't get me off. I felt the frustration building inside me, and with a sudden surge of irritation, I pushed her off. The limo pulled up to the entrance of the nightclub, and we all stepped out into the night air.

"Alright, let's have some fun," Knox said, as our security guards led us through the throngs of people waiting in line. They parted like the Red Sea, their phones popping out to video us as we made our way into the club. Girls were shouting our names and stretching out their hands, but I just ignored it all.

The atmosphere inside was electric. Pulsating beats from the DJ booth filled the air, accompanied by a dizzying array of lights that played upon the writhing bodies on the dance floor. The scent of sweat and cloying perfume hung heavy in the air, as scantily clad women gyrated against one another, their eyes searching for their next conquest.

"Ghost, you okay?" Ryder asked, his eyes narrowing in concern as he noticed my darkened expression. "You seem ... off."

"I'm fine," I replied tersely, my thoughts still consumed by my earlier frustration. "Just need to blow off some steam."

We entered the VIP section, which was cordoned off from the rest of the club. Plush velvet couches lined the walls, while bottles of top-shelf liquor sparkled enticingly behind the bar. The space was already packed with people from the tour.

I downed shot after shot, feeling the burn of the alcohol as it numbed the irritating itch that had settled beneath my skin. I wasted no time indulging in my vices, grabbing an eager girl by the hips and grinding against her as we moved to the rhythm. She giggled, tossing her head back as she pressed herself closer to me, but my eyes sought out Remi among the crowd.

"Ghost, fantastic show tonight," Bash shouted over the music, clinking his glass against mine. Sidney and Trudy were laughing at something Greyson had said, the man looking as handsome as ever, though my mood soured at the sight of him. But at least he wasn't with Remi. Where was she?

My eyes scanned the room, my gaze landing on Remi talking to the photographer from Hollywood Exposé. She looked beautiful, her body encased in a tight black dress that left little to the imagination. And suddenly, I needed to know where I stood with her.

"Excuse me," I murmured to the girl I'd been dancing with, not even bothering to meet her disappointed gaze as I stalked toward Remi.

Her expression was a mixture of concern and annoyance. "Ghost, you're drunk!" she accused as soon as I approached.

"Maybe I am," I slurred, my jealousy fueling my anger. "But that doesn't change what I need to say."

She crossed her arms defensively. "Fine. What is it you want to tell me?"

"Your precious boyfriend," I spat, the venom in my voice palpable. "Are you getting back together with that asshole?"

Remi's eyes widened as pain flashed across her face. "Why are you acting like this?"

"He's a giant douchebag." I sneered. "Didn't he dump you? What is he doing here?"

"Greyson is not an asshole like you," Remi hissed, her eyes flashing with anger. "He's a good person. And you have no right to interfere in our relationship."

My hands balled into fists at my sides as I tried to restrain myself from touching her. "Is that so?" I growled. "That stuck-up celebrity? You think he's some kind of saint?"

"Ghost, you don't know him." Her voice trembled with emotion.

"If you did, you would know that Greyson is a wonderful person."

"Does Mr. Wonderful know we fucked?" I demanded, the hurt evident in my voice.

"Stay out of my relationship, Ghost," Remi warned, her voice cold and detached.

"Is that what you want?" I growled, my hands wrapping around her waist and pulling her flush against my body. My anger and desire mingled together like a volatile concoction, urging me to take control. Her eyes widened in surprise, but she didn't resist as I pressed my lips against hers, kissing her aggressively. Our lips crashed together in a passionate, fiery kiss that left us both gasping for air.

"Tell me," I whispered between heated kisses, my voice rough with need. "Does Greyson make you feel like this?"

"Actually, yes," she replied defiantly, her voice shaking slightly. "I love Greyson. He's the one I want to be with, not some man who fucks around with every girl that crosses his path."

She was right. I had nothing to offer her, but the sting of rejection sliced deep. My heart tightened in my chest. "Is that all I am to you? Just a one-night stand?"

She scowled at me and called my bluff. "You tell me."

What the fuck was I doing? My head was swimming with alcohol and a torrent of emotions I'd never felt before. "Fuck, Remi."

She closed her eyes, disappointed in my non-answer. "I felt something between us. But I can't fool myself into believing we could have something meaningful when you don't do commitment."

"Maybe I don't," I admitted, running a hand through my hair in frustration. "But that doesn't mean I don't feel anything for you, Remi."

"Feelings aren't enough," she whispered, her eyes brimming with tears. "I need more than just passion, Ghost. I need trust and stability, too. I need a partner. You'd end up destroying me."

"Fine," I spat, releasing her and stepping back, feeling the cold reality of her words washing over me like a torrential downpour. "Go be with Greyson. See if he can give you what you need."

"Goodbye, Ghost," Remi whispered, her voice choked with emotion as she turned and walked away, leaving me standing there in the dimly lit club, surrounded by pulsating music and gyrating bodies, feeling more alone than ever before.

Her words cut deeper than any knife, but I refused to let her see how much they affected me. Instead, I turned on my heel and headed back to the dance floor, drowning my sorrows in liquor and the warm bodies of women who meant nothing to me.

Chapter 19

Remi

My heart raced in my chest, threatening to leap out as I tried to make sense of the confusing tornado of emotions that swirled around me. The sight of Greyson's tormented eyes, filled with uncertainty and confusion, had struck a chord deep within my soul. At that moment, I knew, without a shadow of a doubt, that I would always love him — even if he chose to walk away from me forever.

As I stood there, trembling and vulnerable, the memories of my recent confrontation with Ghost flooded back, stirring up a potent cocktail of resentment, longing, and self-doubt. I had known all along that he wasn't offering me anything beyond a casual hookup, and yet, my heart had still fluttered at the thought of being touched by those skilled hands, wrapped up in the enigma that was Johnny 'Ghost' Parker.

The excitement that coursed through me when I was near Ghost mirrored the sparks that flew between Greyson and me, but I couldn't allow myself to be swept away by it. I had to assert my worth and remind Ghost that I was more than just another conquest to him — because deep down, I knew that losing myself in his embrace would only lead to heartache and ruin.

And then, as if to taunt me further, Ghost had pressed his lips against mine while I knew Greyson watched, undoubtedly shocked and hurt. The kiss had been electric, igniting a fire within me that threatened to consume me whole. But despite the undeniable attraction, I could not forget the cold, cruel truth: Ghost didn't want anything more from me. He had made that abundantly clear, and the knowledge stung like a thousand needles piercing my heart.

Now, with the remnants of that heated exchange still lingering on my lips and the weight of Greyson's unspoken decision bearing down on me, I felt like a tangled mess of raw nerves and conflicting desires. My mind raced, grasping for answers and finding only more questions, as I tried to navigate the treacherous waters of my own emotions — and those of the two men who had unwittingly ensnared me in their passionate, complex web.

As I stood there, struggling to make sense of it all, a single tear slipped down my cheek, betraying the fragility that lay beneath my strong, ambitious exterior. And for a brief, fleeting moment, I allowed myself to acknowledge the fear that gripped me: the fear of losing Greyson, of being cast adrift in a sea of uncertainty and unfulfilled desires.

I looked around, emotionally drained, as the room pulsed with the relentless beat of the music. The dimly lit space was suffocating, and I knew I needed to escape before I completely lost myself.

Just when I was about to search for Grey, Larry, my photographer, came over and leaned into my ear to be heard above the music. "I think I've got what I need. I'd like to go over everything with you, but I'd like to finish up at the hotel if that's okay? One of the guys is leaving in a few minutes, so we can catch a ride back with them."

He'd unwittingly thrown me a lifeline, and I was going to grab onto it. "Of course. Give me five minutes and I'll come with you," I replied gratefully, my voice barely audible over the deafening music.

My eyes searched the room for Greyson, finding him sitting on a couch in the VIP area with Trudy. As I approached, he noticed my presence and made room for me to sit next to him.

"Hey, I'm really sorry, but I have to head back to the hotel with Larry to work on something," I shouted into his ear, trying to make myself heard.

Greyson's face fell, but he quickly masked his disappointment. "Do you want me to come with you?" he asked, genuine concern etched on his handsome features.

"No, stay and enjoy yourself," I insisted, forcing a smile. "Sidney and Kaylie are leaving too, so we'll just catch a ride with them. I'm actually exhausted, so I'm not up for talking about serious matters tonight, anyway. I was hoping we could meet for breakfast tomorrow?"

I could tell he wasn't happy about it, but he forced a smile. "Alright," Greyson conceded.

My fingers brushed against his as we shared a brief moment of connection. I hesitated, then asked, "When are you going back to L.A.?"

"Sunday," he replied without hesitation, his green eyes searching mine for any hint of emotion. "I'm free all day tomorrow, but I have to leave Sunday so I can get back on the set Monday. They rearranged the taping schedule, so I only taped half a day on Friday, so I'll be swamped this week trying to make it up."

I searched his face, trying to glimpse a hint of what he was thinking. "Okay. Since you're free, maybe we can spend some time together tomorrow. Enjoy the city. I'm sure I can figure out how to catch up with the tour bus if I stay here a little longer."

"That sounds good, Rems."

Greyson studied my face for a moment, and then finally broached the subject that had been hanging between us all night. "Before you go, I need to know what's going on between you and Ghost," he asked, his voice tense.

"Did you see the kiss?" I asked nervously, my heart hammering in my chest.

"Everyone saw it, Remi," Greyson responded, his jaw clenched.

I sighed, knowing that there was no point in denying it. I'd always planned on telling him, just not like this. "Ghost and I ... we've gotten close during the tour," I admitted, my eyes downcast. "It's not serious. He's not a relationship type of guy, as I'm sure you can imagine. But it's given me some insight about some of the things you were trying to tell me before I left."

"Like what?" Greyson pressed, searching for answers.

"Like how complicated love and attraction can really be. It's not so cut and dried as I insisted," I replied, finally meeting his gaze. "But we'll talk more about it tomorrow, okay?"

"Fine," Greyson agreed reluctantly, though I could tell the conversation was far from over. "I have some things to tell you, too. As long as we're honest with each other, Rems, I think we can work through this."

I was so grateful he said that. It was something I needed to hear, to cling to. I bit down on my lip to keep the tears from spilling. His words gave me just the hope I needed, and I threw my arms around him in an embrace. A small, strangled cry escaped from my lips, muffled by his shoulder. "I want to try," I said, voice thick with emotion.

He wrapped his arms around me, and the warmth of his body engulfed mine. I melted into him and stayed there for a little longer than necessary. He held me in silence for a few moments, as if he could protect me from the world. Finally, with a deep sigh, he let go.

As I got up to leave, a sudden wave of protectiveness washed over me. "Please, don't get into a confrontation with Ghost. Just leave him alone. He's ... fragile right now."

Greyson looked like he wanted to argue but held his tongue. With a final nod, I walked away, my heart heavy and my thoughts still tangled in the chaotic web of emotions that I couldn't seem to shake.

Chapter 20

Greyson

WITH REMI GONE, a heavy weight settled over me as I sipped my drink, looking out over the dance floor from the safe confines of the VIP section. The nightclub's pulsing music and neon lights felt distant and uninviting.

Ghost staggering toward me, stumbling off the dance floor with a pretty girl latched onto his arm. She eyed me with recognition, her gaze wandering over my body before she quickly abandoned Ghost to cozy up next to me. My stomach twisted in discomfort; this wasn't what I wanted.

I retreated to the couch and turned to the girl who followed me. "Would you mind giving me some space?" I asked her gently, trying not to let my unease show. Her eyes flashed with disappointment, but she nodded and slipped back into the crowd. Ghost, now slumped on the couch beside me, scowled at the loss of his companion.

Ghost took another swig from his nearly empty bottle. "What happened to Remi? She disappear on you? Guess she's not too excited to see you." His words were slurred, and his grin held a cruel edge.

"She went back to the hotel with the photographer to do some work," I replied, forcing a calm tone in the face of his mockery.

"Is that so?" Ghost smirked, taking another sip.

"I'm heading back too," I announced. I had no desire to be the subject of Ghost's ridicule while I watched him hooking up with random women. "Do you know which hotel she's staying at?"

Ghost laughed derisively, his dark eyes glinting under the club lights. "What, she didn't tell you?" He taunted, enjoying my discomfort.

"Never mind, I'll find out myself," I muttered, signaling to the security guy who'd been keeping an eye on us from a distance. "Get me a car back to the hotel, please."

"Wait, I ... uh, I need to go back too," Ghost slurred, quickly making up an excuse. "I forgot something at the hotel."

He was probably too wasted to realize how dumb that sounded. "Alright, fine. Let's go," I said, my patience wearing thin.

The security guard, a tall and broad-shouldered hulk of a man, swept the crowd with his eyes and then glanced at me. "The car is ready for you, Mr. Durant. You can follow me when you're ready."

"Thank you." I stood and Ghost followed behind me, still gripping his bottle, completely unaware of the emotional storm brewing within me. I'd be in a car alone with him. I gritted my teeth. Even when he was acting like an utter dickhead, I was still drawn to him.

We exited the club through a private exit and slipped into the waiting car. The leather seat creaked under Ghost as he shifted beside me, the heat of his thigh burning into mine. My heart thudded at his nearness, a volatile cocktail of lust and loathing churning in my gut.

Ghost was searching around the backseat with a frown on his face.

I ground my teeth, staring out the tinted window at the neon-lit streets sliding by. "You don't need anymore to drink."

"What's your problem?" His gravelly voice was a match striking in the dark, igniting my temper.

I bit back a sharp retort, clenching my fists in my lap. I wasn't going to rise to the bait.

"You've always been a big dick," he muttered, his gaze sliding my way through messy strands of hair.

Goddamn, he was such a punk. "Oh yeah? How have I ever been a dick to you or your friends?"

Ghost's eyes narrowed, gleaming shards of obsidian in the shadows. "I'm not impressed by your celebrity status like the rest of the world."

"You're not impressed? Just envious, then." The word was a knife slipping between his ribs, and satisfaction flickered as hurt flashed across his face.

"I don't give a fuck about you. I hate you," he spat, shifting away to stare out the window.

A rumble of bitter laughter escaped me as I pretended his words didn't affect me. "I see the way you look at me, and it's not hatred, Parker."

His head snapped back to look at me. He was sitting dangerously close, his half-lidded gaze smoldering with intensity. His eyes traveled slowly down my body, and I felt a flutter in my stomach.

He glanced at my mouth. "Nobody calls me Parker."

I leaned closer, our shoulders brushing, and relished the hitch of his breath. "Everyone calls you Ghost, but you don't look like a ghost to me." I turned to pin him with a stare, pulse racing. "I see you."

"You're delusional," he scoffed, but his cheeks were flushed, eyes fever-bright.

"Coward." The single word fell between us like a gauntlet, heavy with challenge.

We stared at each other, chests heaving, the air crackling with tension. I was drowning in those fathomless eyes, lost in the swell of his lips and the corded muscles of his neck.

"I'm not afraid of you," he rasped. His voice had an edge of anger to it and was dripping with contempt.

I leaned in, my mouth hovered a hairsbreadth away from his ear, and murmured, "Prove it."

He froze, emotions flickering across his face in rapid succession — surprise, confusion, anger, and maybe even lust. Arousal shot through my veins like fire as my cock hardened painfully in my pants. The aching desire intensified and pulsed throughout every inch of me as I waited to see what he would do.

He surged forward, mouth crashing into mine, and I groaned at the taste of him, whiskey-sharp and intoxicating. Our tongues tangled as my hands fisted in his hair, pulling him closer until there was no space left between us.

He was hard beneath his jeans, and the thought of him being aroused by me sent a bolt of pleasure right to my groin. He pulled away suddenly, and I growled low in protest, my hands grasping his shoulders, not wanting to end our kiss. He pushed me back, and I immediately retreated.

His flashing eyes bored into me, full of hate and loathing. Lifting his chin, he met my gaze defiantly. "Fuck you, Greyson. I'm not afraid of you."

I chuckled darkly as I tried to steady my breath. I was so filled with lust that I had to clench my hands into fists, so I didn't reach out and touch him. He may hate me, but that kiss was pure passion.

I shifted in my seat, desperate to quench the searing passion that had taken over me. My cock was so hard and thick that I felt like it could rip through the fabric of my jeans. Ghost's smoldering gaze seemed to consume me, and the look in his eyes made it clear he wanted to hate fuck me into next week. The thought of an unrestrained night with him ignited a storm of craving within me, and I doubted I'd be able to handle the sheer intensity of it. I would combust.

Ghost said that he hated me, but then he kissed me with such intensity that it was hard for him to deny that there wasn't something more between us. I suspected his intense anger was coming from a place of denial — deep down, he wanted me, but he refused to acknowledge it.

And that knowledge excited me. If his hatred was misplaced, then maybe I could get through to him.

The car pulled up to the entrance of the hotel. Ghost sat unmoving, staring out the window as the driver got out of the car.

"We need to talk about Remi." My voice sounded harsh in the silent car.

Ghost turned to look at me then, his eyes cold and hard. "There's nothing to talk about." He turned back to face the window.

I wasn't going to sit around while he acted sullen and immature, but I was determined not to let this be the end of the discussion between us. I'd come to Boston to resolve all of these feelings I had for him, for good or for bad. I got out of the car and closed the door.

The security guy who drove us wheeled my suitcase over to me. It must have been in the back of the car. One of the perks of being a celebrity was constantly having people take care of all my needs. I hadn't even thought about my suitcase since the airport.

As I was thanking the man, Ghost opened the car door and circled around to my side to enter the hotel.

The security guy asked, "Is there anything else I can do for you, Mr.

Durant? Would you like me to arrange a room for you?"

"No, thank you. I'm good for now." I smiled at the man and then quickly followed after Ghost, who was walking through the nearly empty lobby and making a beeline straight for the elevator bank. The security guard trailed a few steps behind us.

One of the elevator doors slid open right away and Ghost slipped inside, pressing buttons and trying to close the doors before I could get in. I stuck out my hand and prevented the doors from closing before I got onto the elevator, earning a glare from Ghost.

When the security guy tried to join us, Ghost spoke up, "I'm in for the night, Bishop. Thanks."

Bishop stepped back. "Alright, Ghost. Have a good night."

The elevator doors closed, and we rode up in silence. Ghost looked back at me as I followed him off the elevator onto the eighth floor. "Are you stalking me, Grey?"

I wasn't going to let him scare me off. "I'm not leaving until we talk."

He looked away, and I could see the muscles in his jaw clenching. He didn't even respond as he strode down the hallway toward his room. I followed closely behind him, my heart pounding against my chest in anticipation of what I needed to reveal to him.

We reached his room, and he fished the keycard out of his pocket and opened the door. I followed him inside, my eyes immediately drawn to the luxurious suite. To the right of the entrance was a sitting area that boasted a couch with plush velvet upholstery, two armchairs, and a low coffee table. A kitchenette was on the opposite side and straight ahead in the bedroom area sat a king-sized bed with a thick feather-down comforter and too many decorative pillows.

I left my suitcase by the door and found some water bottles in the kitchen. When I came back with one for each of us, Ghost was reclining on the couch with his arms stretched across the back of the cushions, his head tilted back and eyes closed, and his long legs propped up on the coffee table.

I placed a water bottle on the table for him and then sat down in the chair near the couch.

Ghost slowly opened his eyes and stared me down. "You're still here?"

He was stubborn. "I told you, we're going to talk."

"So talk, fucker." He wiped a hand down his face. "I don't have all night."

He wasn't going to make this easy. I opened up my bottle and took a sip, wondering how to say what I needed to. "Why did you kiss Remi at the nightclub?"

He shrugged nonchalantly. "She's hot."

I raised an eyebrow. "Do you kiss every hot girl that you meet?"

"Pretty much." He said it with a cocky flair, but he wasn't smirking. It was hard to read what he was thinking.

"Have you kissed Trudy? She's hot."

He leaned forward and grabbed the water bottle off the table. "What the fuck are we doing here, Grey? I'm running out of patience."

I tried a different angle. "You got up in my face and told me to stay away from Remi."

Ghost had a hard edge to him, but when I looked closer, he seemed lost and not so full of blustering confidence. "This is all about Remi?"

I crossed my arms over my chest. "Not entirely. But she obviously has some feelings for you, and I want to know what's going on."

He scoffed. "Why don't you ask her?"

I pinned him with my stare. "I will when I talk to her, but I'm asking you. Do you have feelings for her? Fuck, did you have sex with her?"

He slouched against the couch cushions, his eyes half-closed and lips down-turned. He exhaled heavily, a contemptuous expression on his face. "If you're going to beat the shit out of me, let's get this over with. But, I'll warn you, I'm not going to just sit here and take it. Let's see how much they love you in Hollywood when you go back with two black eyes."

"Remi doesn't sleep around. She's not like that." The realization that they slept together started to sink in. The emotions surged within me like boiling-hot lava, rising more and more until I felt my face flush with jealousy, my mouth go dry with disbelief, and my stomach churn with anxiety. My voice sounded rough, like it was dragged over sandpaper. "Fuck, you did have sex with her."

Ghost's face tightened and his jaw clenched as he witnessed my confusion. His fists balled up, and his blue eyes flared with anger. "What the fuck, Grey? She told me her boyfriend broke up with her. She was really upset about it, but she never mentioned your name. I had no idea she was seeing you."

"She was upset?" I glared at him. "So you took advantage of her?"

"No. God damn, you're a dick." His fists balled up, and his blue eyes flared with disgust. "I didn't have sex with her the night she was upset. Actually, Grey, if we're being truthful here, it could be said that Remi took advantage of me when I was at a weak moment, but I'm not an asshole and I take responsibility for my own actions."

Remi had slept with him. I needed to push aside the jealousy and hurt that was bubbling up and think more calmly about this situation before I did or said something stupid and caused everything to fall apart.

Remi had feelings for Ghost — that I was sure of. I already knew by the way she talked about him and the way she kissed him, but if she had sex with him, that confirmed it.

It was vaguely amusing because I had feelings for him, too. Remi didn't even know that Ghost was the man I'd been secretly pining for. Was this a big fat joke the universe was playing on me? Or merely a coincidence?

Fear clawed at my insides. Depending on how this played out — it could lead to utter devastation for me. I imagined myself watching from the sidelines as Remi and Ghost got together and fell in love. My heart would shatter as I lost everything that mattered to me.

I wasn't a fan of sitting back and letting the universe do its thing. I liked to take matters into my own hands. Instead of being resigned to fate, I wondered how I could twist this worrisome turn of events into something good.

A text notification sounded on my phone. I pulled the phone from my pocket and glanced down at the screen.

> **REMI:** Finished up with work. Going to sleep. Hope you're having fun at the club.

Ghost was tuning me out, picking at a frayed piece of his worn jeans.

"It's Remi," I said as I typed in a reply.

> **ME:** I left the club. I'm at the hotel with Ghost. We're having an interesting discussion.

Her response came in a rapid succession of texts.

> **REMI:** What? I wanted to talk to you first.
> **REMI:** Ugh, please be careful with him. Ghost is very vulnerable.

Remi: Be angry with me, not him.

I read each text and then looked up at Ghost, who was watching me with interest. Remi was protecting him again, and it definitely piqued my jealousy.

"What's your room number?" I asked.

He slid his feet off the coffee table. "822. Why?"

I began texting back to Remi. "Because I'm asking her to join us."

Ghost expression hardened. "You're going to make her choose?" he spat out.

"Between us? Nah. She already chose me." I gave a smug smirk. "I can give her what she wants — commitment and love. She doesn't think she can get that from you."

I could feel Ghost's rage radiating off of him as he scowled at me. "So you're just rubbing it in my face?"

"No," I answered cooly, gazing down at the new text message from Remi.

"She's on her way. She's rushing over here to protect you." I looked up at him. "She thinks we're fighting."

He exhaled sharply, shaking his head in frustration. "What are we doing?" he asked gruffly, his voice deepening with anger. "Just go. I don't want to talk — to either of you. Just go."

"We're not going to talk," I clarified, a smirk tugging at my lips as a plan began to form in my mind.

"What are we doing, then?" His question was laced with suspicion.

"We're going to give her what she wants." I shrugged nonchalantly, letting the words hang in the air between us.

"Which is?" He narrowed his eyes as he crossed his arms.

I hesitated before finally admitting, "The both of us. We're going to seduce her."

HOW TO CATCH A ROCKSTAR

Surprise crossed his face for a moment before he scoffed incredulously, "What the fuck are you talking about, Grey?"

This was a wild shot in the dark and if I looked as nervous as I felt, it was never going to work. I'd have to project a hell of a lot more confidence than I actually had in this plan. This would be the acting job of my life and a whole lot was at stake for me.

There was a knock at the door. I raised my eyebrow. "You better bring your A game, Parker."

I left him sitting on the couch as I went to answer the door. Remi had changed into jeans and a sweatshirt, but she still looked stunning. I blocked the door so I could talk to her for a few moments without Ghost hearing us.

She chewed on her lip. "What's going on?"

I smiled to reassure her. "I know you have feelings for Ghost, Rems. And I suspect he has feelings for you, though he's shit at expressing his emotions."

She shook her head as if denying it. "Grey, that doesn't matter. I thought you came to Boston to talk about you and me. Do we still have a chance at a future?"

If I were a smart man, I'd take Remi's hand and lead her back to her room. Since I'd seen her again, she'd signaled that she would take me back. We could resume our relationship where we left off. I could stake my claim and not think twice about Ghost again. But after the kiss Ghost and I shared in the car, I knew I could never go back into denial about my feelings for him.

"Rems, there's something I need to tell you," I spoke low, so there was no way Ghost could hear me. "Ghost is the man I was telling you about. The man I've been conflicted about for so long."

Her eyes widened in disbelief and her jaw dropped. She covered her mouth with both hands and let out a gasp of surprise. "Ghost? He's the one? Oh my God!"

I grabbed her hand to pull her toward me and into the room. I leaned in to whisper into her ear, "And he doesn't know it. Not yet, anyway."

Her gaze darted between me and Ghost, who was seated across the room on the couch. A rosy flush spread across her cheeks as she clenched my hand in an iron grip.

I lifted our combined hands and kissed the back of her hand. "Come sit down."

I led her over to the couch and maneuvered her in between Ghost and me.

Ghost rested his hand possessively on her thigh. "Hey, bunny. Your boyfriend and I were just having a nice chat."

Chapter 21

Remi

MY HEART POUNDED AS I sat wedged between Greyson and Ghost on the couch, the tension in the air thick enough to cut with a knife. Greyson had just dropped a huge bombshell on me. Ghost was the man he'd been attracted to for years, the man he couldn't get out of his thoughts, the man that had come between our relationship, but Ghost didn't even know how Grey felt about him. And somehow, I managed to fall in love with Greyson and then sleep with the man that he had those deep feelings for.

Ghost sighed, running a hand through his tousled blond hair. "Well, this is awkward."

He wasn't wrong, and he didn't even know the whole truth. I didn't know where to look or what to do. I clasped my hands in my lap to keep them from trembling.

Grey shifted beside me, the heat of his thigh pressing into mine.

"Doesn't have to be." His gravelly voice sent a thrill down my spine.

I bit my lip, arousal warring with guilt in my gut. How had I gotten into this mess?

Grey reached over, grasping my chin and turning my face toward his. "We could share."

Share? My heart stuttered at the implication, and I couldn't hold back a soft moan. As wrong as it was, the thought of being with them both made me wet.

Ghost growled, low and hungry, his arm snaking around my waist. "What do you say, bunny? Want to be ours tonight?"

I knew this was a mistake. Knew I would only end up hurt. But as Grey nuzzled my neck and Ghost's hand slid up my thigh, desire overruled reason.

I tangled my fingers in Grey's hair, letting him soothe my nerves with a searing kiss before turning to Ghost.

"I—" I swallowed. "I've never done anything like this. I don't know how."

Their answering grins were all teeth, two wolves who had just caught their prey. Tonight, I would be devoured, and I wasn't sure if I should run now or give in to my dark desires.

But before I could make a decision, Ghost's lips were on mine, his tongue exploring my mouth. Grey's hand slid up my thigh, his fingers inching closer to the wetness between my legs. Somehow, between two sets of hands, my shirt came off, followed quickly by my bra.

The moment fingers pinched my aching nipples, I was completely submerged in pleasure. My body responded to their touches eagerly, pushing me into a state of delirium as I felt lips and hands glide over my sensitive skin. My breath came faster until all I wanted was to surrender to the pleasure driving me wild.

"Lift." It was Greyson who was taking charge — who was now

tugging down my jeans and panties until I was completely naked and trembling with desire.

I gasped as both of their hands moved down my body at once, teasing and stroking until I was panting for more. Ghost leaned in closer, his teeth grazing my neck while Greyson shifted lower to lick and suck at my nipples in turn. My breathing grew erratic as they explored every inch of me with their eager mouths, each touch sending pleasure shooting through me like an electric current.

My legs went limp, and I leaned back against Greyson's chest, his hands moving around my waist as he pulled me into his lap. His hard cock pressing against my ass sent a jolt of pleasure through me, and I moaned in response.

Greyson chuckled, the sound vibrating through me. He whispered close to my ear, "How many times are we going to make you come tonight, Rems?"

I let out a soft moan of pleasure as my head fell back against his shoulder, my back arching into his touch. Grey's hands cupped my breasts, his thumbs tracing circles around my nipples.

Greyson tugged at my stiff nipple with his fingers. "Open your eyes, Rems."

My eyelids slowly peeled apart, and I felt a million tiny wings take off in my stomach as Ghost's figure came into focus. He stood back, taking in the sight of me completely unguarded and vulnerable, exposed for him to lay eyes upon. Greyson glided his fingertips down my sides, leaving an electrifying trail that caused me to gasp with pleasure. His hands ventured southward, hovering over my hips before coasting around them and settling on the inside of my thighs.

With gentle forcefulness, he parted my legs, forcing them to stay in the V shape that invited Ghost into our intimate moment. My arousal was now unmistakable; I could feel the heat radiating between my thighs and knew that the slickness would be glistening, as Ghost's eyes raked over my pussy.

Grey pulled my arms back and held me in a locked position. "Fuck her with your tongue, Parker," he commanded.

Obeying his orders, Ghost spread my legs wider and eagerly dove between them to feast. His tongue was a ravenous beast, searching out every inch of my flesh and seeking to bring me pleasure with each slow, tantalizing stroke. He licked, sucked, and teased all the sensitive spots that drove me wild while Greyson fondled my breasts and pressed featherlight kisses against the nape of my neck. My hips began to rock in time to Ghost's licking as I moaned and shuddered, unable to contain the orgasmic bliss that coursed through each nerve ending.

Grey's voice was raspy and dripping with lust. "Eyes open, Rems. I want to watch you come."

How could he possibly know that my eyes were closed? I pried them open and locked gazes with him in the reflection of the mirror. Grey was watching every single second of our carnal act in the glass opposite us. His eyes were drinking it all in; my body exposed and spread out for Ghost, while his head was buried between my legs.

Ghost's tongue flicked across my engorged clit, sending tremors through my body as his finger slid inside me. My hips involuntarily bucked against him as I felt the heat of ecstasy growing with each expertly placed thrust of his fingers. His mouth engulfed my clit, sucking and licking it in perfect rhythm with his thrusts as he pleasured me like no one ever had before. Greyson was holding me firmly in place, squeezing both my nipples.

I met Grey's eyes in the mirror. "I'm gonna—"

The orgasm came upon me quickly and fiercely, engulfing me in an explosive wave of pleasure.

Every nerve in my body felt like it was sparking with electricity, a fire igniting in my veins. I was caught between them, unable to think or move as their hands and lips gently caressed me through the aftermath.

I felt the rumble of Grey's voice in his chest. "Let me taste her."

Ghost pulled away from my limp body and then leaned close to us. He stared at Grey for a few long seconds and something flickered in his eyes that had my heart galloping at high speed again. Then he leaned closer and touched his lips to Grey's.

Grey's hand snaked around Ghost's neck and pulled him in for a long, passionate kiss. I couldn't help but let out a moan of surprise at the sight before me. The heat of their fervor seemed to seep through my skin, burning away rationality and causing me to forget why I was even there. My head rested against Grey's chest, my senses assaulted by the sight of their kiss just inches from my face. So close that I could smell my own scent on Ghost's lips.

Grey's chest heaved against my back as I leaned into him, feeling the insistent pressure of his arousal against my lower back. At that moment, I felt both of their desires, each enhanced by the other until it felt like it belonged to me as well. The earthy growl that ripped from Grey's throat broke through me like an electric shockwave; my orgasm had left me languid, but I thought I might melt all over again as I absorbed Grey's excitement and lust seeping into me like it was my own.

The two finally broke apart, both fighting for breath.

Grey looked absolutely drugged with lust. "You still with us, Remi?"

I buried my head in his neck. "Yes."

He put his arms under my knees and I felt his arm muscles bulge as he stood holding me. My arms wrapped around his neck as he started carrying me toward the bed.

He pulled off the comforter and then laid me on the bed. "Do you need me to use a condom?"

"No." We already had that talk earlier in our relationship and nothing had changed for me. I knew Grey wouldn't risk my health if anything had changed for him.

He nodded and then looked at Ghost. "You're going to need condoms."

I liked that he was taking control of this situation, but I wondered how Ghost felt about it. I wanted to reach out to Ghost, but I wasn't sure of anything, including my role here.

My eyes darted between the two men, Ghost getting a condom from his bag and Greyson staring down at me. They were both still fully dressed. A wave of self-consciousness rolled over me and I reached for the bedsheets to cover myself.

"Don't." It was Ghost's voice. He pulled his shirt off, revealing his toned and tattooed upper body. "Don't cover yourself up, bunny. You're beautiful."

I looked at Grey, but he seemed to be suddenly frozen to the spot. He was mesmerized by Ghost, watching him shuck his pants off. A flicker of unease ran through me. How could I compete with someone like Ghost?

Both Grey and I were eye-fucking Ghost because he had the perfect masculine body. He had an athletic build, toned and muscular, with broad shoulders, a flat stomach, and strong arms. His muscles rippled as he moved, and his arm was covered in tattoos. There was one tattoo on his right side that went from his chest to his hip.

Ghost climbed onto the bed with me. "Bunny, I want your lips wrapped around my cock."

I fought the urge to look at Greyson and seek his permission because I knew Ghost wouldn't like that. Instead, I nodded.

Ghost crawled up onto the bed, and I eagerly opened my mouth as he positioned himself between my awaiting lips. I could feel his hardness against my tongue, tempting me to take him in deeper. His hands grabbed a fistful of my hair as he began to thrust in and out, guiding me up and down with every stroke. His other hand traveled down my spine, slowly making its way down to my backside, squeezing each cheek hungrily. All the while, I kept my lips locked around him, feeling each movement echoing through my body.

Grey was watching us, and I hoped he wasn't angry. I was sucking a cock right in front of him. It was weird, but very, very hot.

"You like watching my cock get sucked, Durant?" Ghost mocked.

That seemed to snap Grey out of his trance. "I'm taking it easy on you, Parker. Don't fuck with me."

He pushed all the way into the back of my throat. "Stop watching and come fuck her pussy, then. If she keeps taking me this deep, I'm not going to last long."

I hummed with pleasure as I sucked enthusiastically on his thickness. My pussy was begging to be filled. Grey swiftly ripped off his clothes, his eyes glazed with hungry desire. All of a sudden, Ghost's gaze shifted away from where my mouth was working its magic and onto Grey.

I knew what Ghost was witnessing. Grey's body was a work of art, his muscular physique perfectly toned and honed for his job. He was sculpted perfection with a broad chest, well-defined muscles, strong arms, and smooth, sun-kissed skin. His six-pack abs formed a v-shaped torso, where he had a treasure trail of dark hair that led down to his gorgeous cock.

He had the looks of a movie star and the body of a god. Even though I was so caught up in the physical sensations of what was happening between us, I still had the mental capacity to sense Ghost's appreciation of Grey's form. I knew that Greyson had lusted after

Ghost for years, but the wildcard here was whether Ghost was into Greyson. From everything I knew about Ghost, he wasn't interested in men sexually, but there was no doubt that he liked what he saw right now. Who wouldn't? Grey was hot.

Grey fisted his cock and Ghost licked his lips. I yanked his attention back to me by sucking him hard until his eyes rolled back into his head. "Ah, fuck," Ghost murmured.

I kept up a brutal pace on Ghost's cock until I felt Grey behind me. "Are you ready for me?"

Ghost grabbed a fistful of my hair, pushing his hard length deep into my throat and clamping a large hand on the back of my head, preventing any escape. At the same time, I felt Grey's finger glide through my wet sex, sending an electric shockwave of pleasure throughout my body. Every nerve in my body lit up and flames ignited from within me. I hummed around Ghost's cock as he held me still.

"Christ, you're soaking wet!" Greyson groaned. "Hold on tight, I got you."

Grey grabbed hold of my hips and thrust his hardness deep into me. I tipped my hips back and pressed into him, intensifying the sensation until he filled me completely. Ghost's hand left my hair, and they both began to move in perfect synchronization, thrusting in and out with wild abandon, fucking my mouth and pussy and pushing me to the brink of ecstasy until I had no choice but to surrender to the blissful sensation.

I could feel the orgasm building within me, starting low and rising higher with each stroke. Before I tumbled over the edge, Ghost cried out with a guttural growl, "I'm gonna cum."

Grey slowed down his thrusts. "Pull out and paint her back. I want to see you cum."

Ghost gritted his teeth as if in agony, but he pulled out of my mouth. He pumped his dick with his fist a few times, and then I felt the hot splatter of his cum hitting my back. Grey let out an animalistic moan and then began thrusting wildly into me. The pleasure was like no other — it pushed me further into the abyss of ecstasy until I couldn't contain myself any longer and screamed out my pleasure.

My cries filled the air, but Grey didn't stop. Grey thrust his hips wildly, harder and faster, until finally collapsing atop me as he released a deep and powerful groan, filling me with his sticky warmth.

The three of us fell onto the bed in exhaustion, breathing heavily to catch our breath and regain our energy. Exhaustion washed over my body as I sprawled across the sheets. Grey and Ghost lay on either side of me, making sure I was okay and whispering the words of lovers in my ear. Their hands roamed in gentle caresses, stoking my blissful state.

My breath came out in contented sighs as I settled into their embrace, feeling nothing but happiness. Soon enough, the weight of sleep pulled me under, and I drifted off into a dreamless slumber.

I don't know what pulled me awake, but suddenly I was aware of lying between Ghost and Greyson in the dark and quiet room. My mind raced as I thought about their hands on my skin, pressing into my sides, holding me as if I belonged to them. Their magnificent bodies were pressed against mine. I was lying on my side, facing Greyson, who was breathing steadily in his sleep. He was so peaceful; his eyelashes fluttered slightly as he dreamed. Ghost was behind me, spooning me, and oh ... I felt something hard prodding against my lower back. He was definitely awake.

Ghost propped himself up on his elbow, leaning in close to my ear. His hushed voice sent shivers down my spine. "Are you still awake?"

"Yes," I answered.

"I want to fuck you nice and slow. Do you want me to, bunny?"

My entire body tingled with anticipation as I slowly nodded in agreement. His hot breath caressed my cheek as he leaned closer. "Don't move or make any noise."

The thought of Ghost fucking me while Greyson slept right there was oddly thrilling. I wasn't sure how much Grey would appreciate it, but he was the one who had instigated this entire situation.

Ghost rustled behind me and then I heard the soft sound of a wrapper tearing. I knew with the movement behind me that he was sliding on a condom. Even though he'd seen Greyson take me bareback, he'd respected me enough to use a condom, considering he had plenty of sexual partners. And, as much as this one night was so amazing, I had to remember that. Ghost wasn't committing to anything here. Hopefully, Grey wasn't under any delusion of a commitment, either.

Ghost turned his attention back to me. He fitted his body tightly against mine from behind and then used his strong hand to lift my top leg up and over his own so that I was exposed to him. His deft fingers began lazily playing with me in a most erotic fashion.

He idly pulled at my nipples and rolled them with his thumb until one by one he had them puckered into two taut peaks, aching for more. His thumb moved in slow circles around my navel, tickling me softly before eventually trailing down toward my already swollen sex. He dragged his fingers through my sensitive folds, eliciting a gasp from me. I shivered against the sensation, my sex growing wetter by the second.

He held himself still, allowing me to adjust to the feeling before finally pushing one finger inside of me. As he stretched me open and filled me up, I could feel him smile against the back of my neck before beginning to thrust in and out with a slow rhythm.

His movements were gentle but not lacking power, as if he knew just how hard I needed him. I felt myself becoming more aroused as each thrust grew deeper and more forceful, sending pleasure radiating through every inch of my body until I was arching into his hand, begging for more.

He suddenly stopped. "Do you want my cock, bunny?" he rasped against my ear.

"Please," I begged.

He pulled back a few inches from me, lining his cock up, and rubbing it up and down my slick folds before he pushed into me with ease.

He began to thrust at an agonizingly slow pace, his powerful body pushing deep into mine. His every movement was calculated and deliberate, sending waves of pleasure throughout my body while his skillful hands caressed my skin. With every stroke, the pressure within me mounted, until I thought I would burst with the sheer intensity of it all. A low moan escaped my lips as he continued to fuck me at his steady, unhurried pace.

It was possibly the most sensual sex I'd ever experienced, and I was having trouble keeping quiet.

My eyes fluttered open and a gasp of surprise escaped my lips. Greyson was now awake. I felt a moment of nervousness, wondering what he would do, but his desire was evident in the lascivious way he caressed my body with his hands, kneading and pinching my breasts until I could feel the electricity coursing through me and centering between my legs.

Grey's lips crashed into mine, my mouth opening eagerly under his bold kiss. His tongue explored me with passionate strokes, claiming me even as Ghost was fucking me from behind. Grey pulled away from our kiss, leaving a trail of smoldering kisses down my body. His touch was electrifying, like lightning charging through every inch of my skin. Suddenly his tongue was on my clit, so close to where Ghost's dick was driving me wild. The combined sensation sent tidal waves of pleasure through my core.

I frantically grabbed fistfuls of Grey's thick locks and bucked my hips in a frenzied rhythm. Ghost felt me get closer to the edge and increased his movements, pushing me further into a frenzy. Bright flashes blinded me as relentless waves of pleasure swept through me, the force of my orgasm crashing over me like an overwhelming wave.

They had worked me over until I was completely boneless — minutes later the aftershocks of pleasure were still coursing through my veins. My muscles felt limp and lifeless yet alive, coursing with energy — radiating a warmth that filled my body with a sense of safety. Sandwiched between them, they were my personal protection against the world outside.

I was overwhelmed by their beauty, mesmerized by the ecstasy between us. I must be the luckiest girl on the planet. I'd tasted paradise, and I'd worry about the consequences of it tomorrow.

With these two gorgeous men on either side of me, I drifted off into a deep slumber — postponing reality that was sure to hit me in the morning.

Chapter 22

Ghost

I AWOKE WITH A start, my heart pounding in my chest. The soft rustle of sheets filled the air as I tried to steady my breath. Remi was curled up in my arms, her head resting on my chest, her dark hair fanned out around her like a halo. A certain warmth filled my chest when I thought about her, which was something that I wasn't accustomed to feeling. My mind raced back to last night's events, and the memories made my cock harder than steel.

Images flashed through my mind — Grey spreading Remi's legs for me to feast on her and Grey's cock sinking into her being the two most prominent. And I recalled the sensation of Remi's lips wrapped around my cock and the riot of nerves that had invaded my stomach when I'd kissed Greyson.

It had been beyond amazing, a night that pushed the boundaries of pleasure and intimacy. A night that left me conflicted and craving more because I had to admit, at least to myself, that I'd been turned on by both of them.

I shifted slightly and felt Greyson's presence against my back. He was sleeping soundly, his arm draped over my waist, pulling me closer to him. My stomach dipped at the thought of him waking up and realizing what we had done. And Remi. She was fairly innocent. She'd freaked out the last time she'd woken up in my bed. I could feel my heart pounding against my rib cage, expecting the worst to come. My stomach dropped as a feeling of dread came over me.

"Relax," Greyson breathed into my ear as his hand squeezed my hip.

Relax? I couldn't relax right now unless I popped a Valium. There was a man in my bed. Make that a naked man who was touching me, possessively. Yes, I was attracted to him, and kissing him had unexpectedly set off fireworks of arousal in me, but I wasn't attracted to men. In fact, after suffering so much abuse at the hands of men when I was a kid, Greyson's presence was setting off some severe deep-seated anxiety.

Last night, his kiss stirred something primal and deep within me. It was so intense that it shattered my numbness in a way that I couldn't even begin to explain. It was like all the walls around me had crumbled in an instant, and I felt strange and free at the same time. But there was also this tingle of fear that crawled up my skin because I knew something deep inside me had changed forever.

This morning, as I felt Grey's dick thickening against my ass, I felt panicky and more than a little ashamed at the tingle of thrill that accompanied it.

I shoved Grey aside roughly, my feet hitting the carpeted floor. My heart pounded in my chest and I felt a surge of adrenaline pushing me forward. Getting up out of bed, I hastily turned back for a moment, contemplating taking a Valium; but I quickly decided against it, knowing that searching through my luggage for one would almost certainly wake Remi up. I didn't want to face her yet. So instead, fleeing seemed like the only option.

I stepped into the bathroom, intent on taking a long shower. I hoped like hell that they'd both disappear while I was in there.

No such luck. Greyson barged his way into the bathroom, closing the door behind him.

I spun around to confront him. "What the fuck?"

My gaze locked with his the second I saw him. His face was chiseled and handsome, with a strong jaw and intense, smoldering eyes. A cascade of black wavy hair tumbled over his forehead and his lips were full and inviting. A day's growth of dark stubble emphasized his masculine appearance.

His perfect features were only rivaled by his amazing body. His skin was smooth and taut, stretched across the large muscles which were visible across his chest and abdomen. He had broad, strong shoulders, and the muscles of his arms bulged as he moved. His body was the perfect mix of power and grace.

He stood there, proud and unashamed, as if daring me to look away. He'd slipped on a pair of black briefs, but I already knew what he was packing beneath them. His gaze met mine, and I felt my heart flutter in my chest. His eyes were dark and full of longing, and his lips curled into a half-smile. I could feel the electricity between us, and I wanted to stay in that moment forever.

Fuck, I was definitely attracted to him. I shook my head to break the spell he had on me. "Leave me alone."

A look of resignation crossed his face. "You're going to run away scared? What about Remi? If you act like this, you'll hurt her. She needs us both to be calm right now."

I kept my voice down, despite the panic I felt threatening to consume me. "Remi's not my problem."

The words felt wrong as soon as they left my lips.

Grey's jaw clenched, his lips pursed in anger and maybe disappointment. "Don't be like this, Parker."

I ran a hand through my hair. I could not do this right now. Fuck, I desperately needed a Valium. I needed my numbness back. "What do you want from me?" I hissed.

He took a breath before responding calmly, "Let's go reassure Remi when she wakes up. The both of us. Together."

I shook my head. "That's your job. I'm not a part of this."

He was gritting his teeth, jaw twitching, as he attempted to maintain his composure. "What do you mean? It sure as hell felt like you were a part of it last night."

"You want me to be the third wheel in your cozy little relationship? Your boy toy?" I spat out the words with a sneer, crossing my arms over my chest defensively.

He stepped closer, and I flinched, taken aback by the intensity of his gaze. "That's not what I want. Not at all. I want more, Parker."

What did it even mean? My heart raced as a tightness twisted in my chest. Each breath became shallow as my anxiety escalated. I turned away from his scrutinizing gaze. "We're finished here, Durant."

I turned on the shower, dropped my towel, and stepped under the spray even though the water was still ice cold. Greyson remained fixed to the spot for a few seconds, but then he turned and left the bathroom. As the door clicked shut, there was a palpable shift in the air. Relief washed over me, but there was also disappointment so thick it felt like honey in my throat.

I tried to clear my mind as the water, now hot, streamed over my body, washing away the remnants of last night's pleasures. I braced my hands on the tiled wall, letting the spray massage my sore muscles. Last night's twisted fantasy and my sexual attraction to Greyson had left me uneasy. Dark memories from my past were lingering like shadows in the corners of my mind. If I let them in, I might not survive. I remained rooted, looking up at the showerhead for a full five minutes, trying to find my way back to the numbness.

Remi slipped into the shower behind me, her delicate hands gliding over my hips. I turned to face her, drawing her into my arms. Surprisingly, her presence filled me with a sense of peace and comfort amidst my chaotic emotions. She tilted her head up, her lips seeking mine. I gave her a slow, deep kiss, savoring the warmth and softness of her mouth.

"Where's Grey?" I asked, pulling back just enough to look into her eyes.

She sighed, leaning her forehead against mine. "He left. He sent me in here. Told me we needed to talk."

Grey was really pushing this thing, and I wasn't sure why. "About what?"

"Us. This thing between the three of us." She lifted her gaze to meet mine. "I don't know what we're doing here, Ghost. Where is this going? Is there even a three of us?"

I exhaled, raking a hand through my wet hair. "I don't know."

Is that what she wanted? A relationship between the three of us? One where Greyson and I shared her? And why would I even consider that arrangement? I was too out of my mind to even consider it right now.

Sleeping next to Grey — hell, just kissing him — had brought back some bad memories that could drown me if I let them.

The memories flickered — a grown man with a sick smile, the smell of alcohol on his breath, another man stroking his dick as he slipped into my bed. And maybe just as damaging, the memory of my father calling me a faggot afterward and taunting me that I liked it.

I shook my head, banishing the ghosts that haunted me. "I've got issues, bunny. The past makes it hard to move forward sometimes."

"Ghost..." Remi whispered, her eyes full of empathy and sorrow. "I know you went through a lot. I hope you know that I'm always here for you — no matter what happens."

"Thanks, bunny," I murmured. "I'm just not in a great headspace right now."

She looked up at me with wide, expressive eyes full of emotion. "Don't overthink this too much. Follow what your heart is telling you. I know we have a connection. I can feel it. But, you and Grey? It's there. I witnessed it last night. It kind of scares me, to be honest."

My brow wrinkled as I tried to figure out her meaning. "What do you mean?"

Remi smoothed her palm over my heart in a comforting caress. "There's something tangible between you two. You light up around him. And, Grey? Well, he feels it, too. And... I feel out of my depth here. You and Grey are so worldly, so experienced. You're both celebrities and I'm just me — nobody special. Why would you even want me in the equation?"

"Don't say that." I tilted her chin up, forcing her to meet my eyes. "You're special to me." My thumb brushed over her lower lip. "To both of us. Never doubt that."

She shrugged her shoulder a little and I could tell she didn't fully believe what I told her. Did she think Greyson and I were going to run off together and leave her behind? It was laughable.

"Remi, I'm the outsider here. I don't know what Greyson wants from me. Does he think the only way he can hang onto you is to include me? I don't get him or what he's up to."

She leaned her forehead on my chest. "Wow, what a mess this is! You feel like an outsider? That's not what Greyson or I think. Or want."

I slid my hands around her back and pulled her closer to my body. She fit perfectly in my arms. "I'm not the outsider that you brought in to spice up your sex life?"

"No!" she gasped. "Is that what you think?"

I chuckled. "Not really. But I barely know Greyson. Why would he even let you near me? I just don't get it."

She ran her hands up my chest and suddenly I was extremely aware of her wet, naked body and her lush curves pressed up against me.

"You should talk to him, Ghost. That's for Greyson to tell you. Just like I think you should tell Greyson about your past, but that's all up to you."

I hadn't even told Maggie my darkest secrets yet. There was no way I was going to tell Greyson fucking Durant. "I don't trust him."

She jumped to his defense. "Grey is a good man. People think he's Colton, but he's not. He's nothing like that. If you knew him like I do, you'd know that he is extremely kind and giving. He wouldn't hurt you."

Colton Grimaldi was the character Grey played on *Devious*. I knew exactly what kind of person Colton was because I'd seen every single episode. Sometime after I'd first met Grey, I'd watched an episode. And then another. Until I was hooked on the stupid show.

As crazy as my life seemed to the outside world, there was a lot of downtime. A lot of lonely time. When we were on tour, I spent hours and hours on the road going from one city to the next. Usually, I filled that time playing guitar and writing new songs. I wasn't big into video games like the other guys in the band. When they got busy playing, I'd retreat to the back of the bus and watch *Devious*.

I didn't really answer her, just grunted a bit.

She traced a finger down my chest. "When I first met him, I expected an arrogant asshole. Like Colton Grimaldi. He was so freaking nice that I thought he had to be acting. Nobody is really that kind. It took me a long time to realize that Grey really was a kind and caring person. That's the real him."

I scoffed in disbelief. "He wasn't exactly meek and kind last night. He was a bossy asshole."

"He's not meek in bed." Even under the warm water, I could see her cheeks redden. "He takes charge in bed. And I really like that."

She reached for the shampoo, beginning to wash my hair with gentle strokes. "He's a good guy, Ghost. He would never hurt you."

I closed my eyes, leaning into her touch. "He hurt you."

"No, he was trying to be honest with me, and I rejected it." She gently pushed me back under the stream of water to rinse out my hair.

I reached for the soap. "Let me soap you up before we run out of hot water."

She closed her eyes and laid her head back, feeling my hands glide the scented lather over every square inch of her body. I wasn't against being devious if it meant getting what I wanted, so I made sure to give extra attention to those areas that made her moan until she was writhing with the need to be touched by me.

Water cascaded down Remi's body as I rinsed off the soap, her wet hair clinging to her face as we finished our shower. When we stepped out, the steam from the hot water filled the room, blurring the lines between reality and fantasy. As she reached for a towel, I couldn't help but be overwhelmed by feelings of lust for her. My desire for Remi was a fire that refused to be extinguished.

"Come on," she whispered, sensing my need, and led me into the bedroom. Our bodies moved in unison, our lips meeting as if they were magnets drawn together. We fell onto the bed, tangled in each other's limbs, our passion consuming us like an inferno.

Afterward, we lay side by side, our breaths heavy and labored. I was still amazed that sex with Remi could feel so different — so much brighter and more vibrant than anything else — like nothing I'd ever experienced before. The heat radiating from her body was a reminder of the intensity of our connection.

She shifted beside me, propping herself up on one elbow and running her fingers through my tousled hair. Her eyes locked onto mine, filled with a mix of desire and determination. "I have to get up. I need to get ready to meet Greyson."

"Greyson shouldn't have sent you to talk to me." I swallowed hard, trying to push down the jealousy that bubbled up inside of me. "Will he be angry we had sex?"

"No." She paused for a moment, her eyes searching mine. "He won't be angry. He knows how complicated things are between the three of us."

Even as we lay in a tangle of sweat-soaked sheets with the scent of our passion thick in the air, I had to ask the question that was burning in my mind. "Are you going to have sex with him?"

"Are you going to judge me if I do?" Remi challenged, her eyes narrowing slightly.

"No, I'm just jealous," I admitted, the raw truth stinging my pride.

She reached out to trace her fingers along my jawline as if trying to put my mind at ease. "We're going to meet up and spend the day together before he goes back to L.A. He's flying back tonight; he has filming early in the morning."

"The bus leaves in a couple of hours," I murmured, staring at the ceiling, feeling the weight of our situation.

As Remi's fingers lingered on my jaw, her touch sent a shiver down my spine. "I'm going to catch up with the bus tonight. You should come with me. Then we could all talk." Remi suggested, her gaze filled with hope.

"I can't," I replied, my voice heavy with emotion.

A silence fell over us, the unspoken words hanging thick in the air. I desperately wanted to let go of my insecurities and follow her, to be a part of the conversation between Greyson and Remi. But the darkness within me held me back, a constant reminder of the broken man I was. This moment, this connection with Remi, was something I could cherish, but it couldn't erase the scars of my past.

She ran her fingertips over my lips. "I know you have a lot going on in your head, but please don't let your past stop you from trying. We can still figure this out."

"Can we?" I questioned, my voice barely more than a whisper. "Or are we just deluding ourselves?"

"Maybe." She sighed, pressing her lips to mine in a soft, tender kiss. "But isn't it worth trying?"

For a moment, the ghosts retreated, fading into the shadows. Right now, there was only Remi — and the solace I found in her arms.

As she pulled away and began to gather her clothes from the bedroom floor, I wondered if she was right. Maybe I was too damaged to ever truly find happiness. Had my past experiences broken me too much, or was there a tiny glimmer of hope that I was strong enough to overcome it?

She slipped into the bathroom and once she was out of sight, my doubts returned. She was scurrying off to see Greyson. A hollow ache settled in the pit of my stomach. I was going to lose her for good.

I jumped out of bed and pulled on my discarded jeans that were laying on the floor. I paced the confines of my room like a caged animal, restless energy thrumming through my veins. Every instinct screamed at me to go after Remi, to stake my claim before it was too late.

With a grunt of frustration, I slammed my fist into the wall. Pain exploded across my knuckles, shards of plaster crumbling to the floor — but the physical ache was nothing compared to the maelstrom of emotions raging inside me.

Jealousy. Longing. A bone-deep fear I couldn't name.

They warred within me, shredding my self-control until all I could think about was Remi and Grey. Remi in Grey's arms, giving herself to him freely in all the ways she never would to me. I couldn't bear it. Couldn't stand the thought of her with someone else, especially Greyson. Just thinking about him stirred something dark in me.

The darkness swelled, blotting out reason and logic until there was nothing left but savage, primal need. I had to claim her, mark her, sink deep inside her tight, wet heat.

And I couldn't even acknowledge to myself what I wanted from Greyson. It was too much. The force of my desires was scary. I needed a Valium or two to calm down these out-of-control feelings. I started searching through my bag, but the bathroom door opened. It was too late. I didn't want her to see me popping pills. Not after that night.

Remi emerged from the bathroom, more put together than she was before. "I'm meeting Greyson for breakfast. Do you have time to come with me?"

I shoved aside the flare of jealousy at the mention of his name.

"We have time for something else," I said, pitching my voice low and rough. I reached for her, pulling her close. She went willingly, molding herself against me with a soft sigh. "He can wait a little longer."

My hands slid down to cup her ass, kneading the firm flesh as I ground my hips against hers. She gasped, eyes fluttering shut, and heat licked through me.

"Ghost..." The word was a breathy moan, full of longing and need.

I took her mouth in a bruising kiss, thrusting my tongue between her lips to claim what was mine. She responded on instinct, clinging to me as she opened for the kiss.

I broke the kiss, nuzzling along her jaw as I caught my breath. Her pulse raced under my lips, matching the frantic beat of my heart.

"Stay," I said again, tightening my grip on her. She made a soft sound of protest, pushing at my chest, though there was no real conviction behind it.

"You know I can't." Her words were for my benefit, not hers. We both knew she would give in if I asked again. "Greyson is expecting me, and the bus—"

"Fuck the bus," I growled, fisting a hand in her hair to tilt her head back. I stared down into eyes dark with desire, seeing my own need reflected in their depths. "And fuck Greyson. You're mine, Remi. You belong to me."

She sucked in a sharp breath, trembling in my arms. I watched emotions war across her face: desire, longing, indecision, fear. When she spoke again, her voice was a thread of sound.

"What are you saying?"

I pressed my lips to the pulse in her throat, feeling it jump under my mouth. "You know exactly what I'm saying."

She shook her head in denial, but she didn't pull away. Couldn't pull away.

I gentled my grip, brushing a soft kiss over her mouth. "Tell Greyson I said goodbye. Then come back to me. Be with me tonight."

"I will." She cupped my face in her hands, staring into my eyes. "Grey will be upset that you didn't come to breakfast, but I'll tell him you said goodbye."

When the door clicked shut behind her, I was all alone with my throbbing fist. Worse, I was alone with the thought that she might never return.

Chapter 23

Greyson

I SAT AT THE restaurant, my fingers tracing the grooves in the wooden table as I waited for Remi. My mind drifted to the night before, to tangled limbs and heated breaths, and I shuddered. Images from our threesome with Ghost flooded my mind — his tattooed skin glistening under the dim light, the way he looked into my eyes right before he kissed me, the intoxicating scent of sweat and lust that hung thick in the air.

After so many years of wanting Ghost, of aching for a single touch or a single scrap of attention from him, I'd had him. I'd had his seductive energy turned on me. For just a moment, it was all mine. Having Remi with me made it a hundred times better.

"Hey, Grey," Remi greeted as she slid into the booth across from me, her radiant smile momentarily pulling me out of my reverie. "You look a little lost in thought."

"Ah, yeah," I stammered, trying to regain my composure. "Just thinking about last night." My heart raced and my cock thickened as flashes of Ghost's body tangled with mine and Remi's filled my mind once more, leaving me astounded by the intensity of it all.

"Me too," she admitted, biting her lip. "It was ... sensational." As she spoke, her eyes held a mixture of desire and uncertainty.

The waiter arrived, notepad in hand, saving us from delving deeper into the previous night's passionate affair. "Can I take your order?"

"Two omelets, please. One with spinach and feta, the other with ham and cheese," I requested, knowing Remi's favorite breakfast dish by heart.

He jotted down our order and disappeared into the kitchen.

"Thanks," Remi said softly, giving me a small smile. She then glanced around the restaurant, seemingly searching for something. Her eyes settled on a couple holding hands across the room, and she sighed.

"Hey," I said softly, reaching out to brush her fingers with mine. "How is Ghost?"

"Confused," she replied, her voice low and conflicted. "I think we all are."

I nodded. I'd gotten the clarity I'd come here seeking, but that didn't make the situation any easier. Somehow, I needed to make Remi understand. I loved her, but I also had deep feelings for Ghost. I was fairly certain I loved him, too. She hadn't understood the first time I'd tried to explain it, but now she had feelings tangled up with him as well.

"Are you...?" Remi hesitated before continuing. "Are you in love with him, Greyson?"

I let out a heavy sigh, knowing there was no point in denying the truth. "I've had feelings for Ghost since I met him years ago," I admitted. "But he always rejected my advances. He hasn't been very kind to me in the past."

Remi nodded, her eyes searching mine for answers.

I'd come to Boston to get answers, not leave with more questions. It was time to lay it all on the line. I needed to see if Remi was on board.

"Listen, Remi," I began, my heart pounding in my chest. "I love you, and I think I could love Ghost if he let me in." My stomach was tied in knots as I watched her face for any sign of her reaction. "I want the three of us to be together."

Her gaze flicked up to meet mine, uncertainty clouding her expression. "Grey, you know I love you. That's never changed for me. I have feelings for Ghost, too. But I don't know if Ghost can make commitments like that, or if he even feels the same way about us."

The weak winter sunlight streaming through the restaurant window cast a warm glow over Remi's face, highlighting her contemplative expression. She hesitated for a moment before speaking. "Ghost has things in his past that he needs to deal with," she said quietly. "And it's not just about being able to make commitments — I think it goes deeper than that."

I furrowed my brow, searching her eyes for answers. "Do you think he could ever love another man? Does he have a fear of intimacy when it comes to being with another man? I would understand it if he couldn't."

"I'm not sure." She hesitated, chewing her bottom lip nervously. "Having a threesome with another man involved is very different from what you're talking about. You're talking about complex emotions, like love. I do believe he has feelings for you, but he's far from understanding that, let alone accepting it. He's still grappling with his own identity and past traumas."

My chest ached, imagining Ghost in pain. I'd always sensed a loneliness in him and felt he might have endured a lot of hurt. I wanted nothing more than to wrap him in my arms and show him he could trust me, trust us, but I didn't want to scare him away.

"Then what am I supposed to do?" I asked, feeling a mixture of frustration and helplessness. "How can I help him if he keeps pushing me away?"

"Talk to him," Remi urged, reaching across the table to squeeze my hand reassuringly. "Open up to him about your feelings and let him know that you're there for him, and maybe he'll be willing to open up to you. But, most importantly, you should give him time and space to process everything."

A server appeared at our table, setting down plates of steaming food before us. Remi picked up her fork and began cutting into her omelet while I poked at my eggs.

As we started digging into our breakfast, I let my mind drift back to Ghost again — the feel of his strong athletic body against mine, the growling sound he made when he'd claimed my lips and plundered my mouth. My desire for him had grown over the years, despite his repeated rejections and distance. But now, with Remi in the mix, my feelings had exponentially increased. The way we connected, the passion we shared — it all felt so right, like a missing piece of a puzzle finally snapping into place.

"Being with him last night, it just felt…" I shook my head, at a loss for words again. "Right. Like we were meant to be together, the three of us."

"I know. I felt it too." Chewing thoughtfully, Remi spoke up again. "Just so you know, I'll be on tour with Ghost for one more week while we get some video footage, then I'll return to L.A. to start working on the whole package."

My heart tightened at the thought of Remi and Ghost spending time together without me. Would they grow closer while I remained thousands of miles away?

"Remi," I said, my voice strained with vulnerability. "I'm not going to lie — the thought of you two being on tour together without me ... it scares me a little."

"Don't worry," Remi said softly, pausing with her fork halfway to her mouth. "I love you. And no matter what happens with Ghost, that won't change. We'll figure this out together."

I nodded, taking a deep breath and forcing a small smile. "You're right. I trust you. It's just ... new territory for me."

"New territory for all of us," she agreed, her eyes flicking between mine, a shared understanding passing between us. "This is scary, but as long as I know I have you, Grey, I'll be okay."

I studied her face, noting the vulnerability that lay beneath her usual determination. It was clear that Remi, too, was struggling with the complexity of our situation. "I've got you, Rems."

She smiled shyly at me before taking a sip of her coffee. "It seems daring to think we could make something crazy like that work." A flicker of anxiety crossed her face. "And I'm not a daring person."

My thoughts drifted back to the night before. The memory of entwined limbs and heated gasps filled my mind — the sensation of Ghost's touch mingled with Remi's as they brought me to the brink of ecstasy. It had been a night of raw passion and unparalleled intimacy, leaving me breathless and aching for more.

Whatever the future held for Ghost, Remi, and me, one thing was certain — I wanted them both, and I would do everything in my power to make our unconventional relationship work, no matter the obstacles we faced.

"Remi," I said, placing her hand in mine, "I know things are complicated with Ghost, but I want you to know that no matter what happens, I love you."

"I love you too, Greyson," she whispered, her eyes glistening with unshed tears. "More than I ever thought possible. I was scared when you said you needed some space to figure things out because I couldn't understand what you were trying to tell me. I truly understand now. You have a certain connection with Ghost. We both do. And it's not just sexual. It's something more. It's love."

Her words resonated within me, stirring a swell of emotion that threatened to overflow. My own love for her was undeniable, a force that seemed to grow stronger each day.

I leaned over the table to press a tender kiss to her lips. "You're my rock, Remi, just as I'll always be yours."

With that, we returned our focus to our meal, comforted by the knowledge that despite the uncertainties lurking ahead, we were united in our desire to explore the depths of our intertwined hearts with Ghost.

We finished our breakfast in comfortable silence. I paid the bill and then we left the restaurant, our fingers entwined.

"So what now?" Remi asked.

The future loomed before us, fraught with uncertainty and the promise of uncharted desires.

"Now, I'll give Ghost some space." I stopped, turning to face her. "You try to be there for him while he works through all of this. When you're back in L.A. next week, we focus on us. If Ghost is interested in something more, he'll know where to find us."

"You're right." Remi smiled, brushing a lock of hair behind her ear. "I'm ready for that. For us. No more waiting."

My heart swelled. "Good. Because you're the best damn thing that's ever happened to me, Remi Sutton, and I don't intend to waste another second we could be spending together."

Remi laughed, throwing her arms around my neck. Her lips found mine, her kisses like fire, burning away any remaining doubts and lighting a blaze of passion that I knew would never be extinguished. Luckily, we were bundled up in winter jackets and hats, so no one was likely to recognize me and ruin our private moment.

We pulled apart, and I grabbed her small hand, lacing our fingers together as we walked along the sidewalk.

As happy as I was, I wished Ghost was here with us. It would feel complete. But I couldn't make him love me.

Ghost had his demons to face, his path to forge. But Remi and I had found our way to each other, and together, we would build a love to stand the test of time. The future was uncertain, but of one thing I was sure — my heart was hers, now and always.

Chapter 24

Ghost

THE AIR IN THE back of the tour bus was thick and humid, heavy with the scent of sex and sweat. Our limbs were tangled together under the rumpled sheets, Remi's head resting on my chest as I traced my fingers along the curve of her spine, her warm breath on my chest lulling me into a sense of tranquility that had been absent for so long.

We'd been wrapped up in our own little world for the past week, coming up for air only for soundcheck or for me to perform on stage. The rest of the time, I couldn't keep my hands off her, craving the escape she offered me from the numbness that had ruled my life for so long.

Remi's fingers danced across my chest, drawing lazy circles around my tattoo. "Again? God, you're insatiable."

"Only with you," I admitted, feeling a mix of fear and excitement at this newfound vulnerability. It was as if she had unlocked something within me, and the numbness that had been my constant companion was slowly retreating.

"Is it always like this for you? This ... intense?" she asked, tilting her head up to meet my gaze, curiosity in her eyes.

"Never," I confessed, pulling her closer to me, not wanting a single inch of space between our bodies. "I've never felt this connected to someone before. You're the only one who's ever made me feel so ... alive."

"Wow," she whispered, her eyes searching mine for any hint of insincerity. But all she found was the raw truth, bared for her and only her. "I never expected anything like this, Ghost."

"Neither did I," I admitted, my heart pounding in my chest at the thought of how deeply entwined our lives had become in such a short amount of time. "I don't want this to end."

The thought of her leaving made my chest ache. I didn't know how I'd go back to the way things were before. If I even could.

Remi tilted her head up, her hair spilling over my arm. "Who says it has to?"

I searched her gaze. Her eyes were clear and steady, filled with a warmth that loosened the knot in my chest.

"I want this, Ghost," she said softly. "I want you. All of you."

My heart swelled at her words, a surge of possessiveness and protectiveness sweeping through me. I caught her mouth in a searing kiss, rolling her under me to settle between her thighs.

She was already wet and ready, her body as eager for mine as I was for hers. A few moments later, after sliding on a condom as quickly as I could, I sank into her in one smooth stroke, swallowing her gasp with my kiss.

We moved together unhurriedly, without urgency, simply enjoying the connection between us. The tension built in my body, slowly escalating with each thrust of my hips. I could feel the hot pleasurable energy gathering in the tip of my spine before radiating outward through my veins like a hurricane. My balls tightened as the explosive intensity coursed through me. With one final powerful surge of pleasure, I let out a deep guttural grunt and released into her.

In the aftermath, I held her close, unwilling to withdraw from the warm cradle of her body as we drifted back to sleep.

When I woke again, I stroked Remi's hair, watching as she slept curled against me. Her features were relaxed and soft in slumber, lips curved in a faint smile. It made something warm and tender unfurl in my chest to know I'd put that expression there.

But too soon, her eyelashes fluttered open, and she stirred with a sigh. "What time is it?" she asked, voice husky from sleep.

I reached for my phone to check. "Nearly noon."

She made a sound of distress and sat up, the sheet pooling around her waist. "Shit, I overslept."

"Stay with me just a little longer," I pleaded, tightening my grip around her waist, not ready to let her go.

"Believe me, I'd love nothing more than to stay here with you all day," she responded, pressing her lips to my chest. "But I have a video call with my boss at Hollywood Exposé at one o'clock, and I need to prepare. And ... I should probably be dressed for that."

Reluctantly, I released my hold on her, watching as she slid out of bed and began gathering her clothes. Though I tried to hide it, tension crept into my expression at the reminder she'd be leaving soon. I'd grown addicted to having Remi with me these past days, and the thought of being apart filled me with an unease I didn't want to examine too closely. Not only would we be apart, but she'd be heading back to L.A. where Greyson would be waiting for her. The thought of them together twisted a knot in my stomach.

Remi noticed my silence; she spun around and cupped my cheek, her eyes soft with understanding. "It's only for a little while. I'll be back before you have time to miss me."

I turned my head to press a kiss to her palm, the warmth of her skin a balm against my lips. "I already miss you, and you haven't even left yet."

She laughed, a sound filled with affection and tenderness, and leaned down to kiss me. I savored the softness of her mouth, the taste of her, imprinting it on my memory.

When she drew back, her eyes were bright with emotion. "I'll miss you too. But we both have responsibilities to attend to, at least for a little while." Her mouth curved. "And the sooner I finish up my work, the sooner I can come back to you."

I nodded, swallowing against the lump in my throat. As much as I hated to admit it, she was right. We couldn't stay cocooned away from the world forever.

She hurried into the small bathroom to get ready for her meeting. I fell back against the pillows, listening to the sounds of the shower running.

As I lay there, the emptiness of the room seemed to press down on me, reminding me once again of the numbness that had consumed me for so long. But with Remi, that numbness was retreating, replaced by an insatiable hunger for her touch, her taste, her love. It terrified me, yet at the same time, it was exhilarating — like waking up from a deep sleep and finally feeling alive.

But no matter how hard I tried, I couldn't shake the nagging feeling in the pit of my stomach — the fear that once she left, Remi would slip through my fingers like smoke, leaving me once again surrounded by darkness.

After Remi left the bus to take her meeting, my stomach reminded me that I needed food. I emerged from the back room, my muscles still tingling from the hours I'd spent tangled up in Remi's limbs.

Ryder glanced up from his phone and smirked. "Well, look who finally decided to grace us with his presence."

Knox leaned back on the couch, eyeing me with a knowing grin. "We were taking bets on whether you two were ever coming up for air."

I flipped them off, but couldn't hold back a smile. Remi had awakened something in me — an insatiable hunger that only she could satisfy. "Remi had a meeting, or I'd be fucking her right now."

"Thank fuck we're staying in a hotel tonight," Ryder said. "At least we won't have to listen to Remi screaming your name all night long again."

I couldn't keep the dopey grin from my face as images of Remi writhing beneath me flashed through my mind. We hadn't exactly been quiet in our passion.

Knox laughed, clapping me on the shoulder as he stood. "We're just giving you shite. But seriously, you're going to have to fumigate the back room, or at least air it out before Summer gets here. Just changing the sheets isn't going to cut it. I'm not dealing with her complaints about the sex smell."

Groaning, I scrubbed a hand over my face. I'd forgotten Summer was flying in to meet up with the tour. With Remi gone and Knox holed up with Summer, the rest of the tour was going to be a drag.

"Yeah, yeah." I waved him off, eager to get away from their teasing. But despite their jokes, I couldn't wipe the smile from my face. After feeling dead inside for so long, Remi had ignited a fire in my blood — and I'd burn the whole damn world down before I let it go out again.

While I was searching through the refrigerator for some food to tide me over before soundcheck, Ryder got a call from Talia. He hopped off the bus to take it, pacing the asphalt outside as he talked to his wife and daughter. The smile that lit up his face left a warm feeling in my chest, and I briefly wondered if I could ever have something like that. I scoffed at the absurdity of it. I was way too messed up.

Knox caught my arm as I turned to head back to my room, his expression sobering. "Hey, can I talk to you for a minute?"

I hesitated, concerned about his sudden change in demeanor. Knox was many things, but solemn wasn't one of them. "What's up?"

He jerked his head toward the front of the bus, away from the open window. I followed him and took a seat on a couch across from him. Knox scrubbed a hand over his head, gaze fixed on the scuffed floor between us. "Look, I know things have been moving fast with Remi…"

My shoulders tensed, and I shifted in my seat. "We're just having fun. No need to give me the big brother talk."

"I'm not trying to lecture you," Knox said. "But you seem really into this lass. More than I've seen you with anyone. Ever. And I want to make sure you know what you're getting into." His eyes flicked up to meet mine. "She's still with Greyson, yeah?"

The question caught me off guard, and I frowned. Remi hadn't mentioned Grey since he'd gone back to L.A. I knew she had spoken to him a few times, but I hadn't asked about him. "What does it matter?"

"It matters because I don't want to see you get hurt," Knox said quietly. "If she's stringing you both along…"

"She's not." The words came out too quickly, too forcefully. I didn't know if it was the truth, only that I needed it to be.

"You sure about that, mate?" Knox asked, watching me closely.

I met his gaze and held it. "I'm sure."

Knox studied me for a long moment, then sighed. "All right. Just …

be careful, yeah?"

"Always am." I forced a grin, hoping to lighten the mood and end the conversation.

Knox shook his head but smiled. "Liar." He clapped me on the shoulder as he stood. "Now go get ready. You need a bloody shower, mate."

I nodded, watching as he left the bus before I headed to the back room. Knox's questions echoed in my mind, sowing seeds of doubt that I quickly shook off.

An hour later, I was sitting in the dimly lit private room the tour manager had arranged for me to use. I pulled up the patient portal video app on my phone and waited for Maggie to answer. My nerves were on edge thinking about our last session, how raw and vulnerable I'd allowed myself to become in front of her.

Only a few days ago, Maggie had flown out to meet me on tour, and I'd confessed to her the dark secret I'd carried for years — my past sexual abuse.

"Hey there, Ghost," Maggie said warmly, her face flickering into view as the video call connected. She looked professional as always, her warm brown eyes framed by a pair of black-rimmed glasses. "How have you been since we last spoke?"

Leaning back against the functional brown couch, I attempted to keep my tone casual despite the weight of our previous conversation. "You know, just living the rock star life. Can't complain too much."

Maggie didn't let my nonchalance deter her, raising an eyebrow before diving straight into the heart of our discussion. "Have you been journaling to identify patterns of negative thoughts and behaviors?" she asked, adjusting her glasses slightly.

I hesitated, glancing down at the leather-bound journal lying next to me on the couch. It was a constant companion these days, filled with scribbled lyrics and messy thoughts. "Yeah, I've been trying to," I admitted, feeling a familiar pang of vulnerability. "It's not easy, but it helps sometimes."

"That's good to hear," Maggie said, nodding encouragingly. "How have you been feeling?"

I sat back and thought about the question. "Honestly, I haven't been thinking about the abuse that much. I've been spending all my free time with Remi. She's making me feel things I've never felt before."

Maggie tilted her head, eyes narrowing slightly. "You don't want to use Remi as a crutch to avoid your feelings. You've taken big steps. I want you to keep pushing forward. Acceptance. Analysis. You've got to own your feelings."

I sighed, dragging a hand down my face. "Alright, if I'm being honest ... I've had a few nightmares, but I've analyzed that stuff in the journal. I'm not actively avoiding my memories or whatever."

Her expression was filled with empathy and concern. "Do you want to talk about the nightmares?"

I shrugged, feigning nonchalance, though my insides knotted with unease. "The nightmares are just loops of memories. Reliving those nights. Hearing my father telling me I wanted it. Feeling..." I trailed off with a shudder, my throat tightening at the memory of calloused hands on my skin. Reliving those horrors made my stomach turn.

"It's normal to have flashbacks about a traumatic experience." Maggie's gentle tone eased some of my distress. "Have you been using the coping strategies we discussed?"

I nodded, refocusing my attention on her face. The familiarity of her features centered me in the present. "Yeah, it helps. I've also been noticing my negative thinking more often. I catch it and logically question it like you told me to. It's crazy how I tell myself negative shit all the time. Just an hour ago, I was thinking that I didn't deserve to have a loving family like Ryder did."

"Yes, those negative thoughts are very corrosive, but just catching and correcting those thought patterns is a very important step in the healing process." She nodded encouragingly. "Remember, it takes time and practice to root them out."

I sighed, feeling the weight of her words settle onto my chest. "It's just ... really difficult sometimes. Like I'm fighting against myself, you know?"

"Absolutely," she agreed sympathetically. "And that's why we're here, to help you develop the tools to overcome those challenges."

She scratched something onto her yellow notepad and then looked up at the screen. "You're making great progress with acceptance and analysis. We should start working on action plans soon, and eventually, we can broach the topic of forgiveness."

My stomach dropped. "Forgiveness?" I repeated numbly.

"I know it's a difficult concept, especially in your situation." Her expression was gentle but resolute. "However, forgiving your abuser is an important step in healing from trauma. It doesn't mean excusing their actions or forgetting what they did. It's about releasing the burden of anger and hurt that you're carrying so you can move forward with your life."

I shook my head, panic and anger warring inside me. "I can't forgive that bastard. What he did..." I sucked in a sharp breath, shaking with an effort not to break down. "He doesn't deserve forgiveness."

"You're right, he doesn't deserve it." Maggie's steady tone cut through my building hysteria. "But you deserve peace. Forgiveness is a gift you give yourself, not the other person. It's about freeing yourself from the past so you can move on to a happier future."

I slumped back against the couch, staring at the ceiling. I knew she was right, as much as I didn't want to admit it. The rage I harbored was a cancer, eating away at me from the inside out. But forgiveness seemed impossible. Unattainable.

After a long moment of silence, I met Maggie's patient gaze. "I don't know if I can do it." My voice sounded small and lost, even to my own ears. "Where do I even start?"

"I'll help you through it, step by step," Maggie urged gently, her voice a soothing balm against the whirlwind of emotions threatening to consume me. "We'll work together to create a plan that feels right for you."

"Okay," I mumbled, my voice barely audible over the pounding of my heart. I fiddled with the silver ring around my thumb, a nervous habit that seemed to soothe my racing thoughts.

As I stared back into Maggie's unwavering gaze, I knew that this next phase of therapy would be the hardest yet. But with each step I took forward, a tiny spark of hope ignited within me that I could conquer my past and find peace at last.

"Now that you're actively working through your thoughts and emotions, you need to remember all the strategies we've discussed to cope with triggers and anxiety." Maggie smiled, her eyes crinkling at the corners. "Things like deep breathing, mindfulness practices, and physical exercise are very effective. If you've let that slide, now is a great time to revisit them. I'd also like you to review your safety plan, in case you have a panic attack or flashback."

I was going to tell her that none of that stuff was necessary, that Remi kept me grounded, but I held back, considering Remi was leaving soon and who knew how I'd cope then.

With Remi always on my mind, it was only a matter of time before our conversation shifted to the tangled web that was my relationship with Remi and Greyson.

When Maggie asked about them, I swallowed hard, feeling the knots of tension forming in my stomach as I began. "I'm not sure how to navigate my feelings for them, especially since Remi is leaving the tour in a few days and heading back to be with Greyson."

"Start by telling me what you feel when you think about each of them," she suggested, leaning back in her chair and studying me intently.

"Remi is... intense," I admitted, my mind filling with images of our passionate encounters. "There's this raw, electric connection between us that I can't deny. I've never felt that way about a woman."

"And Greyson?" Maggie prompted, her fingers tapping against the arm of her chair.

"Greyson is ... different," I murmured, my chest tightening as I thought about our passionate kiss. "I'm attracted to him, but it feels wrong. Dirty. Abnormal."

Maggie listened closely, her eyes reflecting a deep understanding. "And if you removed those negative thought patterns?"

I released a shaky breath, raking a hand through my hair. "Then I'm attracted to him. But, I'm not gay."

Maggie leaned forward in her chair, her gaze never leaving mine as she spoke. "Is that coming from you? Or are you thinking about your father when you say that?"

Her words were like a knife to the gut. I could see my father's face, twisted and ugly, as he taunted me, calling me a faggot and telling me that I liked what those evil men had done after he'd been the one that sent them to my bedroom.

I swallowed hard, squeezing my eyes shut against the burn of tears. "I don't know."

Maggie's eyes flickered with understanding. "Journaling is a great way to work through painful emotions and find clarity." Her voice was soft and encouraging.

We sat in comfortable silence for a moment. I studied the lines of her face, the way her hair fell around her shoulders. She was the only person I'd ever truly let in, and I didn't know what I'd do without her.

"During your next session, I'd like to dig a little deeper into your sexual identity. Eventually, I'd like to disconnect your sexuality from your past abuse." Maggie's voice was gentle but firm. "Give yourself permission to explore the topic in your mind and journal about it this week if you can. I'd like to discuss that and how your promiscuity relates to it all."

Despite the heavy topic, my lips curled up in a smile. "Doc, are you calling me a slut?"

She ignored me. "I'd like to know if you're getting the benefits from the promiscuity that you tell yourself you are."

My fingers absently picked at the threadbare fabric of the couch cushion beneath me. "Sounds like it'll be a fun session."

"You bet it will. And Ghost, I want you to remember that healing isn't linear," Maggie said gently, a hint of concern in her eyes. "There will be setbacks, but it's crucial to keep pushing forward and not let those negative thoughts hold you back."

"Right," I murmured, my gaze drifting to the floor as I contemplated her words. It was a constant battle, one that left me drained and weary.

"Stay focused on your progress." Maggie looked at me with warmth and pride. "Celebrate the small victories, and don't forget to lean on those who care about you for support."

As our session drew to a close, I felt a strange mix of relief and trepidation wash over me. After ending the call with Maggie, I sat staring at the blank screen, lost in thought. So much to process, so much work left to do. But for the first time, real hope flickered inside me. Maybe I could move past this after all.

A knock at the door jarred me from my reverie. "Ghost, it's time for soundcheck."

I scrubbed a hand over my face and stood up, shaking off the heaviness that had settled over me during the call. "Be right there."

Chapter 25

Remi

THE RELENTLESS HUM OF the newsroom at Hollywood Exposé surrounded me, the energy pulsing like a living thing. Phones rang incessantly, my colleagues barked into headsets, and keyboards clattered beneath frantic fingers. Above it all, the large wall-mounted TV screens played endless loops of celebrity gossip and breaking news. This was my domain — a world I thrived in — but today, it felt like a cage.

"Remi," my assignment editor's voice snapped me out of my thoughts. "I need that YouTube Yokels piece by Friday. Don't forget you've got other deadlines coming up, too."

"Of course, Elaine," I replied, forcing a smile. My heart sank as my eyes darted across the piles of paperwork on my desk.

My temples throbbed as the familiar knot of anxiety crept in — the quiet panic of deadlines looming, stories half-written, and dangling unfinished threads that needed to be tied off. Shit, I was so far behind.

I sank into my chair and dug my hands into my hair, worry rising in my chest. The YouTube Yokels piece was a mess. The Ghost Parker package was far from complete — I wasn't even sure of the angle I was going with yet, and I could feel the weight of my other deadlines pushing down on me like a ton of bricks.

I should have done more work while I was on tour with Ghost Parker. Instead, I had been swept away by the intensity of my connection with Ghost, the intoxicating days and nights we spent tangled in each other's arms, but now I was paying the price.

I couldn't lose myself in those memories now. I had a job to do, and my time with Ghost had put me irresponsibly behind.

"Hey, Remi." Linda appeared at her desk next to mine, stuffing her large purse into the side drawer of her desk. The scent of cigarette smoke lingered in the air around her, a stale, sour smell that hung heavy like fog. She must have just returned from one of her many cigarette breaks. "I've been dying to find out. How were the Yokels?"

I didn't have time for gossip, but Linda had a mean streak, and I didn't ever want to be on the receiving end of it. "Let's put it this way, they weren't the backwoods hicks they pretend to be."

Her eyes lit up. "Oooh. Interesting. How was Bubba? All that redneck culture repulses me, but there's something so hot about Bubba."

Refraining from rolling my eyes, I told her the truth about good old Bubba. "He's actually a savvy businessman under all that camouflage."

I watched in real time as the air deflated from her 'Bubba' fantasy.

My phone buzzed, and for a moment, hope and apprehension warred in my chest. But the text was from my boss, not Ghost.

CAROLINE: Where's the draft on the awards

show? You're already two days late.

"Fuck!" I'd completely forgotten about that piece. I started to type an apology but stopped myself. I was already on thin ice after extending my time on the Ghost Parker tour. Excuses wouldn't cut it.

> **Me:** I'm on it. Will have the draft to you before I leave today.

Linda snickered next to me. "It must be tough to come back to reality after traveling with a rock band for weeks."

"Reality bites," I muttered, pulling on a headset and tuning out Linda.

Cracking my knuckle, I pulled up the awards showpiece, scanning the half-written draft. I groaned and then deleted entire sections that were overly florid and fangirlish. I lost myself in my work, fingers flying over the keyboard as I researched, wrote, and edited, chasing the clock. By the time I finished the draft for the editor, it was well past midnight.

Exhaustion tugged at my senses as I packed up for the night. Checking my phone, I bit my lip when I noted there were no new messages, neither from Greyson nor Ghost. I dashed off a text to Greyson, apologizing for missing another night with him, but promising to see him after work tomorrow.

The city lights reflected off the wet pavement as I made my way home on autopilot. My brain tried to process the jumble of thoughts wildly bouncing between work, Greyson, and Ghost.

I couldn't shake the image of Ghost's pleading eyes as I left him while he was still on tour. I had no choice but to return to my demanding job at Hollywood Exposé, but his reluctance to let me go remained etched in my mind. I remembered the way he'd pulled me close and buried his face in my hair. Like he was drowning, and I was his only buoy in a sea of uncertainty. I sensed his quiet panic, the needy desperation for me to stay, that seeped through the cracks of his enigmatic facade.

But then the calls and messages had trickled off. And though I told myself he was just busy, doubt had begun to creep in. Had I misread the situation? Was I just another conquest to Ghost, a way to exorcise his demons before moving on to the next?

A sharp pang of guilt and longing pierced through my chest. Every inch of my body ached to be near him again, to feel his strong arms wrapped around me, his lips pressed against mine. But I knew he was actively working through his past traumas with his therapist; he needed space and time to heal, though it tore at my heartstrings.

As much as I tried to give him room and focus on my career, I couldn't help but feel unsettled by our relationship, or rather, the lack thereof. We parted with a thousand promises and reassurances like most lovers tended to do, but the contact had been purely superficial since we said our difficult goodbyes. The thought gnawed at me, making me wonder if it was just emotionally easier for Ghost to ice me out of his life than to deal with the physical distance between us.

I sighed, pinching the bridge of my nose. Insecurity was getting the best of me as I wondered if Ghost was with another woman even at this very minute. Speculation would only drive me mad. I needed to focus on the work in front of me, on crafting a story with depth and nuance, a glimpse into the world of Ghost Parker that managed to keep the real ghosts haunting the band members dead and buried.

♫♪♪♩♩

I pushed away my half-eaten plate of salmon and asparagus, the stress of the day hitting me all at once. Greyson reached across the table and grasped my hand. "You've been working too hard again."

His touch sent a shiver up my arm. "The YouTube piece has been a nightmare. I don't know why my boss is so obsessed with those redneck posers."

Greyson leaned forward, taking a sip of wine before asking, "So, was the YouTube piece the one you traveled to Tennessee for the other day?"

"Yep," I replied with a sigh, pushing a strand of hair behind my ear. My thoughts were still consumed with the story that felt dishonest and manipulative, a far cry from the journalistic integrity I'd always strived for.

Taking a deep breath, I decided to share the details of my assignment with Greyson. "The YouTube Yokels," I began, my hands fidgeting with the fork in front of me, "they're a family that portrays themselves as country rednecks on their channel."

Greyson leaned forward, his eyes locked on mine. "But you discovered something different about them, didn't you?"

I nodded, a mixture of frustration and excitement bubbling within me. "Yes, I did. They're actually rich, smart, and savvy business people. Nothing like the image they project online."

"Interesting," Greyson mused, swirling the wine in his glass. "So why do you think they put on this façade?"

"Maybe it's because they know it sells," I admitted with a sigh. "People want to see the simple, backwoods lifestyle they pretend to have, rather than the truth."

Greyson nodded knowingly. "Fake reality sells."

"You wouldn't believe their setup," I stated. "They own a huge house on tons of acreage. The house is never shown on video, but the backyard is like a hill-billy movie set. On camera, the family talks with deep country accents, wears camo and John Deere hats galore, shoots guns, rides ATVs, and distills moonshine. In reality, they're far more sophisticated and urban. The accents and camo disappear and they drive luxury cars so expensive their viewers could only dream about."

"Sounds like quite the story," Greyson acknowledged, taking a sip of his wine.

"It could have been," I replied bitterly, clenching my fists beneath the table. "If only my boss would let me tell the truth, the real story. Instead, I spent all day crafting this fake image for the redneck grifters' publicity campaign."

Greyson listened intently, offering silent support as I continued. "It's just ... this is exactly the kind of thing I struggled with when I was a political reporter. It feels like I'm being stifled; that I can't tell the stories that really matter."

I looked away, unable to meet his gaze as I added, "And to make matters worse, Dawn has been breaking major scoops lately, even while she's working on her big Royals in America story. I'm worried that if I don't pull out all the stops for the Ghost Parker story, I'll lose the upcoming promotion to her."

"Remi," Greyson began softly, his voice laced with genuine concern. "You're an incredible writer and reporter. Don't let this one setback define your entire career. You'll have other opportunities to tell the stories you believe in. And as for the promotion, just remember that no one can take away your talent or your passion for telling the truth. No matter what happens, you'll always have that."

I felt a sudden urge to close the distance between us, to jump into his arms and let the warmth of his embrace chase away the lingering shadows of my insecurities.

"Thank you," I whispered, feeling tears prick at the corner of my eyes. God, I was so tired. "Your support means more to me than you know."

"Trust yourself, Remi," Greyson urged, his grip on my hand firm and reassuring. "You have a unique perspective and a gift for uncovering the truth. Don't let anyone take that away from you."

Greyson squeezed my hand, his gaze searching my face with a hint of concern mingling with desire. No matter how many times we were together, that look still made my pulse race. "You need to relax. Come on, let's go sit on the patio. I'll give you a massage."

"That sounds perfect." He knew that was my favorite place. I stood and Greyson wrapped an arm around my waist, pulling me close as we walked outside. The cool night air was punctuated by the gentle rustling of leaves.

We settled onto a chaise lounge, Greyson sitting behind me. He arranged a soft throw blanket over us before his hands slid under my blouse, kneading the tense muscles of my shoulders and neck. I moaned softly, letting my head fall back against his chest.

"You work too hard," Greyson murmured, his lips brushing my ear. I shivered, desire pooling low in my belly. "You need to learn to unwind. Let me take your mind off things for a while."

His hands drifted down to cup my breasts through my bra, thumbs teasing my nipples into stiff peaks. I gasped, arousal burning through my veins. When Greyson's fingers slipped under my waistband, dipping lower, I couldn't stop the moan that escaped my lips.

Maybe an evening of relaxation was just what I needed after all.

I writhed against Greyson — my breaths came faster as his fingers explored my most intimate places. Every nerve in my body was alight with pleasure, the tension draining from my muscles.

"That's it, baby," he soothed. "Just relax and feel."

He pinched my nipples, rolling them between his fingers until I cried out. I was soaked, aching for more, and when his fingers plunged deep inside me, I shouted his name.

"You're always so responsive," Greyson said, nipping at my ear. "It drives me crazy, the way you come apart for me."

"Mmmm. You drive me crazy," I gasped, grinding against his hand. He knew exactly how to play my body, bringing me to the edge again and again. I was floating, lost in a haze of desire, caring about nothing but Greyson's touch.

When he finally let me tumble over the brink, the force of my orgasm left me breathless. I collapsed against him, spent and sated, a contented smile curving my lips.

Greyson kissed the top of my head, his embrace warm and comforting. "Better now?"

"Mmm, much." I tilted my head up, meeting his gaze. "Thank you for always knowing exactly what I need."

"You're welcome." He smiled, tucking a stray lock of hair behind my ear. "But we're not done yet. The night is still young, and I'm nowhere near finished with you."

A delicious shiver ran down my spine at the promise in his eyes. Perhaps relaxation could wait, after all. Some things were worth the sacrifice.

Hours later, I lay in Greyson's bed, satisfied and exhausted. We had explored every inch of each other, bodies entwined in a passionate embrace that left no doubt as to the intensity of our feelings for one another. I'd needed to reconnect with him, especially after spending so much time with Ghost.

"Stay with me tonight." He ran a hand up and down my side. "It's late, and you need sleep. I'll have a driver bring you to work in the morning so you don't have to hassle with the commute. Please, Rems. I haven't spent the night with you since the tour."

"When we were with Ghost." It popped out of my mouth before I thought any better of saying it.

The room was quiet for too long. I turned on my side to face him. "We haven't talked about him much."

Grey let out a heavy exhale of breath. "Ghost hasn't reached out to me at all, Rems. I'm afraid that all along he was only interested in you."

"There was definitely something between you two. I saw it." I rubbed his chest. "Ghost and I got really close on the tour, but now that I'm gone, I think he's pushing me away. He hasn't reached out to me either."

"Did you ever talk about the three of us? About a relationship?" Grey's voice wavered.

Ghost never spoke about Greyson, but I'd witnessed their intense passion for each other. I didn't know whether Ghost would ever be able to overcome the pain of his past and accept a man into his life. He'd confided in me about the sexual abuse he'd endured and that was a trauma that wounded so deeply. I would never betray his trust, yet I wished I could warn Greyson that Ghost may never be able to give him the love he desired.

I answered Greyson carefully. "I was pretty clear with him about what I wanted. What we both wanted. But Ghost never committed to anything. He's still ... working through issues."

Grey sighed. "Okay. I get that," he said with a hint of resignation.

"Maybe you should reach out to him? As a friend?" I suggested.

He thought for a moment before pulling me flush against his hard body. "I need to see him again. When is his tour over?"

"Six more weeks," I answered.

Grey's eyes lit up as an idea came to him. "I can throw a party and invite him — the whole band, of course. If he doesn't come, then I'll know that I'm just deluding myself."

I snuggled closer to him. "Yes, that's a good idea. And in the meantime, you could talk or text with him occasionally. That wouldn't be intimidating if you kept it friendly. Let him get to know you, Greyson."

We settled into a comfortable silence, each with our own thoughts. I couldn't help but remain worried about the dynamics between the enigmatic rock star who had captured my heart and my Hollywood celebrity boyfriend who had loved him from the shadows for years. The complicated triangle between us was difficult to navigate with our tangled pasts and a society that wasn't always accepting of unconventional relationships.

Despite my worries, I quickly drifted off to sleep and woke up facing a long day of playing catch up at work.

By six o'clock, most of my co-workers had already gone for the day. As the newsroom emptied out, the hectic buzz of energy in the room mellowed. I stood up from my chair and stretched, and then went to the staff kitchen to retrieve the turkey sandwich I'd brought for my dinner.

Settled at my desk with my food, I opened up my research notebook and began reading through my notes. As I read, I cross-referenced things in my journal with social media posts and old articles. It was time to figure out what I was going to do for this Ghost Parker story. It was arguably the most important article of my career, and I hadn't been able to focus on it for days.

There had to be a story here, something that wouldn't require me to exploit Ghost and the band members' personal tragedies. I stared at the mess of notes, articles, and social media posts scattered across my desk.

I read through interview notes from some of the road crew that I'd highlighted. Equipment malfunctions, tour bus breakdowns, missing items, and lights flickering probably occurred on every rock tour in existence, but I could spin some of those things to sound more ghostly.

Better quotes were the ones that discussed feelings of being followed or watched, unexplained cold spots, and strange shadows or figures spotted. I could really play up the eerie nature of those incidents. A few other happenings that occurred, like when a crew member was accidentally locked in a room or when a road case mysteriously slid off a dolly and almost crushed a man, were probably due to human error more than ghostly haunting, but I didn't have much to work with.

I had enough material to paint the picture of a ghost with a malicious nature preying on the band. But who was this supposed ghost? Outside of exploiting a few tragedies that would hurt members of the band, I didn't have any suspects.

Surely there was another angle I could pursue? What if the ghost didn't have anything to do with the band? What if the band was just the unfortunate people that the ghost attached to?

A spark of inspiration flickered in my mind. Old theatres often had histories of paranormal activity. If Ghost Parker had ever performed at a venue like that, I had my connection. It was admittedly weak, but it was something.

I spent hours poring over Ghost Parker's early tour dates, cross-referencing venues with reported paranormal activity. My fingers tapped away at the keyboard, my determination growing stronger with each passing minute. If I could find a way to tie their ghostly photograph to a haunted venue, it would be a compelling angle for my story — one that wouldn't involve exposing the band members' private lives.

Long after the last person had cleared out of the newsroom, I finally found what I was looking for: an old theater with a chilling history of unexplained events, including the sudden death of its original owner. Ghost Parker had played there just days before the infamous photo was taken.

"Gotcha," I whispered triumphantly, as a sense of satisfaction washed over me.

I had all the information I needed. Now, I had to weave the disjointed threads into a spellbinding story that would capture the attention of the masses. With a newfound sense of purpose, I closed my research notebook and began typing away on my laptop.

Chapter 26

Greyson

I took a deep breath and steadied my nerves as Lucy entered the bedroom set. This was the first love scene we'd ever filmed together, and while I knew she was a professional, the thought of being so intimate on camera with someone I thought of as a friend made me anxious.

Lucy sauntered over, her silk robe flowing around her legs. She flashed me a reassuring smile as the director called out, "Action!"

I pulled Lucy into my arms, my hands roaming over the curves of her body as our lips met in a passionate kiss. Her mouth opened under mine, her tongue sliding against my own as my fingers found the knot of her robe and pulled it loose. The silk slithered to the floor around her feet, leaving her nearly bare — except for a modesty patch and a couple of pasties — in my embrace.

My hands cupped her breasts, kneading the soft flesh as she moaned

HOW TO CATCH A ROCKSTAR

into my mouth. The sound had my dick twitching enough to make me frantically start reciting the famous 'To Be or Not To Be' soliloquy from Hamlet in my head. I backed her toward the bed, laying her down on the mattress and climbing over her.

This was all acting, I reminded myself. Just another day at work.

I leaned over her, brushing my lips against the curve of her neck.

"Are you ready?" I whispered, trying to ignore the heat pooling in my gut. It was hard to make my body listen to my brain.

She nodded, her hazel eyes meeting mine. "Whenever you are."

I lowered my head, placing my mouth over her pastie as I'd been directed to in rehearsal by the intimacy coordinator. Lucy gasped, arching into me as I rested my mouth against her breast. Her hands slid into my hair and I remembered to sweep my hand down the soft skin of her thigh.

Fuck, this was weird.

Her breath hitched as my fingers crept higher, and I gritted my teeth against the sudden tightness in my jeans.

I kept my movements slow and sensual for the camera, all the while cursing the arousal coiling inside me. This was Lucy, my friend, not some nameless woman I was taking to bed. But in this moment, with her soft moans in my ear, while I kissed a trail across her collarbone, I could almost forget.

"Colton," she whimpered, her nails digging into my arm. "Please..."

The director finally called "cut", so I took a deep, steadying breath and opened my eyes to find Lucy watching me, her cheeks flushed and eyes dark with lingering passion.

This was going to be a long day.

Lucy pulled on her robe and I took a drink of water while makeup touched us both up.

"Ready for another take?" the director called.

I nodded, waiting for Lucy to tie her robe before following her back to the set. We ran through the scene a few more times, the mounting sexual tension becoming easier to ignore with each repetition. It was a good thing because I had to kiss a trail down her entire body about ten times and spend an awful amount of time wedged between her legs before the director was satisfied.

By the time filming wrapped for the day, I was exhausted. Lucy and I retreated to our trailers to shower and change, emerging in comfortable street clothes half an hour later.

"Drinks?" she suggested with an easy smile. I was thankful that she had moved past the awkwardness of our intimate scene as well.

"Sure," I said. We were friends outside of work, and while the lines might blur on set, a drink was a welcome way to decompress after a long day of filming.

We headed to our usual spot, a dive bar within walking distance of the studio where the owner made sure no one hassled the *Devious* actors. The drinks flowed freely as we laughed and chatted, the conversation steering clear of work as we caught up like always.

It wasn't until we were several rounds in that Lucy brought up Remi, her tone turning teasing. "So, how are things with your girl? You told me she was coming back to town, but you haven't really talked about her much."

I tensed, the pleasant buzz of alcohol fading. Remi hadn't been around much recently. She was swamped at work and still trying to put together the package for Ghost's band that could earn her a huge promotion at Hollywood Exposé.

"Things are fine. She's just really busy at work right now," I said, staring into my glass.

"Oh." Her expression turned sympathetic. "I'm sorry to hear she's so busy. You must be lonely."

I shook my head, forcing a smile. "It's nothing. She's fighting for a big promotion. And, our schedules aren't cooperating, you know how it is."

"Well, if you do want to talk, I'm here to listen," she said, her hand covering mine.

I leaned against the worn wooden bar counter, nursing my third bourbon and gazing into the amber liquid as if it held the answers to all my troubles.

Lucy traced a finger down my arm. "That was quite the scene we shot today."

My stomach tightened and warning bells went off in my head. "We're professionals. It was just another day on the job, right?"

"Right." She nodded, though she didn't seem convinced. She leaned closer, lips brushing my ear. "It's just ... there were moments when it seemed like there might be something more. You were ... very passionate."

My pulse stuttered at her admission, and I struggled to find the right words. Whatever this was, I had to shut it down.

"Lucy, you're my friend," I said at last. "What happened on that set stays there. In the real world ... you're one of my best friends. I don't want to jeopardize that."

"I thought maybe I could help take care of your loneliness. I felt a spark between us." Her eyes were burning brightly and for a moment, I didn't see Lucy; I saw Kathryn, the femme fatale that she played on *Devious*. "We could remain friends. I'm not looking for commitment, just some fun."

I shrugged off her touch, irritation flickering in my chest. "I'm not interested."

"C'mon, don't be so boring, darling," she pouted. "You're an adventurous man. Remi doesn't have to ever find out."

I pulled out my wallet so I could pay the tab. "Lucy, I think I'm going to call it a night."

She lifted a sculpted eyebrow. "I hope my proposition didn't frighten you off. I know you've slept with plenty of your co-stars. It never seemed to be a problem before."

"And I'm not friends with any of them anymore. I'd like to remain friends with you." I hoped my answer would put an end to the insane discussion.

Her practiced laughter eased the tension as she launched into a story about her latest Tinder date from hell. I listened gratefully, happy she'd backed down before our friendship was irrevocably damaged.

After paying and saying goodnight, I left Lucy at the bar, making my way into the cool night. As it inevitably did, my mind drifted toward Remi and Ghost while I walked back to the studio to retrieve my car and drove home.

Despite my denials to Lucy, I was lonely. It was true that Remi was really busy, but I wished she could carve out a little time for me. I was sure that once her big assignment was over, we'd be back on track. But Ghost, he was slipping away from me more each day.

Not that I'd ever really had him. I'd admired him from afar for so long, but now that I'd experienced just a small taste of what we could be like together, I couldn't stop obsessing about him. No amount of distance between us could quiet the longing in my heart or dim the memory of how complete I felt as he slept next to me and Remi.

The door clicked shut behind me as I stumbled into my house, my mind consumed with thoughts of Ghost. There was a good chance that Ghost was someone who'd never want me back. My heart felt heavy, and an unresolved ache stirred within me as I recalled the last time I spoke with him. I had basically laid everything on the line when I'd told him that I wanted more than a fling with him and Remi. But he'd been hostile. Scared. Running.

Tossing my keys onto the table, I stripped off my jacket and threw it on the back of a chair, loosening my tie with a sigh. The unsteady rhythm of my footsteps echoed through the empty space as I made my way to the kitchen, pouring myself a glass of water. My hand trembled slightly, causing the liquid to slosh against the sides of the glass.

I took a sip, feeling the cool water slide down my throat, doing little to wash away the lingering taste of whiskey from my earlier drinks. I couldn't sleep, not like this. Not while my mind was racing with what-ifs and should-haves. It was as if a fire had been ignited within me, fueled by the thought of Ghost and everything he represented. I needed to do something. Before he slipped away from me forever.

Liquid courage gave me the push I needed to grab my phone. I scrolled through my contacts until I found his name. My thumb hovered over the call button, hesitating before finally tapping it.

The line rang once, twice, and I squeezed my eyes shut, regretting the impulse that had led me to call him.

Then, "Greyson?" His voice was a rough rasp, seductive and sinful.

I swallowed hard, my throat suddenly dry. "Ghost. I didn't ... I wasn't expecting you to answer."

"Just got off stage," he replied, the background noise of his surroundings confirming his statement. "We're in Columbus, Ohio tonight. Awesome show."

"Is this a bad time?" I inquired, trying to sound casual despite the pounding of my heart.

"No, it's all good. It's good to hear from you."

"You too." I rubbed a hand over my face, trying to gather my scrambled thoughts. "How's the tour going?"

"Long. Lonely. Seems like it's dragging on forever this time." He sighed. "But the fans make it worth it."

A pang of something unidentifiable squeezed my chest. I wanted to reach through the phone and wrap my arms around him, chasing away the loneliness that had crept into his tone.

"I guess I'm a bit lonely, too. I've hardly seen Remi," I said before I could stop myself, my voice betraying a hint of vulnerability. "She's been busy with work."

He grunted wryly. "Well, she's not talking to me either, if that makes you feel any better."

"It doesn't, not really." I attempted to keep my voice steady as I leaned against the kitchen counter.

I heard some people calling out his name in the background. "You sound busy. I should let you go."

"I've got a few minutes." Then it sounded like he partially covered the phone. His voice came out muffled as he spoke to someone with him. "Babe, not right now. Give me a minute."

My heart sank. He was with a woman. Or maybe it was many women. How could I compete with that?

Yet, he had answered. Emboldened by the alcohol in my system, I screwed up the last bit of courage. "I'm throwing a party in a few weeks," I offered hesitantly, swallowing hard before continuing. "You know, just for some friends to catch up and unwind. You and the band are more than welcome to come if you want."

There was a weighted pause before he said, "Send me the details. I'll let you know."

I was squeezing the phone in a death grip. Only due to years of training did my voice come out smooth and natural instead of cracking with strain. "Will do. I hope to see you there."

"Good to hear from you." The line went dead.

Fucking Ghost. He'd been as elusive as ever. He hadn't said no, yet he hadn't said yes.

One thing I knew for sure was that if Ghost came to my party, I would make sure that we had a night to remember.

Chapter 27

Ghost

STRUMMING MY GUITAR ABSENTMINDEDLY, I tried to lose myself in the music, letting the chords echo through the tour bus. Knox and Ryder lounged on the couch across from me, their attention glued to the screen above my head as they played their video game. Their laughter and playful banter filled the air, a stark contrast to the heaviness weighing down on me.

There were still three more weeks of tour left, but a feeling of restless energy had been building up inside me since the beginning of this tour. It was different this time; usually, I loved being on the road, but now it seemed like every day dragged on for an eternity. As if sensing my uneasiness, Knox paused the game and glanced over at me, concern etched on his face.

"You look like you have the weight of the world on your shoulders. Are you doing alright?" he asked, nudging Ryder to get his attention.

Ryder looked up, his eyes full of worry as well.

They both knew that I'd had a video session with Maggie this morning. While I'd confided in Knox about my past, I hadn't told the other guys, but I was thinking about it. So far, Maggie, Knox, and Remi knew and none of them had reacted with revulsion. I actually felt like I was making progress; the more I opened up, the more I seemed to move ahead.

Maggie and I were meeting often. Processing my past and working through her steps was helping me heal what I thought was impossible. Even our talks about my promiscuity must have made an impact on me because I hadn't had sex with anyone for weeks now. It just felt so lurid and cheap now that I wasn't as numb to the world and my own feelings. I was ditching the pills and allowing my emotions to come through without becoming too overwhelmed by them all. Maggie was holding my hand and cheering me on through the whole process and she'd assured me I was making major progress.

At times, though, I felt stripped bare and exposed to the core. Vulnerable and scared. Sometimes I wanted to go back to the comfortable numbness.

Ryder cleared his throat. I must have been taking too long to answer.

I looked up and forced a smile. "Yeah, I'm good. Just antsy to finish this tour."

Ryder sighed, running a hand through his hair. "I feel you. I miss Talia and the baby so much," he admitted, his voice cracking slightly with emotion.

Knox nodded in agreement. "It's tough being separated from the people you love. I can't wait to see Summer again."

We sat there silently, our collective longing for home and loved ones hanging heavy in the air. A few minutes later, Knox and Ryder resumed their game while I stared out the window, watching as the scenery blurred together.

My thoughts were consumed by Remi and Greyson. According to Greyson, Remi was buried under mountains of work at Hollywood Exposé. Despite our schedules, Remi and I had managed to connect a few times on the phone, but we made mostly small talk. I missed having her by my side. When the tour was over, I planned on making her mine.

Greyson called me every couple of days, usually when I'd just finished performing and was pumped up with adrenaline. I'd started to expect his calls and even to look forward to them. I'd tell him about our show — how we had to improvise when Knox had gotten a hand cramp mid-show, how I'd messed up the lyrics to one of our popular songs, and how Bash had lost a drumstick after a stick trick gone wrong.

Grey would tell me about his taping for *Devious* and all the on-set antics. It was weird hearing spoilers that wouldn't air for another couple of months. How the hell would Colton end up scheming with Kathryn to take down Nico?

I still hadn't admitted that I'd watched every episode. Hell, I'd been rewatching old seasons just to see Greyson. Even with the distance between us, I could feel the magnetic pull of his presence in my life, drawing me into a whirlpool of emotions I couldn't quite comprehend. It was something that I'd only just begun to broach with Maggie.

My phone buzzed in my pocket, startling me out of my reverie. Checking the screen, I saw a text from Sidney. Glancing up at Ryder and Knox, I furrowed my brow as I read the message aloud. "Sidney says they've pulled off into a rest area. Their driver told them the tour manager asked them to stop there."

"Really?" Knox raised an eyebrow, his fingers pausing on the video game controller. "That's odd."

"Maybe one of the buses is having mechanical problems," Ryder suggested, worry creeping into his voice.

Pursing my lips, I dialed our driver, waiting for him to pick up. "Hey, Bill, are we stopping at the rest area too?"

"Yup," he confirmed. "Got a message from Darren. We'll be there in a few minutes."

"Alright, thanks." Ending the call, I looked back at my bandmates, unease settling in my chest like an anchor. "We're stopping there too. It's strange, but maybe it's nothing."

"Let's hope so," Ryder muttered, exchanging a worried glance with Knox.

As our bus pulled into the rest area, I noticed the tension in the air, thick and palpable. Something was undeniably off, and I couldn't shake the feeling that this detour was only the beginning of something much darker.

I took a deep breath and checked my negative thoughts, as Maggie would tell me to do.

"Ghost? What do you think is going on?" Ryder asked, his eyes searching mine for any indication of what I might be thinking.

"I don't know, man." I sighed, running a hand through my hair in frustration. "But whatever it is, we'll face it together."

My heart thumped as the bus slowed to a stop, gravel crunching under the tires. Something was wrong.

Sidney and Bash entered the bus with a burst of nervous energy, their faces a mixture of curiosity and concern. Sidney, usually calm and collected, raked his fingers through his disheveled hair before slumping down onto the couch next to me.

Glancing down at my phone, I read the text I'd just received from our tour manager, Darren. "Band meeting in twenty minutes. Wait for us there." I frowned, feeling a knot forming in the pit of my stomach. Something wasn't right.

"Guys," I began, rubbing the back of my neck anxiously. "We've got a band meeting as soon as the tour manager's bus catches up."

Bash leaned against the kitchen counter, crossing his arms. "Wonder what's going on," he mused, furrowing his brow.

"Maybe it's about the next leg of the tour? They're extending the tour?" Ryder suggested, trying to lighten the mood with a grin.

Knox shook his head, his expression serious. "I doubt that," he said. "They've never pulled over our buses to tell us they were extending the tour. It must be something big if they're calling a meeting like this."

"Something must have happened," Sidney murmured, his voice low and tense.

Bash, ever the optimist, tried to lighten the mood. "Maybe we're getting a surprise bonus for selling out all those shows?" He grinned, but his smile didn't quite reach his eyes.

"Any ideas, Ghost?" Ryder asked, turning his gaze towards me.

"No clue, but something feels off," I admitted, my gut churning with anxiety. "I can't put my finger on it, but it's making me uneasy."

The five of us exchanged uneasy glances, each likely running through the possibilities in our minds. A big cancellation. An accident. Some scandal unearthed from our sordid pasts.

My phone buzzed with another text from Darren. Five minutes out. Get everyone on the same page. Be ready to strategize.

Strategize. Fuck. That single word sent a shard of ice sliding down my spine. Whatever was coming, it was going to be bad.

Bash scrubbed a hand over his face. "I don't know about you lot, but I could use a drink. Anyone else?"

"Yeah, I'll take one." I massaged the tension in my neck, my stomach knotting. "Might as well get comfortable. We're gonna be here for a while."

The rest of the guys nodded, a heavy silence filling the bus as Bash poured whiskeys all around. We each claimed a seat, staring into the amber depths of our glasses and waited.

Ryder's phone buzzed in his hand, breaking the tense silence in the room. He glanced at the screen and frowned before answering. "Talia?" he asked, concern lacing his voice.

His brow furrowed as he listened to her, his hand gripping the phone so tightly that his knuckles turned white. "Oh fuck," he muttered under his breath, his voice taut with worry.

"Hey, hey, calm down," Ryder tried to soothe her, gripping the phone tighter. "What's going on? Talk to me."

As he listened to her frantic words, his face turned pale, and he muttered a string of curses. "Oh, fuck ... You're kidding, right?"

Whatever Talia said in response wasn't good. Ryder's eyes widened, and he swore under his breath. "Shit. How did this even happen?" He listened for a moment, cursing again. "Okay, just stay inside the house with Zoe. I'll have someone out there as soon as I can."

"Ryder, what is it?" I demanded, my patience wearing thin as my anxiety threatened to consume me.

"Remi," he replied tersely, pinching the bridge of his nose. "Hollywood Exposé."

I sat forward, dread pooling in my gut. Remi. Fuck. And if it was about to break on Hollywood Exposé, there was no containing it now.

My stomach dropped as I realized the implications of his words. Remi's story on the band wasn't supposed to be published yet, but something had clearly changed. Something that had left Talia — and now all of us — on edge. Something that had stirred up a shitstorm.

"Okay, Angel, just take a deep breath," Ryder said into the phone, his voice wavering as he tried to calm Talia down. "We'll figure this out, I promise. I'm going to get someone from Vector out to you now. Don't worry about the rest."

Ryder ended the call, his face pale. "That was Talia. Remi's story is hitting the internet as we speak. And it's bad."

"How bad?" Knox asked, voicing the question on all our minds.

He hesitated for a moment, his expression pained as he relayed what little information he had gathered. "Apparently, reporters have been calling her nonstop about the article. It's chaos. Paparazzi are camped outside our house and won't leave them alone. They're being aggressive. I've got to get them some security."

"Fuck," Sidney spat, echoing my thoughts. "What's got them so worked up?"

"Something about me having a secret affair with Greyson Durant and my marriage to Talia being a sham. Apparently, there's sordid shit in the article about all of us." Ryder tossed his phone onto the table with a humorless laugh. "We're fucked."

I snatched my own phone from the table and quickly pulled up the internet. The rest of the band followed suit, each of us searching for whatever had caused Talia's distress.

"Shite!" Knox cursed, scrolling through his phone. "It's all over the internet!"

Sid groaned as he found the article, his expression a mixture of disbelief and anger. Bash just stared at his screen, his jaw clenched so tight I thought it might shatter.

I clicked on the article *Who's Haunting Ghost Parker?* with the byline Remi Sutton. The headline was accompanied by a photo of me and Ryder in our younger, more reckless days, looking strung out and surly.

I quickly scanned the words, feeling a cold fury building inside me.

"What the fuck?" How could she have done this to us? To me? I thought we had something special, something real. Was it all just a lie? A means to an end?

"Ghost, man," Ryder's voice was thick with sympathy as he looked at me, sensing the pain that coursed through me like a river of ice. "I'm so sorry."

"Did she play me this whole time?" I whispered, my voice raw with hurt and betrayal. "Just to get the story of a lifetime?"

"Let's not jump to conclusions," Sid said cautiously, placing a hand on my arm. "Maybe there's more to it than we think."

"Or maybe we're just fools for trusting her in the first place," Knox spat bitterly.

It felt like a dagger had been plunged into my heart, twisting mercilessly with each word I read. Remi, the woman I was falling in love with, had betrayed me — us — in the worst possible way. I couldn't shake the image of her smiling face, the warmth of her touch, the sound of her laughter. And now, all that remained was the cold reality of her deceit.

Chapter 28

What is Haunting Ghost Parker?

YOU'VE SEEN THEIR FACES everywhere: posters, T-shirts, the internet, and on stage. Ghost Parker is the latest one-hit wonder band that has stuck around longer than a pesky fly at a picnic, because let's face it, they're pretty to look at.

I spent weeks embedded on their concert tour trying to solve the mystery that has haunted them for years — who or what is the ghost in THAT photo? You know the one I'm talking about: the eerie negative of the five band members with a chilling and otherworldly presence lurking in the background. A fan spotted it, the internet went wild, and ever since, we've all been dying to know: who's haunting Ghost Parker?

As I wove through the twisted tales and haunted histories of these popular musicians, the truth became ever more elusive. Was it a vengeful spirit, a long-lost family member, a jilted lover, or simply a figment of our collective imagination? As the nights grew darker and the shadows lengthened, it became clear that there was more to this haunting than met the eye. One thing was for certain — Ghost Parker's eerie aura wasn't going anywhere, anytime soon.

So, as we delve into the mysterious world of Ghost Parker, remember that the truth is often stranger than fiction. Who knows what secrets lurk in the hearts of our favorite rock stars, or what scandalous tales are yet to be uncovered? In a world where ghosts linger in photographs and dark whispers echo through concert halls, anything is possible. And remember, dear readers, sometimes the most terrifying ghosts are the ones we create ourselves.

My time on tour with the band was a whirlwind of late nights, electric performances, and scandalous secrets. It felt like I was living in a real-life rock 'n' roll soap opera. And let me tell you, there's no shortage of potential ghostly suspects among the colorful cast of characters surrounding Ghost Parker.

As I traveled on tour with the band, I was privy to the whispers and legends that swirled around them like fog on a moonlit night. Everyone had their theories about the ghost, each more spine-tingling than the last. From tragic love stories to vengeful spirits, the tales of Ghost Parker's spectral companion grew wilder and more enthralling with each passing day. It seemed everyone had a stake in uncovering the truth behind the phantom in the photograph.

As we peel back the layers of Ghost Parker's haunted history, we delve into the realm of scandalous affairs and tragic losses. First off, there's Trudy, the band's PR rep, who is known for her fierce loyalty and iron grip over keeping the band's image squeaky clean. The woman, who is known for her ability to spin any story, appears to be hiding a secret of her own. Behind closed doors, Trudy has been cozying up with one of the band's bodyguards, a hulking Adonis with a penchant for tattoos. Unnamed sources say they've spotted the pair sharing more than just late-night strategy sessions (talk about mixing business with pleasure).

Then we have Johnny Parker, (ironically nicknamed Ghost) the enigmatic lead singer with a voice that can make angels weep, who experienced his own share of heartbreak. His stepbrother, a fellow musician with dreams of joining the band, tragically took his own life when he realized he wasn't quite talented enough to make the cut. Some whispered conversations among the crew even suggest that this tormented soul is now exacting his revenge on the band by haunting them from beyond the grave.

As the Ghost Parker tour bus rolled through the dusty back roads of America, I dug deeper, uncovering a veritable Pandora's box of potential ghostly suspects. Take, for instance, Ryder, the rhythm guitarist with a tragic family history. This rocker from Ohio had a cousin who always dreamt of joining the band but unfortunately succumbed to an opioid overdose. Could the restless spirit of this lost soul still be haunting the band, seeking the fame and fortune it was denied in life?

Meanwhile, Knox, the lead guitarist, has his own melancholy tale to tell, a love story that would make Shakespeare weep. Our dear Knox was engaged to a beautiful Scottish lass who tragically died in a car accident just days before their wedding. She too had dreams of traveling to America and living the rock star life alongside her betrothed. It's whispered among those close to the band that her restless spirit is causing trouble, perhaps furious over being left behind. Is she lingering among the living, unable or unwilling to accept her untimely demise? It's a chilling thought that even the most hardened roadie can't shake off.

While the Ghost Parker tour continued, a rollercoaster ride of thrilling performances and spine-chilling mysteries, I found even more secrets lurking in the shadows and more suspects emerged from the pasts of the band members themselves.

As for Sidney, the bassist with a troubled past, he grew up in the harsh world of foster care, where he endured years of abuse before finding solace in music. But his life took a turn for the better when he married Kaylie, the little sister of the band's drummer, Bash. Rumor has it that the three are inseparable — with whispers suggesting that Sidney, Bash, and Kaylie share a highly unconventional relationship — adding another layer of intrigue to the already mysterious group.

As the curtain of mystery surrounding Ghost Parker's spectral stalker continues to rise, our pile of ghostly suspects grows bigger. Bash himself is not without his own ghostly baggage. Father to a son named Kody, Bash brought the boy along on tour, exposing the child to the darker side of the rock and roll lifestyle. Kody's mother, according to an anonymous source within the road crew, is currently serving time in jail for dealing drugs. The source revealed that she dabbled in black magic. This revelation sent shivers down the spines of several crew members, who now wonder if she put a hex on the band out of spite from behind bars.

Meanwhile, Ryder, our tall, dark, and handsome guitarist with the chiseled jawline, must find it hard to leave his beautiful wife Talia and their newborn baby behind as he goes on tour. But, dear readers, it appears that he has found some solace in the arms of none other than Greyson Durant. Yes, THE Greyson Durant, famous for his portrayal of Colton Grimaldi on the long-running nighttime soap, *Devious*.

Greyson's sexual orientation is Hollywood's worst-kept secret — sorry, ladies, he's not interested in you. Old photos show him hanging out with the band, and recently he was spotted at their concert in Boston. The whispers of him being in a secret relationship with Ryder have only grown louder, casting a new light on Ryder's marriage to Talia. Could she be playing the role of a beard in this clandestine love triangle? Our sources claim that the trio once shared a shore house in

Huntington Beach — how very cozy indeed.

But wait, dear readers, there's more to this wild ride of Ghost Parker's escapades. While we've uncovered a plethora of haunting suspects and closely guarded secrets, it seems there's another specter lurking in the shadows — one that could bring the entire band to its knees.

As the members of Ghost Parker took to the stage one night in a packed stadium, their fans screamed and cried out for the band they adored. But as the opening chords of their hit song, *Okay Babe* echoed throughout the arena, one couldn't help but wonder if the real ghost haunting Ghost Parker was something much more mundane than spectral visitations: their lack of talent.

That's right; I'm putting it all on the table here. Their hit song, *Okay Babe*, serves as a perfect example. One might describe it as pure bubble gum pop served up to the masses — catchy, but with no originality or soul behind the music. The band's tunes may be infectious enough to keep fans coming back for more, but the band's music is as lifeless as the supposed ghost that haunts them.

As Ghost Parker continues to churn out assembly line hits, one can't help but wonder if they are merely puppets in the hands of a larger commercial machine. Are they simply selling their souls for fame and fortune while sacrificing their artistic integrity? It's a tale as old as time in the entertainment industry, and Ghost Parker appears to be just another cautionary story in the making.

So, as we delve into the murky waters surrounding the band's personal lives and supernatural encounters, let us not forget the most damning specter of them all: mediocrity. Is the eerie figure lurking in the shadows of their viral photograph a lost soul seeking revenge or redemption? Or is it simply a manifestation of the emptiness found within the band's superficial lyrics and uninspired melodies?

For in the end, no matter how many ghosts or scandals may haunt Ghost Parker, it is their lackluster music that will ultimately leave them to fade into obscurity.

And who knows, maybe somewhere along the line, they'll find a way to break free from the specter of mediocrity that haunts their every move and tap into the raw talent and passion that lies dormant beneath the surface of their glittering façade. Only time will tell.

And there you have it, folks — your latest dose of guilty pleasure from the world of Ghost Parker. As always, we'll be keeping our ears to the ground for any new developments in the lives of these troubled rockers. After all, who doesn't love a scandalous secret or two? Stay tuned!

Chapter 29

Ghost

My hands trembled as I scrolled through Remi's article, bile rising in my throat with every word. She'd betrayed our trust, twisted the truth, and even called into question our talent all at the same time.

I reread the story, this time slower, feeling the stab of betrayal with each new insult I uncovered. Remi had even managed to drag Trudy, the woman that had befriended her on the tour, into the dirt and imply that she was a slut. I read further and swallowed hard against the ache in my gut as I read about my stepbrother's suicide. Remi knew that Adam's death was a particularly painful part of my past, and yet she'd served it up to the masses as a mere tidbit of titillating gossip while suggesting that the band was somehow to blame for it.

"Fuck," Sidney growled, reading on his own phone while digging his hands through his hair in frustration.

Next, Remi hinted that the ghost could be Knox's fiancée, Aila, who'd died in a car accident just days before their wedding. I knew how damn hard Knox had struggled with grief, guilt, and shame. He'd come a long way, but the renewed scrutiny was bound to set him back. Remi so callously going after Knox, someone I considered a brother, hurt me even more than what she said about Adam, who could never be hurt by this world again.

Bash grunted. "Remi fucked us. She fucked us all. I've got to call my lawyer."

Bash must be reading the part that I was reading right now. Remi had exposed the abuse Sid had received when he was in foster care. And, oh fuck, I kept reading — she inferred that Bash, Sid, and Kaylie were in some kind of incestuous love triangle. Holy fuck!

Or maybe Bash was a faster reader than I was because what came next was just as bad. In reality, Bash didn't even know who Kody's mother was, but Remi stated that she was serving prison time for drug charges. Oh, and she was a voodoo witch on top of that.

"She even fucked over Greyson," Ryder added. "Fuck, it's as bad as Talia said it was."

I got to the part about Ryder and Greyson's secret relationship, which, of course, was a complete fabrication. With her breathless gossip, she'd essentially outed Greyson, a Hollywood megastar, as gay to the entire planet, even though she'd claimed to love him.

The cherry on top of this shit sundae — after manipulating the truth and outright lying to hurt everyone I cared about most in this world — she'd managed to shit all over our talent as a band. What. A. Fucking. Bitch.

Betrayal gutted me, sharp as a blade. I swallowed hard against the ache in my chest, struggling to breathe. How could she do this? I thought I'd finally found someone I could trust who'd understood the gnarled wreckage of my soul. But she'd only seen a story to exploit.

I hurled my phone across the room. It bounced against the wall, cracking the glass. "Fuck!" The curse tore from my lips as I gripped my hair, chest heaving. She didn't care about me. She never had. I was just a means to an end, a way for her to advance her damn career.

I stalked over to the counter and splashed whiskey into my glass, downing it in a single swallow. The liquid fire did nothing to dull the razor edges shredding my insides. I poured another drink with a shaking hand. I was a bomb on the verge of detonation.

"This is all bullshit. A bunch of lies. What are we going to do about it?" Bash asked, his voice tight with concern.

"Let's wait for Darren," Knox suggested. "They should be here any moment."

Bash was right, the article was mostly fabricated scandal, but the world would now view it as the unvarnished truth.

When the tour manager's bus finally pulled up, we all exchanged anxious glances. Darren and Trudy stepped onto the bus, their grim expressions confirming what I already knew. My stomach knotted as I braced myself for the fallout. I could sense the tension in the air as they glanced at each one of us, clearly aware that we'd already seen the damning article.

Scratching the back of his neck, Darren spoke first. "I can see you've all read the article," he said, his voice low and steady, trying to maintain some semblance of calm.

"She completely fucked us over, Darren," Ryder growled.

"Trudy will handle the PR side of things, but I've already talked to BVR. The label wants to milk this for all the publicity they can," Darren stated, holding up a hand to prevent any objections. "The tour will go on as planned, but we're boosting security at the venues. Reporters and fans are already swarming the next location."

I frowned. We were about to walk into a media shitstorm and then we were expected to perform as usual? Fuck.

Darren continued, "That's why we stopped — so the security team could get ahead of us and set up parameters for tonight's venue. Reporters and fans are already gathering there."

My chest tightened at the thought of facing that chaos. Bad enough I had to deal with the inner turmoil churning through me, but now my most private struggles were splashed across tabloid pages for the whole damn world to see.

The tension within me was palpable, like an invisible force choking the air around us. My fists clenched and unclenched by my side.

Trudy cleared her throat before addressing the band, her tone serious and business-like. "Vector Security has someone en route to Ryder's house in L.A." Her eyes flicked to Ryder briefly. "Paparazzi have gathered there too, but we're monitoring the situation closely. Unfortunately, it seems that Greyson is taking the brunt of this mess, but that is good for us."

"Fuck." The word escaped my lips before I could stop it. I clenched my fists, feeling the anger and worry churn inside me like a storm. The ramifications of Remi's betrayal were already spiraling out of control.

Trudy sighed, her gaze soft with sympathy. "I'm working on a response strategy to mitigate the fallout from the article. We've had a lawyer from BVR speak with Hollywood Exposé, threatening legal action."

"Is that going to work?" Knox asked, his brow furrowed with concern.

"Unfortunately, the wording of the article makes taking it to court unlikely," she admitted, her gaze steady despite the troubling news. "But I assure you, we will do everything in our power to get through this."

"I'll leave the buses stopped so the security team can get into place at the next venue," Darren said. "We'll get to the venue and then we act like it's business as usual. Except, we'll need to follow strict security protocols. I suggest you keep your after-show partying to a minimum. In fact, it might be better to remain low-key and come back to the buses right after the show."

"We've already canceled your media spots until we get a read on how this is going to play. For now, just stick to the plan," Trudy said. "Don't make any comments to the press. Go on with tonight's show like nothing's happened."

Easier said than done. I swallowed hard, fighting back the urge to punch something ... or someone. But she was right. I had a job to do, and giving the media a sign of weakness was the last thing I needed.

Ryder slammed his hand down on the table. "Shouldn't we release a statement that it's all bullshit? They're harassing my wife and daughter, and I can't even help them."

Trudy turned to him. "I know this is hard, Ryder. Vector will keep them safe. And, we have to be very measured with our response. We'll be speaking with Greyson's team shortly to coordinate. It'll be a lot better for everyone if we're all on the same page."

Knox held out his phone for us all to see. "Christ, look at this."

It was a video clip of Greyson getting mobbed by the press outside his studio. They were shouting out all sorts of crazy questions, including speculation about who he'd slept with. It was sickening.

My hands curled into fists as a wave of anger rose in my chest. Those leeches had no right to invade Grey's privacy like that or to put Talia and Zoe in their crosshairs. They didn't deserve to be dragged into this mess. None of us did.

But there was no escaping it now. The story was out, the damage done. All that was left was the fallout and the sinking realization that nothing in my life would ever be the same again.

"Right now, the best thing we can do is put on a killer show tonight," Darren replied, his eyes meeting mine. "We'll handle everything else. Just focus on giving the fans what they came for."

I knew he was looking to me to lead the band right now. "Alright," I agreed, forcing myself to sound more confident than I felt. "Let's give them a show they'll never forget."

Trudy's gaze softened with sympathy. "I know this is hard, but try to stay focused on the show. Your fans are counting on you."

It would be easier said than done. My fans were the last thing on my mind. But I couldn't lose myself in this chaos. I had to stay strong, stay in control. Letting the darkness win wasn't an option.

"Trudy and I need to get back to our bus. We have a lot of work to do." Darren eyed us. "Call if you need anything, but stay on the buses. When we get the all-clear from Vector, we'll be heading to the venue."

Trudy made her way to the door, pausing to glance over her shoulder before she stepped out. "You'll get through this. Just remember why you're here."

The door slid shut behind them, leaving us alone in a silence that echoed with the tangled mess of Remi's betrayal. I sank onto the leather couch and dropped my head in my hands. I couldn't help but let my thoughts wander to dark places, my past demons clawing at my insides.

After everything I'd survived, all the work I'd done to leave the past behind, I was right back where I started.

"Remi," I growled, fury lashing through my veins like fire. "Fucking Remi."

Disgust curdled in my gut. She'd played me, exploited my trust to further her own ambitions. I should have known better than to let her get close.

The weight of her betrayal anchored itself in the pit of my stomach, dragging me down into a dark chasm devoid of light. A torrent of emotions raged within me, threatening to tear me apart from the inside out. My mind raced as I stared at the phone Sid had handed back to me, with Remi's article plastered across the cracked screen, highlighted by the number of likes and shares that only seemed to multiply by the minute.

Tension rippled through my muscles as I clenched my fists, knuckles turning white with the force. My breaths came in shallow gasps, my lungs struggling to take in enough air as my chest tightened painfully. The world seemed to close in around me, suffocating me with the crushing realization that Remi had betrayed me in the worst possible way by using me to hurt my friends. The memory of her touch, her taste, was forever tainted by the bitter sting of her deceit.

"I've got to get back to my bus before Kaylie finds out about this. She's going to be upset." He put his hand on my shoulder. "If we all stick together, we're gonna be fine."

"I'll come back with you." Bash's voice was subdued compared to his usual playfulness. I could tell that he, too, was feeling the weight of the situation. "We've got this. Just tune out the noise and give a good show tonight."

"Yeah, mates. We're in this together," Knox reminded us, reaching out to squeeze my shoulder. "We'll come back here after the show to talk it out. We'll grab some booze and weed and chill. Just the five of us, like old times."

"What about hot chicks?" Bash asked.

Ryder flinched. "No chicks. Not tonight. Let's keep a low profile until we get this figured out."

I scrubbed a hand over my face, weariness seeping into my bones. At that moment, I didn't know how the hell I was going to face the crowd that night. How was I supposed to pour my heart out on stage when it was ripping me apart inside? But Trudy was right. My fans deserved better than that. They'd stood by me through good times and bad, and I wouldn't betray them now. Tonight, I'd give them what they came for. A performance they'd never forget.

I nodded to my bandmates, forcing a small smile despite the turmoil brewing inside me. We were a family, bound by the music that flowed through our veins and the love that held us together. No matter what Remi had done, no matter how much her betrayal stung, I knew I wasn't alone. We would face this storm together, as a band, as a family. And somehow, we would survive.

"Let's do this, guys," I said, my voice laced with renewed conviction. "Ride or die."

"Ride or die," they all repeated, full of grim determination.

Chapter 30

Remi

I SAT ACROSS FROM Jenny, the cat video queen, who animatedly described her process of creating thought bubbles for her feline star, Mr. Whiskers. The coffee shop hummed with the chatter of patrons and the grinding of espresso machines, but I remained focused on my interviewee.

"Timing is everything," Jenny insisted, brushing a lock of hair behind her ear. "You have to wait for that perfect moment when the cat's expression just matches the message you want to convey."

"Thank you so much for your insights, Jenny." I closed my notebook, signaling an end to the rather serious and in-depth interview I hadn't been expecting. I had more than enough material to work with. "I think our readers will really enjoy learning about your creative process."

Jenny beamed, gathering her belongings. "It was great talking to you, Remi. Can't wait to read the article!" With that, she left, her stylish bag swinging at her side.

While I was gathering my things into my leather satchel, my phone buzzed in my pocket again. I fished it out, only to find several missed calls and texts from Caroline, my boss.

A flicker of unease rolled through me as I tapped the call-back button, trying to prepare myself for whatever crisis had emerged.

"Remi! Where the hell have you been?" Caroline barked before I could get a word in. "The lawyers are already threatening to sue us, and the board is demanding your head on a platter!"

"Sorry, I was interviewing Jenny, the cat lady—" I started, but she cut me off.

"Jack Hoffman is furious with me." She spat out the words like venom. "How could you do this to me after the chance I took on you? I'll be lucky if I have a job at the end of the day."

"Caroline, slow down." I gripped the edge of the table, my knuckles turning white. "I have no idea what you're talking about. What did I do?"

"Your article on Ghost Parker has caused a giant clusterfuck of massive proportions. How could you publish it without consulting me? Lawyers from their record company are threatening to sue Hollywood Exposé!"

As Caroline's words washed over me, a cold dread settled in my chest. I hadn't shown that article to anyone yet, let alone published it. My mind raced, trying to make sense of the situation while she continued berating me.

"Caroline, I don't know what you're talking about. I haven't submitted anything on Ghost Parker," I insisted, my voice wavering.

"Are you serious?" She scoffed, her disbelief palpable. "It's already online! You were clearly trying to upstage Dawn and get some pre-buzz for your story package, but you should have come to me. You've put the entire company in jeopardy. Hoffman is furious that you tried to scoop Dawn like this."

Fear clawed its way up my throat, choking me as I struggled to comprehend the situation. My hands shook as I gripped the phone tighter, sensing the severity of the predicament I found myself in. "I swear, Caroline. I didn't publish anything about Ghost Parker."

Silence. Then a heavy sigh. "I don't know what kind of game you're playing, Remi, but it's not going to work." She seethed, her anger palpable through the phone line. "You have a history of going rogue and Hoffman knows this. You're a liability to us now. He wants your resignation on his desk by the end of the day. We'll be releasing a statement that Hollywood Exposé disavows the article and the statement will also say you no longer represent us. It will either say you resigned or you were fired. It's your choice."

The line went dead. I stared at my phone in numb shock, her last words echoing in my mind. They were going to fire me over an article I didn't even write. The coffee shop seemed to tilt and spin around me, Caroline's words fading into a dull roar. None of this made any sense.

My trembling fingers pulled up the browser on my phone, searching frantically for the article. As it appeared on the screen, I felt my world shatter around me. It was all there in black and white. "What is Haunting Ghost Parker?" the headline screamed at me, my name prominently displayed beneath it. A cold tendril of dread unfurled inside me. I hadn't written this. I hadn't submitted this.

My heart pounded in my chest as I began to read the words written as if by me, each sentence a stab of betrayal. While I read, my mind frantically tried to work out where this article came from. Of course, my first thought was Dawn, but how could she have gotten all this information?

A bitter taste filled my mouth as I read each line, a mixture of anger and despair threatening to consume me. Somehow, Dawn had twisted my research into a weapon that not only got me fired and would ultimately destroy my career, but she'd betrayed everyone I had grown close to — Ghost, each guy in the band, and even Greyson.

The suicide of Ghost's stepbrother, the death of Knox's fiancee, Ryder's cousin, and the history of Sid's foster care were all things I'd researched extensively. I'd researched Kody's mother but hadn't come up with anything. As far as I knew, the information in the article about her was pure fabrication, as were the rest of the prurient insinuations about the band.

The smears about Greyson gutted me even more than the others did. I had no idea why he'd been included in the hit piece, except maybe because I was dating him, but linking him to Ryder? It made no sense. There were a few pictures of Greyson and Ryder together embedded in the article, but there was no hint of scandal in any of those pictures.

The other photos that had been used in the article were all pictures that had been lifted from fan sites of Ghost Parker. I recognized them from my research on the band. They weren't particularly good photos; they were curated photos with the sole purpose of painting the band members as reckless, out-of-control, drunken, and drugged-up rock stars.

The article concluded by questioning the band's talent in a cruel fashion that I knew would crush some of the guys in the band. It was as if I'd betrayed their trust, stabbed them in the back repeatedly, and then kicked them in the head when they were already down. It was extra vicious.

I had no doubt that Dawn was behind the piece. My mind raced, trying to piece together how she could have obtained everything she needed to create the scandalous story. Somehow, she'd gotten access to my research notes and twisted the facts in cruel ways or outright fabricated malicious tabloid fodder. Nausea churned in my gut, knowing that the publication of this article was a turning point in my life — just not in the way I had originally hoped.

Tears welled up in my eyes as I realized just how much damage had been done. The article was already exploding all over the internet with most of the comments being about Greyson and his sexuality. Oh my God! There was no way Greyson would believe I'd done this to him. Was there?

My heart raced as panic surged through me, my breaths coming in short gasps. I glanced around the coffee shop, suddenly feeling exposed and vulnerable.

Damn you, Dawn. A seething rage boiled just beneath the surface of my anguish. She was the only one who could have done this — orchestrated my downfall with calculating precision.

As I left the coffee shop, my thoughts scrambled, trying to formulate plans for damage control — desperate attempts to salvage my career and relationships from the ashes of betrayal. But deep down, I knew that nothing would ever be the same again.

I had no idea how I'd prove that Dawn was behind this, but I couldn't even think about that right now. First, I had to contact Greyson and Ghost and make sure they both realized that I hadn't done this to them.

♫♫♪♪♪

Neither Greyson nor Ghost answered any of my numerous calls. I couldn't blame them. According to clips I'd seen on the internet, they were dealing with a lot of fallout from the damn article.

I'd retreated to my apartment, furiously making phone calls while monitoring the fallout. First, I'd contacted a termination lawyer who'd advised me to craft a resignation letter that denied authorship of the article.

As I was typing up my resignation, I received a bevy of e-mails from Hollywood Exposé. Human Resources requested that I turn in my company badge and laptop by tomorrow morning. At that time, I would be given a few minutes to pack up my desk of all my personal property.

The email from HR was followed by multiple emails from company lawyers reminding me of the confidentiality agreements in place, the intellectual property on my laptop and any research conducted during my employment as belonging to Hollywood Exposé. Another email reviewed my employment contract and highlighted my legal indemnity clause.

Worried about my legal liability, I called the lawyer who had originally reviewed my contract. Luckily, he'd pushed back on Hollywood Exposé's standard clause and got a mutual indemnification clause agreed to. Still, my lawyer explained to me, if I got sued over this article and lost, I was financially screwed.

If any party named in the article proved defamation and could prove harm such as pain and suffering, damage to reputation, lost wages, or even personal harm such as shame, humiliation, or anxiety, I'd be found liable.

The lawyer explained if Ghost Parker canceled the rest of their tour, that was considered lost wages. If Greyson's studio had to delay taping because of paparazzi, that was lost wages. And anyone would reasonably conclude that these types of false allegations resulted in reputational and personal harm.

God, it was a nightmare. I'd likely have to go up against Hollywood Exposé. My lawyer was preparing a letter demanding they publicly correct the false attribution of my name to the article, but they were heavy guns and I had no way of proving I didn't author the piece. In the meantime, I was advised to publicly disavow authorship of the article on my personal social media accounts as I'd been locked out of access to Hollywood Exposé.

The lawyer told me my best hope was that the entire thing blew over quickly, but from what I could see, it was doing the exact opposite. It was blowing up like crazy. Ghost Parker and Greyson were getting a lot of blowback. Items from the article were being repeated and spread everywhere.

Even if they believed me that I didn't write that malicious article, the legal clusterfuck didn't end there, because suing me might not be in their hands anymore. Their businesses were being harmed. Greyson's studio or the band's record label could start a lawsuit.

My mind was spinning. With everything moving so fast, I had little time to prove my innocence in all this. I needed to find out how Dawn accessed my research. My co-worker, Linda, turned out to be no help. She hung up on me after informing me that she couldn't afford to associate herself with a disgraced employee. Proving my innocence when I had no access to work any longer seemed impossible.

It was past dinner time when I finally finished with all the urgent matters my lawyer had advised me to do. I hadn't eaten all day, but my stomach was too tangled to even think about food.

I still needed to explain the situation to all the people it'd affected. Ghost Parker was performing in Alabama tonight. With the time difference, Ghost should be done with the show by now.

My heart pounded as I dialed Ghost's number, my fingers trembling over the keys. What would I say to him? How could I possibly make this right?

The phone rang once, twice, and with each unanswered ring, my anxiety spiked. Finally, it went to his voicemail. I hung up. I'd already left him two messages and several texts.

Greyson was definitely done taping for the day by now. He hadn't called or texted me back either after I left him messages, but I didn't blame him.

I took a deep breath and dialed his number, my heart aching with the weight of everything that had happened. The phone rang only once before he answered, his voice strained and tight. "What do you want, Remi?"

I swallowed past the lump in my throat. "Greyson, I'm so sorry. I didn't write that story. I would never hurt you like that." I insisted, clutching the phone tighter.

"You have no idea what kind of train wreck you've caused." His tone sliced through me like a knife, sharp and unforgiving. "Everything is in shambles because of you. Everyone is breathing down my neck — the media, the paparazzi, even reporters harassing my parents at their house!" Greyson continued, his voice reaching a crescendo. "My agent and the people at *Devious* are in talks, and with my contract up for negotiation soon, this could be the final nail in the coffin for me on the show. And it's not just me, Remi! My coworkers are upset too, since the studio is now surrounded by a swarm of media vultures. And for what? So you could get your big break?"

"Greyson, I swear it wasn't me." My voice cracked, tears welling up in my eyes. "It must have been Dawn. She did it somehow."

I could feel the weight of his disbelief pressing down on me. His words were like a slap to the face, cutting deep. "Only you had that information, Remi. How could Dawn possibly know any of it?"

"Maybe she hacked my computer. Maybe Linda helped her get my password," I suggested, desperate for him to believe me. "I got fired from Hollywood Exposé because of this, Greyson."

"That's your own damn fault," he said coldly. "I told you not to let your ambition get in the way of doing the right thing. You hurt so many people with that story, including Ghost."

The image of Ghost, his haunted eyes reflecting the torment within, seared into my mind. My heart twisted at the thought of causing him pain, and the unfairness of it all threatened to consume me.

It had all spiraled so far out of control, and at the center of it all was my own ambition. But I hadn't written that story — someone else had twisted my words, my work, and used it against me.

I bit my lip, struggling to find the right words. "Greyson, please," I begged, my voice barely above a whisper. "I'll prove I didn't write the story. I still have the draft I was working on, and it's nothing like what was printed."

"Everyone is suffering because of you, Remi." As he spoke, I could hear the strain in his voice and the barely concealed fury. "Rampant speculation about my past male lovers is everywhere. And to throw Talia and Ryder into the mix — Talia's trapped in her house with her baby, with the vultures circling, waiting to pick them apart. Why would you do this to us?"

"Greyson, I didn't—" I started, but he cut me off.

"Save it, Remi," he snapped, his voice cold as ice. "I don't know what you were thinking, but you've caused enough damage already."

I felt my heart break at the sound of Greyson's anger and hurt. Even if I hadn't written the story, I knew that my actions had played a part in this disaster. And now, not only was my own life falling apart, but I'd dragged the people I cared about down with me. I closed my eyes, wishing I could reach through the phone and comfort him somehow.

"I never meant for any of this to happen," I said softly, gripping the phone as if it were my lifeline. "You have to believe me. I would never do something to intentionally hurt you. I love you!"

"Well, you did." His voice cracked, and for a moment, I thought I detected a hint of anguish behind the anger. "You broke my heart, Remi. I trusted you, and you betrayed me."

The word 'betrayed' hung in the air, heavy and suffocating, making it hard to breathe. A sob escaped my lips as I struggled to find the right words. But there were no right words. No way to undo the harm that had already been done.

My mind raced with all the things I wanted to say — apologies, explanations, excuses — anything that would make him understand that I never meant for any of this to happen. "Greyson, please..." I whispered.

"Enough, Remi!" His sudden outburst startled me, and I could imagine the fiery anger flashing in his eyes. "You have no idea how much damage has been done! I'm too busy trying to pick up the pieces of my life right now ... I can't keep doing this with you."

The line went silent. When Greyson spoke again, his voice was flat and unyielding. "Don't contact me again, Remi. We're through."

Tears began to stream down my face as images of our steamy encounters flashed through my mind — the way his muscular arms held me close, his passionate kisses setting my body aflame. I couldn't believe that the man I'd grown so close to was now so distant, unreachable behind a wall of hurt and betrayal.

"Alright," I managed to say, my voice trembling as I struggled to maintain my composure. "If that's what you want, Greyson. I'll leave you alone for now. But I won't give up on trying to clear my name, and ... and I'm not giving up on us."

I could hear the conflict in his breathing, the hesitation wavering between forgiveness and self-preservation. "Goodbye, Remi," he finally said, his voice barely above a whisper.

The line went dead, leaving me with nothing but the sound of my own ragged breaths and the knowledge that I had destroyed everything around me.

"Goodbye," I murmured to the empty room, the silence echoing around me. I sank to the floor, my entire body trembling with grief and fear.

Greyson's face swam before my eyes, his parting words echoing in my mind. He didn't believe me. He thought I had betrayed him, betrayed his trust, and broken his heart. The thought was unbearable. He thought I'd betrayed him all for the sake of a byline.

And now I had lost him forever.

I let myself cry for a few moments, allowing the torrent of emotions to wash over me before taking a deep, shaky breath. I couldn't afford to wallow in despair; there was work to be done, and I knew that every moment wasted brought me further away from the truth — and from any chance of salvaging what was left of my relationship with Greyson.

Chapter 31

Greyson

THE MERCILESS GLARE OF camera flashes assaulted my eyes as I pushed through the throng of paparazzi outside my house. I'd retreated to my beach house for the weekend, trying to escape the horde, but they'd caught on pretty quickly.

Their voices rose in a cacophony, each question more invasive than the last.

"Greyson, are you dating Ryder from Ghost Parker?" one reporter shouted, shoving a microphone toward me. I gritted my teeth and clenched my jaw, attempting to ignore their relentless questioning.

"Is Talia just a beard for you and Ryder?" another voice chimed in. The weight of their assumptions bore down on me, heavy and suffocating.

I wanted to go check to see how Talia was doing, but I couldn't even visit my friend without setting off a firestorm of fresh speculation. It was all so maddening.

"Are you gay, Greyson? Why have you been hiding it?" My heart thundered in my chest, but I refused to give them the satisfaction of a response. I could feel the sweat pooling at the base of my neck, the heat of shame and anger mingling with fear.

"Are you ashamed of who you are?" The words cut deep, stirring up years of confusion and self-doubt. I forced myself to keep moving forward, each step feeling like wading through molasses.

"Go fuck yourself!" I growled, my voice cracking under the strain. With a surge of adrenaline, I shoved past the final barricade of photographers.

My hands shook with fury as I fumbled with my keys, desperately seeking solace in my home. Once inside, I slammed the door behind me and drew in ragged breaths, trying to calm the storm raging within me.

The stress of the last week was catching up with me. Remi's betrayal had unleashed a media frenzy — my sexuality dissected and scrutinized for all the world to see. New articles were citing "anonymous sources" claiming I'd had affairs with various celebrities over the years. Each accusation felt like another knife in the back, twisting to cause maximum damage.

Men I didn't even know were coming out of the woodwork to grab their fifteen minutes of fame. All they had to do was claim we'd had a torrid love affair, and the media ate it up.

"Greyson Durant's secret love life revealed" — the headlines were relentless, their words sinking their teeth into my flesh like vultures feasting on carrion. I didn't actually mind my sexuality being outed — it was the way it had all unfolded — the knife in my back twisted by someone I loved — that left me reeling. The extreme scrutiny of my life was suffocating, but what hurt me the most was the realization that despite our love for each other, Remi chose her career over me, knowing full well the damage she would cause.

I slammed my hand against the wall, the pain momentarily grounding me in reality. The chaos outside my door was stifling, and I needed some semblance of control. Desperate to shield my parents from the relentless prying of reporters, I booked them on a vacation in the Caribbean. Their grateful smiles had done little to ease the bitterness in my heart. They were just another of Remi's victims.

Instead of welcoming all this publicity, *Devious* had been ruffled. My agent wasn't certain *Devious* would renew my contract for the new season. In light of the media stories, *Devious* had asked me to do some LGBTQ+ advocacy and got angry when I declined. My personal life was not theirs to dictate.

My usually unflappable agent had pushed back when the show had suggested that my sexuality had tarnished the image of my character, Colton, and had warned that the fan backlash from killing him off would be a far greater firestorm.

Devious had made me a big star, and I was confident I'd get work if I was dropped, but the show had been my life for the last 12 years and the cast and crew were like family.

I made my way into the kitchen and sat down on the island stool. Remi's betrayal had sunk deep, leaving me feeling shaken and lonely. Wrecked.

I dialed Ghost's number for the umpteenth time, my heart pounding with a mix of anxiety and hope. Frustration twisted my insides as I listened to the ringing tone, only to be met once again by his voicemail. "Hey, it's Ghost. Leave a message,"— the words sounding almost mocking.

"Ghost," I sighed, pressing my fingers against my temple, "it's Greyson. I ... wanted to talk to you about everything that's happened.

HOW TO CATCH A ROCKSTAR

Please, call me back." With a heavy exhale, I ended the call and tossed the phone onto the counter, feeling the weight of rejection settle on my shoulders.

Ghost hadn't returned any of my calls. I thought maybe he blamed me for this mess because I was close to Remi. But deep down, I knew the truth — he was afraid. Afraid of being dragged into the spotlight, of having his life picked apart any further by vultures hungry for gossip.

I couldn't really blame him. If our positions were reversed, I might do the same. Still, his silence stung.

I couldn't shake the memory of Ghost's lips on mine, the intensity of his touch that set my entire being alight. My attraction to him was overwhelming, yet so was my love for Remi. My feelings for both of them hadn't disappeared overnight because Remi had betrayed me, which just made everything so much more painful.

I needed to clear my head. Grabbing a beer, I stepped onto the deck, hoping the sound of the ocean waves in the distance would offer an escape from the chaos surrounding me.

I gripped my beer bottle tightly, the cold glass numbing my fingers, as I stared out at the churning gray waves and felt the ocean breeze on my face.

As I took a swig, my phone rang, pulling me back into reality. Glancing at the screen, I saw Jonas Steel's name flash before my eyes. A mix of anticipation and dread filled me as I answered, memories of our passionate encounters lingering in the recesses of my mind.

"Grey, I've seen the latest media coverage about you. How are you holding up?" His cultured tones were smooth as silk, as hypnotic as ever.

"As well as can be expected." I kept my own voice neutral, not about to give him the satisfaction of knowing how much Remi's betrayal had gutted me.

He clucked his tongue as if in faint disapproval. "I'm so sorry you're going through this. I'm sorry your supposed girlfriend ... that reporter ... stabbed you in the back."

He continued, his tone bordering on condescending, "Trusting her was ... naïve."

"Thanks for the reminder," I snapped, bitterness creeping into my voice.

A beat of silence. When he spoke again, his tone had sharpened. "You should have known better than to trust her. She's an ambitious little snake, just like the rest of us."

Anger burned hot in my chest, scorching away the hurt, but I wasn't going to give him the satisfaction of a reply.

"Look," he continued, a hint of urgency in his voice, "I need to ask you a favor. I don't want our past ... relationship to come out. You know how this industry can be. There's a lot at stake for both of us, and I'd rather not be dragged into this mess."

The weight of his words settled like lead in my chest. "Alright."

"We can't afford to be linked together right now. Keep your distance, Grey," he finished, his voice softening slightly. "Please."

"Fine," I gritted out, clenching my fist around the phone. "I'll keep my distance."

"Thank you, Greyson," Jonas said, relief evident in his voice. "Take care of yourself." The line went dead, leaving me with a bitter taste in my mouth.

Breathing hard, I leaned against the railing of my deck and stared out at the waves crashing against the shore in the distance. The salty breeze teased my face, but it did little to quell the storm raging inside me. Jonas was right about one thing — I should have known better. But Remi wasn't the only snake in the grass. There were far too many people willing to use me for their own gain.

As I stood there, lost in the incredible hurt Remi had inflicted on me, and the ache of losing my true love, I caught a glint of light from the beach below. My eyes narrowed, focusing on the paparazzi with long-range camera lenses and those cone-like devices designed to eavesdrop on conversations from far away. They were pointed up at my deck, hoping to catch every word, every emotion.

My blood boiled. Their prying eyes and intrusive lenses were violating my privacy once more. This house, which had become my refuge from the madness of Hollywood, no longer felt like a sanctuary.

Gripping the railing, I fought to control the surge of anger coursing through me. I stormed back into the house, slamming the door behind me. These vultures had no right to invade my life like this, to feast on my heartache for their own gain.

Was there no end to this nightmare? I sunk into an armchair, feeling more alone than ever before. The walls of my safe haven now seemed to close in around me, smothering me beneath the weight of betrayal and loss.

So much had changed in the last week. My life felt torn to shreds, my privacy obliterated, all because of Remi's betrayal.

I took a long swig of beer, the bitterness coating my tongue. I shouldn't have trusted her. I should have known her ambition would trump everything else.

Including me.

Everyone wanted a piece of me, but no one gave a damn about the man behind the facade.

As the shadows lengthened across the room, I found myself lost in the depths of despair. I was left alone to face the darkness within, betrayed by the ones I loved and abandoned by those who claimed to care.

I thought of the paparazzi surrounding my house, the men emerging from my past to claim their fifteen minutes of fame. But beneath the anger and betrayal simmered a newfound freedom. A chance to take control of my destiny once and for all. Despite it all, a small spark of defiance still flickered within me.

Let them speculate all they wanted. I was done playing their games.

Done with the lies and betrayals. Done with giving my heart to people who only wanted to break it.

No more deceit or manipulations. No more facades or masks. I was going to live my truth and damn the consequences.

I told myself that Remi hadn't shattered my heart into a million pieces.

But it was a lie. And I was tired of lying to myself.

I would survive this storm, and when the waves finally receded, I would come out stronger in the end.

Chapter 32

Ghost

THE POUNDING BASS AND flashing lights of the club thrummed through my body. A mass of sweaty bodies gyrated on the dance floor, lost in the pulsing rhythm of the music. My bandmates were scattered around the VIP section, shots in hand as they laughed and joked, repelling the never-ending advances of handsy women.

I hung back in the shadows, nursing a glass of bourbon. The ache in my chest had nothing to do with the alcohol. Remi's betrayal still gnawed at me, ripping into my heart like a savage beast. I thought I'd finally found someone who could see beyond the rock star facade, who genuinely cared for me and could see the real man beneath. But she'd only seen a story. A way to advance her career.

Despite the energy surrounding me, I felt somewhat disconnected, a quiet observer amidst the chaos. Maggie had been working hard with me in therapy, trying to keep me from sliding back into emotional detachment, but there was no doubt I was retreating. All of my hard work, clawing my way out of an emotional black hole, had been shattered by Remi.

She'd really done a number on me. The first time I let anyone into my life and my heart got trampled on. What a fool I was.

Knox sidled up next to me, concern etching lines on his forehead. "You gonna join the party anytime soon?" He followed my gaze to where Bash had some blonde on his lap, her hands roaming freely over his body. "Or are you just gonna keep brooding in the corner all night?"

I shrugged, the movement tense. "Not really in the mood. I'm going to head to the hotel early."

Knox sighed, dropping a heavy hand on my shoulder. "Can't say I blame you. But you can't keep punishing yourself like this. Remi's the one who fucked us all, not you. And we're all surviving this. We'll be okay."

"Doesn't change the fact that I let her in," I said, jaw clenched. "I should've known better."

"How? By being a normal human being for once and actually caring about someone?" Knox shook his head. "Don't do that to yourself. You deserve to be happy, and someday you're gonna find someone who actually gives a damn about you for you, not for who you are on stage."

I stared at the amber liquid in my glass, a maelstrom of emotions churning inside me. Maybe Knox was right, and Remi's betrayal said more about her than me. But after being burned so badly, a part of me wondered if I'd ever take that risk again. If I'd ever be able to open myself up enough to find that connection Knox spoke of, or if I was doomed to remain alone in the shadows.

"I'll grab us some new drinks. " Knox grinned, clapping a hand on my shoulder before leaving to hunt down our server.

I downed the last of my drink, deciding to make an early exit before Knox returned to stop me. I'd put in enough of an appearance and Knox would understand. He knew that I never enjoyed partying after a show as much as performing on stage. It always felt like a letdown after such an incredible high.

Bishop was by my side in an instant after I signaled, ready to escort me to the hotel. He led me out of a back exit of the club to a private parking area. The black SUV was already pulled up to the curb and waiting for us. I slipped into the backseat and waited for Bishop to get into the driver's seat.

Instead, he opened the back door and poked his head inside. "Talia's out here. She wants to talk to you."

Talia? I groaned. I had almost made my escape. "Sure. Tell her to hop in the car. I'll only be a few minutes."

Talia, Ryder's wife, slid into the backseat next to me and closed the door. "I saw you sneaking out, Johnny Geronimo."

My lips twitched at the corners, despite the heaviness in my chest. I think she was the only person that knew my middle name. "My powers must be fading, Natalia Rose."

"I'm only staying for a few days, so I wanted to make sure I got a chance to talk to you." Her luminous eyes were filled with concern.

"How's Zoe doing?" I asked, trying to keep the conversation light.

"She's awesome." She smiled warmly as she thought of her daughter. "I asked my parents to watch her for a couple of days, so I could come to support Ryder. I thought it was important to be here with him."

"I'm sorry for all the trouble Ryder and you are going through because of the damn article." Their lives had become collateral damage in this whole mess.

Talia waved a hand, dismissing my apology. "Don't worry about us. As long as Ryder and I have each other, we'll be fine. How are you holding up?"

I sighed, running a hand through my messy hair. "I've been better, but thanks for asking."

She paused, studying my face with concern. "We're all worried about you, Ghost. I know Remi hurt you, but we're here for you." Her hand settled over mine, squeezing gently. "If there's anything Ryder or I can do, you know you only have to ask."

I nodded, my throat tightening at her kindness. "Thank you. That means a lot." When I finally met her gaze, the understanding and compassion in her eyes nearly undid me. I cleared my throat roughly before I continued. "I've been thinking about my stepbrother a lot. I miss him. Sometimes I feel so lonely. But it's nice to know that my friends care about me."

"You're not alone, Ghost." Talia brushed a strand of blonde hair behind her ear. "It must be hard for you — having his suicide out in the open like that."

My stomach twisted at the reminder, old guilt and sorrow welling up anew. I looked away, jaw clenching. Some wounds never fully healed, even after all these years. "It's not something I ever wanted to be public knowledge. It's a painful part of my past, not tabloid gossip. But we're all dealing with our own hellish versions of that, thanks to Remi."

Talia studied me, concern etched into her delicate features. "I'm glad the five of you have each other to lean on. You'll pull through this. Greyson's reeling from the aftermath too, you know. And he's all alone."

"Greyson?" The mention of Greyson's name sent a spike of warmth through the icy numbness inside me, immediately followed by a stab of guilt. He'd reached out to me repeatedly since Remi's article came out, and I'd ignored each call and text. Not because I blamed him for Remi's actions — I knew he'd been just as blindsided as me — but because the mere thought of talking to him made the ache of loss and betrayal flare to life once more.

"He's been really hurt by everything that happened as well," Talia said, her voice gentle but insistent. "You know he's one of my best friends, right? I've spoken to him on the phone, but I can't even visit him without feeding the flames of the rumor mill. He's going through a lot right now, more than any of us can imagine."

I hesitated, guilt creeping in. Greyson was dealing with even more fallout than I was, and yet I'd been avoiding his calls. "Greyson's called me, but I haven't answered," I confessed.

"Maybe you two should talk," she suggested gently. "It might help both of you to heal. Remi betrayed him, too. He could use a friend who understands right now."

"Maybe," I mumbled, my mind racing with the thought of reconnecting with Greyson.

"He's a good person. I know it's hard to trust people right now, but you can trust him," Talia insisted, her eyes locking onto mine with intensity. "He's been really shaken up by this whole thing." She hesitated for a moment, biting her lip before adding, "I know he really ... respects you, Ghost. Talk to him."

I looked into Talia's eyes and saw the sincerity there, urging me to take that leap.

"Thanks, Talia. I'll think about it," I murmured into her hair as she hugged me tightly before climbing out of the car.

I thought about Greyson during the car ride to the hotel, mostly remembering our night together with Remi. When I got to my room, I picked up my phone to call him.

Was he feeling just as hurt and lost as I was? I'd seen clips of some of the media circus surrounding him, and I wondered how he was holding up. Guilt washed over me. I was such a coward. I was dealing with my own shit, but I should have answered his calls.

I sank onto the end of the bed and rubbed a hand across my face. Quite suddenly, I realized that calling wasn't enough; I needed to see him in person. The more I thought about it, the more urgent it seemed, and the more determined I became to make that happen.

Instead of calling Greyson, I called our tour manager, who picked up on the first ring. "Darren, I need to fly out to L.A. as soon as possible. Find a gap in our schedule and make the arrangements so the tour isn't affected."

He sighed. "Shit. This is important?"

"Yeah," I confirmed. "You know I wouldn't ask if it wasn't. Get me at least four hours in L.A. Make it happen."

"Alright," he grumbled. "Whatever the fuck you're doing, you're taking Bishop with you."

Two days later, I was boarding a plane to L.A., my heart pounding with anticipation. I'd only told Knox where I was going, and he seemed to think it was a good idea. My mind raced at the thought of seeing Greyson again.

As the car pulled up to Greyson's house, I noticed the chaotic swarm of paparazzi and reporters surrounding the entrance. I pulled my hood up and put on a pair of sunglasses before I stepped out of the car. Bishop got me through them without incident, though I could hear the mob erupting into chaos behind us as they realized someone had slipped past.

The adrenaline coursed through my veins as we finally approached Greyson's front door.

Opening the door with a look of disbelief on his handsome face,

Greyson stood in the doorway, clearly taken aback by my unexpected visit. "What are you doing here?" he asked, his voice trembling slightly with surprise and concern.

"Can we come in?" I asked urgently, glancing over my shoulder at the ever-present paparazzi. Nodding without hesitation, Greyson quickly ushered us inside, closing the door firmly behind us.

"Is everything okay?" Greyson asked, his brows furrowing as he took in my disheveled appearance. Running a hand through my hair, I tried to gather my thoughts before diving into the conversation that had brought me all the way to L.A.

"I had to see you," I said bluntly. My heart was pounding, nerves and anticipation warring within me. "We need to talk."

Bishop cleared his throat. "I'll give you some privacy. Ghost, when would you like me to return?"

I glanced over at the man. "Thanks, Bishop. I'll text you when I'm ready."

Leaning against the wall, Greyson crossed his arms defensively. When Bishop left, he spoke. "I assume that this is about the article Remi wrote?"

I nodded. "Yes, it's been bothering me. I have to know why she did it. It doesn't make sense. I haven't spoken to her. Have you?"

He studied me dispassionately. "Can I get you something to drink?"

"Yeah, whatever you have is fine."

Greyson led me to a room in the back of the house with plush carpets and antique furniture. In the center of the room was a large mahogany desk with a tall leather chair behind it, and two comfortable chairs sat in front of a crackling fireplace. The walls were lined with bookshelves filled with an impressive collection of books. Thick curtains were closed over the windows, making the room look dreary until Greyson flipped on the light switch.

He indicated that I should sit in front of the fireplace while he fixed us some drinks from a bar cabinet. "I'm not sure if it was a good idea for you to come here. If anyone is able to identify you—"

"I don't give a fuck anymore," I said, and I realized I meant it. "How could it get any worse?"

Greyson crossed the room, handed me a tumbler of whiskey, and then sat down on the chair that was facing mine. "How is everybody doing? Talia told me a bit, but I feel like she's shielding me from the full extent of how it's affecting the band."

"Bash is worried sick about losing custody of Kody even though his lawyer has assured him that wasn't likely. Knox had to relive the worst moment of his life when the story of his fiancée dying in that car crash resurfaced and got picked apart in the media." I clenched my fist, feeling anger bubble up inside me. "Sidney's painful early life in foster care was exposed for the world to see."

I paused, swallowing hard, before continuing. "And then there was that fake story she spun about Ryder and you being in a relationship, about Ryder's marriage being a sham. It hurt all three of you." My voice cracked, betraying the depth of my emotions. "She played with our lives and livelihoods, Greyson. I just don't understand how she could do that to us."

"Did you know Remi was gunning for a big promotion when she wrote it?" Greyson asked hesitantly, his gaze holding mine captive. I shook my head, feeling a wave of anger wash over me as I realized how calculating Remi had been.

"She was hoping to become the face of Hollywood Exposé, but her little stunt ended up getting her fired."

I froze, my mouth falling open in surprise. "She got fired?" I repeated, disbelieving. I hadn't heard a hint of this news before now. "Jesus," I muttered, rubbing the back of my neck. "So she betrayed us both just to get ahead in her career and ended up getting fired? It's sickening."

"Unfortunately, that's the world we live in," Greyson sighed, his shoulders slumping.

Closing my eyes for a moment, I tried to make sense of Remi's twisted motives. "So, everything with her was fake? The time we spent together? It felt real. That's the hardest part."

"I understand how you feel." He took a slow sip of his drink. "I wanted to marry her. I even had the ring and was ready to propose before she went on assignment with the tour."

My brow wrinkled with confusion. "I thought you broke up with her?"

Grey leaned forward, studying me as he spoke. "We did take a break. I had some confusing feelings for someone else that I needed to sort out. I was honest with Remi. She knew that."

Something in his heated look made me squirm despite the sudden bolt of jealousy I felt. Christ, what was it about this guy?

"Did you know that she was going to do this to me? To Ghost Parker?" I had to know.

"No. I knew she was writing an article, but she insisted she wasn't going to hurt anyone." He rested his glass against the armrest of his chair. "I spoke to her briefly after it was published. She actually denied writing the article. She claimed that someone was setting her up. She begged me to believe her."

I sat up in my chair. "What? Why would someone do that?"

He shrugged. "She was in competition for the anchor spot with a colleague who was very competitive. Remi thought that woman had gotten ahold of her research somehow."

"But you didn't believe her?" I asked.

"I was dealing with a lot. The media was suddenly breathing down my neck. *Devious* said they might not renew my contract for next season. Men were coming out of the woodwork, claiming they slept with me." He was staring into the flames of the gas fireplace as he spoke. "It was all due to that article. And I was still reeling from the shock of her betrayal. I didn't give her denial about writing it much thought."

Fuck. Maybe I was just too weak to face what she'd done, but I latched onto Remi's denial like a lifeline. "Have you thought about it since?"

"Yeah." He said softly. "I'm still puzzled by some of it. Like why would she make up stuff about me when she knew things that were actually true and far more damaging? She could've had the story of the year, yet she made up that stuff with Ryder and Talia. Something about that seems off to me."

I swallowed the rest of my whisky in one gulp. "Grey, is it possible she was telling you the truth? That someone else published the article with her name on it?"

"If they had access to Remi's files, maybe. It seems preposterous, but why would she bother to deny that she wrote it after the fact?" He stared into space for a few moments. Finally, he released a frustrated sigh and said, "Frankly, I'm still struggling with it. I'm around actors all day — if she was lying about loving me, she's one of the greatest actresses of all time."

My mind was racing with my own thoughts about Remi, but what I asked Greyson next surprised me. "What secret did Remi know about you that she didn't use?"

I held my breath as I waited for his reply. His eyes narrowed with suspicion as he tapped his fingers on his glass and then ran a hand through his hair. After a long silence, he sighed and shifted in his seat, his eyes meeting mine with a mix of fear and uncertainty. "Okay," he said quietly. "I'll tell you."

Exhaling the breath I'd been holding, I gripped the arms of the chair, waiting for his confession.

"Jonas Steel." His posture was tense, as if bracing himself, waiting for my response. "He was my longtime lover and Remi knew that."

Holy fuck! It was a bombshell. Jonas Steel was a major movie actor. A-list. Greyson and Jonas. My mind spun with the implications. "So, the article was right? You're gay?"

Greyson chuckled bitterly. "I consider myself bisexual. You didn't know? Apparently, it was Hollywood's worst kept secret."

My head sunk into my hands as I rubbed my temples. "No ... Maybe. I don't know."

Greyson had had relationships with men. Had I sensed that? Was that why I was always so nervous around him? Snippets of memory — of me being abused — flashed through my mind. I grimaced. Fuck, I was spiraling into a bad place.

His voice was strained. "You're disgusted."

I looked up and saw the pain in his eyes. "No. I just didn't know."

The color drained from his face. "You're worried that we slept with Remi together and now you think that makes you gay."

"No," I denied. "Stop putting words in my mouth."

He stood up, his shoulders slumped, and his hands tucked into the pockets of his jeans. Without looking at me, he spoke in a flat, emotionless voice. "You should just leave. It's safer for you that way."

I didn't feel like I'd gotten what I came for, and yet I wasn't quite sure what it was I was chasing. Greyson was right; it was safer for me to walk away right now. But, I was sick of running from everything. Maggie had shown me I was strong enough to face reality.

"Do you want me to go?" I asked.

He fixed his curious gaze on me for a few moments before replying in a measured voice. "The press would have a field day if they found out you were here."

My jaw clenched. "I don't care."

Why did I want him to tell me to stay so badly? I was still so fucking confused.

He turned away from me to face the fire. "They would speculate that we were together. It would ruin your reputation."

I stood up and threw up my hands in disgust. "Who the fuck cares? Nobody cares about that kind of shit anymore. Your fans don't. Mine don't. They can print whatever the fuck they want. I don't care. The media is all smoke and mirrors nowadays. Fake bullshit. Everyone knows that."

He flinched as if I'd struck him, eyes closing in pain. "I might as well tell you everything."

My stomach churned with anticipation as I waited for him to break the silence. Every muscle in my body tensed up as if warning me of what was about to come.

"You were the person Remi and I broke up about. Remi didn't know it was you until I told her in Boston, but you were the other person I had feelings for."

"What?" I inhaled sharply, my heart pounding like a wild drum in my chest as I stared at him with incredulity. Shock and confusion raced through me, leaving me frozen in place and unable to move. Questions that had been lurking on the edges of my consciousness for weeks now bubbled up to the surface, but I couldn't form even one into words.

Greyson's face twisted in agony, his eyes full of emotion. "It's always been you. I felt it from the moment we met. Even while you couldn't stand to be in my presence, I've always felt … something, a deep connection to you."

I stood there, staring at Greyson as he spoke those words. His eyes bore into mine with a fierce intensity that left me feeling exposed and vulnerable. Every fiber of my being wanted to deny what he was saying, to push him away and run as far from him as I could. But there was a part of me that couldn't deny the truth in his words, a part of me that had always been drawn to him despite my best efforts to resist.

"I don't know what you're talking about," I said, my voice barely above a whisper.

"You do," Greyson said, taking a step closer to me. "You've always known, just like I have."

I could feel his breath on my neck, sending shivers down my spine. I wanted to run, to hide, but I couldn't move. My body was frozen, trapped between the past and the present, between my fear and my desire.

"I can't," I said, but Greyson didn't seem to care. He pushed me up against the wall, his hands pinning mine above my head.

"You can," he said, his voice low and commanding. "You want to, just like I do. We both know it."

I closed my eyes, trying to block out the memories that threatened to overwhelm me. But Greyson's touch was like a flame, igniting a fire within me that I couldn't ignore.

I began shaking. My world was tilting on its axis. Greyson's lips were on mine, his tongue demanding entrance. I wanted to resist, but it was like trying to hold back a tidal wave. I opened my mouth, allowing him to deepen the kiss. His hands were everywhere, exploring my body with a hunger that matched my own. I moaned into his mouth, feeling my body come alive with pleasure.

Greyson finally pulled away, his eyes searching mine for an answer. I was still shaking, my heart pounding so hard I thought it might burst from my chest. He must have sensed the fear and uncertainty that threatened to consume me because he smiled and stepped back.

"I know you're not ready," he said, his voice low and gentle. "But you do want this, Parker. There's no use denying it."

Panic bubbled up inside me, my father's mocking voice echoing in my head. You liked that, didn't you? You little faggot. I shook my head, trying to clear the hateful words that kept running through it.

Fuck. I shoved hard against his chest, pushing him back.

Chapter 33

Greyson

I stared at him. I could see the emotions swirling in his eyes, hurt, confusion, anger. He felt the undeniable chemistry we had, and he rejected it.

"You're a coward, Parker," I rasped.

Hatred burned in his eyes. "Fuck you, Greyson."

He automatically stepped back when I leaned toward him, but his back was up against the wall now. He had nowhere to go. I crowded up against him, letting my anger and disappointment take over. "You'll never find happiness hiding from life."

"Who's hiding from life?" he lashed out at me. "I get up on stage night after night and rip my heart open for my fans. But you? You're acting. Pretending to be someone you're not. Colton Grimaldi, badass playboy when you're nothing but a weak piece of shit pussy."

Anger blinded me to all else. My forearm pressed against his chest, holding him against the wall in a threatening manner. "You don't know a goddamn thing about me. So fuck yourself, asshole."

Ghost wrenched at my arm, but my anger gave me a whole other level of strength.

"I know that I hate you." He spit the words at me like venom.

The air left my lungs as if a boot had landed in the pit of my stomach. My throat closed up tight, attempting to choke back the sudden hurt that was threatening to spill out of me. "Why?" It was a simple question. That one word hung between us like a palpable force.

His lips parted, but he didn't speak. One moment, my arm pressed against his chest, the energy I felt surging through me almost enough to tear him apart piece by piece, and the next, he was staring at my lips. I felt the anger and tension between us shift abruptly, a palpable energy radiating off of him and onto me. His eyes still burned with that same intensity, but something else had been sparked in their depths — an almost animalistic hunger that sent my heart racing. The anger in my veins shifted quickly into a different kind of heat.

The next thing I knew, Ghost had grabbed the back of my head and pressed his lips against mine. It was a fierce kiss — full of anger and hurt and so much passion that I could barely keep up. His tongue swept over my bottom lip, demanding entry into my mouth, and without thinking, I opened for him.

My hands instinctively gripped his shoulders, and I kissed him back with as much intensity as he was giving me. My legs felt weak, my heart raced, and a heat coursed through my veins that I'd never felt before. I was completely consumed by the moment, pushing everything else away and focusing on the sensation of Ghost's lips against mine. His hands moved from my head to my back, pulling me closer to him until I was flush against his body.

The kiss was a fight for dominance between us. Our lips moved in an almost desperate frenzy, neither of us wanting to come up for air. We were locked in this moment, and I felt my body trembling with desire as he squeezed me tighter against him. My eyes closed and my breathing became shallow as I felt Ghost's arousal pressing against me. My heart raced with the thrill of pure energy surging through my veins. A fire ignited inside me and I felt unstoppable in that very moment. It was a sensation I ached to keep alive and hold on to forever.

Time seemed to stand still as we kissed with a hunger that neither of us could deny. I wanted to take it further — to explore every inch of his body — but mostly, I just wanted to hold him close and revel in our connection.

He roughly grabbed my throbbing dick through my pants. I groaned as white-hot desire shot through me. Lust was quickly overtaking me; I could barely think.

I pulled my head back, breaking our searing kiss, and dragged in a deep breath. "What are you doing?"

The air pulsed with an almost tangible electricity. His eyes glowed, and his cheeks had taken on a slight flush. A seductive smirk curved his lips, but his voice still simmered with anger. "You want to fuck me? Then just fuck me."

"What are you talking about?" My eyes frantically scanned his face for a sign of his intention, but I only found confusion. He was offering something I desperately wanted, but I knew he didn't want the same thing.

Ghost shoved me hard in the chest with the palm of his hand, pushing me back a step. "Just fucking do it already." He tore his hoodie off and threw it on the ground.

My heart raced as I stumbled back a step. Sweat prickled down my neck and I could feel the panic swirling in my chest. What was he doing? Of course, I'd wanted to fuck him for years, but not like this.

He was a straight guy, or so he believed, at least. "I'm not going to fuck you, Ghost."

"Why the fuck not?" He growled, his eyes pierced mine, and the heat from his gaze seemed to curl around me. "You want to. I know you do."

I shook my head slightly, struggling against the overpowering urges coursing through my veins. I gritted my teeth in a desperate attempt to restrain the raw and primal urges bubbling up inside of me. "Not like this."

He threw his head back and let out a laugh, heavy with disbelief. The corners of his mouth were turned down, and the brittle sound echoed through the room.

"I only fuck guys who want to be with me. And, you don't." I said evenly, trying to keep my emotions in check.

He stared at me for what felt like an eternity, his gaze heavy with something I couldn't quite put my finger on. His features softened and his body relaxed slightly before he stepped forward and brushed the back of his fingers against my cheek.

I didn't have time to react. Lightning quick, he slammed me up against the wall, crowding me with his body. His mouth found mine again — this time with a ferocity and intensity that rendered me speechless. His hands gripped the back of my neck as his tongue swept over mine in a passionate tangle that sent shivers of pleasure up my spine.

Ghost kissed me with an aggression that left me gasping for breath. His lips were soft yet demanding, his tongue exploring every inch of my mouth. I felt lost in the sensation and completely consumed by the emotion behind it. He pressed himself against me, his hard body filling me with a warmth that spread through my veins like wildfire. His hands moved down my body, slipping underneath my shirt to caress the skin on my back and stomach. His touch was electric, and I felt myself melting into his embrace.

I could feel Ghost's heart pounding against mine as he slid his hand inside my jeans, his rough fingertips sending sparks of pleasure through me. I gasped into the kiss and finally let go, surrendering to the overwhelming sensation coursing through me.

His hands moved faster as he frantically started to undress me, his teeth grazing my neck as he tore off my shirt. His lips left trails of fire down my body, and I felt myself trembling with anticipation. His fingers grasped at my belt, and then he worked the buckle open. I wanted to slow him down, but I was losing all control.

I grasped onto his shoulders and buried my face into the crook of his neck, shaking as he slipped his hands into my pants again. I moaned loudly as his fingers slid across my exposed flesh, causing every hair on my body to stand on end. My breath came in ragged gasps as I felt his hand fisting my aching cock.

I panted against his neck, my hands sliding down his shoulders to his arms as I tried to steady myself. "We're not doing this."

"Yes, we are." He spoke through gritted teeth.

His hand moved faster, his fingers working my dick in a way that made my head spin. Ghost's hands on me were the most erotic thing I'd ever felt. I could barely think as my body tensed with pleasure beneath his touch. He leaned forward to kiss me again, and I could feel the heat radiating off his body.

But something stopped me. I pushed him away, my hands trembling as I looked into his eyes. He was breathing heavily, with a wild and unfocused look in his eyes. Even when he looked so lost, an aura of power radiated from him. He looked like an angel of vengeance, beautiful beyond comprehension, but bent on destruction.

He was as aroused as I was, but he didn't want this like I did.

"No," I said firmly, taking a step back. "I don't want this."

Ghost blinked as if he had been jolted from a trance, his eyes focusing. He stepped back and ran a hand through his hair, looking away from me.

"Not like this," I said, more gently this time.

"Fuck!" he shouted as he retreated, picking his sweatshirt up from the floor. "I'll call Bishop and be out of here in a few minutes."

My chest tightened with panic. I couldn't let him leave like this. Not until he understood how I felt about him.

"Stay for dinner." I pleaded. "Just to talk. My housekeeper left me a feast — it would be a shame to let it go to waste."

Ghost stopped in his tracks and slowly turned around. His expression had softened, and he looked almost relieved to be given a choice to stay. He nodded and stepped back towards me.

"Alright," he said softly, looking into my eyes with a hopefulness I hadn't seen before. "I'll stay for dinner."

Chapter 34

Greyson

I stared at Ghost across the table, my pulse racing with a mixture of longing and apprehension. After that searing kiss we'd shared, I didn't know where we stood. I wanted him with an ache that went bone deep, but I was afraid of scaring him off.

I cleared my throat. "So, uhm ... how's the tour going?"

He shrugged, gazing into the depths of his wineglass. "Same shit, different city."

An awkward silence fell. My hands trembled as I set down my fork, the food in front of me now ashes in my mouth.

Ghost sighed. "There's something I want to tell you." He ran a hand through his scruffy hair. " I... I told Remi something dark ... something about my past that I've kept hidden for so long. It was worse than what she revealed about my step-brother's suicide."

The tension flowing between us was almost palpable. Under the table, I nervously clenched and unclenched my hands, trying to control the pounding of my heart.

"Whatever it is, you don't have to tell me. Just know that I'm here for you. No matter what."

Ghost stared at me for a long moment, his gaze piercing. I felt stripped bare under the intensity of it, as if he could see into my soul.

Then he looked away, shoulders hunching. "When I was a kid, my father..." His voice wavered, and he took a deep breath before continuing. "He would drink. A lot."

Fuck. His father was an alcoholic and his step-brother had taken his own life. His childhood must have been rough. I had sensed that his scars ran deep, and now I knew why.

Swallowing hard, he finally looked up at me, his eyes filled with pain and vulnerability that made my heart clench. "My father ... he used to let men ... do things to me ... when I was a kid." Ghost's voice trembled, and he squeezed his eyes shut, taking deep breaths as if attempting to keep his composure.

I gaped at him, bile rising in my throat. A wave of nausea and horror washed over me as the implication of his words sank in.

"He ... he pimped you out?" I rasped.

He nodded, but his eyes were downcast, avoiding my gaze.

He looked up at me with those soulful blue eyes, and I saw aching vulnerability in their depths. "Afterwards, he'd call me horrible names. Tell me how much I loved it — what a little faggot I was for letting those men touch me."

He choked on a sob, his body shaking, and I fought the urge to reach out and comfort him, fearing my touch would only remind him of his trauma. My heart shattered into a million pieces for him. All the pain and trauma he'd endured was unthinkable. No wonder he had such a hard time trusting people or letting anyone get close to him.

"Jesus Christ," I whispered, my stomach twisting into painful knots. Anger and sadness swirled within me like a raging storm. "I'm so sorry, Ghost.

The room grew eerily quiet as my mind raced, struggling to process what Ghost had just revealed. The darkness that had always surrounded him suddenly made sense, and I understood why he had been so hesitant around me. My heart ached for the little boy he'd once been, and the lasting damage that had been done to him. But I also saw the strong, complicated man he'd become, despite it all.

I forced myself to stay grounded in the moment, focusing on Ghost's needs rather than my own swirling emotions.

"Ghost, you didn't deserve any of that," I whispered fiercely. "You're not your father's twisted perception of you. You're so much more than that."

My words unleashed something in him — a flood of anguish and rage he'd bottled up for so long. He shuddered, slamming a fist on the table. "He ruined me. I'm so fucked up because of him."

"No, don't say that." I scooted my chair closer and wrapped an arm around his shoulders, relieved when he didn't pull away. "You're not ruined or fucked up. You're strong, brave, and amazing. I won't let anyone hurt you like that again. I promise."

His eyes were haunted, staring into the distance as if reliving a particularly painful memory. "It's just ... fucking hard. I still struggle with the memories, and sometimes I worry that I'll never be able to escape them."

"Then we'll fight those demons together," I promised, squeezing his shoulder. "No matter how long it takes or how hard it gets, I'll be here for you."

We sat in silence for a while, the weight of his horrific past heavy in the air. I was heartbroken for the suffering he had endured, and I vowed to myself that I would do everything in my power to help him heal from the scars of his past.

♫♫♪♪♪

Resting my head against the cool window, I stared out at the city lights as they blurred together like a watercolor painting. The tension in my chest had been building all night; I wasn't sure how I could help Ghost. I could feel his gaze on me, but I didn't know what to say or do.

I snapped the curtains closed against potential prying paparazzi lenses and turned to the room, which was dark except for the soft glow of the fireplace flames.

Bishop would be arriving shortly, so I didn't have much more time alone with Ghost. I wanted to say so many things before he left and went back on tour, but nothing seemed appropriate for the situation.

I swallowed hard, my throat tight. "Have you spoken to someone about this — someone professional — that can help you?" I prodded gently.

He leaned back in the chair, seeming much calmer now. "I have. I've been seeing Maggie, my therapist, for years, but I only recently told her the entire story after I told Remi. And I was doing really well. At least until Remi betrayed me. Betrayed all of us." His voice broke on the last word, and he looked away, jaw clenched.

I sat in the chair across from him, sliding my hands down to my lap to keep myself from reaching out to him. "So, talking to the therapist is helping?"

"Yeah." He nodded. "She has all these strategies — coping strategies and stuff about negative thinking — and it's weird, but they work.

And I've been working hard to stop popping pills to numb the pain."

"That's good," I encouraged.

His foot bounced nervously on the ground. "I've kept this all a big secret because I was so fucking ashamed and I was worried that people, my friends, would be horrified — that they'd judge me. Maggie didn't react that way — of course not — she's a professional. But, Knox. He was supportive, not disgusted. Actually, Remi was the person I first told. I don't even know why."

Hearing Remi's name was like picking at an old scab. Even though she'd hurt us all, I still had lingering feelings for her. It was hard to understand.

"I don't get it." Tightness crept into the corners of his mouth and his chin quivered as he flicked his gaze towards me, brows furrowed in confusion. "Why didn't she publish the story about my sexual abuse? It's much more scandalous than that made-up story about my stepbrother being rejected by the band. Remi knew that Adam died well before Ghost Parker even formed. It wasn't even a good lie because it's easily proven false."

I didn't want to ask, but I had a sinking suspicion that Adam's death was related to the abuse, and that made the situation all the more tragic if that was even possible.

The images that Ghost's confession had conjured twisted my gut — the thought of anyone, let alone a child, enduring such horrors was sickening. Ghost and his brother had suffered a lot and then Ghost had been left with survivor's guilt on top of it all.

I just couldn't imagine Remi using something so horrific for her own gain. "Ghost, only an absolute monster would exploit something like that."

He rubbed his face like he was wrestling with something. "Or someone who'd do anything for a promotion. And I don't think that person is Remi. I don't think she was ever like that."

The silence seemed to stretch on forever before I cautiously asked, "What do you mean?"

Ghost was staring with concentration at the dancing flames like he was trying to put together a puzzle. "Remi knew about Adam. She'd found out when she did some background research. She knew a lot of stuff about the band before she even came on the tour. It was all in that blue notebook."

I was curious as to what he was getting at. I encouraged him to continue. "Yes, the week before she joined your tour, she traveled to do research on the band. I know she was in Ohio and Georgia, probably some other places."

"Yeah, the information about Adam's suicide was in that notebook from her research. But when she asked me about Adam in an interview, I shut her down. I was pissed that she'd found out that info about him." He glanced up at me, gauging my reaction.

"Okay."

"It was after that when I told her what Adam and I had both endured and how it broke him." His foot was bouncing up and down, expending nervous energy. "I told Remi. She knew everything, but I'd told her personally. It wasn't a part of her research."

I arched an eyebrow. "So you think she was holding on to some personal integrity by not publishing it?"

"I don't know." He shook his head. "I just know that the only stuff that made it into her article were things she'd dug up before the tour. The other stuff was completely fabricated."

"That's a fucked up code of ethics. On the one hand, she didn't use the stuff you'd told her privately, but on the other, she completely made shit up?" I let out a bitter bark of laughter.

"I'm just saying, if someone got a hold of her research, they could have written that story." He looked at me with such desperation in his eyes, almost begging me to agree. "You said Remi denied writing the article. If someone had access to that notebook she was always writing in…"

I kept my tone measured and even, despite my skepticism. "That seems a bit far-fetched. Wouldn't Hollywood Exposé have some way of checking who published the article?"

Ghost jumped up from the chair and started pacing. "I don't know, Grey. She knew about you and Jonas Steel. That would have been a bombshell, but she didn't publish that. Instead, she made up that weird story about you and Ryder. It doesn't make sense."

I stroked my chin, trying to think logically. "We both still have feelings for her. That makes it hard to accept what happened. I think—"

Ghost's phone pinged with a text. "Fuck, Bishop is here. I've got to get to the airport."

He typed a return message and then sent it. "I've got 10 minutes before he comes in to get me."

I stood up and approached him cautiously, not wanting to come on too strong. "Will you answer my calls while you're on tour?"

He ran a hand through his hair. "Yeah. When I can."

I moved closer. "Then focus on finishing your tour. Call me anytime. I'm here any time you need me. When the tour is over, we'll figure out where this is going."

His brow furrowed as he glanced away, and a trace of insecurity crept across his features. "That's it? After everything I told you tonight? I came here…"

My heart ached for him. I cupped his cheek, stroking my thumb over the sharp angle of his cheekbone. "Do what you need to do. Talk to your therapist about us. After your tour, I'll come with you to a therapy session if that helps. But, if you decide we can only be friends, that's okay. I care about you, not just physically. I'm always on your side, Parker."

A tremor ran through him. "You don't think I'm too fucked up to bother with?"

"I think it's going to be a long three weeks. And no, you're not too fucked up." My hand moved from his cheek to rest on his shoulder. "Thank you for trusting me with your past. I know it must have been incredibly difficult to share. But just remember, you're not alone anymore. You have me — and I'm not going anywhere."

Leaning in, I brushed my lips over his, a feather-light caress. He made a soft sound low in his throat, hands coming up to grip my waist.

I pulled back, but Ghost yanked me towards him until our bodies were in full contact. Our mouths met with a suddenness that caught me off guard, his full lips moving feverishly against mine. I was nearly lost in his hungry demands, but I fought against the desire that was coursing through me until I managed to break away.

He made a sound of frustration deep in his throat, a guttural growl that seemed to echo around us. His nostrils flared, and his eyes were black and feral.

I placed my hands on his shoulders, holding him back from me, yet not letting him go. "I would love to be with you, but we have to take this slow. I'm only restraining myself, so I don't completely mess this up."

"You're an asshole," he rasped.

I chuckled. "We're back to that again?"

He shrugged out from under my grip. "Come back with me. On the tour."

My cock was rock hard in my pants and ached for release, pleading for me to say yes, but knew I couldn't. "We both know that would be a huge mistake."

"Fuck the paparazzi and the media. I don't give a shit." The words came out of his mouth like bullets, but the venom was absent from his voice. He didn't mean it fully.

I approached him slowly, pulling him into a hug. "I'm going to call you tomorrow after your show. You're going to answer. We'll talk for the next three weeks. It'll give us time to work through some shit." I spoke directly into his ear, "I promise, Ghost, I'll be here when you're done with the tour."

We stood there, embracing for a few silent moments. I felt his shaky inhale of breath against my neck as my hand slipped down his back, under his shirt, and over the smooth, warm muscles of his spine. Closing my eyes, I reveled in this feeling of closeness with him as my heart pounded against my rib cage. I was grateful, and a bit surprised that he didn't pull away from me, despite the fact that he must have felt my throbbing cock pressed against his body.

The doorbell rang, and his muscles tensed up. I let him go.

He looked at me with a gaze so powerful it felt like it could reach my soul. It sent a wave of warmth through me that was full of yearning and emotion, a tenderness I could both see and feel. His soft lips curved into a small, sad smile as he drew me in with an invisible force.

"Okay, Durant. I'll catch you later."

I didn't want him to walk out that door. I swallowed the lump in my throat. "Take care, Ghost. I'll see you soon."

He nodded and stepped away, turning towards the door. He pulled out his sunglasses and then pulled up the hood of his sweatshirt. He didn't look back as he left my study.

I hoped like hell I was doing the right thing letting him go.

I would be there for him, in any way he needed, and together we would move beyond the demons of his past.

Chapter 35

Remi

THE HEAVY MAHOGANY DOOR opened with a creak. I stepped into the lushly appointed boardroom, my pulse racing like a freight train. Seated at the long, polished table was Mr. Hoffman, the CEO of Hollywood Exposé and lawyers for both Hollywood Exposé and Black Vault Records, Ghost Parker's record label. A few of the sour-faced lawyers noted my entrance, but most of them ignored me.

My lawyer, a middle-aged man with graying temples, patted me on the shoulder. "You ready for this, Remi?" he whispered, his voice tense. My palms were sweaty, but I nodded, attempting to project confidence.

"Let's get started," the lead lawyer for Hollywood Exposé said, shuffling papers on the table before him. "As we've discussed, we're here to finalize the out-of-court settlement between our client, Hollywood Exposé, and Black Vault Records."

"Ms. Sutton," another lawyer chimed in, directing his ice-cold gaze at me, "in order for this settlement to proceed, you must agree to a full retraction of the article, admit that the article was false, and apologize in writing."

I clenched my jaw, feeling my anger rise like a tide. This wasn't fair; I didn't even write that damned article, but I didn't have a shred of evidence of that and no one believed me. Swallowing hard, I forced myself to nod, knowing that if I didn't, it could cost me everything.

"Furthermore," the lawyer continued, "you will be required to sign a non-disclosure agreement, effectively gagging you from discussing this topic further."

"Fine," I spat, my hands shaking as I reached for the pen. I signed the necessary documents, each stroke of my signature feeling like a betrayal to my career.

"Congratulations, Ms. Sutton," the lead lawyer for the BVR record label sneered, extending his hand to shake mine. "You've just saved yourself a fortune in restitution."

"Your career, however," he continued as he gave my hand one pump, "may not be so fortunate. After what you did to my clients—"

"Enough," my lawyer interjected, putting a protective hand on my shoulder. "We've done what you've asked. This meeting is over."

I stood up abruptly, the harsh scrape of my chair against the floor echoing through the room like an accusation. I could feel their eyes boring into my back as I turned to leave. My every step was heavy with defeat.

"Remi," my lawyer said gently, catching up to me as we stepped out of the boardroom. "You did the right thing."

My knuckles turned white as I clenched my fists, rage and humiliation warring inside me.

After weeks of legal wrangling and sleepless nights, this was how it ended — not with the vindication I craved, but with defeat.

I scrubbed a hand over my face. "I can't believe this. My career ... my reputation ... It's all in shambles now. How did it come to this?"

My lawyer sighed. "I know it's difficult, but this was the pragmatic choice. Dragging this out in court could have bankrupted the magazine and destroyed your career. This way, at least the magazine's insurance covers the settlement and you're shielded from further lawsuits from BVR or the rock band."

I turned on him, eyes blazing. "My career is already destroyed! Did you miss the part where I have to get on my knees and beg for forgiveness for something I didn't even do?"

He didn't meet my gaze, staring at the floor. Even he didn't believe I was innocent.

"Listen to me," he urged, his voice firm yet sympathetic. "We had no choice. Fighting this would have led to financial ruin. You can rebuild your career or branch out in a new direction."

I stared down at the papers in my hands, the weight of my decision settling into my heart like a stone. It was like déjà vu. Years before, I'd been forced out of my dream career and had worked so hard to build a new one. I didn't know if I had the heart to do it again. The injustice of it all felt like a deep, bottomless hole in my heart. Even though I wanted to fight for what was right, a part of me felt defeated and resigned.

"Maybe you're right. I was never going to win this fight," I conceded, wiping away a stray tear. "But that doesn't mean any of it is fair."

"Give it time, Remi," he reassured me, before walking away. "You'll bounce back from this."

No one believed that I didn't write that article. My lawyer, Caroline — my boss, and my co-workers all scoffed at my denials. What hurt the most was that Greyson and Ghost believed I could write such a malicious and hurtful article about them.

Why would absolute strangers ever believe me when the people closest to me hadn't? Once the retraction and apology were published, my reputation and credibility would be shattered. I'd be lucky to land a job writing obituaries for the local free newspaper.

Everything I'd worked for was slipping through my fingers, and there wasn't a damn thing I could do to stop it. I felt tears burning behind my eyes, but there was no way in hell I'd cry here, at Hollywood Exposé.

I hurried down the hall, eager to escape the legal sharks that were all mortal enemies in court, but were probably high-fiving each other for doing virtually nothing yet earning tons of money off this stupid settlement.

When I heard a door open behind me, I quickly ducked through the door marked ladies' room on my right. I needed to get my emotions under control before I ran into anyone I knew. Then, I'd make a beeline for the exit.

This ladies' room had a small, secluded anteroom set off to the side, with plush chairs, a large ornate mirror, and an antique chandelier hanging from the ceiling. The sitting area was lit by a series of small sconces, giving it a warm ambiance of quiet luxury.

Taking a deep breath, I sank into one of the plush chairs. I'd lost.

I'd done everything I could think of to prove my innocence, but nothing had worked. In the end, without Hollywood Exposé's cooperation, it had been an impossible task.

Admitting my guilt in the settlement had not only ruined my career but also my chances of getting Greyson and Ghost to believe me. Now what was I going to do? I wouldn't give up on them, but the task seemed nearly insurmountable now.

Tears slid down my cheek. I had lost them both. Two men that I loved. Who wouldn't even take my calls any longer. I cried for the injustice of it all. Most of all, I cried because I was alone. There was no one left to stand beside me, to tell me everything would be okay. I was broken; I'd lost everything that mattered.

The ladies' room door creaked open, and there she was — Dawn Chambers, in all her calculated glory. My stomach churned at the sight of her perfectly coiffed blonde hair and Cheshire cat grin. A predatory smile spread across her face as she spotted me, her eyes gleaming with malice.

Dawn sauntered over to the chair I was sitting in, her stilettos clicking against the floor like nails on a chalkboard. "Well, isn't this cozy?" She purred, glancing at me from the corner of her eye.

I gritted my teeth and stared straight ahead, surreptitiously swiping at my damp face. I wouldn't give her the satisfaction of seeing how much she'd ruined me.

"Cat got your tongue?" Dawn leaned closer, her floral perfume overwhelming my senses. "Or did Greyson steal that too, along with your journalistic integrity?"

My heart thudded in my chest. That bitch. I wanted nothing more than to claw her smug face, to make her feel a fraction of the pain and humiliation she's caused.

Instead, I took a deep breath and met her icy blue gaze. "Jealousy doesn't suit you, Dawn."

A flicker of anger flashed across her face before she regained her composure. "Please. I have no reason to be jealous of a disgraced hack like yourself." She flicked her blonde hair over her shoulder.

She turned around and faced the ornate mirror, pretending to fix her hair. "I heard you were in today, signing the settlement that admits you defamed Ghost Parker. You're the talk of the newsroom. It's a sad day for Hollywood Exposé that an employee, well, ex-employee now, would stoop so low. Quite an embarrassment, but we'll survive once we set the record straight. I've been assigned to report on your horrible misdeeds."

I gritted my teeth, refusing to give her the satisfaction of a reaction, but her words cut deep.

"Did I mention it's official?" She said casually, watching me in the mirror. "I'll be taking over Mindy's anchor spot. We're already transitioning. You can catch me. I'll be anchoring all next week while my Black Sheep Royals in America package airs. Take notes. You'll see what real entertainment journalism looks like."

She was like a vulture circling its prey, swooping in to pick at the carcass of my career. I wanted to scratch her eyes out. As she continued taunting me, I surreptitiously reached into my purse and hit the record button on my phone, praying for some kind of leverage against her.

Dawn examined her reflection, smoothing a stray hair back into place. "It's a shame you lost your job. You went a bit overboard with the competition for the promotion. You should have just stuck to the truth."

"The truth?" I couldn't stop myself from snapping back. "You wouldn't know the truth if it punched you in your smug, self-serving face."

Dawn turned to face me, eyes glinting. "Careful, Remi. Insulting a colleague could damage your reputation even further. Oh wait…" She smirked. "You don't have a reputation left to damage, do you?"

I surged to my feet, rage boiling over. "You lying, manipulative bitch!" I shouted. "I know what you did! I'm going to prove it. And I'm going to make you pay for destroying my life."

Dawn's eyes widened briefly, but she recovered quickly, her smile turning icy. "Good luck with that," she said coolly. "You have no proof of anything."

My fingers tightened around my phone, hidden from her view. I needed to remain calm if I wanted to outsmart her. I took a deep breath, feeling the cool air fill my lungs before letting it out slowly.

"Is that all you came here for, Dawn? To rub salt in my wounds?" I asked. I had to keep her talking.

"Of course not, darling," she said, feigning innocence as she inspected her nails. "I just wanted to make sure you knew how well things were going for me. After all, you've always been so supportive of my work."

The sarcasm dripped from her voice like venom. It took every ounce of self-control not to lash out, to stay focused on the task at hand — getting her to reveal her true nature, and to catch it all on tape.

"Well, I'll admit, it was a bit surprising to see you go so far." She turned back to the mirror and began reapplying her bright red lipstick. "How's Greyson doing with all this? It was incredibly cold to out your own boyfriend to the whole world like that. But even I have to admit, it was quite the scoop. Frankly, I didn't think you had it in you."

My jaw clenched at the mention of Greyson's name. "I didn't and you know it, Dawn. My only question is: how did you do it? How did you get all that information to write the article and pretend it was me?"

Her laughter echoed off the cold marble. The predatory smirk on her face only intensified my desire to wipe that smugness away. "I didn't do anything. You imploded your career all by yourself."

"Really?" I questioned, my voice barely hiding the bitterness I felt. "You expect me to believe that you had nothing to do with it?"

She regarded me with mock pity. "Why should I bother getting my hands dirty when you're so good at sabotaging yourself?"

"I know it was you, Dawn."

Her eyes narrowed, and for a moment, I thought I'd finally managed to rattle her composure. But then she just laughed again, shrugging nonchalantly as she examined her manicured nails. "Oh, Remi," she sighed, shaking her head. "Always so desperate to believe that everyone else is the villain."

I searched her face for any sign of guilt or fear, anything that might give her away. But all I saw was cold, calculated confidence.

"Some people in the newsroom have been talking. Not everyone thinks you're so innocent." It was a total bluff, but I was growing desperate.

Her eyes locked onto mine, and for a moment, we just stared at each other — two predators sizing each other up, waiting for the other to make the first move. Then, finally, she broke the silence.

"Believe what you want, Remi," she said coolly, her gaze never wavering. "But if you think I had anything to do with your downfall, you're sorely mistaken."

Damn her! I was running out of time. I glanced down at my phone tucked safely inside my purse, seeing the seconds tick by as it recorded our conversation. This was my last hope — I just needed her to slip up. To admit what she'd done. But Dawn was cunning, cautious. She wouldn't be easily baited.

"You think you're going to record me confessing the whole thing?" she asked suddenly, her tone dripping with disdain. "Please. You're still playing checkers while I'm playing chess. Your Scooby Doo tactics won't work. No wonder you're disgraced from the industry. Really, Remi, I thought you'd be a more formidable opponent."

Fuck! Her words stung, but I refused to let her see the effect they had on me. My eyes locked onto hers, searching for any hint of vulnerability. But she offered none. She was a fortress, impenetrable and unyielding.

"Maybe you're right," I admitted, attempting to feign defeat. "Maybe I'm not as clever as you. But if you didn't do it, then who did?"

She rolled her eyes as if my question was beneath her. "Not my problem, sweetheart."

"Of course it isn't," I said, my voice laced with sarcasm. "Why would it be? You got what you wanted — my job, my reputation ... all of it."

"Life's a game, Remi," she replied coldly, straightening up and adjusting her blazer. "And unfortunately for you, I play to win."

She took a step toward me, her eyes flickering with cruel amusement as she leaned in closer, her breath hot against my cheek. "If you want to know what happened, I'll tell you. Make sure you record this," she sneered, pressing closer to me. "You were a busy little bee digging into all the dirt on the band and then you were shocked to find out that your boyfriend had a thing for another man. That's why you outed him because he was in love with the guitarist, Ryder. Grey went to Boston to visit his lover, and you pitched a fit."

I clenched my fists, nails digging into my palms as anger bubbled up inside me like molten lava. My heart raced, fury and hurt wrestling for dominion as I stared into Dawn's smug face.

"You're twisted, Dawn," I spat, unable to hold back any longer. The words tasted bitter on my tongue, but they were nothing compared to the poisonous lies she'd woven around me.

Dawn's smile only widened, her eyes gleaming like polished obsidian. She stepped back, releasing me from the vice-like grip of her presence, only to circle me like a vulture honing in on its prey. As she moved, I felt the weight of her gaze, scrutinizing every inch of my being, searching for weaknesses to exploit.

"Am I?" she asked, feigning innocence. "Or am I hitting too close to the truth?"

I gritted my teeth, swallowing the fury that threatened to spill over.

HOW TO CATCH A ROCKSTAR

I needed to stay focused, to gather enough evidence to pin her down. But with each passing moment, it became harder and harder to think clearly.

"You were jealous of Ryder stealing your man," Dawn continued, her cruel eyes never leaving mine. "That's a rough one. You couldn't keep Greyson satisfied, so he turned to Ryder."

Her words stung like tiny needles jabbing at my heart, but I refused to let her see the pain they caused. I fought back the urge to scream. The look of pure satisfaction on her face only fueled the fire burning in my chest.

"Greyson didn't deserve what you did to him," I whispered, my voice trembling with the effort it took to keep my emotions under control. "Neither did Ryder, nor his family. You used them, destroyed their lives for your own gain. And for what? A promotion? To bring me down?"

She retreated back to the mirror. "Remi, darling. You're delusional. It was your article that did all that damage. Is that why you threw Ryder's cousin under the bus, too? You had the perfect motive." Dawn sneered, her voice dripping with disdain.

She snapped her compact closed with a loud click. I was afraid she was going to leave without saying anything incriminating.

I had to keep her talking. "What are you talking about?"

She shrugged. "You wanted to get back at Ryder for stealing your man, so you went after his dead cousin, making tenuous connections, at best, to the ghost being the cousin who supposedly died of an overdose."

Supposedly died. Something about those words stood out to me. "How would that be getting back at Ryder?"

Her laughter sliced through the air like a razor-sharp wind, and her eyes narrowed into slits of contempt. The sound was sharp and mocking, with an edge of superiority as if to emphasize how foolish I was.

"What do you think the dead cousin's parents felt when you exposed to the whole world that the coroner's report stated that he died of autoerotic asphyxiation? That's kind of low, even for you."

A cold shiver ran down my spine as I realized the full implications of Dawn's words. She'd just exposed herself. The smug expression on her face seemed to mock me, but it was her casual mention of autoerotic asphyxiation that truly caught my attention. That bit of information about the coroner's report was in my notebook, but it wasn't in the article and wasn't public knowledge. Dawn had just proven that she'd read my notebook and it was only a small leap to deduce that she was the one who wrote the article.

I could barely breathe, my heart pounding in my ears as the realization of Dawn's misstep hit me like a ton of bricks. "How did you know he died from autoerotic asphyxiation?" I asked, my voice steady despite the pounding in my chest.

Dawn's eyes flickered with panic for a split second before she recovered. "What? Because I read it in the article, of course!"

"Except that wasn't in the article," I replied cooly, my pulse quickening as I watched her facade begin to crack.

Her eyes widened for a split second before her expression smoothed over, trying to maintain her cool façade. She tilted her head slightly, feigning confusion. "What are you talking about, Remi?"

"Autoerotic asphyxiation wasn't mentioned in the article," I continued, staring her down. "That piece of information was only in my notebook."

Dawn's eyes narrowed, a bead of sweat forming at her hairline. She hesitated for a moment before responding, her voice wavering despite her best efforts. "You — you must be mistaken."

"Face it, Dawn. You just exposed yourself." My words were hard and unyielding, like steel. "You've been caught."

As I glared into her desperate gaze, I could almost hear the gears turning in her mind, scrambling to come up with a plausible explanation. But there was none — she had just given herself away, and she knew it. Her carefully constructed house of cards was starting to crumble, and I could sense her panic rising beneath the surface.

"Are you seriously suggesting that I read your notebook?" she scoffed, attempting to maintain her air of superiority. "Get real, Remi. You're grasping at straws now."

"Am I?" I countered, my voice steady despite the whirlwind of emotions churning within me. "The fact is, you shouldn't have known how Ryder's cousin died unless you had access to my research."

"Your accusations are absurd," Dawn spat, her poise slipping with every passing moment. "You're just bitter because you lost everything, and you're looking for someone to blame."

"Except I didn't write that article," I shot back, my voice dripping with disdain. "And now I have proof that you did."

Her chest heaved with each ragged breath, and I saw the unmistakable glint of fear in her eyes. But she was nothing if not tenacious, and even now, she refused to go down without a fight.

"Even if I did know," she spat, her voice laced with contempt, "it doesn't prove anything. It's your word against mine, and who do you think they'll believe?" Her eyes gleamed with a sinister light, daring me to challenge her.

I stared back at her, my heart pounding in my chest like a primal drumbeat urging me forward. No longer would I stand idly by while she twisted the truth to suit her whims. No longer would I allow her to manipulate me and those I cared about.

"Maybe it is my word against yours, Dawn," I said, my voice low and dangerous, "but I'm not backing down this time. I'll find a way to expose you for the liar that you are."

Dawn sneered, her eyes cold and calculating. "You're welcome to try," she hissed, grabbing her purse from the table it sat on and slinging it over her shoulder.

She turned back to me with a sickly sweet smile plastered on her face. "It was lovely catching up with you, Remi. I won't keep you. I'm sure you have another exposé to fabricate." She sauntered toward the door, then paused, glancing at me over her shoulder.

"Oh, and Remington?" Her lips curled into a cruel smile. "Say hello to Greyson for me."

She left me staring after her with a mix of triumph and trepidation on my face. The battle was far from over, but I finally had a solid lead to expose Dawn's deceit. Determination surged through my veins like liquid fire. Dawn may have outplayed me before, but she had just given me the ammunition I needed to fight back. The recording in my possession could potentially expose her for who she truly was — a manipulative, scheming opportunist.

The only thing that tempered my triumph was that she'd called me Remington. It was a warning shot. She knew about my past — she was the one who'd left that threatening message years ago, warning me to watch my back. I had to be cautious. Dawn was cornered like a wild animal, and she was sure to lash out unpredictably.

Before exiting the restroom, I made sure to stop the recording, saving it securely on my phone. The next move was mine, and I knew it needed to be calculated and precise. One slip-up could mean the difference between victory and utter defeat.

My lips curled into a victorious smile. I couldn't help but feel a sense of hope.

I got her.

Chapter 36

Ghost

I paced the living room of my apartment, my hands running through my hair as I tried to quell the anxiety building in my chest. I hadn't seen Greyson in weeks, but we'd spoken to each other almost every night while I was still on tour. Knowing he was there, to reach out to whenever I needed, made the tour a little less lonely.

The fervor surrounding the article about the band had finally died down, and the paparazzi had mostly moved on to new scandals. Paparazzi had not been camping out at Greyson's door anymore, but he still wanted to be careful, so he insisted on coming to my apartment. He was adamant about shielding me from his scandals.

I'd told Maggie that I was attracted to Greyson and wondered if I could have a physical relationship with a man after the abuse I'd suffered. In true Maggie fashion, she'd jumped straight into helping me work through my issues.

As much as I was thinking non-stop about Greyson, I was also still fucked up with lingering feelings for Remi. She'd left both Grey and I messages asking to talk to us. I've decided that I want to see her again, at least to talk, and I was worried that Greyson wouldn't understand, but I needed answers from her.

The doorbell rang, shattering my thoughts and causing my stomach to crash to the floor. I answered the door and Greyson stood before me, looking as handsome as ever in black jeans and a tight gray T-shirt with an almost predatory smile on his face.

His body was a testament to his dedication to fitness, and his eyes — dark and filled with a hunger that matched my own — bored into me. My heart raced as an unsettling mix of arousal and fear coursed through me.

"Hey, Ghost," he greeted, stepping inside and closing the door behind him, his gaze never leaving mine. I could feel the heat emanating from his body as he stood closer.

"Hi," I managed to choke out, my throat tight with nerves. Greyson's presence had a way of making me feel exposed, vulnerable, and yet so alive. He raised an eyebrow, sensing my unease.

The tension between us crackled like electricity, making it difficult to think straight.

Greyson closed the distance between us, grabbing my arm and pulling me toward him. His breath was warm on my neck as he whispered, "Stop looking at me like that."

"Like what?" I asked, feigning innocence.

He gripped my hips and pulled me closer. "Like you want to devour me."

Our lips crashed together, a clash of teeth and tongues. He kissed me back fiercely, desperately, like a drowning man gasping for air.

His hands were in my hair, gripping tightly, and my hands roamed over the hard planes of his chest and his back, pulling him impossibly closer.

I groaned into his mouth as arousal flooded through me, hot and urgent.

He was just as affected — I could feel his erection straining against his jeans, pressing into my hip. I plunged my tongue into his mouth and he moaned, the sound shooting straight to my cock.

After weeks of denial, we were finally giving in to this madness between us.

And it was so much better than I'd imagined. My body trembled as I felt the overwhelming desire for Greyson surge through me like a tidal wave. I couldn't resist giving in to my carnal needs any longer.

My hands roamed over his muscular body, feeling the power beneath his skin. I wanted him more than anything, but the fear still lingered, threatening to smother the flames of desire. As if reading my thoughts, Greyson pulled away, his breath ragged.

"Ghost, we don't have to do this if you're not ready," he whispered, his eyes filled with concern. But despite my trepidation, I needed him — needed the connection that only he could provide.

"No." Our breaths mingled with the charged air between us. Dropping to my knees before him, I fumbled with his belt. "I want this, Greyson. I want you."

"Ghost," he gasped, taken aback by my sudden submission. But I didn't let his surprise slow me down. With trembling hands, I unzipped his pants and released his throbbing erection from its confines. A delicious shiver ran down my spine as I took him into my mouth, savoring the taste of his need for me.

"Fuck," Greyson moaned, his hands tangling in my hair as he pushed himself deeper into my throat. His hips bucked forward uncontrollably, driven by pure instinct. The sensation of his length filling my mouth only fueled my own arousal, pushing me further into the abyss of desire.

But before I could fully lose myself in the moment, Greyson's grip tightened, pulling me back from my lustful haze. He forced me off his cock, leaving me gasping for air, my lips swollen and slick with saliva.

"Enough," he growled. He pulled me up to my feet, his eyes ablaze with a mix of frustration and yearning. "I want more than this, Parker."

Before I could reply, he backed me up against a wall with his body. My heart raced as he trapped my wrists above my head, pinning my arms in place with one hand. It was a dominating move that only served to further ignite the fire within me.

The raw desire in his eyes made my stomach clench with need. "Don't move," he growled, dropping to his knees.

Anticipation swelled inside me as I stared down at Greyson. He was flushed and breathless already, desire etched into the lines of his face. I ached to touch him, to run my fingers through his hair and grip tight, but I stayed still. I wanted to give him this — to give him everything.

He undid my belt with deft fingers and tore open my jeans. My cock sprung free, hard and leaking, and I choked back a moan. He looked up at me with an intensity that made my breath catch in my throat. He reached out and took hold of my cock, stroking it with a practiced hand while maintaining eye contact.

"Tell me what you want," he demanded, his voice rough and seductive.

"Fuck ... I need you," I choked out between pants, my chest heaving as my need for him threatened to consume me.

Greyson's eyes flicked up to mine, darkened with lust, and he licked his lips. "I'm going to suck you off until you come down my throat."

Fuck. Just the thought of Greyson's perfect mouth wrapped

around my cock was enough to make me dizzy with need.

Without another word, Greyson swallowed me whole, taking me into his warm, wet mouth. The sensation was almost too much to bear, and I struggled to keep my hands above my head as instructed. His tongue swirled around my length, teasing and tantalizing me further into submission.

"God, Ghost ... you taste so fucking good," he murmured against my skin, his breath hot and heavy on my throbbing cock. I could see the lust and desire clouding his eyes, driving him just as mad as it was driving me.

Without warning, he sucked me into his mouth again. Wet heat enveloped my length, and I threw my head back with a groan, my hips jerking helplessly. I gripped the wall behind me, knuckles white, as I fought not to grab Greyson's head and fuck into that delicious heat.

He hummed around my cock, the vibrations shooting straight to my balls, and started to move. Up and down, his tongue was swirling over the head and tracing the vein on the underside. He took me deep, throat relaxing, until I was completely enveloped in silken heat.

"Fuck, Greyson," I gasped, breathless and trembling. I'd never felt anything so good in my life. He was going to destroy me.

Greyson pulled off slowly, a wet pop as my cock left his mouth, and looked up at me through heavy-lidded eyes. His lips were swollen and slick with saliva, and I groaned at the sight.

"Tell me what you want," he rasped, voice rough. He wrapped a hand around my length and stroked firmly.

I blinked at him, lust-addled mind struggling to understand. He wanted me to tell him what to do? Fuck. The thought of directing Greyson, of him obeying my every command, had heat pooling low in my gut.

"Suck me," I growled, burying my hands in his hair and guiding him back to my cock. He went willingly, eagerly, swallowing me down again. "Just like that, fuck yes."

He moaned around me and picked up the pace, head bobbing over my lap as he took me deep with every stroke. The lewd, wet sounds of his mouth on my cock echoed in the room, punctuated by my bitten-off groans.

The heat coiled tighter and tighter, building at the base of my spine. I was close, so fucking close, the pleasure blinding me to everything but the sweet suction of Greyson's mouth.

"Grey," I panted, tugging at his hair in warning, but he only moaned again and redoubled his efforts. His tongue was swirling over the head of my cock on every upstroke, pushing me closer and closer to the edge.

"Fuck, I'm gonna come," I gritted out. The coil snapped, and I came with a shout, spilling down Greyson's throat as my vision went white behind my eyelids.

He swallowed it all, lips sealed tight around my cock as I pulsed inside his mouth. By the time he pulled off, I was trembling and oversensitive but sated in a way I'd never known.

Greyson pulled back, wiping his mouth with the back of his hand. His pupils were blown wide, lips red and swollen. He looked thoroughly debauched.

He rose to his feet, pulling me into a brutal kiss that left me dizzy and reeling. As our tongues tangled together, I tasted myself on his lips — a heady combination that left me panting and desperate for more.

"Well, fuck." His chest rumbled against mine. "I wasn't expecting that. Are you okay?" his voice was laced with concern.

"That was fucking incredible," I mumbled against his lips. "But what about you?"

I reached between us to palm the hard line of his cock through his jeans. His hips bucked up into the touch, a broken moan spilling from his lips.

"That was for you." His lips grazed my jaw as he pulled my hand away from the bulge in his pants. "I wanted to make you feel good. I'm not going to let you do anything you're not ready for."

"Why are you always deciding what I'm ready for?" I huffed a laugh and kissed him again, softer this time. When we parted, I brushed my thumb over his lower lip, watching his eyes flutter closed at the touch.

"I'm claiming you, Parker," Greyson whispered harshly against my lips, his grip on my waist tightening. "And there's no going back."

My heart thundered in my chest, equal parts of fear and excitement coursing through my veins. Despite the anxiety stemming from my past threatening to swallow me whole, I knew one thing for certain: I wanted — no, needed — Greyson to claim me, to make me his in every way possible.

I stepped back from him, giving him space, while he adjusted himself. "Do you want a beer? I haven't had a chance to go shopping yet, so I don't have much to offer. We'll have to order something for dinner."

"About dinner," he looked up, "Talia invited me over. I was hoping you'd join me."

"At Talia and Ryder's house?"

"Yeah," he confirmed.

A sliver of unease ran through me. "Won't that look weird to them — if we come together?"

"Talia is my friend. She's known about my feelings for you." His lip turned down in a frown. "Unless you're more comfortable keeping everything completely under wraps from our friends?"

I blew out a breath, not knowing what to say. Nervous energy vibrated in my veins.

He spread out his hands in a calm and soothing gesture. "There are few people I trust. Talia is one of them. And Ryder. But it's up to you."

"I don't even know what we are doing," I said, feeling lost in a whirl of emotions.

"We're dating," he retorted with a smirk as if it was the most obvious thing in the world.

"Dating?"

"Have you ever dated someone before?" he asked with genuine curiosity.

I shrugged and looked away. "Not really." Never was the correct answer.

He laughed at my obvious discomfort. "Dating is getting to know each other. Taking things slowly. I'll buy you a few dinners. We'll watch a few movies together. I'll try to cop a few cheap feels here and there. It's a time-honored tradition."

I forced myself to relax. "Ok, so we're dating. I'll go to dinner with you, but let's just keep things cool."

"Got it. Cool." His eyes danced with laughter. "No grand announcements that we're together. No PDA."

I felt myself bristling at Greyson's teasing. "Jesus."

He came over and draped his arm around my shoulder. "Don't worry, Parker. I've got your back."

We arrived at Ryder and Talia's house on the beach several hours later. Ryder answered the door and didn't even blink at seeing me with Grey.

Ryder led us into the great room where Talia jumped up from the floor, where she was sitting next to Zoe, and greeted Greyson warmly, giving him a long hug. I was nervous, wondering if Talia was going to ask what I was doing with Greyson, but instead, she pulled out of Greyson's arms and turned to me.

"Johnny Geronimo, I'm happy to see you." Her bubbly personality immediately put me at ease. She stepped over and threw her arms around me.

I squeezed her in a hug, picking her up off her feet for a few seconds. "Natalia Rose, you're looking good."

"Johnny Geronimo?" Greyson croaked out. He was staring at me and Talia with a decided frown on his face.

I quickly let her go. "Yeah, that's my name."

Greyson looked back and forth between us, a flash of jealousy crossing his features. So much for playing it cool. For a world-renowned actor, he was certainly wearing his heart on his sleeves.

"Grey! Oh my God! Look at your face." Talia snickered.

Greyson rubbed a hand down his face, still looking a bit unnerved.

Talia's eyes were sparkling with mischief. "What would you do if I kissed him on the cheek?"

She raised up on her tiptoes and planted a kiss on my cheek.

I winced at the look of pure jealousy on Grey's face. Christ. He couldn't hold it in. He actually made a growling noise.

"You are jealous!" Talia exclaimed.

Ryder was sprawled in an oversized armchair, his eyebrows knitted together. He shifted his eyes from me to Greyson and asked with confusion in his voice, "Wait. Are you two together?"

I glanced over at Greyson, wondering if he'd deny it to protect me. But he kept his mouth shut, leaving it up to me. Shit, I wasn't ready for this.

Ryder saw my hesitation. "I knew you two were talking — the tour bus is small; there's no hiding anything. But, an item?"

I swallowed. "We haven't really determined that yet. I'm working through some stuff. I'm sure you heard me talking to Maggie non-stop this tour."

He nodded. "Yeah."

"I suffered sexual abuse as a kid and I kept it all bottled up until recently." I held my breath, waiting for his reply.

Ryder's jaw dropped. He slumped back in the chair and closed his eyes for a moment, muttering, "Oh fuck. I didn't know."

Tears welled up in Talia's eyes, and she embraced me, her hands gently rubbing my back.

Greyson moved to stand next to me in silent support. I didn't move; I stood rigidly, waiting to see what Ryder would do. He was one of my best friends and I worried he'd look at me differently.

"I can't believe you were going through all this and I didn't even know. I knew you were talking to Maggie a lot, but..." He threw up his hands in disgust. "Why am I always the last to know?"

He looked so put out that I actually had to suppress a chuckle. "You're not. I only told Knox just recently. Grey knows. And now, you and Talia. I was afraid to tell anyone. Afraid of how they'd react. Afraid of judgment."

He blinked slowly, trying to comprehend the situation. His head shook slowly in disbelief. "Why would people judge you?"

"I don't know." I shrugged. "It really fucked me up, Ryder. I'm just starting to figure out just how much with the help of Maggie."

He stood up and approached me, pulling me in for a hug. "I'm sorry that happened to you, but I'm here for you, brother. Whatever you need."

He pulled back, and I felt a lump of gratitude in my throat. "Thanks."

"Whatever you've been doing with Maggie, keep doing it." He slapped my shoulder. "I've seen some sparks of life in you. You've been like a different person these past few weeks. Maybe that's Greyson. And, if he's good for you, Ghost, then I'm behind you one hundred percent."

Ryder put his arm around Talia's shoulder and then his other on mine. "Get in here, Grey. Huddle up."

Greyson laughed but then stepped to our sides, closing off the circle.

Ryder looked around at all of us. "On three, ride or die."

"Ride or die," we vowed.

After dinner, we returned to the great room with drinks. Greyson was holding Zoe on his lap and playing silly games with her. It was weird watching him playing with and holding a tiny baby. He was a big, aggressive guy, but was so gentle with Zoe.

Talia came into the room, sat on the couch next to Greyson, and tucked her feet under her. "I don't want you to get mad, but I kind of did something that you may not like."

Greyson's goofy smile meant for the baby slid off his face. "Christ, Talia. What did you do? And Ryder, did you know about this?"

Ryder held up his hands. "I couldn't stop her if I tried."

She scrunched up her nose in preparation for Greyson's reaction. "I had lunch with Remi."

The sound of her name sent a stampede of butterflies fluttering through my stomach.

"Remi?" Greyson choked out her name.

"Don't kill me, Grey. She told me she's been trying to contact you." Talia swung her head around to look at me. "Both of you. And neither of you would return her calls or messages. I don't blame you, but she swears she didn't write that article."

Greyson's jaw squared. He stood up and handed Zoe to Ryder. "She publicly admitted to it, Tal. It's been all over the news. She apologized for all the lies and Hollywood Exposé had to pay out big bucks in a settlement."

"I know. But I talked to her and I believe her. I don't think she did it," she said, a glimmer of hope in her eyes. "She has something she wants to show you. She's waiting nearby right now. It's up to you, but I think you should listen to her."

Remi was actually here? Despite my anxiety, there was a spark of excitement; I couldn't deny that I wanted to see her. Remi was the only person who could make my heart race as fast as Greyson did.

Greyson shot a worried look my way, dragging his hand through his hair. "She's here?"

Talia nodded. "She'll be here in ten minutes if I text her."

I made a decision. I had to know the truth for myself.

"I want to see her," I announced.

Greyson and Talia both looked at me in surprise, but then Greyson conceded. "Okay. Let's do it."

Chapter 37

Remi

THE LOW HUM OF the espresso machine and the soft murmur of conversations around me did little to calm my nerves. I sat in the corner of the dimly lit coffee shop, clutching my lukewarm latte as if it were a lifeline. My heart hammered in my chest as my gaze darted between the window and my phone, praying for a text from Talia.

Earlier, she'd mentioned that Ghost had arrived with Greyson at her place, and my mind went into overdrive, wondering what that could mean. The image of our three entwined bodies haunted me, sending tendrils of desire creeping up my spine. I wanted — no, needed — to see them both, to confront whatever twisted reality we were tangled in together.

My phone buzzed with an incoming message. I caught my breath, fingers trembling as I unlocked the screen. It was Talia. 'They agreed to talk. Come over.'

"Thank God," I exhaled softly, relief washing over me. Pushing aside my now-cold drink, I gathered my belongings and hurried out of the cafe, thoughts racing through my head. What would I say? How would they react? Would there be anger or understanding?

A wave of nausea rolled through me as I approached Talia's house, taking note of the sleek, black car parked outside — a sure sign of their presence. I hesitated for a moment, gathering my courage before knocking on the door.

"Come in, Remi," Talia greeted me warmly, though I could sense the tension in her voice. "They're waiting for you in the great room."

"Thanks, Talia," I said, my throat tight with anxiety. "If you're willing, I'd like for you and Ryder to listen to what I have to say. It affects you both, as well."

She offered a reassuring smile. "Ryder is just finishing putting Zoe to bed. I'll give you some time alone with the boys. We'll be down in about ten minutes. Okay?"

I took a calming breath. "That's great. Thanks."

She showed me to the massive room with breathtaking views of the coast before hurrying off.

As I stepped into the comfortable, but stylishly decorated space, my eyes immediately locked onto the two men seated on the plush sofa. Ghost, his intense, brooding gaze piercing through me like a dagger, and Greyson, his muscular frame tense with anticipation. The palpable energy between them made the air feel thick and charged, their desires and fears mingling like a storm ready to break.

"Remi," Greyson said, breaking the silence. "We didn't expect to see you tonight."

They sat together, a formidable and united front, and I sensed a guarded hostility coming from them both. I couldn't blame them. They thought I'd published that malicious and hurtful story.

"Greyson, Ghost," I acknowledged them both, struggling to maintain my composure. "I ... I needed to talk to you both. About the article."

"Which part, Remi?" Ghost raised an eyebrow, his voice tinged with bitterness. "The part where you ripped to shreds the talent of my band or all the lies you printed about my friends?"

Tears burned like acid in my eyes, but I refused to let them fall. The contempt from those around me was unbearable. "I didn't write the article. Or publish it."

Greyson grimaced, clearly frustrated. "You admitted it, Rems! I read the apology statement."

I threw up my hands in despair. "I didn't write that either. But, I agreed to it. As part of the settlement."

Ghost remained silent, the intensity of his gaze pinning me in place. Finally, he spoke. "For the defamation lawsuit with Black Vault?"

"Yes," I answered. "Look, I'm not allowed to talk about the settlement. I had to sign an NDA. But that settlement had nothing to do with the truth. It was a product of all the corporate lawyers — BVR's and Hollywood Exposé's. The settlement shielded Hollywood Exposé's culpability while protecting BVR's assets, which is the band. I get that, but both sides of lawyers were working together to pin it all on me and earn their big payouts."

Ghost fixed me with an icy cold glare, his expression giving away nothing. "So, you're not really sorry? You only apologized because of the settlement?"

"I'm sorry for everything you all went through because of that article. All of you. The band, Talia, Trudy, everyone that article hurt." My chest was heaving with emotion. "I'm sorry that a lot of it came from my research. If I hadn't been given that assignment or been in that stupid competition for the promotion, it wouldn't have happened.

But, I didn't write it, I swear."

Just then, Talia and Ryder descended the staircase, joining us in the large room.

"I'm sorry for interrupting, but Remi asked us to join because she wanted us to hear, too." Talia looked tentatively at Greyson and Ghost.

"Fine," Greyson nodded. "Let's get on with it, then."

I struggled not to squirm under the weight of their scrutiny. I owed them this explanation, even if they never wanted to speak to me or see my face again.

"Let me start with a little background so you understand all this." I looked around the room. Talia was listening intently. Ghost had leaned back on the couch and folded his arms over his chest. Greyson's thigh was pressed up against Ghost's leg and when he glanced over at Ghost almost possessively, my heart skipped a beat.

"Mindy Blakedale is retiring from Hollywood Exposé. The company was having trouble deciding on a replacement for her. My boss, Caroline, was gunning for me and Jack Hoffman wanted Dawn Chambers."

I tucked a hair behind my ear and continued, "They decided to run a competition. Whoever came up with the better story would become the new face of Hollywood Exposé. We were each assigned a topic from Jack's rejected story pitch file and obviously, I got the story about a ghost that was haunting a rock band."

"And you said Dawn was a real conniving bitch," Talia interjected, obviously trying to help me out. At least, I had one person on my side and she still didn't even know the full story.

"Yes, Dawn warned me that she'd do anything to win the anchor spot. I knew she was a pit bull of a reporter, but I thought she'd stick to the lanes of her own assignment; I didn't think she'd interfere in mine."

Greyson leaned forward. "You're saying Dawn did this? That she wrote the story and claimed it was you?"

I nodded. "She did. Somehow, she got ahold of my notebook." I reached into the satchel purse hanging on my shoulder and pulled out my slightly battered notebook with the teal leather cover with gold embossed vines that my mother had bought for me. My mom had bought it as a reminder for me to reach for my dreams and as a good luck gesture for my potential promotion. Instead, the notebook had led to my downfall, both professionally and personally.

I tapped the cover of the notebook with my fingers. "This notebook contained all my research on Ghost Parker. All the research I did before I even joined the tour, all the interviews I conducted with the band and crew members, research about your past tours — anything I could dig up."

Greyson arched a brow at me, completely nonplussed by my words. "Does that notebook have information about my affair with Ryder? About how Ryder and Talia's marriage is a sham?"

"No!" I groaned in frustration. "There's nothing in here about you. Dawn just made up that stuff to hurt me. I think she saw the photo of you and Ryder in Boston on one of the fan sites and ran with it. She made up a lot of stuff, as you all know."

Ghost was playing with a ring on his finger and Ryder's leg was bouncing up and down. I was losing them. I needed to get to the point before I lost them for good.

Nervously, I bit my lip and continued. "I don't know how she got it. I always locked it in my drawer at work when I went to the restroom or got a cup of coffee in the breakroom. Maybe she had a key to my desk somehow."

Greyson was staring at me. "Rems, that sounds a little far-fetched."

"I believe her," Ghost blurted out.

Wow. Only seconds ago, I'd felt his hostility as he challenged me.

My heart swelled with gratitude for his support. He had no reason to trust me or take my side, yet here he was — giving me strength when I thought that all hope was lost. We locked eyes, and I felt that intense connection. It was his faith in me that bolstered my courage and gave me the strength to press on.

"Thank you." I took a deep breath, not missing the surprised looks the others were giving Ghost.

Greyson tilted his head, his mouth curled into a grimace of doubt. "You think Remi's co-worker stole her notebook and wrote that story to get her fired and get the promotion?"

Ghost turned to Grey. "We talked about this. Nothing about that article made any sense."

It wasn't Ghost's words that froze me to the spot, but the way his hand grazed Grey's thigh. It wasn't a sexual touch, but an intimate one.

I could see it then. It was clear. These two men, both of whom I loved fiercely, had formed a relationship together. Maybe it started off with a mutual grievance about that horrible hit piece, but it had grown into something more.

The looks that passed between them, the body language, and even how close they were sitting to each other all telegraphed how close they'd become. They had bonded over the suffering I'd brought upon them.

Now, I was the outsider, and it felt like a dagger in my heart. I was the outsider, not the glue that brought them together as I'd been before.

I was truly happy for them because I wanted the best for both of them. But that didn't mean I didn't feel a pang of jealousy. Actually, it wasn't as simple as jealousy. It was more like an aching despair. I wanted to be a part of their relationship, but I'd lost. Even with Ghost saying he believed me, I didn't know if I could ever be a part of what they now shared.

I choked back the tide of rising panic and sorrow. My heart strained against my ribs, battered from the maelstrom of emotions churning inside me. All I wanted was another chance, a glimpse of hope that I could make things right.

I wouldn't give up now. I was going to fight like hell. First, I needed them to listen to my recording.

"The story I was working on was about the New Palace theater, which is supposedly haunted. Ghost Parker performed there years ago. I have all the research right here in my notebook. When Dawn published that defamatory hit piece, I sent the real story I was working on to Greyson right away. It was nothing like what was published."

"I read it, but you could have written both." Greyson's voice was tinged with disappointment, cutting through me like a knife. "It doesn't prove anything, Rems. That could have been an earlier draft that you didn't go with because it wasn't sensational enough. You even told me you had to up your game because Dawn was getting good scoops."

"You're right. I couldn't prove anything. That's one of the reasons I had to agree to the settlement or risk financial ruin."

I took a deep breath, determination flooding my veins, white-hot and razor-sharp. "After I signed the settlement, I was leaving Hollywood Exposé and Dawn cornered me in the ladies' room to gloat. I managed to record most of that conversation, and I got her to slip up."

Talia gasped. "She confessed?"

I was so focused on Greyson and Ghost that I'd almost forgotten she and Ryder were still in the room. "It wasn't exactly a confession, but it makes it pretty clear she was guilty."

Ryder raised an eyebrow, glancing over at Ghost. "Okay. Let's hear it then."

I turned to face Ryder. "It has a lot to do with you, Ryder. And some of it may be ... painful."

Talia had been leaning against the armrest of Ryder's chair, but she gently slid onto his lap.

"Me?" He slid his arms around Talia's waist and locked his fingers together in front of her.

"It's about your cousin, Rocky."

Talia turned her head to the side to ask Ryder, "Was he the one from the article? The one who overdosed?"

Ryder nodded and answered softly. "Yeah."

"I found out something about him," I started tentatively. "It's in the notebook. I wasn't ever planning on revealing it because it's not necessary for anyone to ever know. I think it was a lie made up to spare the family shame or embarrassment."

Ryder's jaw was rigidly set. "What is it?"

I started pacing back and forth while I talked. "When I was in Ohio researching your background, I found out about your cousin's death. I needed a ghost for the assignment, someone that died who was connected to the band in some way, and I thought the cousin might work. It was stupid to think about exploiting someone's death like that."

I glanced around the room, and when no one spoke, continued, "According to local media reports, your cousin died of a fentanyl overdose, which isn't very uncommon, especially in the area where he lived. No one questioned it. Why would they?"

"You're saying it wasn't a fentanyl OD?" Ryder eyed me warily.

"The cause of death said nothing about drugs," I confirmed. "In fact, your cousin didn't die of a drug overdose at all. I'm sorry, Ryder, if this is hurting you."

He shifted in his seat. "I wasn't very close to Rocky. Or my aunt and uncle. What did he die of?"

I hesitated for a second. "Autoerotic asphyxiation."

The silence that followed felt like an eternity until Talia finally spoke up. "Isn't that like ... cutting off your air supply while ... masturbating?"

"Uh, yeah." I nodded.

Ryder's mouth twisted into a sneer of revulsion. He grunted; his expression one of surprise and disgust. "What an absolute dumb fuck!"

Ghost agreed. "Yeah, it's absolutely risky as fuck. They don't call it the 'grim reaper reach around' for nothing."

Ryder's shoulders slumped, and he sighed heavily with exasperation. "The guy was as dumb as a box of rocks, but damn! You have to be pretty stupid to take those kinds of risks."

"The chokey-strokey," Ghost added.

Ryder was still shaking his head in disbelief. "All for some high-risk wanking."

"Okay," Greyson cut in. "So the guy managed to strangle himself. What does that have to do with Dawn?"

I pulled out my phone and found the recording, which I also had multiple copies on other devices for safekeeping. "I'll play you the recording, but remember, only a few people know the actual cause of death. It's not reported anywhere; I checked. Ryder didn't even know, but it's in my notebook."

I turned up the volume and hit play. Remembering Dawn taunting me about my Scooby Doo tactics, I felt a bit like Velma, about to rip off the mask on the culprit. My eyes ping-ponged around the room, watching everyone's expressions as they listened.

At first, I hadn't been able to get Dawn to crack, and she'd stuck remarkably to the story, making me look bad even though it highlighted her taunting, nasty nature. But eventually, we got to the crucial part.

Grey's lips pressed into a thin line as he listened to Dawn's voice.

... he was in love with the guitarist, Ryder. Grey went to Boston to visit his lover, and you pitched a fit.

Talia shook her head as she listened. "This woman is a complete bitch!" she muttered.

We came to the part where Dawn's accusations were about to expose her.

... threw Ryder's cousin under the bus, too? You had the perfect motive.

Ghost was leaning forward on the couch, Greyson's hand on his arm as if to hold him back. Finally, the words I'd been waiting for spilled out of Dawn's mouth as we listened.

... that he died of autoerotic asphyxiation? That's kind of low, even for you.

The recording went on for a couple more minutes with Dawn's sputtering denials and vicious attacks.

... it doesn't prove anything. It's your word against mine, and who do you think they'll believe?

They sat in stunned silence, absorbing all that they heard. I inhaled deeply, feeling some of the burden I'd been carrying lifted, a small sense of vindication.

Talia broke the heavy silence. "She obviously wrote the article. But, I don't get it. The autoerotic asphyxiation wasn't in there. Why would she bring it up?"

I paced over to the straight-back chair and sunk into it, the surge of relief making my legs suddenly weaker. "My guess is that she got access to my notebook, but she didn't have a lot of time to look it over. She read through it quickly and got some information I was researching — most of the true stuff that was written." I glanced over to see that Ghost and Greyson were listening intently. "Then she wrote the article pretty quickly. It wasn't well written and its sole purpose was to inflict damage. She filled in any gaps by flat-out inventing stuff. I think she read about the autoerotic asphyxiation in the notebook but forgot to put it in the article, later thinking that she did."

"That's fucked up," Ryder cursed under his breath.

"I can't think of any other explanation of how she'd know about Rocky's death except for reading it in my notebook. And, I know I didn't write that article. I'm positive it was her." I clenched my jaw, waiting to see how they would react.

Talia snorted, "Remi, it's obvious after listening to that tape that she wrote it."

Ryder agreed.

I turned to face the two men who mattered the most to me. "Even if you never want to speak to me again or see my face again, I wanted you to know. It wasn't me. I wouldn't do that to any of you."

Ghost stood and approached me, his boots thudding heavily on the hardwood floor. My heart pounded as he stopped in front of me, his piercing blue eyes scanning my face.

"Remi," he began, his voice gravelly, "I'm so sorry." His words held a sincerity that broke through the walls I had built around myself, and I could no longer contain the tears that welled in my eyes.

Tears sprang to my eyes at his words, the knot of fear and hurt in my chest unraveling. I threw my arms around his neck, clinging to him as I tried to tide the stream of tears, blurring my vision. His strong arms encircled me, pulling me close to his hard chest.

After a long moment, I leaned back to look at him, wiping the tears from my cheeks. "This has been a nightmare that I didn't know how to wake up from. I was so scared that you'd hate me forever.

Ghost shook his head, brushing a stray strand of hair from my face. "My instincts knew all along that you'd never do that. I should have listened to them."

Greyson, who had remained silent throughout the entire exchange, finally spoke up. "I'm sorry, Remi. It's just ... hard to process everything right now." I peered at him through tear-streaked lashes, noting the way his jaw clenched and unclenched as he tried to keep himself composed. It was a subtle gesture, but it spoke volumes about the turmoil brewing beneath his carefully controlled exterior.

My heart ached to erase the distance that had grown between Greyson and me. "I don't blame anyone for believing I wrote that story. I would have, too, in your position." Frowning, I glanced over at Grey. "Even though Dawn did it, I still feel guilty for bringing her into your lives. I still feel responsible."

Talia and Ryder exchanged a glance before Talia cleared her throat. "You can't blame yourself for actions other people took. You had no control over any of that. Dawn really screwed us all over. The best thing we all can do is get past it without letting it interfere with our lives anymore," she said, offering me a small smile.

Her words, though genuine, did little to ease the tension that still lingered in the air. Greyson had taken the brunt of the damage from that article, and I wasn't sure he'd ever be able to separate me from that pain.

Ghost pulled me against his hard length. "Fuck, Greyson," he growled. "Get over here. We've got our girl back."

His words sent a rush of adrenaline running through my veins. I held my breath, praying Grey would come to us.

He stood and crossed the room in a few long strides, pulling me away from Ghost and into his arms. "You don't have to say anything else. I'm just glad this nightmare is over." He pressed a soft kiss to my forehead, warmth flooding through me at his touch.

His words echoed in my mind as I clung to him, desperate for the reassurance that everything would be alright. And for the first time in what felt like an eternity, I allowed myself to hope — to believe that maybe our love survived the storm.

I felt Ghost pressing up behind me. Sandwiched between these two men I loved, my heart surged with joy. I was home.

Chapter 38

Greyson

THE TENSION IN THE room was stifling. Ghost stood by the window, staring out at the city skyline. Remi perched on the edge of the black leather sofa, her knee bouncing nervously.

After leaving Talia and Ryder's house, the three of us met back at Ghost's apartment to talk through our issues. We were all edgy. None of us knew how to bridge the gap that had grown between us. The awkward silence only further highlighted how far we'd grown apart.

"This is ridiculous," I grumbled.

Ghost turned, eyes hooded. Remi bit her lip.

I strode across the room, grabbed Ghost by the collar, and crushed my mouth to his. For a moment, he resisted, then he was kissing me back, hard and hungry.

Our kiss was brutal and claiming, all clashing teeth and warring tongues. Ghost kissed like he lived, fast and hard and out of control, but I set the pace now. I dominated his mouth as I dominated his body, pinning him in place against the wall.

Remi gasped and my heart thudded crazily as I slid my hand into Ghost's hair, the silky strands slipping through my fingers. He growled, low in his throat, and pressed against me.

He moaned into my mouth, the sound vibrating through me, and his hands came up to grip my shoulders. I broke away with a nip at his lower lip and grabbed his wrists, slamming them back against the wall above his head.

"Keep them there," I growled, "or I'll stop."

Defiance flashed in his eyes, but he nodded once. I released his hands to trail mine down his chest, relishing the feel of firm muscle under my palms. His abdominal muscles clenched under my touch and I grinned, dropping to my knees.

"Greyson, don—"

I cut him off by unzipping his jeans and freeing his cock. He was already hard and leaking, and I couldn't resist leaning in to swipe my tongue over the tip, tasting salt and something uniquely Ghost.

A strangled groan escaped him as his head thumped back against the wall.

His hands remained in place, clenched into fists, and I rewarded him by taking him deep into my mouth. I set a hard, driving pace, hollowing my cheeks on every upstroke and humming encouragement.

I broke off only long enough to growl out an order, "Remi, you're next. Get undressed."

When I was satisfied that she was obeying me, I turned back to Ghost and redoubled my efforts. I'd unleashed the wild beast inside me and it wasn't easily slaked.

Ghost was close already, thighs trembling under my hands when I slid one hand back to grip his ass, urging him deep into my mouth.

"Come for me," I demanded, and that was all it took. He shuddered and came with a bitten-off cry, spilling down my throat.

I sucked him through his orgasm until he whimpered in surrender, then climbed back to my feet. Ghost sagged against the wall, eyes closed, chest heaving to drag in air.

I leaned into him. "Look at me." My voice was rough with desire, my own need throbbing between my legs.

Ghost opened his eyes, glassy with sated pleasure, pupils blown wide. "Greyson."

My name on his lips was satisfaction and surrender, and I claimed his mouth again in another searing kiss.

When we finally broke apart, panting, Remi was only a few feet behind me, her lips parted slightly and her eyes glassy with lust. She'd taken off her jeans and sweater but was still dressed in her matching bra and panties.

"Take it all off, Remi," I ordered.

With shaking hands, she unsnapped her bra and let it fall to the ground. Then she slipped out of her panties. She shivered under our gazes as both Ghost and I looked over her lush curves. I couldn't wait to sink into her tight heat.

I looked back at Ghost, who looked completely decadent with his messy hair, swollen lips, and his hands still raised over his head, like an offering. I wanted to fuck him, too, but I was still worried about his past. We needed to talk about what he wanted and needed from me, and until then, I would take things slowly with him.

"Rems, take his shirt off." I wanted to see all of him.

My eyes were focused on Ghost's face, watching how his eyes hooded when Remi approached, how the simple touch of her fingers affected him. While Remi pulled Ghost's shirt over his head, I kicked off my jeans and fisted my angry cock.

HOW TO CATCH A ROCKSTAR

Ghost captured Remi's lips in a hungry kiss and my cock pulsed just watching them. I stepped toward them, not wanting to be separate, but with them both. Grabbing Remi's ass, I ground my hard length against her.

I tried to wait for their kiss to finish, but I was impatient. I wanted to be inside her. Now. "Turn around, Rems."

She spun around in Ghost's arms. Her eyes were fixed on the cock in my hand, so I gave it a few strokes while Ghost watched over her shoulder. His hand smoothed up her side and then he palmed her tits, squeezing and lifting them. She moaned softly when he started pulling at her nipples, making them harden into sharp points.

God, I was ready to explode. "Lift her up."

I didn't have to explain; Ghost knew exactly what I wanted. He gripped Remi under her thighs and lifted her, pinning her in place. His tanned and tattooed forearms made a gorgeous contrast against her pale skin, but I could hardly concentrate on it because my eyes zeroed in on her pretty pink pussy. It was a mental picture I'd probably remember until the day I died.

It only took me a few seconds to line up my aching cock with her entrance. Remi's breath caught as I entered her in one hard thrust.

So tight. So wet.

I groaned, withdrawing slowly before slamming back in. Remi cried out, her nails digging into my shoulders. I pounded into her, our bodies colliding, slick with sweat.

Each snap of my hips sent jolts of pleasure through me, the tension coiling tighter and tighter. Remi writhed between Ghost and me, her breasts bouncing, soft moans escaping her parted lips.

Ghost growled behind her, the sound adding to the stimuli overwhelming my senses. I sunk into Remi and then stole a ravishing kiss from her before my mouth landed on Ghost's lips. I could not get enough of these two.

"Greyson, please..." Remi begged.

Pulling away from Ghost's mouth, I drove into Remi harder, faster, chasing the release I craved.

Within a minute, Remi tightened around me, her body going taut. A strangled cry tore from her throat as she came unraveled.

I followed after her, spilling deep inside her clenching heat. My vision whited out, and for a moment there was only blinding pleasure and the roar of blood in my ears.

When I came back to myself moments later, I was slumped against Remi, barely held up by Ghost's grip on her thighs. I eased out of Remi with a groan, and Ghost lowered her legs so she could stand on shaking limbs.

She sagged against me, her chest heaving as she struggled to catch her breath. I wrapped my arms around her, pressing a tender kiss to her temple.

Over Remi's head, my gaze met Ghost's. Heat and longing simmered in his pale eyes, a promise of things still to come. This was everything I'd wanted, everything I needed. The three of us, together at last, with no more walls between us.

I pulled back and smiled at Remi, who seemed to be in a state of blissful exhaustion. "Let's move this party to the bedroom," I suggested. I could feel her legs shaking against mine and knew that she probably needed a break from the intensity of the moment.

Remi looked up at me, her eyes wide and maybe a little nervous. "I thought you wanted to talk?"

"You've got about the next ten minutes to talk before my dick turns into a heat-seeking missile again. We can do all the talking you want tomorrow. Tonight is for fucking."

Ghost chuckled. We were on the same page.

Remi put her hand on her hips. "You're so bossy, Grey."

"You fucking love it." With those words, I scooped her up in my arms and started walking toward the bedroom.

I stopped at the first door and saw the bed. Before I could step inside, Ghost said, "That's the guest bedroom. Next door on the right."

If Ghost wanted us in his bed, I was more than happy to comply. I moved down to the door he indicated and stepped inside the large room.

I turned to him and frowned. "You don't make your fucking bed?"

He lifted his broad shoulders in a lazy shrug, not concerned by my grumbling. "This is my first day home after a long-ass tour. I had a lot of things to do."

I put Remi down on the rumpled sheets. "Jesus, Ghost. How about getting a housekeeper if you can't—"

Remi cut in, "For someone who didn't want to talk, you're sure talking a lot, Grey."

"How are we going to get him to shut up, bunny?" Ghost asked.

"Well, he said something about not talking when his dick was hard, so..."

Ghost gave me a shove. "On the bed, Durant."

They were teaming up on me, and even though I liked to be in charge, I complied and sat down in the middle of the bed next to Remi. Her nimble fingers worked open the buttons of my shirt, pushing the fabric off my shoulders, and soon I was as bare as the other two.

Ghost joined us on the bed, pushing on my chest until I lay down.

"God, you're so beautiful," he breathed, as he pressed his lips against my chest.

It was exactly what I was thinking about him. My fingers traced the patterns on his skin as I marveled at the contrast between his inked and unmarked flesh. He moaned in response, leaning down to taste my mouth.

I was ready. My lips crushed against Ghost's, devouring him in a kiss that obliterated all thought. Tongues dueled and tangled as I grasped his hair, angling his head to gain better access. His taste — whiskey and smoke — intoxicated me, firing my blood until I shook with need.

His cock pressed into my hip, hot and insistent, spurring me to grip him tighter. I wanted to mark him, to sink my teeth into the pale column of his throat and taste his essence. The urge shocked me, but there was no denying the savage hunger clawing inside my chest.

While Ghost had kept me occupied, Remi's soft hands stroked my dick and fondled my balls until I was once again pulsating with need. I was surprised by just how quickly the two of them had me panting and desperate for relief.

Ghost slid down my body and I missed his attention, but then Remi straddled me, her pussy hovering inches from my mouth. Her intoxicating scent, musky and feminine, wafted around us.

I glanced down at my cock, standing at attention, thick and veined, the tip glistening with precum. Ghost's calloused fingers wrapped around my length and began stroking it. Our eyes met, blue on slate gray, and a spark ignited between us.

Hunger.

Lust.

Possession.

He lowered his mouth around my cock, inch by inch until it hit the back of his throat. Sparks danced across my vision, heat pooling low in my belly. I was close already, the intensity nearly too much.

Remi gasped and then pressed down on my face. I didn't hesitate before I grabbed her hips and buried my tongue between her folds.

The sounds of sucking and licking filled the room, punctuated by

Remi's breathy moans and the wet smack of my lips greedy on her flesh.

She rode my mouth without mercy as Ghost worked me relentlessly. It was too much and not enough. I was drowning, flying, coming apart at the seams.

My release slammed into me, wrenching a muffled shout from my throat. Remi clenched around my tongue, finding her own peak. We shook together, pleasure ricocheting between us.

My whole body felt liquid and boneless. I barely registered Ghost flipping Remi over onto her hands and knees and sliding on a condom before entering into her from behind. When I finally came to my senses, I slipped a hand between Remi's legs so I could play with her clit while I enjoyed the visual of Ghost's perfect physique pounding into her.

The sounds of her moans and his guttural groans echoed through the room, a symphony of pleasure that just felt right. This was everything, the three of us together with no barriers left between us. I'd walk through fire for moments like this.

Remi's keening cries hinted at her impending orgasm, and I knew exactly how her sweet pussy was clamping down on Ghost's dick like a vice when I saw his face. The muscles on the side of his neck were strained as he thrust into her.

I pinched Remi's clit, and she detonated exactly the way I knew she would. Ghost thrust into her a few more times before he threw his head back in his own ecstasy.

They collapsed in a tangled, sated heap at my side. I pressed a kiss to Remi's sweat-slicked temple and the corner of Ghost's mouth, infinitely content in the arms of my lovers. Tonight, we had all gotten exactly what we needed.

Only a few minutes passed before Remi stirred in my arms and then sat up, looking like a debauched temptress. "I better use the bathroom before I fall asleep."

I let her get up and watched while Ghost took care of the condom. He climbed back into bed and didn't hesitate to slide up right next to me. I couldn't hide the lazy smile that crossed my face as I pulled him against my chest.

"I hope this fancy apartment comes with an equally fancy bathroom with a giant tub and shower," I spoke into his neck, breathing in his scent.

"It does," Ghost confirmed. "I've never used the tub before."

"Hmmm. We dirtied Rems up tonight." I snickered. "We'll have to get her thoroughly cleaned up tomorrow."

His hand slid over my chest and I sucked in a breath. "What's wrong with right now?"

"We're out of luck, Parker." I chuckled. "She's about to pass out for the night. I guarantee it."

Remi came out of the bathroom with her face freshly scrubbed. "I hope you don't mind, but I used your toothbrush. I couldn't find any extras, and I didn't want to snoop through your stuff."

She didn't really wait for an answer, but crawled into bed, pushing her way right between Ghost and I.

I held in my laughter at Ghost's pouty expression, and within a few minutes, I could tell that Remi was sound asleep.

A few minutes later, Ghost spoke quietly, "I never go to sleep this early."

He was used to late nights on the tour. He was probably restless. "You can get up if you want. I don't want to leave Remi. She probably wouldn't wake up — she sleeps like a log, but just in case, I don't want her waking up alone."

He rolled onto his side to face me. "I don't want to leave either."

The room had darkened, but the door was open and we'd left the lights on in the apartment. Remi's face was turned into my shoulder, leaving Ghost's face only inches from mine, even though Remi was trapped between us.

"Do you think this can last?" he asked after a long silence.

"Do you want it too?"

"Yes." His gaze was intense, a piercing blue that held me captive.

My heart melted with the raw emotional connection I suddenly felt. "So do I. This isn't just about sex for me."

He closed his eyes, suddenly looking overwhelmed by it all.

I reached my hand out and cupped his cheek. "Are you okay?"

When his eyes opened, they were burning like fire. "I don't want to be treated like a victim."

I paused a moment before whispering, "I don't want to hurt you. Ever."

His jaw set and a spark of determination glinted in his eyes. "I'll tell you to stop if I need to."

"Okay," I said, but I wasn't so sure I believed him.

He narrowed his eyes. "I'm not always going to let you take control."

"Let me?" My thumb swiped over his lip. "You have no say."

"The fuck I don't," he growled. He turned his head and captured my thumb in his mouth, sucking it in.

I groaned at the sensation. Jesus, my cock was stirring again. I pulled my hand away, wondering if he knew how much power he had over me.

"I want to protect you." I glanced down at Remi, still sound asleep. "Both of you."

Ghost made a scoffing noise with his throat.

"She's not very ... experienced. I know she's nervous about being with both of us at once. She has to know that I'd never force something on her she wasn't comfortable with."

"Of course not," he added.

"She can say no to anything. What we shared tonight was amazing. We don't need to do anything else and I'd be okay with that," I continued, needing to get my point across. "That goes for you, too. I'm not going to push you into anything. I'm happy just being with you like we were tonight."

He let out an impatient puff of air. "I want it all, Greyson."

"I want to go to therapy with you and see what Maggie says—"

He kissed me fiercely, silencing my words. "Go to sleep, Durant. We'll talk in the morning."

♫♪♩♩

Remi's sleepy voice woke me up in the morning. "Where's Grey?"

I popped my head up to look over Ghost's body, which was wedged in between us. "I'm right here."

She pinned Ghost with a glare. "How did you get in the middle?"

A sly smile spread over Ghost's lips, but he just shrugged his shoulders, acting clueless. I knew he liked being the center of attention.

I decided to give him a little attention. My hand slid down his back and over his toned ass before slipping across his hip. His cock was already rock hard and poking into Remi's back. I wrapped my fist around it and relished the way it made Ghost drag in a ragged breath.

What a fucking amazing way to wake up.

Chapter 39

Ghost

My eyes fluttered open as the sun peeked through the curtains, its golden light caressing my skin. A tangle of limbs greeted me — Remi nestled into my side, her breaths slow and even, Greyson's arm slung over my chest, his face buried in the crook of my neck. The scent of sweat and sex still hung heavy in the air, remnants of our passionate night together.

A smile tugged at the corner of my lips. Being sandwiched between them was my new favorite way to wake up. I buried my nose in Remi's hair, seeking her sweet scent while reliving the pleasures we shared the night before.

"Ugh, Ghost," Remi groaned, squirming beneath the covers as she tried to escape my possessive embrace. "How did you end up in the middle again?"

I feigned innocence, trailing a finger down her spine. "No idea, bunny. Must have rolled over in my sleep." The lie slipped off my tongue easily. I didn't roll into the middle — I crept between their sleeping forms, craving the warmth and comfort of their bodies. The truth was, I couldn't get enough of them. Of this. I wanted it to be permanent.

Greyson's chest rumbled against my back as he let out a low chuckle. "Liar." His lips brushed the skin of my neck, sending a shiver down my spine. "You were wide awake when you wedged yourself between us."

His fingers lazily traced patterns along the curve of my hip. The sensation sent shivers down my spine, awakening a familiar hunger within me. I knew he felt it too; our shared desire for one another was undeniable. As his fingers continued their exploration, I could feel my body responding, my cock swelling with anticipation.

"Oh, my God. You two are insatiable." Remi teased, her voice thick with sleep. She reached out to gently stroke Greyson's arm, her fingertips brushing against my chest. "If you two are thinking of going at it again, you're gonna have to do it without me. I'm pretty sore."

"Why don't you take a long soak in the tub, Rems?" Greyson wrapped his hand around my cock and gave it an experimental stroke. My hips bucked off the bed.

"That does sound wonderful." Remi's eyes were focused on Grey's hand. She lifted an eyebrow. "Are you two trying to get rid of me?"

"Never." Grey stroked my cock again, this time with a firmer hand. I clutched at the bedsheets, trying not to groan. "In fact, we need a shower. I'm going to clean him up and you can watch."

She licked her lips, her eyes dark with lust. "Ooh. That sounds like a show I'd love to see." She slid from the bed, the sheet pooling at her feet. My gaze roamed her naked body as she sauntered toward the en suite bathroom. Over her shoulder, she said, "Make sure it's a good one."

Greyson chuckled, his breath hot on my neck. "Don't worry, Rems. It'll be so good."

The click of the bathroom door closing echoed in the silence. I shifted to face Greyson, desire simmering in my blood. He cupped the back of my neck and brought our mouths together in a searing kiss. Our tongues tangled and danced, stoking the embers of desire in my belly into flames.

"Fuck, Grey." The curse fell from my lips with a hiss. "Let's get in the shower. Now."

Nostrils flaring, he stood. I followed him into the bathroom, the air thick with steam as the tub filled while Remi brushed her teeth. Greyson started the shower water while I found some new toothbrushes for everyone.

Remi moaned with delight as she stepped into the luxurious tub. She was a vision, water sluicing over the curves of her body.

When I finished brushing my teeth, I stepped into the shower and immediately crowded Greyson against the tiles, capturing his mouth in a bruising kiss. Our cocks slid against each other, creating delicious friction.

My fingers traced the contours of his chest, lingering over his defined pectorals before teasing his nipples. A shiver ran through him, his breath hitching as he bit back a moan. It thrilled me — this power I had over him, the knowledge that I could bring him to his knees with just a touch.

"Remember who's watching," I whispered into his ear, my words both a tease and a challenge. "Do you want Remi to see how much you crave my touch?" The thought of her there, just beyond the glass, sent a thrill down my spine — a voyeur to our most intimate moments.

Greyson's response was a low growl. He grabbed the shower gel, pouring it into his hands before slathering it onto my body. As he lathered up my chest, his fingertips danced across my sensitive flesh, igniting a fire deep within. My breath caught in my throat, the desire building inside me threatening to break free.

"Is that what you want, Parker?" he murmured, his voice barely audible above the roar of the water. "You want her to watch you beg for more?"

I turned my head to see Remi. She lounged in the luxuriously deep bathtub opposite us, her eyes fixated on our interplay, her lips slightly parted in anticipation.

"Let's see if you can handle this, rock star," Greyson whispered into my ear, sending shivers down my spine. His soapy hand wrapped around my cock, stroking it slowly, teasingly."Because I'm going to make you beg for it."

The hot water sluiced over my skin as Greyson pushed me against the shower wall, pinning my wrists above my head. Our cocks ground together, slick and hard, sending sparks of pleasure up my spine.

"Who's in control here?" His voice was a low growl against my ear that made me shiver.

I smirked, rolling my hips to slide our lengths along each other in a slow grind. "You think you are."

He bit my neck in retaliation, teeth sinking into the corded muscle. I groaned, the bite of pain sharpening my arousal. "Keep pushing me, Ghost, and I'll have to teach you a lesson."

I twisted in his grip, shoving him back against the opposite wall of the shower. If Remi wanted a show, I was all too happy to give her one.

We grappled for dominance, hands roaming over wet skin as the water beat down on us. My cock throbbed with need, leaking against his hip. I wanted to fuck him, to claim him, to wipe that smug look off his face as I pounded into him.

I captured both his hands with mine and this time it was my hand imprisoning his above his head. My other hand was wrapped around both of our cocks, stroking firmly.

Precum slicked my movements as a groan tore from his throat. "Fuck, Ghost."

My breath was hot against his ear, my voice rough with lust. "You're mine, Greyson. Say it."

He gritted his teeth, writhing in my grip as my fist pumped faster. Pleasure coiled in my gut, the edge looming close.

With a growl, he surrendered. "Yours. I'm yours."

A dark chuckle. "That's right. Now cum for me."

My command threw him over the edge. Release roared through him as he came with a shout, spilling over my hand in hot spurts.

While he still floated in the haze of his orgasm, I whispered in his ear. "I'm not done with you."

The hunger inside me grew, threatening to consume me entirely. I knew what I wanted, but a tremor of fear ran through me. I didn't have to do this. I could tell him to drop to his knees and suck me off, and he'd do it in a heartbeat.

The water cascaded down Greyson's body, highlighting the contours of his muscles as he smirked at me, that deliciously wicked glint in his eyes. I knew that he could push his way out of my grasp; that he was allowing me some control. Somehow, that made it all the more exciting.

My pulse quickened, my arousal becoming uncontrollable with each passing moment. We were a swirling tempest of pent-up desire and unspoken need. But I wanted more than just to be caught up in the storm — I wanted to master it.

"I'm going to fuck you," I growled, grabbing a condom from the shower caddy and ripping open the foil packet. My fingers slipped on the slick surface, but I managed to roll it onto my throbbing erection. The sensation of the latex encasing me only heightened the anticipation, and I could feel my heart pounding like a drum against my chest.

Greyson's gaze remained locked on mine as I stepped closer, our wet bodies pressed together, his breath hot on my skin. He leaned his head back against the cold tiles, exposing the column of his throat — a tacit invitation for me to stake my claim.

"Ghost..." he whispered, his voice barely audible above the sound of the water. "Are you sure about this?"

As I squeezed my throbbing erection, I couldn't help but let out a low moan. "You want this, don't you?"

Greyson attempted to maintain his composure, but the lust in his eyes betrayed him. "More than anything," he whispered, his voice ragged.

"Good," I replied, my lips brushing against his as I spoke.

Remi, unable to tear her eyes away from the scene before her, bit her lower lip and squirmed in the bathtub. The sight of her desire only fueled my own, and I pressed in closer to Greyson.

"Fuck, Ghost," he gasped as our mouths met again in a feverish dance. Our bodies pressed together, slick with soap and water, and the heat between us threatened to consume us both.

"Say it, Greyson," I demanded, my voice low and commanding. "Tell me what you want."

He hesitated, struggling to maintain control even as his body betrayed him. His chest heaved with anticipation, his eyes shining with a mix of vulnerability and desire. "I want you, Ghost. I want you to fuck me."

♫♫♪♪♩

I lay on the end of the bed after putting on a pair of boxers, my rubbery legs dangling over the side. I was exhausted but in the best possible way. Greyson and Remi were still in the bathroom cleaning up, and I had two things on my mind: food and more sex.

Water droplets glistened on Remi's skin as she sauntered into the bedroom, fresh from her bath, steam still clinging to her body. I watched her movements with a predatory hunger, taking in the way her hips swayed and how her damp hair clung to her neck. She joined me on the bed, lying close enough that I could feel the heat radiating off her.

She turned to look at me with her big brown eyes. "I love that you and Greyson have gotten close. He's such a good person, Ghost. And he cares about you. About us." Her lips twisted into a smile. "Even if he can be bossy at times, it looks like you figured out exactly how to deal with that."

"Bunny," my voice came out as a low rumble. "You didn't mind that we did that ... without you?" My heart tightened at the thought of having crossed a boundary, yet I couldn't keep the memory of our tangled bodies from invading my thoughts.

She bit her lip before answering. "It was a very good show." A wicked smile spread across her face as she trailed her fingers along my arm. "I'm not gonna lie; it turned me on watching you two."

Yet, there was something lurking behind her eyes — an insecurity gnawing at her. "I just wonder sometimes if you and Greyson don't need me," she admitted softly, vulnerability seeping through her words.

As her confession hung in the air, I felt a pang of guilt for causing her to doubt her place in our lives. I pulled her closer, wrapping my arms around her and pressing my lips to her forehead, wanting to absorb her fears and replace them with reassurance.

"Remi," I whispered into her damp hair. "I want to be with both of you. You're everything to me, and so is Greyson." The truth resonated within me, forming a knot of certainty that I couldn't deny.

My heart raced as I leaned down to capture her lips in a searing kiss, letting the heat of our connection consume us. I wanted her to feel the depth of my desire, to understand that our bond transcended physical pleasure — it was a connection that weaved its way through our souls, binding us together.

As our lips parted and I gazed into her eyes, I hoped she could see the truth of my words mirrored in my own. This wasn't just about sex — it was about love, trust, and the raw vulnerability that came from baring ourselves to one another, both physically and emotionally. At that moment, I knew our tangled hearts would forever be intertwined, and nothing could ever change that.

My stomach chose that moment to rumble with hunger. "I think we could both use some food after last night." I felt her nod against my chest, a slow smile spreading across her lips.

"Definitely," she agreed, her fingers tracing lazy circles on my skin. "What did you have in mind?" My stomach grumbled in response, making Remi laugh softly.

"Let me see if I can dig something up," I offered, reluctantly pulling away from the warmth of her body. "You and Greyson can join me in the kitchen when you're ready."

"Can I borrow one of your T-shirts?" She sat up, her hand already reaching for the edge of the blanket. The sight of her like that, naked and vulnerable, stirred something inside me, a raw desire that threatened to ignite once more.

"Of course," I replied, trying to keep my voice steady. "You're welcome to anything in my closet. Same goes for Greyson." I hesitated for a moment, then added, "You know you're always welcome here, right?"

She smiled, her eyes softening with gratitude. "Thanks, Ghost. That means a lot."

I didn't bother with a T-shirt for myself as I made my way to the kitchen. I loved the way Remi and Greyson's eyes roamed over my body.

My thoughts lingered on Remi, the taste of her lips still fresh in my mouth, the way her body felt pressed against mine. The hunger I sought to satisfy went beyond just food — it was a craving for connection, an insatiable need to be close to the people I loved. And with Remi and Greyson by my side, I knew I had found that connection.

I rummaged through my cabinets, searching for food, when the buzzer rang. It was Knox, and I thought about turning him away — hiding my relationship with Remi and Greyson from him, but then I buzzed him up. I wasn't going to be ashamed of our relationship when it made me so happy. Besides, he said he had breakfast with him.

When I heard his knock at the door, I left the kitchen, tugging at the waistband of my boxers as I made my way to answer it. I had been expecting Knox, but when I swung the door open, surprise filled me as I found both him and Summer standing there.

Summer pretended to shield her eyes from the sight of me. "Come on, Ghost, put on some clothes. Feels like we're back on the tour bus," she teased, her eyes traveling down my half-naked frame.

I gestured them inside. "What are you guys doing here?"

Knox raised his eyebrows, grinning. "We were shown an apartment that just opened up in your building. Corner unit, lots of light." He stepped inside, pulling Summer along with him. "Summer's place has been getting a bit tight for the two of us, and the neighborhood isn't what it used to be. I can't believe I left her there alone while we were on tour."

Summer patted his shoulder. "How did I manage to survive for so long without you?"

"This building is so expensive, though," he added, frowning slightly.

"Christ, man, you can afford it," I needled him, enjoying the light-hearted banter.

Knox rolled his eyes, but a smile still played at the corners of his mouth.

"Anyway, we brought breakfast," Summer announced, holding up some bags of food triumphantly. A growl erupted from my stomach as the scent of bacon and eggs wafted through the air. She grinned knowingly. "Knox said you wouldn't have gone shopping yet after the tour."

"Guilty as charged," I admitted, rubbing the back of my neck sheepishly. "I guess Knox wins the bet."

Knox raised his eyebrows in a suggestive manner. "I'll be collecting my winnings later. For now, I'm hungry." He dug his hand into a bag and pulled out a muffin.

Summer shook her head at Knox and then looked at me. "We've got bacon and eggs, tons of pancakes, bagels, and muffins. Hopefully, you have coffee."

I liked Summer, especially after getting to know her better on tour, but it was only after connecting with Remi and Greyson that I could appreciate just how good she was for Knox.

"Grey is not going to like all these carbs," I predicted.

Knox choked on his muffin. "Grey?"

As if saying his name conjured him from thin air, Greyson walked into the room, drawing my gaze away from Knox and Summer. He was wearing my clothes, which hugged his sculpted body like a second skin. His damp hair clung to his forehead, accentuating the sharp lines of his chiseled jaw. My heart hammered against my chest as desire surged through me.

Summer's eyes widened, her lips parting as she took in the sight of Greyson. Knox raised an eyebrow, a knowing smirk playing on his lips. "Grey, do you remember my girlfriend, Summer? You met her at Talia's baby shower?"

Greyson flashed a charming grin, nodding at Summer, who seemed to have forgotten how to breathe. The tension in the room thickened, and I couldn't help but feel a pang of jealousy at the attention Greyson garnered.

The moment was interrupted by Remi's entrance. She wore my clothes too, but they hung loosely on her slender frame. Confusion flickered across Knox and Summer's faces, making the atmosphere even more awkward.

Remi stopped in her tracks, taking in the scene.

Summer raised the bags in her hands again. "We brought breakfast."

"Terrific! I'm starved." Remi glanced over at me as if asking for help. "Summer, come help me make coffee in the kitchen?" She gestured towards the doorway with a slight tilt of her head.

As Summer hesitated, I caught Greyson's eye and gave him a pointed look. "Grab me a shirt, will you?" I needed a moment alone with Knox.

Greyson nodded, disappearing down the hallway. The women left for the kitchen, leaving Knox staring at me in bewilderment.

"Is this what I think it is?" he asked.

I moved closer to him, not wanting anyone to overhear our conversation. "Yes."

"Oh. Okay." He stared into the distance with his brow furrowed and ran a hand through his hair.

Knox's eyes flashed with curiosity, his breath warm on my face as he leaned in. "Mate, what do I think this is?"

Laughter bubbled up within me, a strange mix of relief and amusement. "You know, Knox," I said, feeling the weight of my own vulnerability in admitting it, "Remi, Greyson, and I ... we're together."

Knox's eyebrows shot up just as Greyson walked back in, his eyes darting between Knox and me. He took in how close we were standing to each other, and jealousy sparked in his eyes. As subtle as a bull in a china shop, he stepped between us, using the excuse of handing me a T-shirt to create distance.

"Easy there, Grey," I smirked, noticing his possessiveness. "Knox and I have been friends for years. Hell, he's seen me naked before. The tour bus was like a sardine can on wheels; there were no secrets there." My heart raced, questioning if I should share more. "In fact, I'm pretty sure back in the day, Knox and I ..." I trailed off suggestively, a wicked grin on my lips.

"Ugh! Rock stars!" Summer interrupted, having just returned to the room. She covered her ears, wrinkling her nose. "I don't want to know!"

Greyson's jaw clenched, betraying a jealous streak that made my cheeks flush with excitement. His possessiveness sent an unexpected thrill surging through me.

I put on the plain black T-shirt with the silhouette of a guitar on it that Greyson picked out for me, feeling his eyes on me as he watched me dress.

"Knox," Summer interjected, waving a hand to get his attention. "Remi told me she didn't write that article. It was a co-worker who set her up." She directed her gaze at me and raised her eyebrows. "Ghost, you should have led with that. I was so confused."

I glanced over at Remi, who was nervously picking at the hem of her T-shirt. "Oh, sorry. A lot has happened in the last couple of days."

"No kidding!" Summer retorted, her eyes scanning the three of us. "What's going on between you guys?"

My stomach churned with a blend of trepidation and excitement as I shared a glance with Remi and Greyson. This was our moment to be open, to embrace the connection that had formed between us. But in doing so, we risked judgment and misunderstanding.

"Summer," I began, my voice barely above a whisper, "the three of us ... we're together. In a relationship."

As the words hung in the air, I braced myself for the unknown, my heart pounding in my chest. There was no turning back now. Remi came to stand next to me, silently offering her support.

Summer's brow furrowed, her eyes darting between me, Remi, and Greyson. "The three of you?" she asked, hands on her hips. "All together? Like a triangle? Is it an equilateral triangle or more like an isosceles triangle?"

My heart hammered in my chest, the uncertainty of their reactions sending a shiver down my spine. I glanced at Remi, her fingers entwined with mine, and then at Greyson, who stood tall with an air of confidence. They were my rock, my foundation.

"Equilateral," I finally replied, swallowing hard. "We're together in every way."

Knox crossed his arms over his chest, his lips quirking up in a smile. The silence hung thick in the air, suffocating me.

Then Summer broke into a wide grin and clapped her hands together, the sound echoing through the room. "Oh, that's wonderful! I'm so happy for you guys!"

Knox slapped me on the back. "Yeah, Ghost, if you're happy, we're happy too." He turned to Summer. "Isocoles triangle, lass? What the bloody hell are you talking about?"

A wave of relief washed over me, my muscles unclenching as I let out a breath I hadn't realized I'd been holding. I'd gone from numbing the pain of my past and sleepwalking through life to this — to learning to experience it fully with Remi and Greyson by my side.

"Thank you," I whispered, my voice barely audible, but the gratitude within it was immense.

Remi squeezed my hand and leaned in to press a soft kiss against my cheek while Greyson wrapped an arm around my waist, pulling me close. Their touch, their presence, sent warmth spreading through my body, igniting my senses and grounding me in the moment.

As I looked into their eyes, I saw love, acceptance, and understanding reflected back at me. And as I stood there, enveloped in the embrace of the two people who had taught me to embrace life's complexities and allowed me to explore my desires without fear or judgment, I realized that this was what happiness felt like.

Deep within my heart, I knew that the journey ahead would be filled with challenges and uncertainties. But with Remi and Greyson by my side, I also knew that I was strong enough to face them head-on. And at that moment, as Summer and Knox's laughter filled the room, I finally understood that I was no longer alone — I belonged to something greater than myself: a love that defied conventions and transcended boundaries.

And for the first time in my life, I was truly free.

Chapter 40

Ghost

I LAY BACK ON my lounger, feeling the warmth of the sun on my skin. Remi and Greyson were lounging beside me, their bodies glistening with sweat.

The sun's rays cast a golden glow over the tropical oasis. We had staked out a prime location on the edge of a natural pool with its crystal clear water and soft sandy bottom. A waterfall cascaded down from the dark rocks above, creating gentle ripples in the water and providing a refreshing mist. At the edges, lush tropical plants and bright flowers spilled down and cast their cool shadows across the pool.

My eyes traced the gentle sway of palm trees that encircled the exclusive resort, the scent of tropical flowers teasing my senses. I lounged between Remi and Greyson on soft, plush recliners, soaking up not only the sun but also the intoxicating energy of their presence.

Months had passed since the three of us decided to become exclusive, but the novelty of being together still hadn't worn off. This vacation was exactly what we needed to escape the stresses of our lives.

I stretched out my legs, feeling the heat warm my muscles, and sighed with contentment. Our lives had become chaotic — me, caught between rock tours, producing a new album, and dealing with the ghosts of my past; Remi, unemployed but pouring her heart into a fictional political thriller inspired by the scandal she'd investigated early in her career; and Greyson, his character "killed off" in *Devious*, enjoying a long break from filming while the world remained ignorant of his impending return from the dead.

As I closed my eyes and let out a contented sigh, I felt a hand on my chest. Opening my eyes, I saw Greyson leaning over me. He grinned and leaned down to kiss me, his lips hot and demanding. I couldn't resist him, and I pulled him closer, kissing him deeply.

Remi cleared her throat, and we both turned to look at her. Her lips curved into a half-smile as she tried not to laugh. "Are you two going to make out all day? And why does Ghost always get to be in the middle? It's not fair."

We laughed and settled back into our loungers, enjoying each other's company. I watched Remi, my eyes tracing the outline of her wet bikini against her tan skin. My heart raced as she brushed a strand of hair behind her ear, revealing her slender neck. A bead of water rolled down from her collarbone to her chest, and I fought the urge to lean forward and taste it.

Remi noticed my attention and leaned over, her fingers tenderly caressing my thigh. Her touch ignited a familiar warmth within me, a belonging. She smiled softly, her eyes dancing with affection, before returning to her book.

Greyson, looking every bit the TV star with his chiseled physique and sun-kissed skin, reached for his water bottle, taking a slow sip as he glanced at me. His gaze was heavy with unspoken emotion, a testament to the deep connection we shared.

Greyson had been patient with me when I didn't even know I desperately needed it, taking things slowly and opening his heart to me. As promised, he joined me in a few therapy sessions with Maggie so he could understand how to help me best. I could tell that Maggie really liked Grey, and that ticked me off. I guess I was just as jealous as Greyson got, but at least I could keep it under wraps. Grey never hid his jealous streak.

I closed my eyes, basking in my contentment. As I lay there, sandwiched between these two gorgeous people who had opened their hearts to me despite my many flaws, I felt an overwhelming sense of gratitude. Our love was unconventional, a tangled web of passion and trust, but it was ours. And for the first time in my life, I felt truly alive, anchored by the powerful force that bound us together.

A sudden shift in the warm breeze caught my attention, and as I turned my head, I noticed a sultry woman sauntering toward us. Her hips swayed seductively, her eyes locked onto Greyson as if he were prey. My pulse quickened, an unexpected surge of possessiveness coursing through me.

"Colton! Oh my God, I can't believe it's you!" she exclaimed, stopping next to Greyson's lounger. She was stunning, with long blonde hair and curves in all the right places.

Grey lifted his shades, his expression betraying mild amusement but also a hint of discomfort. I could almost hear the gears turning in his head, weighing the pros and cons of engaging with this stranger who was clearly taken with his on-screen persona.

"You're even hotter in person," she purred, eyeing Greyson hungrily. "How about you and I go grab a drink?"

I sat up, my protective instincts kicking in. "Sorry, but he's already taken."

Her gaze snapped to mine, and I felt her eyes ravishing every inch of me. "By you? I can work with that. How about the three of us go get that drink?"

"By both of us," Remi chimed in, shifting on her lounger.

The woman's eyes widened, taking in the intimacy of our loungers pressed together. She scoffed, crossing her arms. "Sorry, I'm not interested in women."

Remi snorted with disgust. "Who asked you?"

I allowed myself a small smirk as I tilted my head toward the pool where Bishop, my ever-present bodyguard, was wading in the crystal-clear water.

Yes, I'd seen both Remi and Greyson checking him out earlier, but damn, I couldn't blame them. He was ex-military, and the dude was all muscle. We managed to convince him to let his hair down and enjoy the resort amenities for once since most of the clientele here had more notoriety than we did.

"However, that guy over there is single," I informed her, noticing how her eyes lit up at the sight of Bishop's muscular form. She hesitated for just a moment before flouncing off in his direction, her indignation replaced by eager anticipation.

I glanced at Greyson and Remi, their faces mirroring my own relief as we basked in our reclaimed privacy.

Greyson looked over at us. "Are you sure you want to tell people that we're together? She could sneak some pictures. Talk to a tabloid. Then the whole world would know."

"I don't care," I forced out through a tight throat, each word a biting blade. "I'm tired of hiding it. I'm not ashamed of being with you two. Anyone who doesn't like it can fuck off."

HOW TO CATCH A ROCKSTAR 431

Remi reached for my hand and squeezed it. "I don't care either. As long as I have you two, I can get through anything."

As we lay there, a renewed sense of unity enveloping us, I realized just how far we had come. I couldn't help but think that this was just another test of our unconventional relationship, a reminder that the outside world would always be ready to challenge our bond. It was up to us to hold fast and weather the storm together.

As the day wore on, the simmering arousal between us grew to a near boil. The heat seemed to amplify everything, making me more aware of each lingering touch. While the sun-warmed water lapped at my chest, I gazed over at Remi and Greyson, their wet skin glistening under the midday sun. My cock twitched with rising lust at the sight of Remi's full breasts, barely contained by her bikini top and the bulge in Greyson's swim trunks.

An ache started low in my belly, heat pooling between my legs. I wanted them. Now.

Greyson's eyes met mine, a smoldering look that sent lust shooting through my veins. He stood, water sluicing down his tanned torso, and slid his hand onto Remi's thigh, his fingers tracing circles against her skin.

He caught my stare with a knowing grin and leaned in to whisper something in her ear. Her face flushed, and she bit her lip, glancing over at me. The tension between the three of us was palpable, and I knew we wouldn't be able to keep our hands off each other for much longer.

"Let's go back to the villa," I suggested, my voice raspy with desire. Remi nodded, her eyes darkening with lust, and Greyson pulled her against his body, her hips brushing against his cock.

I was drawn towards them as if by an invisible force. Greyson ran a hand down my chest, his touch igniting sparks that shot straight to my groin. I arched into him with a groan, craving more. Remi shifted beside me, the rustle of her bikini straps sliding down her arms, making my cock twitch.

She leaned over and whispered in my ear, her breath sending a shiver down my spine. "I want to suck your cock while Greyson fucks you."

My gaze locked with Greyson's. Heat and promise simmered in his eyes, reflecting the hunger gnawing inside me. "Then let's get out of here."

In silent agreement, we left the pool and retreated to our villa. The moment the door closed behind us, Remi was on her knees in front of me, freeing my cock from my trunks. Her warm mouth closed over the head, sucking hard, and I groaned.

Greyson came up behind her, tugging at her bikini bottoms, revealing her bare ass. He caressed the pale globes, slipping his fingers between her folds. Remi moaned around my cock, the vibrations sending shockwaves of pleasure through me.

I tangled my hands in Remi's hair, guiding the pace of her ministrations. The sight of her on her knees, Greyson fingering her from behind, was almost too much.

"Bed. Now." My voice was strained, lust evident with every syllable.

Remi released me and stood on shaky legs before pulling me toward the bed. Greyson gently pushed me back onto the bed, and Remi followed, straddling me as she shed her bikini top. My hands caressed her breasts, my thumbs teasing her nipples as she arched her back and moaned. Greyson's lips found her neck, leaving a trail of kisses down to her chest as he took one nipple into his mouth.

"God, you're beautiful," I whispered, watching Remi's face contort with pleasure as Greyson's tongue flicked against her sensitive skin.

Greyson moved down, tugging off Remi's bikini bottoms and tossing them aside. He glanced at me, his eyes filled with desire, and together we removed our own swim trunks, leaving the three of us naked and entwined.

Skin to skin, the rest of the world faded away until there was only the three of us, chasing pleasure and ecstasy in each other's arms. As waves of unthinkable pleasure coursed through my body, electrifying every nerve ending, I struggled to catch my breath.

Remi's skilled tongue slicked over my cock with practiced precision while Greyson's strong hands gripped my hips, his powerful thrusts driving him deeper inside me. The intensity of their combined touch left me reeling, grasping at the sheets beneath me, the fibers tearing slightly under the force of my grip.

Remi's lips tightened impossibly around my throbbing arousal, her eyes never leaving mine as she took me deeper into her mouth. The intensity in her gaze only fueled the fire raging within me. The sensation of her tongue dancing against my sensitive flesh sent shivers down my spine, causing me to moan.

"God," a hoarse whisper escaped my lips, my voice an unrecognizable rasp. The quivering in my legs intensified as Greyson's rhythm quickened, our bodies colliding with an intoxicating mix of urgency and desperation. Remi's tongue swirled around me, her luscious mouth working in tandem with Greyson's relentless pounding. Her fingers dug into my thighs, anchoring herself to me as she delved deeper, consuming me with reckless abandon.

"Greyson…" I gasped, clutching at the sheets beneath me. The tension coiled tighter within me, threatening to shatter the last vestiges of my control. He responded with a growl and leaned forward, his heated breath ghosting across my neck as he whispered into my ear.

"Let go, Ghost. We've got you."

My heart pounded in my chest, every nerve ending screaming for release. The pressure built to an unbearable crescendo, threatening to tear me apart from the inside. It was as if my very soul were being pulled in two different directions, stretched thin between the tantalizing touch of these two lovers.

And then, just when I thought I could take no more, the storm broke within me. The dam of my restraint shattered, and I was flooded with a torrent of euphoria that threatened to drown me in its depths. My vision blurred as the waves of pleasure crashed over me, every muscle in my body tightening before finally giving way to sweet release.

Remi's soft moan vibrated against me as she swallowed my offering. Grey growled deep in his throat before finding his own release.

A guttural cry tore from my throat as my body trembled, racked by violent spasms that seemed to last an eternity. Time itself seemed to slow as the sensation coursed through me, a wildfire leaving searing pleasure in its wake. For a moment, we hung suspended in time, three souls lost in the throes of passion.

As the aftershocks subsided, I struggled to catch my breath, my chest heaving with the effort. In that moment, vulnerability threatened to consume me, a weight pressing down on my chest. Greyson's strong arms wrapped around me, pulling me close as he whispered soothing words into my ear. Remi's gentle touch traced patterns across my trembling thighs, her eyes filled with unspoken understanding.

I let the remnants of my defenses crumble, allowing these two incredible people to see the raw, unfiltered version of myself that I'd kept hidden for so long. My heart swelled with gratitude, an overwhelming sense of love and belonging wrapping around me like a warm embrace, one that went beyond the physical pleasure our bodies had just shared.

We collapsed onto the bed, our bodies tangled together, slick with sweat, and spent from our passionate encounter. Lazily, I combed my fingers through Remi's hair. Being with them filled a void inside me I never thought would heal. With them, I was no longer broken.

Exhaustion settled into my bones, the aftermath of our passionate encounter leaving my chest heaving with each breath as I felt Remi's head resting upon it and Greyson's arm draped over her waist. The intimacy of our connection was palpable, a moment I wanted to hold on to forever.

Greyson's fingers traced lazy circles over my ribcage, his heartbeat pounding against my side. "I love you both. You know that, right?"

Remi's breath hitched, her arms tightening around my waist. I swallowed hard, my throat burning. Greyson had never said those three words to me before.

I buried my face in his neck and breathed deep, the scent of sex and sandalwood calming the riot in my blood.

"I love you, too," Remi whispered. Her lips brushed the nape of my neck and I shuddered.

Her words hit me like a tidal wave, and I found myself struggling to keep my own emotions in check.

Greyson's hand slid up to cup the back of my head, his gaze searching mine. Waiting.

The words stuck in my throat, too huge and frightening to give voice to. But as Greyson's thumb stroked my jaw and Remi's fingers laced with mine, the truth burst free.

"I love you both," I rasped, my heart pounding wildly. "So fucking much."

A smile lit Greyson's eyes as he surged up to kiss me, hard and deep. Remi made a soft sound of pleasure against my skin, her whole body relaxing into mine.

When Greyson finally released me, I was breathless. "Then let's make this official. Move in with me," he said softly. "Or we'll get a new place of our own. Whatever you want. I just ... I need to know you'll both be there when I wake up every morning."

My chest ached, overflowing. A place to call home. A family to call my own.

After all these years, I'd finally found it.

"Yes," I whispered and kissed him again.

"Let's do it," Remi whispered, her hand finding mine and giving it a reassuring squeeze. "Let's move in together."

I let out a slow breath, contentment seeping into my bones. This was right. However unconventional, the relationship I'd found with Remi and Greyson had healed wounds I'd thought beyond repair. Made me feel alive again in the best possible way.

Greyson's palm slid down my chest, coming to rest over my heart. "You're thinking too loudly again."

I huffed a laugh. "Just ... happy."

The word felt strange on my tongue, unfamiliar. But true.

Remi kissed my shoulder, a sweet, undemanding press of lips. "I'm happy too," she murmured. "Happier than I ever dreamed I could be."

"We're going to take such good care of you," Greyson promised, rolling until he blanketed my body with his. "Give you everything you've ever wanted. Everything you deserve."

Heat sparked low in my gut, arousal and something more twisting together. Emotion clogged my throat, too much to give voice to.

Remi sat up and straddled my hips, rubbing her slick pussy up and down my length until I was panting with need.

Greyson came up behind her, trailing kisses down her neck. One hand fondled her breast while the other slid between her legs, circling her clit while she impaled herself on my cock.

While Remi rode me hard, Greyson's lips crashed into mine. I tangled my hands in his hair, crushing to my mouth. He met each of my slow, deep thrusts into Remi with a plunge of his tongue into my mouth.

And when release came, it was shattering. Beautiful. Binding us all together in a way I knew could never be broken.

At that moment, I finally understood.

Home wasn't a place. It was Remi's smile. Greyson's embrace. The love and acceptance I'd found in their arms.

And I would hold on to it — hold on to them — forever.

The End

Next in series

Bad Boys of Rock

Book 5:

(Keep turning the pages for an excerpt!)

HOW TO MARRY A ROCKSTAR

Wild nights lead to even wilder consequences.

What happens in Vegas doesn't always stay in Vegas...

After a wild night in Vegas, I wake up in a tangle of sheets with ... Bash. He's the hot-as-sin drummer for the chart-topping rock band, Ghost Parker. He's also a long-time friend. I'm nothing if not resourceful, so

I turn this disaster into an unexpected bonus — an adventure on the kinky side.

When the rhythm of desire meets the beat of passion...
Juggling fame, fortune, and fatherhood hasn't been easy. When Lacey tells me she wants to turn our reckless night in Vegas into a steamy friends-with-benefits arrangement to explore her hidden kinky side, I'm all in. But what begins as a lustful adventure threatens to become something so much greater.

Grab your **backstage pass** to meet the boys of Ghost Parker and get ready for this sizzling story of a friends-with-benefits arrangement with a kinky twist. Turn up the volume and prepare to be utterly consumed by this rockstar romance — a steamy and glittering tale of erotic exploration, secret desires, and friends becoming lovers amidst the chaos of stardom.

Keep turning the pages to read an excerpt from
HOW TO MARRY A ROCKSTAR

Arabella Quinn Newsletter

Let's keep in touch!

Sign up for my newsletter and be the first to know about new releases, sales, giveaways, and other exciting news. As an added bonus, you'll receive a FREE ebook as my thank-you for signing up!

Arabella Quinn newsletter
https://subscribepage.io/ArabellaQuinn

Bad Boys of Rock Series

Who doesn't love the tattooed bad boys of rockstar romance? **Get ready to toss your panties on stage — it's gonna get wild!**

Book 1: HOW TO SEDUCE A ROCKSTAR — A mind-boggling case of mistaken identity sets the stage for a scorching hot romance between Ryder, the sinfully sexy guitarist of a famous rock band, and Talia, the unsuspecting woman who stumbles into his life. After the erotic encounter with the mysterious and sexy stranger in his bed, Ryder's world is rocked.

Book 2: HOW TO TEMPT A ROCKSTAR — Forbidden desires ignite in this sizzling romance between Sid, the tattooed bad-boy bass guitarist, and Kaylie, his best friend's little sister. When a tiny bundle shows up at Sid's door, Kaylie reaches out to help as his world turns upside-down. As the lines between love and lust lose focus, they must weather the tempest of forbidden desire and hidden truths to see if their love can survive the ultimate test.

Book 3: How to Date a Rockstar — In this sizzling rockstar romance, enemies become lovers while secrets threaten to tear them apart. Knox, the lead guitarist with the irresistible Scottish accent, becomes entangled in a fake dating scheme with Summer to appease her meddlesome mother. When the lines between fake and real blur, Knox must confront his tragic past and face the truth that he's been battling. Can their budding relationship survive the harsh glare of the spotlight and the ghosts of the past that haunt them? Or will the truth shatter their hearts beyond repair?

Book 4: How to Catch a Rockstar — Passions burn hot when Ghost, the enigmatic lead singer of a popular rock band, becomes ensnared in a tempestuous love triangle between Remi, a woman who ignites his dormant emotions, and her boyfriend, whom he despises. As lust and hatred collide with betrayal, can the three navigate the treacherous waters of a passionate love triangle and find redemption amidst the chaos of stardom, or will their dangerous games leave them shattered? The only question is—who will be left standing when the music stops?

Book 5: How to Marry a Rockstar — Bash, the reckless and carefree drummer of a chart-topping rock band, is busy juggling fame, fortune, and fatherhood. Lacey, the sultry vixen, has been friends with Bash and his band for years. Their lives take an unexpected turn when one reckless night in Vegas changes everything, leaving them entwined in more ways than one. With their secret passions and insatiable cravings unleashed, they embark on a steamy friends-with-benefits arrangement with a side of untamed kinks.

Also By Arabella Quinn

BAD BOYS OF ROCK SERIES

How to Seduce a Rockstar

How to Tempt a Rockstar

How to Date a Rockstar

How to Catch a Rockstar

How to Marry a Rockstar

ROCK ME SERIES

Rock Me: Wicked

Rock Me: Naughty

Rock Me: Crazy

Rock Me: Sexy

ROMANCE NOVELS

My Stepbrother the Dom
Impossible (to Resist) Boss
Being Jane

THE WILDER BROTHERS SERIES

(small town romance)

Fake Marriage to a Baller
Luke – coming soon

Other Novels by Arabella Quinn

MY STEPBROTHER THE DOM

A sizzling stepbrother romance with a twist:

For years, I had the worst crush on my stepbrother, Cole Hunter. We used to ride bikes, skateboard, and go fishing together — now I couldn't even be in the same room as him without my pulse racing. One cocky half-grin from Cole would have my face blushing while my panties melted. It was insane — and completely humiliating.

It was a painful secret that I guarded fiercely. Cole was off-limits. *Forbidden*. If he knew how I felt, I would die of embarrassment.

I avoided Cole for years, until one wild night, when my best friend took me to a club. I thought I was going to see a grunge band, but it turned out to be a much kinkier kind of club. A club where anything goes, and well, things got a little crazy. Make that a lot crazy.

No one would ever know what I'd done, right?

Then I discovered who the man behind the mask really was...

Impossible (to Resist) Boss

A sexy billionaire CEO. His headstrong secretary. And a computer file that exposes her most secret and dirty fantasies about him.

Lilliana

I hate my boss.

He's an inconsiderate and demanding tyrant. I hate his juvenile rules, his micro-managing ways, and his selfish and unapologetic manner. But most of all, I hate how insanely sexy he is — how all the women around him can't help but fawn all over him.

He's a wealthy, ego-driven maniac that has a new bimbo at his beck and call with the mere snap of his fingers. Despite these irrepressible naughty fantasies I keep having about him, I wouldn't stroke his ego for all the money in the world.

Jason Kaine

I may have found the one.

After years of fruitless searching, I've found the perfect secretary. She's scarily efficient, not afraid of hard work, detail-oriented, and best of all, she doesn't complain about my important rules. She's a dream come true.

So why can't I keep the image of her, deliciously naked and spread out invitingly across my desk, from invading my head? I didn't get to where I am today by being stupid. I've got plenty of willing women to choose from who understand my absolute no-strings policy.

Lilliana is strictly off-limits, but I see the way her eyes devour me. I see how her pulse pounds whenever I get near. I know she's ripe for the taking, but that would be disastrous for both of us. It might be the worst mistake ever, but something's bound to give.

About the Author

Arabella Quinn is a *New York Times* and *USA Today* bestselling author of contemporary romance. When she's not busy writing, you can often find her clutching her Kindle and staying up way past her bedtime reading romance novels. Besides contemporary romance, she loves regency, gothic, and erotic romance — the steamier the better. She also loves thrillers, especially psychological thrillers. She saves reading horror for when her husband is away on business but doesn't recommend that. She averages about five hours of sleep per night and does not drink coffee. Also, not recommended!

Arabella Quinn newsletter
https://subscribepage.io/ArabellaQuinn

Excerpt

HOW TO MARRY A ROCKSTAR

Chapter One

Bash

"More! More! More!" He chanted.

I glanced sideways at the little tyrant standing on his chair at the table in our eat-in kitchen. "Manners, Kody."

He giggled. "Please."

"I'll get you some more, but please sit down. No standing on the chair."

I missed the ugly plastic booster seat he used to sit in. At least then he was buckled in and couldn't escape, but cleaning that thing was a giant pain in the ass. At three-and-a-half years old, Kody's baby days were long behind him. Now, he was a master at getting into mischief, making enormous messes in record time, refusing to take naps, and changing his food preferences on the daily.

I pulled the second slice of bread from the toaster, slathered it with peanut butter, and then added a few banana slices on top of it.

When I turned back around, Kody was sitting on top of the kitchen table, his big toe pushing a mushy banana slice around his plate.

I grumbled under my breath. "Kody, I said, sit down."

He grinned. "I am, Dad."

"I meant on your chair, you little stinker. We don't sit on the table."

I placed his new slice of toast on the table and then scooped him up into my arms. I hugged his wiggling body for a few seconds and then deposited him back into his chair.

Before he could take a bite of his toast, his eyes lit up, and he shrieked, "Jojo!"

Josie came into the kitchen and rumpled his hair. "Good morning, kiddo. I told you I was going to be here in the morning."

Kody nodded happily and then went to work stuffing the toast into his mouth.

Josie's eyes swung over to me. "The question is: what are you doing here? I wasn't expecting you home so early."

Ha! Neither was I.

Josie had come over to babysit last night because I'd had a date with a woman I'd met a few weeks ago. Usually, Kaylie and Sid took Kody overnight when I needed them to, but Kaylie was very pregnant with twins and due any day, so I'd enlisted Josie's help.

She lowered her voice and looked around. "She's not here, is she?"

"No!" I replied, a little too defensively. "I came home last night. You were already sleeping."

"So, did the date go well?"

I pinched the bridge of my nose. "Not as well as I'd hoped it would."

If I thought Josie would let it go at that, I was sadly mistaken. "It was date number three, though. Did you take the bald-headed gnome for a stroll in the misty forest?"

"Huh?" It was too early in the morning to understand what Josie was going on about. Whatever it was, it was probably a dig at my expense.

Josie wiggled her eyebrows up and down. "You know, the four-legged foxtrot."

Kody spoke up from the table. "More, please." He was busy licking his fingers clean.

I glanced at his empty plate. "Jeez, Kody. How much toast can you eat?"

Josie bustled over to the kitchen counter where a large Tupperware container was sitting. "I made your favorite, Kody — banana-chocolate chip muffins. Do you want one?"

He nodded his head vigorously.

Josie pulled a muffin out of the container and peeled off its baking paper before she plunked it down on the plate in front of him.

He chirped out a thanks and then began demolishing it.

She turned to me with hands on her hips. "So, did you attack the pink fortress?"

I grimaced. I had a vague feeling I knew what she was getting at, but I didn't want to discuss it. Especially not with her.

My hand tunneled through my hair in frustration. "What in God's name are you talking about, woman? Just say what you mean."

She tilted her head in Kody's direction. "I was trying to spare little ears. But I take it from that grumpy response that there was no hanky panky involved. You struck out, huh?"

"I didn't strike out," I grumbled. "She didn't live up to expectations."

HOW TO CATCH A ROCKSTAR   453

"Oh!" she drew out the word sarcastically. "So, you did play hide the salami, but she didn't meet the standards of the master delicatessen owner?"

Christ. Josie knew how to needle me like no other. I felt a headache coming on.

Kody crammed the last bit of muffin into his mouth and then began climbing down from the chair. Before he escaped, Josie wrangled him over to the sink to wipe his face and wash his hands. As soon as she set him free, he scampered off to find some toys in the other room.

Josie turned to me, waiting for an explanation. She was like a junkyard dog with a bone.

"We had a nice dinner and then I came home. End of story."

"Nothing happened?" She didn't sound convinced. "I thought the entire purpose of me staying overnight to watch Kody was so that you could make the beast with two backs?"

"Let's just call it sex! Or fucking. Your choice. And it didn't happen last night. Are you satisfied?"

"Jeesh," — she threw up her hands — "don't take it out on me!"

"Sorry. I just had high hopes the night would end differently."

I met Addison at a party about a month ago. She zeroed in on me right away. She was full of energy and really sexy, so it'd boosted my ego a bit since I was in a serious dry spell as far as women went.

My entire lifestyle changed virtually overnight when I found out I was a father. Since then, sure, I'd had sex with groupies while I was on tour, but they'd all been fast, soulless transactions only meant to slake my thirst. I hadn't spent more than an hour with any of them. I always felt the need to get back to Kody as soon as a show was over, so sex was quick and dirty.

Off-tour, my sex life was non-existent. When Sid and I used to live together, we were partying every night. Now Sid was married to my little sister, and they were expecting twins. My other bandmates were no better. Ryder had a wife and an eight-month-old baby. Knox was talking about getting married to Summer. Hell, even Ghost was in a serious relationship, even if it was with two other people. Hanging out with all of them was still fun, but it was completely different from the old days.

In a way, I felt like I was getting left behind. I'd started thinking that maybe it was time that I settled down, too. I was 32 years old and had a kid. Maybe it wasn't completely fulfilling to stick my dick in any willing hot chick. Maybe it was time to date around and find the woman that I wanted to spend my life with. I'd watched my bandmates fall in love with incredible women and damn if I didn't feel a bit of jealousy. I wanted that, but I wasn't sure how to get it.

So, after hanging out with a bunch of couples for too long after our last tour, I jumped at the chance to go to a party. I'd become friends with Davis, a guy in an upcoming band that I'd met on tour last year. He was as wild as I used to be.

He was in town between tours, so he invited me out a few times. I met Addison one of those nights when I was out with his crew. She and I ended up fucking that night in the coat room.

I was intrigued by her. She was flirty and sexy, making me feel special. The sex was quick, but it had been hot, so I got her number.

I thought about her a lot, so after a few days, I gave her a call. She was going out with friends, so she invited me to meet her at a club. That second meeting, she gave me a quick and dirty blowjob in a car full of drunk people.

Maybe that should have been my warning. I didn't really give a shit who saw her give me a blowjob, but why didn't she? They were her friends. If I was being honest with myself, it made me slightly uncomfortable. I tried to brush it off. She was younger than me, around 25 years old, and she still partied hard. It's not like I wasn't like that when I was 25.

The next time we met, she was out with her friends again. She was hammered by the time I got there. I left after I made sure she got home safely, despite her slurring pleas for me to fuck her.

That led me to last night. I had asked her out to dinner so that I could get to know her better. On a real date. Just her and me.

Dinner was great. She was sweet. She asked about my music, my friends, and my experiences with my band, Ghost Parker. I even told her about Kody. She seemed really interested in everything I had to say.

I found out more about her. She told me about growing up in southern California and about her large family. She and her friends hung around the underground rock scene in L.A. — that's how she knew Davis and his band. Addison was younger, so she did talk a lot about partying and had thought little about her future, but that was okay.

She knew that I'd booked a hotel room so that we could spend the night together. I wanted to take my time and explore every inch of her. I had a feeling she was used to taking everything fast, and I wanted to show her that slow and thorough could be amazing.

While we were sipping wine, gazing at each other across the candle-lit table, I had the brief thought that I should have invited her to my home for our date. I could have impressed her with my fancy house and my cooking skills. I could have woken up with her in my bed, given her an orgasm or two, and then impressed her with a fancy breakfast.

My mother had always said to my sister growing up that a man who cooked was a man that you should marry. Out of necessity, I'd learned a lot about cooking over the last couple of years. It didn't make sense to hire someone to cook for me when I was on the road with the band so much. It had been easier to figure it out on my own.

Taking her out to dinner had been great. Getting to know each other without either of our friends around had been fun. I'd stepped way back from the spotlight the past few years and now hardly anyone ever recognized me out in public. After witnessing all the shit my bandmates had to go through, I was grateful.

I was excited to get Addison back to my hotel room. She went to the restroom while I was settling the bill. As soon as she got back to the table, I knew something was off with her.

Josie broke into my thoughts about the date. "What happened? You two didn't have a good time together?"

I slumped into the chair at the kitchen table. "Dinner was great. We were getting along fine. I thought we really had a connection. Then she went to the ladies' room."

"And?" she prompted.

"When she got back to the table, she was suddenly talking up a storm. Jumping from one subject to the next. When she wiped her nose with the back of her hand, I fucking knew. My insides froze." I closed my eyes, trying to blot out the memory. "When I looked closely, I saw that her eyes were bloodshot. Her pupils dilated. And there were traces of white powder under her nostril."

Josie sniffed her disapproval. "Cocaine?"

"And to think I almost brought her around Kody!" I moaned with frustration. "I can't believe how fucking stupid I am."

"Don't beat yourself up about it." Josie placed her hand on my shoulder. "You did everything exactly right. When you have a son to think about, it's true, you can't bring home women willy-nilly. You've got to vet them first, which is exactly what you did."

"But we were getting along so well. I really liked her. She made me feel good." I moaned and put my face in my hands. The dumb shit coming out of my mouth was just giving Josie great ammunition to use against me. I was sure she was memorizing every dumb word to throw back in my face someday.

"There's plenty of fish in the sea."

I looked up. "Kody's getting older. He's going to start noticing the kind of women I have in my life. I can't just keep hooking up with fast, easy women. Who I bring into his life is important."

"So, what you're saying is that you're looking for a girlfriend and not a fuck buddy?"

While I was talking, Josie refilled my coffee mug and fixed a coffee for herself. Then she put some of her muffins on a plate and brought it all back to the table.

"Something like that." I made a face, just for the fact that Josie just said fuck buddy. "I need to get to know a woman a little better before I fuck her. Vet her, like you said. Take her out with my friends and see if they get along. If she passes the test, then maybe we can take Kody places together and I can see if Kody likes her."

She pulled up a chair across the table from me and sat down. "Whoa. You're getting ahead of yourself. First, you have to just start dating."

"That's the problem. I don't know how to date."

She slid a muffin over to me. "What are you looking for in a woman?"

I eyed the muffin like it was poison. I had an irrational hatred of raisins and Josie knew that. She was forever trying to sneak raisins into my food. Kody loved them — the little traitor — and never warned me. I eyed the chocolate chips with suspicion before I took a bite.

I thought about what I wanted in a woman while I chewed on the delicious muffin. "She has to like kids. She has to enjoy the music scene and everything that comes with it. And, of course, she has to like sex.

A lot of sex."

"Kids, music, and sex," Josie summarized. "Does she have to look like a model?"

"No," I answered right away. "But I have some standards. She can't be hideous. I don't want to have to fuck her with a bag over her head."

"Very funny."

I smiled. "I'm not as hung up on looks as I used to be. Personality is more important than appearance." I really couldn't believe the shit coming out of my mouth today.

I took a sip of my coffee and frowned. It was black; there was no flavored creamer or sugar added to it; yet, it had a weird taste to it. A sweetness that tasted off.

Josie smiled. "I think I know someone who meets those criteria. I'll set you up. Even if it isn't a love match, it could give you some good dating practice."

"I don't know, Josie. I don't think set-ups are my thing. I rather find women to date by myself."

"And how's that working out for you so far?"

I refused to answer, but she had a point. I took another gulp of coffee, immediately tasting the off-putting flavor. As I swallowed, something small and lumpy knocked around inside my mouth. I gagged.

It was a fucking raisin.

I sprang to my feet and rushed to the sink. My stomach heaved; I was about to throw up. I spit the foul black demon out of my mouth and began retching while my eyes watered. Later, I found out that the entire cup of coffee was loaded with them. Fuck, it was nasty.

When I could finally speak again, I looked over my shoulder at her with disgust and just the tiniest bit of admiration. "You better watch your back, woman. This means war."

Her smile was cunning. "You know, Kaylie offered to pay me triple what you pay. You're going to miss me when those twins are born."

Chapter Two

Lacey

I stepped into the swanky reception area of the doctor's office in Beverly Hills. I'd waited close to six months for this appointment and it couldn't have come at a better time.

Walking across the white marble floor, I approached the reception desk to check in, right on time.

The lovely receptionist, with her incredibly flawless skin and blindingly white teeth, smiled up at me. "I'm sorry. The doctor is running late today. A few complications arose with a procedure this morning, so he's behind. The wait will be at least another 45 minutes. Would it be more convenient for you to reschedule?"

No, it wouldn't be more convenient to reschedule. At all. It had taken me forever to get a consultation with this world-renowned doctor. I wasn't going anywhere.

I'd been waiting long enough. The clock was ticking. Figuratively — I looked down at my Blancpain diamond watch with the mother-of-pearl dial and ostrich leather strap — and quite literally.

"No, I'll wait."

She nodded serenely. "Can I get you anything to drink? Coffee? Perrier?"

"No, I'm fine."

Her head tilted slightly. "Please have a seat and we'll get to you as soon as we can."

The waiting room wasn't utilitarian, like an ordinary doctor's office. Everything was done in shades of white, including the walls, curtains, furniture, and floor, but it didn't feel sterile. It was elegant.

HOW TO CATCH A ROCKSTAR

The furniture was plush and inviting – small tufted sofas with throw pillows — instead of the vinyl-covered chairs that you'd normally see. Elegant lamps lit the room and expensive artwork broke up the white walls. Soothing music was gently playing in the background and the scent of lavender was diffused into the air.

The entire effect should have been calming, but I was a bundle of nerves.

I sat down on one of the small sofas and crossed my legs. There was one other person in the room, presumably another patient who was waiting to be seen. A quick scan of her ivory suit, obscenely expensive handbag, shoes, and jewelry told me that she was quite wealthy. She was probably thinking the same exact thing about me as she looked me over. She smiled faintly and then returned her attention to her phone.

As I sat on the couch and waited, I wondered what people would think if they could see me now. What would my father think? Or my 81 employees? What would the posse of kickass girls — the one that shrunk every year as they got married off — the posse that worshipped me as their 'queen b' think? Or how about the many men whose hearts I'd crushed under my lethal stilettos over the years?

Would they feel sorry for me? Think I was pathetic? Or would they be impressed with what an empowered woman I was? Probably a mixture of all of that. I wasn't even sure what I thought of myself, but I wasn't going to dwell on any insecurities I was harboring. I was a tough bitch — an expert at pushing away any unwanted emotion.

The white door across the room opened, and a nurse poked her head into the room and addressed my silent companion. "Mrs. Davis? We're almost finished up in here. We'll be ready for you in about ten minutes."

The lady in the white Chanel suit raised her hand in acknowledgment. It trembled faintly as she placed it back on her lap.

I averted my eyes, but it was too late. She had caught me watching.

"I'm here to see if my embryo transfer was successful." Her face remained neutral, but her voice wobbled slightly.

"Oh." I was startled that she'd shared that with me. "Good luck to you."

She placed her long fingers at the base of her throat as if trying to ease the tension there. "This is our second attempt. The first one failed. We just got married, and we're trying to have a baby. I'll be 44 in a month."

I folded my hands on my lap, not quite knowing what to say. "I hope it works out."

She nodded. "It's a real bitch going through this. Don't wait."

I pressed my lips together but didn't say anything.

My 34th birthday was coming up. It had crept up on me silently until suddenly, the realization slammed me in the face.

I'd spent my twenties proving to the world that I'd earned my position in my father's company through merit, not nepotism. I'd climbed the corporate ladder until I was running the A&R department. Even though I was called a savant at finding and signing talent, it came down to more than natural ability and instinct. I'd worked my ass off.

I was known as a barracuda in the industry and I wore my success and confidence like a shield around my heart. Thoughts of babies or families never crossed my mind. I used men sexually and needed nothing else from them. I sowed my wild oats and had no regrets.

In my early thirties, I began noticing people around me pairing off. Getting married. Starting families. I felt nothing but a smug satisfaction that I was better than them. Stronger. I'd been promoted to Executive Vice President of Castle Music. I was at the top of the food chain. Revered and feared by most of the company. Women hated me because I took what I wanted. Men hated me because they wanted to be like me. Did. not. care.

I'm not sure when I started questioning everything. Maybe it was after I'd spent another lonely night after I'd kicked a man out of my bed. Maybe it was after one of the many dalliances I'd had with the members of the rock bands I worked with. After I'd tangled with a few members of Ghost Parker, a noticeable disquiet started seeping in. I'd felt a pang of rejection. It was foreign and ugly. I didn't like it. That was the first hairline crack in the armor.

In a frenzy to bury these insecurities, I started seeing a 22-year-old, hot-as-fuck, bad-boy rocker. He was covered in tats and attitude, with a body to match. His infatuation with me was like a balm to my bruised ego. He couldn't stop coming back for more and he kept me extremely satisfied.

Until I walked in on him fucking a girl. A young, dumb girl. Someone who'd so far achieved nothing in life except existing. The girl squeaked like a mouse when she saw me. Without missing a thrust, he asked me if I wanted to join in. God, I felt every one of my 30+ years at that moment.

I wasn't devastated or mad, more like letdown. My ego checked hard. I was surprised to realize that I felt this possessive towards him. I couldn't blame him too much. He had no concept that I might actually feel any emotion. It was twisted, but I never showed any vulnerabilities to a man. He fucked her simply because he could; we'd never talked about being exclusive. There was nothing real between us. I ended up signing his band to Castle and then making sure never to cross paths with him again.

That was a moment of revelation. An epiphany. I didn't love him, but something that we had was important to me and it wasn't sex. I went through what I classified as a minor heartbreak.

On the other side of that moment, I became more human. Right about that time was when I helped Kaylie through some rough times. I'd never had a friend before, but now she was my best friend who'd co-founded an amazing charity, Cyber Angels, with me. She'd gone through a lot, but now she was married to a man I had a brief hot fling with long ago.

After my epiphany with the hot rocker, I decided to settle down. As I did with everything else in my life, I methodically approached my new relationship goals. I was looking for commitment.

I found the guy who checked off all my boxes: successful, attractive, charismatic, assertive, social, driven, mature, and not involved in the music industry. Theo was all of those things, and he wasn't threatened by my success. I'd never been swept away by romance before, and it was exhilarating. He was always telling me how gorgeous I was and how lucky he was to find me. He even called me 'beautiful' as a nickname, and it made my heart melt each time he said it. And the cherry on top — he was extremely skilled in bed. I was smitten. I really thought he could be the one.

Until we went sailing on a yacht with his work buddies, who he was trying to impress. I thought there would be some other women there, but it ended up being me and him with three other guys.

He'd asked me to wear a particular bathing suit that was his favorite. The suit was almost obscene with how little skin it covered. I protested. That suit wasn't something I usually paraded around in. Somehow, he managed to convince me. He told me I had a rocking body, and he wanted to show me off. All the other girls would look hot, so I couldn't show up wearing some frumpy get-up.

I reluctantly went along with it, but then felt uncomfortable when there were only guys on the boat and they were all ogling me like a piece of meat. I'd never been shy about my body, but something about the whole thing felt off.

The entire afternoon, Theo was plying me with drinks. I almost suspected that he was trying to get me drunk. He was so insistent that I'd started dumping them overboard when no one was watching.

I closed my eyes and the horrible day came back to me with a clarity that was painful.

♪♫♪♪♪

Theo joined me on the deck of the yacht. He handed me a new drink. I felt dizzy. The yacht was anchored, but it still swayed slightly in the waves. I hoped it was the boat moving and not all the alcohol I'd consumed. I'd been secretly tossing most of it since Theo was bent on everyone having a good time and wouldn't take no for an answer.

The boat pitched — or was that me? — and Theo grabbed my waist as I awkwardly stumbled to keep my balance. He pulled me closer and then slid his hand into my bikini bottom.

My fingers curled around his wrist to stop him. "No, Theo. We're not alone."

"No one's here right now." He began nibbling on my ear and I could smell the alcohol on his breath.

"But they could be here at any moment."

His hand slid up my back and before I knew what was happening, he yanked on the string that was the only thing keeping the two tiny triangles of fabric over my breasts. "You've got me so horny, beautiful, I can't help it."

I scrambled to cover my tits with my hands and he laughed.

He gently tried to pull my hands away. "You've got a gorgeous body. Show it off for me. Let everyone see what is mine."

I gasped. This didn't seem like him. "No. I don't want to."

"Don't be a prude." His hand tangled in my hair and he pulled my head up to look at him. "I want to fuck you good. Let them watch. They'll be standing back there with their dicks in their hands while I've got you. I'll fuck the shit out of you. It'll be so good, beautiful."

I pushed against his chest, but he didn't even seem to notice. His other hand had encircled my waist and pulled me tight against his erection. He pulled my bikini bottom halfway down my thighs and then lightly smacked my ass with a growl. Lust was blazing in his eyes.

I tried to reason with him. "Theo, you're drunk..."

He licked his lips. "I'll lick your pussy while they watch. Tell me that doesn't turn you on. I bet you're soaked right now just thinking about it."

The idea was turning me on, but somehow his presentation was turning me off. He just wanted to show me off? "No, Theo. What if someone took a video?"

He growled. "I bet we look so hot together. Fuck, Lacey. You can't prance around in that bikini all day and not expect me to get horny."

Theo spun me around in his arms and I realized that one of his friends was standing not even ten feet away from us, watching while he drank his beer. Theo's forearm was resting under my breasts, pinning my back to his chest. His other hand pinched one of my nipples, before snaking down my stomach and then sliding between my legs. His fingers began stroking me, circling my clit teasingly before penetrating my pussy over and over again. In and out.

He was groaning in my ear. "You're so fucking wet. You like this, baby." It was a statement, not a question.

I couldn't pull my eyes away from the guy watching us and I wondered briefly if he was going to join in, but I wasn't sure if I wanted him to.

I fought the orgasm that I felt building, but Theo knew exactly how to touch me. It didn't take long before my head was tossed back against Theo's shoulder and I was coming. I clamped my mouth shut, not making a single peep.

"Fuck, beautiful, I've got to get inside of you."

He yanked my bikini bottom all the way down my legs, then spun me around so that I was facing the railing. By that time, I noticed that the other two guys had joined the first to watch the show.

Theo placed my hands on the warm metal railing. "Hold on tight, beautiful."

I stared at the bouncing waves while he pulled his shorts down. He kicked my legs further apart, thrust his dick into me from behind, and then began fucking me like a pornstar. This time, I didn't orgasm. It felt like forever but probably was only a few minutes when he finally pulled out and shot his load on my lower back and ass with a caveman-like grunt.

I spent the rest of the time on the yacht below deck. Several times, Theo tried to get me to join the men, who were up on the deck drinking, hanging out, and laughing like nothing happened. I told him I was tired and he let me be.

♫♪♩

That was the beginning of the end for Theo and I. When I confronted him about it later, he claimed that what we did wasn't so bad, just a little kinky.

That was true. It wasn't even close to the kinkiest thing I'd ever done. My heart wanted so badly to give Theo the benefit of the doubt. We were both drunk. And I'd hoped that he was going to be the one for me. I was starting to think about marriage and babies.

But I couldn't stop that niggling of suspicion. I was suspicious of his motives. After remembering what Kaylie went through, I started worrying that there might be hidden cameras in his bedroom. I just didn't trust him anymore. I wondered if he was cheating on me during all his business trips.

I dumped him about a month after that sailing trip on the yacht. He didn't put up too much of a fight, so I obviously did the right thing. Fuck him and fuck men. Why did it have to be this hard?

Kaylie helped me through that heartbreak. Did I mention that I'd had a threesome with Kaylie's husband and her brother back in my wilder days? That was all firmly in the past. She and Sidney were meant to be together. They were soulmates. And I was lucky to be the maid of honor at their wedding.

During that awful breakup with Theo was when Kaylie told me she was pregnant with twins. That's when the biological clock really began to tick. It was ticking with an urgency. Somehow, time had crept up on me. I was 34 years old. I needed a plan. Hopefully, the doctor could give me some options.

The lady in the white suit glanced over at me and then smiled faintly. She was nervous.

I held back for a second, then it all just came sliding out. "I'm thinking of getting my eggs frozen. Or maybe just skipping over that part and getting pregnant using a sperm donor."

She arched an eyebrow. "How old are you?"

"Almost 35."

She nodded. "Get pregnant as soon as you can."

I don't know why I kept talking. "I'd prefer for my baby to have a father in the picture. But all the men I know are weak assholes. If I wait for prince charming to come around..." I shrugged.

The room was silent for a minute or two.

"I don't love my husband. He doesn't even have the faintest clue how to satisfy me in bed. He's just the sperm donor in my case."

It seemed like an awfully harsh thing for her to say about her husband. "I, uh, I don't know what to say. That's..." My voice trailed off.

"Sad? Nah. I chose my husband specifically for his ability to be a good father. I get all the sexual satisfaction I need elsewhere."

"Oh." I didn't know her situation, so I wasn't about to get all judgy on her.

"My therapist told me that sometimes very strong women have trouble giving up control in bed." She cocked her head as if in thought. "Let me ask you, have you ever been in love?"

I thought for a long moment. "No, not really."

She nodded sagely. "I recognize myself in you." She paused for a few seconds and then pressed on. "Did you work to earn your money, or did you inherit it?"

I raised my eyebrows at her boldness but then answered. "Both."

"Ahhh. Even worse than I suspected."

What did how I came about money have to do with anything?

She dug into her purse and then pulled out what looked like a business card. "I had to learn how to be more submissive in the bedroom before I could really feel free. Of course, it takes an experienced, dominant man — or woman, if that's your thing — to safely take the reins to allow that complete surrender. It's changed my whole life. Giving up that control is freeing. It's the greatest feeling in the world. Absolute nirvana."

"You're talking about a BDSM relationship? Dom/sub type of thing?"

Honestly, I couldn't ever imagine submitting myself fully to someone else. It wasn't just laughable to me; I almost found the thought repulsive. I just wasn't made that way.

Some of my thoughts must have shown on my face, because she smirked knowingly.

Just then, the door across the room opened again. "Mrs. Davis, we're ready for you."

The woman stood up. She handed me the card from her purse. "My advice is to choose the sperm donor."

I looked down at the card in my hand. One word was written in red script on the black business card: Scarlett. There was a phone number underneath it. The rest of the card was empty, including the back. I wasn't even sure what Scarlett was. I'd probably toss the thing as soon as I could.

The woman walked across the room and, just before disappearing behind the door, she turned back to me and winked. "And don't throw away the card." The door shut behind her and she was gone.

Chapter Three

Bash

Date #1

I should have pulled the plug on date #1 right away. As soon as I opened the door, I noticed Maryellen wasn't the type of girl I would have normally chosen to go out with.

She might have been attractive if she'd put a bit of effort into it. She was wearing a faded blue T-shirt covered with short, white animal hairs and a pair of jeans that had weird stretched-out, drooping knees. It was a hot sunny day; how the hell was she wearing denim without overheating? The most distracting thing about her was the way her brunette hair was cut and styled. Her bangs were super short and stubby – a look even really edgy girls could rarely pull off. They looked like Kaylie's bangs had that time she'd taken a pair of scissors to them when she was six.

Altogether, her features weren't ugly, but when she smiled, her painfully crooked row of bottom teeth stood out. When I introduced myself, she held out a hand for me to shake. It was awkward.

Not sure what to do, I invited her inside. Unfortunately, that choice to be a nice guy instead of ending it on the spot led to an awkward get-together of pure agony. Fuck. It was brutal.

She stepped inside my house. "Wow, you're so not what I expected!" She seemed excited. "Josie told my grannie that you play drums in a band? That's neat."

I was about to answer when her phone rang. She held up a finger for me to wait and then she turned her back to me before she lifted the phone to her face. "All clear, Nugget. Thanks."

She giggled and then turned back around to face me. "So, yeah, I used to play the trombone for years. I was in the marching band in high school. My mom wouldn't let me go to band camp with the cool kids, because ... well, you know. But I went to a lot of competitions. Even some overnights!"

"Huh." I was at a loss for words.

She kept babbling. "Yeah, I was thinking about bringing over my trombone. Maybe you'd want to jam together? I mean, I was thinking about doing it, but I really wasn't. Besides, my trombone playing is probably really rusty, so ..."

Rusty trombone? Was she trying to make sexual innuendos? I wasn't sure, but my dick was busy trying to burrow into my body in hiding. I was definitely not attracted to her.

How did I ditch her without being a complete asshole? She was looking at me expectantly. I panicked. "Would you like a drink? Water, beer, wine?"

"Oh!" Her eyes widened. "I don't drink alcohol. Well, maybe one drink would be okay. Social lubrication, and all that. But, I'm driving. So, water would be good."

Did she just look at my junk when she said lubrication? Or was I just freaking out? "Water. Okay. One moment."

I bolted out of the room toward the kitchen, hoping she wouldn't follow me. I grabbed a cold bottle of water from the refrigerator and then took a few deep breaths.

So, it was obvious this wasn't a love match, but I didn't need to be a dick to her. I would be a gentleman.

But I was going to kill Josie for this.

When I went back into the living room, Maryellen was holding a framed photograph of Kody that usually sat on the side table.

Her face was scrunched up with confusion. "Is this your brother?"

Brother? "No, that's Kody, my son."

Her eyes widened. "You have a kid?"

"Yeah."

She looked around the room. "Are you married?"

She seemed to be shocked, so I kept my answer simple. "No."

"Does his mother have custody?" She peeked over at me. "You see him every other weekend or something?"

My lips pressed together. "I have full custody. You don't like kids?"

She let out a high-pitched squeak. "Meep. I'm just not used to them. It seems like a lot of responsibility to take care of them. I've got a Pomeranian and taking care of Sookie is overwhelming at times."

She put the picture of Kody down and then swiped her phone a few times before pointing the screen at me. "That's my Sookie."

It was a picture of a white ball of fluff. A tiny dog sitting on a couch. "Cute," I mumbled.

"Let me guess, you're a cat person? Dogs are so much cooler! Do you want to see Sookie's Insta page? She's got a ton of followers. I don't do social media — my therapist told me to give it up, too much anxiety — but I help Sookie out with her page." She gave me a wink and then added, "If you follow her, she'll follow you back. Sookie_Pom."

I took a step back. "I don't really do social media either."

Her eyes widened with surprise. "You don't! Wow, we really are compatible. Do you love animals? I thought we could go to the zoo for our date. I mean, who doesn't love animals?"

Fuck. I wasn't about to spend all day at the zoo with this crazy girl just to be a nice guy. I had my limits. "Honestly, I'm not really a zoo person. I had a bad experience there once."

"Oh shit!" She nodded. "I saw a male gorilla humping a female gorilla right behind the glass when I was a kid. He was huge. I mean, crazy big. And it happened like five feet away from me. It was really traumatizing. And that would be so awkward if that happened on a date."

My hand tunneled through my hair. I was starting to sweat. "Maryellen, I couldn't help but notice that you didn't seem comfortable that I had a son."

She couldn't meet my eye. "It was quite the surprise. Josie didn't mention that to my grannie."

"He's a big part of my life. Actually, he's the biggest part of my life." I kept my tone nice and even. "So, I'm not sure that we are all that compatible."

Her hand flew to her forehead. "I'm really sorry! I hope you aren't too upset. I just ... it's not you, it's me. You seem so great. I just..."

I started leading her to the door. "It's okay. Thanks for being honest with me."

Just as she got to the front door, she stopped. "I have this friend, Nugget. She really loves kids. I could give you her number?"

"No, that's okay." I bit my lip. "I think I'm going to take a little break from dating."

She nodded. "I understand."

I pressed my phone to my ear as I listened to it ring and ring.

"Pick up," I muttered.

Finally, Josie answered, "Did you get lucky?"

"Cancel the date you set up for Saturday," I growled into the phone. "I'm not spending another minute of my time with some whack job you set me up with."

She gasped. "Maryellen is not a whack job."

"Fuck, Josie. You did that on purpose, didn't you?" I accused.

"You said you weren't looking for a model! Maryellen may not be that gorgeous, but she's got nice titties. Perky!"

I paced around the room, trying to let off steam without yelling. "I wouldn't know if she had nice tits; I couldn't see past all the dog hair on her chest."

"Oh yeah, she loves that dog. Dresses him up in pink tutus and stuff. What's his name? Nookie?"

I let out a huff of breath. "She was telling me all about her glory days in marching band–"

"See, she likes the music scene. You said that was important to you."

I ignored her and continued my rant. "And she wouldn't shut up about her dog's Instagram page. And watching gorillas mate at the zoo."

"Aha! She likes sex. That was important to you. I mean, she named her dog Nookie, so that tells you something."

My teeth were clenched so hard, I was surprised they didn't crack. "I'm not into gorilla porn. Christ, Josie, you set me up with a complete nutter!"

"So far, you two sound perfectly compatible. The both of you share a love of music and it sounds like sex might be kinky with her. What's the problem?"

I took a calming breath. "Well, she absolutely freaked out when she found out I had a son."

Josie paused for a moment. "Huh. I didn't know that about Maryellen. That's too bad. "

"Yeah. Too bad." I sounded like a petulant dick, but I no longer cared. "So, please, for the love of God, cancel the thing you set up for Saturday. I'm done with dating."

"No can do. Angelique already has your address, and she made dinner reservations. It's too late to cancel."

I had to put my foot down. "Look, I refuse to go out with another girl you set me up with. I don't trust your judgment."

She wasn't backing down an inch. "I happen to know Angelique loves kids. She's beautiful and 'hot to trot', as you kids would say."

"No one says that. Not even old people."

She ignored me. "So, Angelique loves kids. She loves sex. That meets two of your criteria. And I bet she loves the music scene, too. She's got piercings. Two that are visible. Maybe you might be able to find some others? Some hidden ones?"

"She's got piercings," my tone dripped with sarcasm, "so that means she into the music scene?"

"Exactly!" she agreed. "That means she checks all of your boxes. And she's way sexier than Maryellen. Trust me."

I grunted. That wasn't saying all that much.

"C'mon, Bash. Just go to dinner with her. How bad could it be?"

Chapter Four

Bash

Date #2:

I'd been texting with Angelique for days. She seemed cool, and she'd been a little flirty with her messages, but we hadn't exchanged photos, so I was still a bit nervous. Josie said she was hot, but … I didn't put too much stock in that.

The plan was that she'd pick me up because the restaurant she made reservations at was closer to my place. When the doorbell rang, I was so fucking nervous. I was half expecting a hideous hag to greet me when I opened the door.

I was pleasantly surprised and very relieved at the same time. She was attractive and age-appropriate. Thank God. She had dark hair cut in an edgy bob, a stud on the side of her nose, and a lip piercing. She was dressed in a white blouse with a flouncy, short skirt, and combat boots.

Angelique let out a nervous little laugh. "I was worried, but Josie really undersold you. She said you were a little out of shape, but not too hideous looking. Frankly, I was worried you'd be fat and sweaty, but you're hot. Is this your house?"

I waved her inside. "Yeah. This is home."

She looked around. "Wow, it's really nice. You're not a complete deadbeat loser. When Josie said you played the drums in some band, I had my doubts, but you must do nicely for yourself."

I smiled. "Yeah. I do okay."

"I love musicians!" There was a sparkle in her eye. "I love the creativity and the energy surrounding them. I'd love to hear you play sometime. A drummer! That's badass!"

My cock was waking up, responding to the praise. "I have to admit, I was a bit worried about who Josie was setting me up with, too."

She chuckled. "How do you know Josie?"

"She's my nanny."

She scrunched up her face and groaned. "You have a nanny? Shit."

A burst of laughter escaped. She was so cute. "I meant my son's nanny."

Her eyes widened. "You have a son?"

My gut tightened with anxiety. "Yeah. He's three years old. Do you like kids?"

She didn't hesitate; she was emphatic. "I love kids!"

I gestured to the picture of Kody on the table. "That's my son. Kody."

She walked over to get a better look. "He's so cute."

I'd followed her, so when she spun around, we were only a few feet apart.

She bit her bottom lip. "The last time Josie set me up, this guy in a three-piece suit showed up at my door." She made a disgusted face. "He brought me flowers. I mean, why bother — they'll just die, anyway."

I made a mental note never to buy her flowers. Jesus, dating was complicated.

"And, then—" she was chewing on her lip now. "I saw something. It was..." She trembled slightly. "... just bad. Kind of traumatic."

She stepped closer to me and rested her hands on my chest. I placed my hands on her elbows, not sure how to comfort her. "What did you see?"

HOW TO CATCH A ROCKSTAR 479

She shook her head and then pressed her whole body up against me. Her arms circled around my neck and then she smiled at me with perfectly straight teeth.

She felt amazing pressed up against me. I slipped my hands down her body until they were cupping her ass cheeks over her skirt and pulled her tighter against me. I was sure she could feel my hard cock trapped between our bodies. Hopefully, I wasn't scaring her off by being too forward.

"Can I see your dick?"

I was stunned. I guess I wasn't being too forward then. "Like, right now?"

"Yeah," she whispered.

I squeezed the globes of her ass. "You want me to take it out?"

She nodded.

I was hard as a rock now. "Okay, sweetheart. I'll show you my dick."

Well, this was promising. I'd only met her for five minutes and already my dick was throbbing. I unzipped my pants.

She dropped to her knees, dragging my pants and boxer briefs down with her. She certainly wasn't shy.

Her mouth was inches from my dick while she inspected it with wonder.

"It's beautiful." I could feel her warm breath as she said it. "It's a great size. And you've got two balls! Thank God!"

It was the weirdest fucking thing a girl on her knees had ever said to me, but it was making my cock pulse with need.

"You have the perfect dick." Her words were coming out all breathy. "It's making my mouth water."

Fuck. "You want a taste of it, sweetheart?"

She glanced at the smartwatch on her wrist. "By my estimate, we've only got about four more minutes, but that should do the trick."

Four more minutes for what? I had no clue what she was talking about, but I didn't care because she was licking her lips and unbuttoning her shirt.

"I really like my nipples played with while I suck cock. It gets me off. Pinch and squeeze them, both of them, but not too hard."

Okay. She knew what she wanted and wasn't afraid to ask for it. This was a bit fast and unexpected, but it was exactly what I wanted right now. Damn, this girl was perfect.

She opened her shirt and then pulled her bra cups down under her tits. She didn't have huge tits, but they looked gorgeous raised up as if in offering, especially propped up by her bra. It was a beautiful sight. My dick certainly appreciated it. I was seeping and Angelique hadn't even touched me yet.

I tweaked both her nipples gently at the same time, and she let out a hum of appreciation as she slid her hand into the waistband of her skirt.

"You're going to touch yourself, sweetheart?"

She nodded.

"Then, I want to watch. Pull your skirt up so I can see."

"Yessss," she hissed. She pulled up her skirt, and she wasn't wearing anything under it. She spread her knees wide on the floor so I could get a good look. Then she slid her finger over her sex. Her flesh was glistening and pink. I could smell her arousal.

Fuck, this date was turning out better and better.

First, she checked her watch and then slid her lips over my cock. She felt like heaven. She was fairly skilled, taking me deep, working with my rhythm as I thrust into her mouth. Since my hands were busy playing with both of her nipples, I couldn't anchor her to get any hard thrusts in. Even though my thrusts were shallow, her cheeks were caving in as she hoovered me hard. Watching her touch herself was the icing on the cake because this girl was not shy. She was fucking herself with her fingers and moaning around my cock. It was hot, and I was already imagining all the things I wanted to do to her.

Suddenly, she stopped bobbing on my cock and brought her wrist up to her face to check her watch. She stopped for a moment to read a text. I patiently waited, even though it felt like torture, softly running my thumbs over her taut nipples.

She pulled her mouth off my cock. "Sorry, time's up. If you want to cum, you've got about one more minute. So hurry up."

One more minute? What the hell?

She sucked my cock back into her mouth and started bobbing on it frantically. I took one of my hands off her stiff nipple and wound my fingers through her hair, so I could guide her head back and forth on my cock as I thrust hard into her mouth.

She was fucking me deep with her mouth and she had no trouble taking it all. She reached up and started fondling my balls. That should do it. Another few thrusts. She pressed a finger against my asshole and two thrusts later, I spurt down her throat.

She milked me for everything I had, pulled off, licked her lips, and then asked where the bathroom was. While she was gone, I got myself together. I was feeling loose-limbed and fantastic.

She came back, kissed me on the lips, and then her lips trailed across my jaw toward my ear. She whispered, "I didn't cum, so you owe me one, lover-boy."

I grinned at her. "Give me a few minutes and I'll have you screaming, sweetheart."

She patted my chest. "I'll hold you to it. We've got to go now."

I remembered she wasn't wearing any panties, so my hand slid down to her ass as we exited my house. Living out in the suburbs, there was no one around to see my hand as it slipped under her skirt and grabbed a firm ass cheek. I half expected her to playfully bat my hand away, but she didn't.

There was a minivan in my driveway and it took me a few seconds to realize it must be hers. It wasn't the type of car I expected her to have.

Then, as we approached, I realized there were kids in the car. Lots of kids.

I was puzzled and a little uneasy as I got into the passenger seat. The kids, all clearly under the age of ten, were either yelling or crying.

When Angelique got behind the wheel, the oldest one, a boy about seven years old, yelled, "Mom, that took way too long. I'm so hungry!"

She turned around in her seat to address them. "Everyone settle down. I'm sorry it took so long. I had to finish something important, but we're ready to go now. Kids, this is Bash. He'll be having dinner with us tonight."

Oh my God. What was happening?

"These are all your kids?"

I turned around to study them. There were four of them. I couldn't get a good look at one of them because they were in a car seat facing backward. A toddler boy, younger than Kody, was buckled into another car seat. Two older kids were in the back row, sitting in booster seats.

She started the car and began backing out of my driveway before I had the chance to escape. "Yep. These are my babies. Charlie and Harper are my little ones. Amelia and Will are the ones in the back."

Will shouted from the back, "Mom, I'm really hungry!"

Angelique pulled out onto the road and then glanced in her rear-view mirror at her son. "Good thing you're hungry, because we're going to Pop'em Possum for dinner."

My ears almost started bleeding with the high-pitched shriek of glee they all let out.

Pop'em Possum was a local restaurant franchise geared toward kids that was known for its giant opossum mascot, greasy microwaved pizza that tasted like cardboard, and arcade games. I'd never been there, but the local billboards and TV commercials made it look horrifying.

I gripped the armrest. "I thought you had reservations somewhere?"

She looked over at me and smiled reassuringly. "I have a friend who works there. I get a good discount and can get the kids some tokens. It keeps them busy and out of my hair. They love it."

It was loud in the car. The kids were constantly yelling. As soon as we got out of my neighborhood, I realized that Angelique was a terrible driver. She was cutting people off, not braking soon enough, and flipping off people who beeped at her. It was twenty minutes of a white-knuckled car ride from hell.

It took a considerable amount of wrangling to get the kids all checked in with hand stamps and wrist bands and then to get them seated. All six of us were crammed into a booth together. Will spilled his soda all over the table while we were waiting for the food, so there were wads of wet napkins all over the place.

Angelique's kids were busy coloring on the paper tablecloth and fighting. Complete pandemonium was going on all around us: kids running and screaming everywhere, horrible carnival music blaring, and a nightmare-fuel, giant opossum wandering around to freak out the kids who were already hopped up on junk food.

I skipped the "pizza" and only nibbled at the soggy french fries. The kids slammed down their food in record time. When we were about done eating, a greasy-haired guy who looked as high as a kite came over with a bucket of tokens for the kids. After a collective squeal of delight, all but the littlest one ran off to play arcade games.

"Thanks, Karl." She knew him by name. And I was pretty sure she was giving him some kind of weird eye signal.

It was ridiculously hard to communicate since it was so damn loud. There was a strange blue light pulsing in the background, which was making me feel queasy. Or maybe that was the fries? Either way, I was convinced I was in the 7th circle of hell.

Angelique was busy on her phone. I was wondering how I could escape. Before I could come up with a plan, she stood up.

"Would you keep an eye on Harper for a minute? I have to use the bathroom."

"Sure." I looked warily at Harper, but she seemed to be fairly content picking at the food left on her plate. As soon as she realized her mom was gone, she let out a giant wail.

I tried to soothe her, but after no success, I knew I had no choice. I unbuckled her from the seat and lifted her up. She looked me over, but then thankfully stopped crying.

For at least five minutes, I held Harper in my arms, trying to keep her calm. When she got fidgety, I walked over to the arcade area to check on the other kids. When I found Will, I asked him to point out the other two, because I couldn't pick them out in the swarm of kids. They were all wearing their wristbands, and they couldn't get out of the place without the matching wristband of the parent. It was a pretty secure setup.

Our table was still empty when I returned. Where the hell was Angelique? Was everything okay? Maybe the horrible food was not sitting well in her stomach?

Then I had a terrifying thought. My gut twisted. What if she abandoned her kids? Left them here with me and took off — just like Kody's mom had abandoned him. It was a crazy thought. I tried to shake it off, but where the hell was she?

I couldn't keep still. I was antsy. I headed to the bathrooms. Girls and their moms were coming and going from the ladies' room. It was too crowded to go in there and look for Angelique, so I asked a young mom to check if she was okay.

She came back a few minutes later and told me there was no Angelique in the bathroom. I was starting to panic.

Out of desperation, I checked the men's room. I was a bit uneasy about bringing Harper in there, but I was too worried for it to stop me.

I poked my head inside the door. A row of urinals, most of them the shorter urinals for little dudes, lined the wall. Each of them was decorated with a hissing opossum face as a target to pee on. I thought the bathroom was empty and was about to leave until I heard a rustling of movement behind one of the stall doors.

It only took me a few seconds of listening carefully and seeing the arrangement of feet under the stall door to realize that someone was having sex in the stall and I had a pretty good idea who it was.

"Angelique" — my angry shout startled Harper, so I modulated my voice to a gritty snarl — "Get the fuck out here right now."

I waited outside the restroom door for her to come out, hoping like hell she'd get out before I had to stop any kids from going in there while she was having sex. I was no angel, but having sex in a restroom at a kid's restaurant crossed a line.

The greasy-haired employee came out first. He walked by without a care in the world. A minute later, Angelique strolled out. Silently, I handed Harper off to her.

She looked at my clenched jaw and laughed. "What? You wanted to be exclusive or something?"

I bit back my response.

She snorted. "I don't do monogamous. I'm polyamorous."

♪♫♩♪♪

I waited about 30 minutes for my car to pull up after I booked it on the ride-sharing app on my phone. When I got settled in the car, I called Josie, needing to let off a little steam.

I started right in when she answered. "I'm done dating. Never set me up again. I don't care who it is; I won't go out with them."

"Huh! I wasn't too surprised about the 36-year-old virgin dog lover; she may not have been the perfect match. But Angelique? She's perfect! She likes kids, she likes sex and I'm sure she could handle your rock star lifestyle. She meets all your criteria of what you wanted in a woman."

I blew out a frustrated breath and growled into the phone. "She's a polyamorous 27-year-old that already has four kids."

"You are too picky!" She tsked. "And what's wrong with being polyamorous?"

"She was having sex with some other guy on our date!" I couldn't keep the heat out of my voice.

"Don't be such a bigot."

"Josie, you drive me crazy."

She laughed.

"I think I want to remain single forever."

How to Marry a Rockstar

Printed in Great Britain
by Amazon